Knight
An *Impossible* Novel

By Julia Sykes

D1520059

For Laura Oliva,
fabulous author and fabulous human being.
Thanks for being the best Convention Husband a girl
could ask for!
XXX

Prologue

Smith

Drawing on years of practice, I mastered the anger that burned within me. It sizzled through my veins, threatening to surge forth and consume my careful control. But I had learned how to curb my more volatile emotions a long time ago, honing and channeling them so they could be released in purposeful bursts of measured violence. The anger became a low thrum, sharpening my focus as I harnessed it rather than being ruled by it.

My rage was bred from disgust at what was being allowed to happen at Decadence, the BDSM club my fellow FBI agents and I were raiding. With the help of owner Derek Carter, the Latin Kings had been trafficking drugs through the club. Agent Sharon Silverman had been investigating the place undercover for a month, but she had gotten in over her head. Now the FBI finally had the information we needed to move in on the Kings, and we were ending this op tonight.

I took a deep breath and summoned up my control. I had a job to do, and I couldn't let my own emotions rule me.

Finding BDSM was what had saved me from falling prey to my own addiction twelve years ago. The sense of control – not only over a willing submissive but also over myself – that I got from being a Dominant had been the antidote to the powerlessness I had felt when it came to the allure of drugs.

The people who frequented this club warped everything that the lifestyle was supposed to be about. The fact that some of the assholes here dared to call themselves Doms filled me with fury. They were supposed to be responsible for the well-being of their submissives. How could they possibly exercise the necessary control when they were intoxicated? Even worse was the fact that they allowed their subs to use. The trust a submissive placed in her

Dominant was a beautiful thing, and the idea that a "Dom" would violate her trust by jeopardizing her health was loathsome.

We had the patrons lined up against the back wall. Anyone who was intoxicated or had drugs on him was going to find himself – or herself – facing some very serious charges.

I coldly surveyed the people I was about to question, taking note of the ones who looked especially nervous or unsteady on their feet. My eyes were drawn to a woman who was standing in the darkest corner of the room, and my anger threatened to overwhelm me. She was frail, thin to the point of being almost emaciated. Her sunken cheeks and the dark shadows under her eyes were all too familiar to me. She bore all the hallmarks of an addict.

But what really goaded my anger was the fact that she bore all the hallmarks of a submissive as well. She was dressed in nothing but a sheer black lace dress that did little to conceal her gaunt figure, even though its long sleeves covered her arms and the hemline came halfway down her thighs.

Even more so than her revealing clothes, her stance identified her as a sub. She stood rigidly, her arms held behind her back in a way that thrust out her small breasts. Her head was held high, but her eyes were downcast.

And a heavy iron collar encircled her slim neck.

I was struck by the strong desire to brutally mangle the man who dared to call himself her Dom. But no one was standing near her. I was going to find out who she was and who her asshole Master was so I could be sure to put him through hell.

My heart twisted as I approached her. I was going to have to arrest her, but it was clear to me that the woman was a victim. If she was involved with the Latin Kings in any way, it had obviously been to her detriment.

She didn't look up at me, not even when I came to a stop directly in front of her, invading her personal space. Now that I was closer to her, I took in her appearance more carefully. Although her skin was sallow, the delicate lines of her face gave her an almost elfin appearance. Her full lips were dry and cracked, and her eyes – although downcast – were obviously large, with dark, thick lashes. A mass of wavy, light brown hair framed her face and hung almost to her waist. It might have been lustrous once, but now the color was muted and dull. Despite the way her addiction had cruelly marred her, she was still beautiful. She must have been absolutely stunning when she was healthy.

With great effort, I kept the ire from my voice as I addressed her gently.

"What's your name, sweetheart?"

She didn't respond in any way; she maintained her stiff stance and didn't look up at me. It was as though she hadn't heard me.

"I'm Smith James. I'm a Special Agent with the FBI," I said, my voice a bit more formal as I flashed my credentials. I didn't want to frighten her, but she needed to take me seriously. "If you cooperate, I'll make sure the Bureau goes easy on you. If you resist, things won't be so pleasant for you." I glanced at her skimpy outfit. She obviously didn't have any ID on her. "I need your name."

Her brows drew together, and she bit her lip. The dry skin cracked open, and a crimson line appeared on her nearly colorless lips. I hated the sight of this beautiful woman who had been destroyed by her addiction. And now she was forcing me to treat her more harshly than I would like.

If the broken woman wouldn't respond to kindness, then maybe the submissive in her would respond to the direct order of a Dominant.

"Your name, girl," I demanded, my voice sharp and authoritative. "Tell me. Now."

Fear flashed across her features.

"F-fucktoy," she whispered tremulously.

I let out a low growl. She thought she could play games with me? Well, I wasn't about to let her get away with that.

She had no idea who she was trying to fuck with.

Chapter 1

Slave

I used to think pain wasn't real. At least, not in the sense of being a tangible thing. It was just the result of my primal brain's in-built response to inform me that damage was being inflicted on my body. If I trusted the person who was giving me pain, then I knew he wasn't going to damage me. If I understood my pain, it stopped being something to fear and became something... interesting. I could master the hurt and ride the high of the adrenaline that flooded my system. I could enter subspace, that gloriously blank place where nothing existed but the sweet endorphins released by the pain that I embraced.

But then He came along and turned that all on its head. He enjoyed administering pain to torture, not to pleasure. And I couldn't trust Him not to inflict damage. He claimed He didn't like it when I forced Him to damage me; He didn't want to mar his property. But that didn't mean He wasn't willing to do so in order to get what He wanted.

I had tried to fight the pain for so long, to hold on to my conviction that it wasn't real. It couldn't hurt me if I didn't let it. But He gave me so much that it overwhelmed me, claiming all of my senses until my whole world was agony. I was perpetually trapped in some twisted, inverted form of subspace where nothing existed but the pain, but it gave me no pleasure.

My only reprieve was the sweet reward that came with the merciful sting of a needle. If I was good, if I obeyed and screamed prettily enough, then He would give me my reward. I lived for it; that was the only time I *was* alive.

But I had become so dependent on it that now the denial of my reward was just as terrible as the agony He gave me. It had been so long since I had gotten my last fix.

Tonight, Master was testing me. He wanted to see just how obedient I was. He wanted the satisfaction of seeing just how thoroughly He had broken me.

I was broken. And I didn't even care. All I cared about was my reward. Right now, my need for it was so acute that my insides were twisting and my skin was on fire. I was desperate to give Him whatever He wanted so I could get my fix. If He hadn't ordered me to stand in the corner quietly and wait for Him to return, then I would have been curled up on the floor sobbing.

But I wasn't ensconced in the stark loneliness of the pitch black dungeon that had become my home, and I didn't have the luxury of going to pieces. His order for my silence denied me even the right to voice my agony. He had brought me out in public for the first time, and I recognized the place where He had brought me as a BDSM club. He would be able to torment me here in front of dozens of strangers, and no one would stop Him.

The thought of calling out a safe word or screaming for help didn't even cross my mind. All I could think about was when He would come back and doing my best to please Him so that He would grant me my reprieve. He had been gone for so long, and I was starting to panic.

Something wasn't right. The sounds of intoxicated laughter and whips hitting flesh had given way to shouts and chaos, and now the club was going quiet around me. I was anxious for Master to return. He had promised He would come back for me.

"Stay here and don't make a sound, whore. Know that I'll be back for you, so don't you dare say a fucking word."

I had been on my best behavior, but the phone call He received just before He left my side had enraged Him. My arm throbbed where His fingers had dug into me. The fresh bruises would be obscured by my lace dress, as were the rest of the marks He left on my body.

Even though I feared His anger, I was desperate for His presence. I could endure His retribution so long as He gave me my fix.

But now a strange man was talking to me, threatening to hurt me if I didn't tell him my name.

I didn't have a name. If I did ever have a name, I didn't remember it now. I was a slave, and slaves don't have names.

"Your name, girl. Tell me. Now."

I recognized that authoritative tone, and I knew better than to refuse a direct order. This man wasn't my Master, but maybe Master had sent him to test me. Fear gripped me. Master had ordered me to remain silent, but if He had sent this man, then I would be in trouble for defying him. And the stranger had threatened to hurt me if I didn't obey him. I already hurt so much. I didn't think I could take any more without screaming.

He wanted a name.

"F-fucktoy," I whispered. That was what Master called me sometimes.

The man growled his displeasure, and I suppressed the urge to flinch. I wasn't allowed to move.

"Whore," I tried again. "Slave."

"Don't play games with me, girl. You won't like the consequences. Tell me your real name."

Hot tears stung at the corners of my eyes. I didn't understand what he wanted from me. Sometimes Master toyed with me like this, asking me questions for which there were no answers, giving me tasks that were impossible to carry out. He enjoyed punishing me when I couldn't comply. I had to do whatever I could to earn this man's forgiveness. My back was on fire from where Master had reminded me of the consequences for disobedience before bringing me to the club. He actually had damaged me this time. But that burning paled in comparison to the inferno that was consuming me from the inside out.

I dropped to my knees before the strange man, my shaking hands fumbling at his belt. It wouldn't be the first time Master had shared me with another man. I prayed I wouldn't be punished for acting without permission, but if I gave this man enough pleasure, he might tell Master that I deserved my reward.

My fingers had hardly touched the leather of his belt when his hands encircled my wrists, stopping me short.

"What the hell do you think you're doing?" He snarled, fury bleeding into his tone.

The tears spilled over. I didn't know what this man wanted. I didn't want him to hurt me. I felt utterly lost without

Master's commands. I had broken His edict to remain still and silent, and now that I didn't have any further orders I didn't know what I was supposed to do.

The fear that gripped me made it difficult to draw breath, but I forced the words out, desperate for instructions.

"Please, Sir," I said anxiously. "I'll do anything you want. Tell me what you want."

The stranger crouched down in front of me, releasing my wrists so he could place his fingers beneath my chin, forcing my head up. I automatically put my hands behind my back, gripping my elbows in either hand and straightening my shoulders. My posture had obviously displeased him.

"I want your name," he said harshly.

My body began to tremble as fear and pain threatened to overwhelm me. This man was toying with me. He wanted to hurt me.

My mind searched frantically for the correct answer. "I don't have a name," I finally replied.

I stared at the line of his strong jaw, and the downward twist of his full lips made my terror ratchet up a notch. He applied more pressure under my chin, lifting my head further. Oh, god. I knew what was coming next.

"Look at me, girl."

The only times Master commanded me to meet his eyes were when he wanted to see the pain in my own.

But I couldn't refuse his direct order. That would only make things so much worse for me. Dread pooled in my roiling stomach as I lifted my gaze. I couldn't help flinching when my eyes met his. They were pale blue shot through with silver, ringed in indigo. They reflected the light like the glowing eyes of a wolf, a predator. Although they were mesmerizing, they were crystalized ice that made me shiver as they cut into me.

I didn't know what I was supposed to do. He didn't want me to give him pleasure. At least, not in the physical sense. I suspected he would take his pleasure from my pain. If only he would give me instructions, then I might learn how best to avoid a more agonizing punishment. I might get my reward sooner.

"Where is my Master?" I asked, both craving and dreading his return.

The lines around the man's eyes tightened, and ire flashed in their multifaceted depths. I resolutely resisted the strong urge to shrink away.

"What's his name?" He bit out the words.

Oh, no.

I was beginning to realize I had made a grave mistake. If this man didn't know Master and I had tried to touch him, I would be in deep trouble. Master might not give me my fix.

"Master. He is Master," I answered tremulously, praying that I was giving him the answer he wanted.

"I won't tolerate this game much longer, girl." He nearly bared his perfect white teeth as he delivered the threat.

I was supposed to remain silent, but I couldn't hold back my desperate sob. The stranger didn't know Master. He wasn't going to give me my reward. Every inch of my body twisted and burned; my need was threatening to tear me apart from the inside out.

The wrenching pain was so acute that my stomach convulsed. I jerked away from the man only just in time to avoid getting sick on him. My insides heaved, but there wasn't much within me to give up.

My stomach writhed, making my vision go red. I felt the coolness of the floor beneath my cheek as I pulled my knees up to my chest in an attempt to hold my body together. My need was ripping me apart. I wanted to scream out my agony, but Master would be angry if I drew more attention to myself. Oh, god. He had ordered me to remain still and silent, and I had defied Him. I hadn't meant to, but that wouldn't matter to Him. He had never pushed me so hard before, had never tortured me for this long by withholding what I needed.

"Breathe, girl," the man commanded. "Breathe."

I tried to comply, but forcing my lungs to expand was excruciating.

"I need a medic over here!" The stranger barked out. He placed a hand on my back, and more fire lashed at me as he pressed into the open wounds where Master's whip had bitten into me. I whimpered, and the man jerked back from me with a curse.

Blinking hard in an attempt to clear my vision, I looked up at him beseechingly through my watering eyes. He was staring at the wet crimson line on his hand with disgust.

"Please, Sir," I begged raggedly. "Tell Master I was good. I tried to be good." Giving in to the impulse that had been riding me hard, I raked my nails over my tingling arms, longing for the singular kiss of the needle that would cause the pins sticking into every millimeter of my skin to abate. "I need my reward. I need it. I tried to be good."

The stranger grabbed my wrist, pulling my arm away from my body so he could push back my sleeve. A string of curses erupted from him as he took in the small marks that the pinpricks of the needle had left on my skin. His anger hit me like a physical blow.

The terror finally ripped the agonized screams from my throat that I had so desperately been holding in. Once the first was released, they were impossible to hold back. Pain claimed me.

I had thought that my entire world, my life in my dungeon, had been torture. But this was just as horrific as the beating that had finally broken me.

Reality fell away, the torment blotting out even the terrifying stranger.

Chapter 2

Memories assailed me, so sharp that I was forced to relive the most horrific scenes of my torturous existence. The only thing that pierced my delirium was a large, warm hand firmly gripping my own as a deep voice murmured words of comfort and reassurance. But this small mercy only punctuated the lucid horrors for a few minutes at a time, and I wasn't sure which was the harsher torture: the fear and agony I endured or the false promises that everything was going to be okay. The kind reassurances gave me flashes of cruel hope before the pain claimed me again.

* * * *

It was the first time I could recall the woman I had been before I was broken. But remembering her was almost as agonizing as the memories of what had been done to her. She had been strong and brave and defiant. She would have found what I was now to be abhorrent. That woman would rather be dead than be what I was.

That woman had sought out a Master, but she dreamed of a loving, caring relationship of reciprocal pleasure. She had wanted to give her submission willingly as a gift to a man who she trusted implicitly with her body and her heart.

But He took her and twisted everything she had so fiercely desired.

"You want to be beaten, whore. I've seen how much you enjoy it. This is your fantasy. That's why I chose you. The others didn't last long, but I think you'll take it. You will take it. It would displease me if you died. And you don't want to disappoint me. You'll learn that soon enough."

He had found her at a BDSM club. She had even noticed him briefly at the beginning of the night. He wasn't exceptionally beautiful, but he was handsome enough in a generic sort of way. But something about the strange light in his hazel eyes had put her off. Besides, she preferred tall, dark, and dangerous men to unassuming blond guys. If only she had realized that he was the most dangerous man at the club, she would have run screaming.

She didn't notice him watching her that night. He had seen how she found joy in pain, but he didn't understand the first thing about why she enjoyed it. And truthfully, he didn't want her to enjoy it. He just wanted her to be strong enough to take the agony he gave her.

On the first night of her incarceration, she had awoken to find herself locked in a cage. The world was pitch black, and the only way she realized her confinement was her inability to move. The cage was so small that she couldn't even sit up or stretch out her legs. She had beaten against the iron bars until her hands were bloody, and her terrified screams had echoed through the darkness until her throat was raw and burning. They tapered off to wracking sobs, and eventually even those quieted as her tears dried up.

Only then did he come to her for the first time. Even the dim light of the spare light bulb that provided the room's only illumination seared her eyes when he turned it on. Although he spoke softly, his voice boomed throughout the room, assaulting her eardrums after the long, dark silence.

He didn't explain where she was or why he had taken her. He offered to release her from the cage, to give her food and water and the chance to use the toilet. His only condition was that she remain silent and not attempt to escape him. She had nodded in agreement, doing her best to covertly take inventory of her prison. The walls were built of dull grey concrete blocks that matched the concrete floor. The dank quality of the air let her know she was underground. There was a toilet in the corner of the room and a showerhead mounted to the wall. She shuddered as she took in the provisions that indicated he intended to keep her here for a prolonged period.

Even more terrifying were the apparatuses that she usually associated with the thrill of BDSM that were spaced throughout the room. There was a St. Andrews Cross pushed up against the opposite wall, and she recognized a bondage table and a crude spanking bench. Only this bench was crafted of rough wood, and it didn't have any padding. Chains hung down at various points, looped through thick ringbolts that were embedded in the heavy wooden beams above.

But there were stairs leading up to the door through which he had entered. That was the only route to freedom, and she intended to fight tooth and nail to attain it. The prospect of not reaching that door was too horrible to contemplate.

He watched her carefully when he released her from the cage, but he didn't touch her in any way. Keeping up her end of the bargain, she was compliant and didn't speak as she stretched her muscles and took the water and protein shake he offered her. Even though she desperately needed to relieve herself, she was too repulsed by the idea of using the toilet in front of him to put off her plan any longer. She had taken self-defense classes, and she knew the most efficient ways to incapacitate a man.

Her hand shot out, aiming to drive her palm into his nose, hopefully breaking it. But she never made contact, and she didn't even get the chance to bring her knee up into his groin. He caught her wrist almost lazily before the back of his hand cracked across her cheek with sickening force.

She screamed and cried and begged, but he just laughed as he tore off her clothes. Despite her best efforts, he easily blocked all of her attempts to fight him off.

That was the first time that he raped her. Even though she lost count of the times he forced himself on her, she still thought of it as rape.

But that was before she had broken. Now she accepted that she belonged to Master, and it was His right to use His property as He saw fit.

* * * *

The world was brightly lit and the air was sharp with antiseptic. My body was still on fire, my need consuming me. The pins were digging into my arms again, and I strained to gouge them out from under my skin. But soft restraints held my wrists at my sides, preventing me from seeking relief. I hated when Master tormented me like this, tying me up and denying me my reward for an agonizingly long period of time. He reserved this punishment for my gravest infractions.

"Please, Master," I whined. "I'll be good. I promise I'll be good."

A pair of familiar silver eyes appeared above me. The man gently brushed my sweat-dampened hair back from my forehead.

"It's okay, sweetheart," he said softly. His deep, rumbling voice should have been soothing, but I didn't trust the comfort it promised. "I know it hurts, but you have to ride it out. You'll be okay. I'll be right here with you."

"What did I do wrong?" I asked, desperate to give him what he wanted. "I'll do anything. I'm sorry. I'm so sorry."

"You have nothing to be sorry for, sweetheart. And you don't have to do anything for me." His words were spoken gently, but fury blazed in his eyes.

I hadn't done anything wrong, but he was telling me there was nothing I could do to make the pain stop.

"I don't understand," I sobbed. "Why are you punishing me?"

His anger spilled over, tightening his features into something fierce and terrifying to behold. Rage pulsed off of him like a palpable thing. This new Master was even crueler than the first. He spoke to me so kindly while torturing me mercilessly.

"Please, Master," I gasped out. "Tell me how I can please you."

"I am *not* your Master," he snarled.

He was so angry. My behavior was so displeasing that he wouldn't even claim me as his slave. What would it take to win his approval? How could I possibly avoid pain if he wouldn't give me any instructions?

Despair overwhelmed me, and I succumbed to my dark memories once again.

* * * *

Master had tried for weeks to break me. To break *her*.

The dark isolation in which she lived had been almost as terrible as the pain he gave her. Sometimes, she forgot what sight was until he came and turned on the light. The sight of him became the only real thing in the world. After long days of captivity, she was disturbed to realize that she almost longed to see him, if only to cling on to her deteriorating sanity. He reminded her that the world existed outside of her own head, even if that world was steeped in torture and violation.

The silence was almost worse than the blindness. In her waking hours, she talked to herself aloud, just to remember what sound was. She desperately clung to the memories of her life before she was taken, recounting them to herself as though telling a story to a close friend.

But after a while, the words began to lose their significance, and she would laugh at the strange, meaningless sounds that issued from her mouth in the semblance of coherent expression.

At times, she was tempted to surrender to the madness, to at least escape mentally. If he wouldn't allow her body to die, she could destroy her own mind. If he used her after that, she wouldn't really be *her* anymore. That way, he wouldn't have truly conquered her. Her existence would end on her terms.

But she knew her body would survive, and he would continue to abuse it and use it for his own pleasure until it finally expired. She couldn't abandon herself to that fate. Everyone else might have given up on her, but she wasn't going to give up on herself.

Everything became so much harder when he introduced her to the drugs. She wasn't sure how long she had been imprisoned when the needle first kissed the crook of her arm, but time became even more meaningless after that.

He had tied her over the spanking bench and beaten her most vulnerable areas, inflicting the maximum pain possible without breaking the skin. Splinters had dug into her as her body twisted against the rough wood. He usually demanded that she call him "Master," claiming he wouldn't stop until she did so.

She couldn't hold back her screams, and she was ashamed when she begged him to stop. But she wouldn't call him Master. He didn't deserve that. Ceding control of her body and mind to her Master was supposed to be a beautiful thing, borne of a relationship based on trust and mutual respect. She had never given anyone that gift. If she surrendered that to her tormenter, with that one word she would surrender her soul.

Although the pain he inflicted was horrific, he always stopped before she called him Master. He was too concerned with compromising the beauty of his slave to scar her permanently.

But on that day, he tried a new tactic. He said nothing as he strapped her to the spanking bench and beat her mercilessly. His silence set her teeth on edge. The absence of his furious demands was almost more terrifying than the sound of his harsh voice booming through the room. All she could hear were her own agonized screams, and without his commands, it was much more difficult to muster up her defiance as a mental shield.

It was only when he was finished with her that he finally spoke.

"If pain won't break you," he said roughly, "maybe pleasure will. I'm going to make you my obedient slave, whore. One way or another."

She barely felt the prick of the needle; the tiny sting was nothing in comparison to the throbbing of her enflamed flesh. But even that fire was wiped out by the warm bliss that surged through her veins almost instantaneously.

God, the heroin was a beautiful thing.

But what was the sweetest relief would soon become the most powerful weapon he wielded against her.

* * * *

The brightly lit room flashed back into existence as I returned to my current reality. I remembered I had been released from my prison only to be brought to a new one. And I had a new Master as well.

I shuddered at the memory of his cold cruelty, and I squeezed my eyes shut again, longing for the darkness of my dungeon.

Although I wasn't ready to face the fresh horrors that awaited me, I forced myself to take inventory of my body.

Inconceivably, the pain of my denial had lessened incrementally. My new Master must be tiring of torturing me. That could only mean one thing: he would want my body soon.

Despite my fear of him, I would accept him. Defying him wasn't an option. I prayed he would allow me to please him so he wouldn't use me too harshly. I would do anything I could to avoid further punishment. I would prove to him that I was a good slave.

My pain might be abating, but the skin on my arms was crawling. It felt as though thousands of fire ants were roving over my flesh, their tiny serrated jaws leaving little burns behind. I raked my fingernails against them, desperate to claw them off me.

My wrists were caught up by one large hand, preventing me from scraping at my skin.

Oh, god. My new Master was right beside me.

I was too frightened to look up into those disturbing silver eyes. They were so beautiful and yet so cruel. The dichotomy was far worse to behold than the lust-filled eyes of my previous Master: brown mingled with green, recalling the muck of a muddy pond. And there was always a light in them that was just *wrong.*

"Please," I whispered, unable to resist tugging against his strong hold. I needed him to release me so I could soothe my crawling skin.

He ran his fingers through my hair, but his other hand still held my wrists fast, pressing them against my chest.

"It's okay, sweetheart," he said gently. "You'll pull through."

How could he be so tender and yet so cruel? I had thought my previous Master was insane, but this man was something even more maniacal.

Burning tears slipped from the corners of my closed eyes, but I forced myself to stop struggling. I didn't want to anger him further.

"That's a good girl. Just breathe."

His rumbling approval was jarring. My former Master never offered words of praise.

I pushed back my confusion, focusing on his command to breathe. He had finally given me an order I could follow. Thinking for myself always led to trouble. It was far easier to blindly obey without contemplating my reality too closely.

"Shouldn't she be restrained?" I didn't recognize the voice of the new man.

"I made the nurse remove the restraints," Master said angrily. "Do you know how much they upset her? I would expect you to understand, Vaughn."

"And you holding her down is better?" The man – Vaughn – asked, disapproval evident in his tone. "Do you really think that she wants any man to touch her right now?"

"She shouldn't be alone," Master ground out.

"She wouldn't be," Vaughn countered. "The nurses could watch her twenty-four/seven if you hadn't intimidated all of them into staying out of the room."

Nurses? What were they talking about?

Don't think, I reminded myself. *Just accept what's happening.*

Breathe. I continued to comply with the one order he had given me.

"They don't understand. And neither do you," Master said sharply.

"I understand that the staff members here are trained to deal with recovering addicts. I understand that they're medical professionals. You're a field agent with the FBI, Smith, not a nurse."

"You've always been the perfect goddamn Boy Scout, Vaughn," Master spat. "Some of us aren't as pure as the driven snow. I know what withdrawals feel like; I know what she's going through from firsthand experience. I don't need a fucking medical degree to understand the hell she's in right now."

"Okay," Vaughn's voice was softer now, placating. "I get why you feel a connection to her. But I'm worried about you, buddy. You should go home and get some sleep."

"I'm not leaving her alone. I can't." Master's voice was strained. "She's been tortured. By someone like us."

"I am nothing like the bastard who hurt her," Vaughn said, fury bleeding into his calm tone. "And neither are you. It's not on you to make amends for what he did."

"You've seen the marks, but you weren't there when I found her." Master said angrily. "She moved like a trained submissive. That fucker even collared her. She called him 'Master,' but she was clearly terrified of him." He sounded disgusted.

There was a long pause before Vaughn spoke again. "I think it might be best if you're not on this case at all. You obviously can't approach it with any sort of objectivity."

"How the fuck am I supposed to be objective when that asshole has used what we do and twisted it to destroy her? We use pain and pleasure to bend submissives to our will, but he's perverted those methods and fucking broken her, Vaughn. Her eyes… It's like there's nothing there, nothing left inside her. She doesn't even know her own goddamn name. And it makes me sick that I know just how he did it. The doctors here can't understand that. So no, I can't be objective when it comes to this case. And if you were a real Dom, you couldn't be either."

There was a pause.

"May I speak with you in the hall, James?" Vaughn asked calmly, politely.

Master squeezed my wrists gently to reinforce his control. "Don't scratch at your arms, girl. I'll be right back."

I swallowed hard. This command would be much more difficult to follow than his order to breathe.

As soon as he released me from his restraining hold, the ants seemed to double in number, tormenting me, tempting me to disobey. I clenched my fists, forcing myself to keep my arms pressed to my chest where Master had left them.

Don't think. Don't think about it.

Breathe. Don't scratch your arms.

I allowed the commands to become a litany running in the background of my mind. In order to distract myself from the horrible burning itch, I focused on my surroundings. Since I was keeping my eyes resolutely closed, my sense of hearing was heightened, and I honed in on Master and Vaughn's distant conversation.

Master's voice was harsh, and the occasional expletive punctuated his muffled statements with sharp clarity. He placed emphasis the curse words, making them discernable when the rest of what he was saying was garbled.

In contrast, Vaughn's voice was quieter, softer. He spoke in steady, even cadences.

Eventually, Master's voice turned more subdued in the wake of Vaughn's unrelenting calm.

I heard only one pair of footsteps returning to me, and I instantly recognized Master's touch as he gripped my hands gently, rubbing soothing circles across my palms.

As much as I feared my new Master, I was suddenly glad that my former Master had given me to him. He offered words of praise and gentle, rewarding touches.

A chilling thought struck me. Maybe I hadn't been given to him; maybe he had taken me without permission. If my former Master found me and discovered that I had been disloyal, he would hurt me.

Which punishment would be worse? The retribution of my former Master or the cruelty of my new one?

But was he cruel? He had tortured me by denying me my reward, but he certainly wasn't being cruel to me now.

Yes, I preferred this treatment. I had to ensure that my new Master would keep me.

I opened my eyes so I could meet his silver ones. "I'll be good for you, Master. I promise."

His expression twisted in fury. "Don't call me that," he snapped.

I cringed away from him, squeezing my eyes shut again. I had looked at him directly and spoken without permission. I braced myself for pain, but I was shocked to feel his fingers running through my hair again in a soothing rhythm.

"It's okay, girl," he said more gently. "You're okay. Just rest."

I had made the right choice. Although his ferocity terrified me, that same ferocity would protect me once I convinced him to accept me. Master would keep me safe from His retribution if He returned for me.

I just hoped my new life wasn't more painful than the last.

Obeying Master's order, I fell into sleep.

* * * *

I relived the day I came into being, the day the woman I had once been had finally given up.

She had been in the dark for so long. The only time she was blessed with the light was when he came to hurt her, to violate her. She dreaded that blessing.

And she dreaded the high of the heroin almost as much as she craved the sweet hours of release from her reality, from her pain. Every time he hurt her, every time he fucked her, he forcibly gave her the drug as her "reward."

She was terrified to realize that she was coming to see it as just that: a reward for enduring what he gave her. He wanted her to willingly accept what he did to her, to beg him to use her so she could attain that sweet release.

Even *she* didn't understand how she was clinging on to her last vestiges of defiance.

She didn't know how long she had been trapped in her prison, but she was beginning to fear that no one was coming to her rescue. Her family hadn't known where she was on the night she was taken; they would have been disgusted if they found out she was exploring the BDSM lifestyle. And her slim hope that one of her friends from the club had witnessed her abduction was waning. She had left the club fairly early, and no one else had been in the parking lot when she walked out to her car. The last thing she remembered was retrieving her keys from her purse before something sharp pierced her neck and the world disappeared.

Even more upsetting was the realization that it would have been her family who reported her missing rather than her friends at the club. No one from her "real life" knew about her forays into the world of BDSM, and it was unlikely anyone would trace her disappearance to the club. Her friends in the lifestyle didn't even know her last name.

Despite her fear that she wouldn't escape her hellish new reality, she still resisted her captor. He had mentioned others that he had tortured before her. They had died.

Once, she had tried to die. But he wouldn't let her.

He allowed her to refuse food and water to the point that she was so weakened she could barely move. Then he took advantage of her weakness, forcing sustenance down her throat. Once he had revived her, he hurt her worse than ever. It was one of the first times he had really damaged her, striking her with a cane until her skin broke and wept blood.

She ate and drank compliantly after that, but she still fought him every time he tried to take her, her battered body doing its best to resist him. If she ever managed to land a blow on him, she would be returned to the cage when he was finished with her. Otherwise, he kept her secure with a manacle around her ankle. It was attached to the wall by a short chain, but it gave her the freedom of movement she needed to reach the toilet and the showerhead. He insisted that she wash herself, and although she wanted to defy him, she hated the feel of grime on her skin.

She had abandoned the notion of privacy in her first few days of incarceration. He had taken her clothes so that she never had the option of hiding her body from him. She had never been shy about being naked; she used to be a bit of an exhibitionist. But the sensation of his eyes studying her flesh made her skin crawl. It was just one more of her pleasures he had corrupted.

He had taken so much from her, but he hadn't taken her free will, her defiance. Not until the day that he brought in his Mentor.

She heard the dreaded creak of the door opening at the top of the stairs, and she closed her eyes in anticipation of the light that would sear them.

"Keep your eyes closed, whore. If you look at me, I'll make sure you never see anything again. And if I hear you utter one word without express permission, I'll cut out your tongue."

The man's voice was unfamiliar to her, and although his timbre was warm and rich, his words chilled her to the core.

The insides of her eyelids flared red as the light was flipped on, but she kept them shuttered. She already dreaded seeing the man who had made her life a living hell, so it wasn't difficult to avoid the sight of him. What was more difficult to resist was the impulse to identify the new man who was entering her prison.

"But Sir. She's my property. I like how she looks. I don't want her permanently damaged." She recognized the voice of her jailor, and she was shocked to realize he sounded almost petulant.

"Do you want a pretty whore or an obedient slave?" The new man asked harshly. "You've had her for nearly two months, and she has yet to call you 'Master.'" He sighed. "I have to admit I'm disappointed in you. I thought I had taught you better than this."

"The others broke," her tormentor said defensively.

The man who she would come to think of as "the Mentor" spoke disparagingly. "Yes, but the others didn't survive, did they? You chose this one because she was special. I would say you've chosen well if it weren't apparent that you have no idea how to truly master a woman. You should have taken great pleasure in breaking this one, but instead you've allowed her to frustrate you and defy you at every turn."

"Yes. I know that." Her captor struggled to keep his tone deferential, but frustration bled into it. "That's why I've asked for your help."

The Mentor's voice was low and soft. "If you don't remember to speak to me with proper respect, I'll take her for myself. Then you can find another toy that breaks easily and wastes away in a matter of weeks. If you keep going through them at the rate you have been, people are going to start taking notice. And I won't save you if they come for you. I'll put you down before they can even get to you. I will *not* allow you to take me down with you. Do you understand me?"

"Yes, Sir. I'm sorry." His tone was so meek, she barely recognized the speaker as her jailor.

"Don't make me regret my decision to teach you how to channel your urges. You've only survived this long because of what I've given you. I've never been known for benevolence, and I've already afforded you any scraps of it that I might possess." The Mentor's voice was flat, devoid of any emotion. It was more chilling than her captor's cruel bark or enraged shouts.

"And I'm so grateful for that, Sir. I won't fuck up again. That's why I need your help. Please." She was shocked to realize his words were ragged with fear.

Oh, god. If he was frightened of the Mentor, what might the man do to her?

"I have to admit your attempts with the heroin were a good idea. It will prove an effective way to ensure her loyalty. But only once you break her. You've demanded she call you 'Master,' but you stop giving her pain before she does so. Why would she give in when you can't follow through on your threats?" The Mentor spoke disparagingly, and he sounded more than a little disappointed.

"String her up," he ordered his student. "And if you want your eyes to remain in your head, I suggest you keep them closed, whore," he warned her.

She did as he commanded, keeping her eyes shut tight when her captor grasped her wrists, pulling her up. That didn't mean she was going without a fight. She jerked against his hold, trying to kick out at him. Her blindness and her terrified trembling rendered her efforts laughably ineffective.

But neither man laughed. She would have preferred that cold, cruel sound to the way they spoke about her as though she wasn't even there, as though she wasn't a person.

She was already crying by the time the manacles encircled her wrists and her body was stretched taut so that her toes were barely touching the floor. Her captor usually restrained her with padded cuffs to avoid breaking the skin, but this time cold metal bit into her.

Her eyes flew open when the bullwhip cracked across her back for the first time. She wasn't sure which man had struck her; they were both standing behind her, out of her line of sight.

But she wasn't thinking of them in that moment. Her mind was completely overwhelmed by the shocking, searing line of fire that licked across her back. The blow robbed her of her breath, and she wasn't even able to scream out her pain.

Her screams began soon enough.

Blood streamed down her back and legs in hot rivulets as the men punished her flesh with the whip, cutting at her with impunity. She wanted to beg them to stop, but the agony was so all-encompassing that she was incapable of forming words.

She had thought her entire world had been misery before, but now she truly understood how merciful her captor had been with her. The pain assaulted her relentlessly, until her mind couldn't recall a time before the pain had become her existence. She was powerless to resist its onslaught, and she was so tired of fighting. She couldn't remember why she had been fighting. It was such a pointless endeavor.

She surrendered to the agony, accepting that there was nothing else in her world. Her screams ceased, but she wasn't aware of it; her own voice had long since lost its significance.

Her captor's voice was at her ear, oozing into her battered mind with insidious intent.

"Do you want your Master to end your pain?"

Yes. Yes, she wanted that more than anything. She hadn't even thought that possible. A low whine escaped her in an attempt to answer in the affirmative.

"Beg me, slave."

She swallowed, struggling to remember how to form words.

"Please," she forced out her final words raggedly. "Please make it stop, Master."

Cool, heavy metal encircled my neck, and the click of the lock resounded in my ears, a sound of finality. The tears I wept were joyful as the needle pierced my skin, blessing me with sweet oblivion.

Chapter 3

When lucidity returned to me, the horrors of my past were blotted out by fear of my present. The internal fire had been doused, and the prickling of my skin had abated. The persistent pain had been replaced by a pervasive ache that left my muscles feeling weak and watery.

I didn't have to open my eyes to know he was there. My new Master.

It didn't seem he would grant me the merciful loneliness afforded to me by my former master. He was always there. He had remained with me to witness the entirety of my torment.

And now that he had allowed the pain to abate, he was sure to want my body.

His thumb brushed against my sore, cracked lips.

"Open up, sweetheart. You need to drink this."

His words were so tender that I wanted to cry. It was so much easier to accept abuse when orders were delivered as detached commands.

But it didn't matter that I was upset and frightened. *Don't think.*

I parted my lips obediently, opening my jaw wide to accept his cock. I kept my eyes closed and braced myself for the salty taste of his pre-cum on my tongue.

"Close," the order was a growl.

There was nothing in my mouth. Was he simply testing my obedience?

Don't think. Obey.

But that mantra was becoming difficult to follow. My mind was clearer than it had been since the day I had come into existence, and I dreaded that this new acuity would make my reality that much harder to endure.

Now it was fear rather than hope for a reward that prompted my compliance. I pressed my lips together, only to realize that something small and round had been placed between them. My eyes opened of their own accord, my long-forgotten curiosity driving me to discern what was happening to me.

I knew better than to meet his silver eyes, but I perceived that his beautiful features were taut with anger. I had done what he had asked. How had I displeased him?

My eyes began to burn. I hoped he enjoyed the sight of my tears as much as my former master.

He brushed the wetness from my cheeks with a feather-light touch.

"Don't cry, sweetheart."

I took a deep breath through my nose, trying my best to push down my emotions.

Don't cry. Don't cry.

I blinked rapidly, clearing my vision until I could see the dark stubble on his strong jaw once again.

He sighed heavily, and the downward twist of his mouth seemed almost sad.

"Look at me." His voice was cajoling rather than commanding, but the power in his tone communicated that it was an order nonetheless.

My eyes snapped up to meet his. My mind couldn't comprehend the unfamiliar, soft light in them.

"I'm not going to hurt you," he said firmly. "I need you to drink this. It's just diluted Gatorade. You need the electrolytes."

I had no idea what that meant, but I realized that the object between my lips was a straw. While his soft expression confused me, it was easy enough to understand his words.

Drink this, or I will hurt you.

Suppressing the urge to tear my gaze from his, I obediently took a pull of whatever liquid it was that he wanted me to drink. It didn't matter what it was; I was going to drink it. I was too terrified of his capriciousness to do otherwise.

The lushly flavored liquid washed through my parched mouth and down my sore throat like the sweetest elixir. I drew in more and more, suddenly eager to comply with his order. God, it tasted so *good.* I hadn't drunk anything but water in longer than I could remember, and that had been hard with minerals. This was sweet and somehow bright. It tasted like joy.

All too soon, he pulled the drink away from me. I could feel that my disappointment was evident in my expression, but I didn't protest.

"You can have more in a little while, sweetheart," he told me gently. "I don't want you to drink so much that it makes you sick."

He hadn't given me permission to speak, but I knew I was supposed to thank him. I actually *wanted* to thank him. I was beginning to have an inkling of what that light in his eyes meant: it was kindness. And I craved more of that even more acutely than I wanted more of the sweet drink.

I was ready to give my body to him, but I was shocked to realize that I was wearing some sort of thin cotton gown. I wasn't supposed to hide my body from my Master. Grasping at the garment's hem, I shifted so I could tug it up over my legs and bare myself for him.

The gown only slid a few inches up my thighs before he took my wrists in his hands, halting my progress.

"What are you doing?" His tone was gentle, but his eyes had turned hard. I shrank back from him, but I wasn't allowed to look away.

"I-" My voice caught in my throat.

Look at him. Don't cry.

"I'm sorry I covered my body. I want to thank you, Master."

His brows drew together, but his grip on my wrists didn't tighten with his anger. When he spoke, his voice wasn't harsh, but it was deep and imbued with authority.

"Let's get a few things straight, girl. If you want to thank me, all you have to do is say 'thank you.' And you have every right to wear clothes."

I frowned slightly, confused. I had no concept of having rights.

"Let me be clearer: you don't have permission to remove your clothes. You are not allowed to do anything for me – or anyone else – that is sexual. I'm not going to hurt you. No one is going to hurt you. Tell me you understand that."

I didn't understand. Nothing he was saying made any sense. What did he want me for if he didn't desire me for sexual pleasure or to take pleasure from hurting me?

But he hadn't asked me whether or not I understood; he had ordered me to tell him that I did.

"I understand, Master."

"I've told you not to call me that." Given the harshness of his expression, I expected him to snap at me. But his voice remained cool and controlled. "My name is Smith. Smith James. I'm a Special Agent with the FBI. I found you at the BDSM club Decadence when we went in on a drugs bust. Do you remember that?"

I cast my mind back, shying away from my hazy recollections of my former life to find the disjointed memories of the night I had met my new Master. They were steeped in pain and fear, but I could clearly remember the first time I had seen his remarkable eyes.

"Yes, Ma-" I stopped myself just in time. "Yes. I remember." He had told me his name, but he hadn't given me permission to use it.

"You've been very sick for a long time, sweetheart," he informed me gently. "We brought you to St. Paul's Hope for detox and rehab. You've gotten through the withdrawal period, so the hardest part is over. I need you to understand that the pain of the withdrawals wasn't a punishment."

Detox? Withdrawals?

The significance of his words began to coalesce in my mind: I wasn't going to get my reward again. I wasn't sure if the emotion that flooded me was relief at the fact that denial could no longer be wielded against me as a punishment, or grief that I would never again be granted that release from reality. My chest heaved as my confusion overwhelmed me.

Look at him. Don't cry. Don't cry. Don't cry...

But I couldn't follow both orders. If I couldn't break from his gaze, then I couldn't blink back the tears. I shuddered in dread as they spilled down my cheeks.

"I'm sorry," I gasped out.

His hand cupped my cheek, his thumb brushing at the wetness there. "It's okay. I'm going to help you get through this," he said softly. "Don't cry, sweetheart."

"I can't help it," I choked back a sob as I stared into his eyes. "I'm sorry."

He cursed under his breath. I braced myself for the blow that I knew was coming, but – to my utter shock – he wrapped his arms around me instead.

"You can cry as much as you want, girl. You have nothing to be sorry for."

He held me against him, his hand cupping the nape of my neck so my face was pressed against his chest. With his permission, I let myself go. I cried and cried until his white collared shirt was thoroughly soaked with my tears, and he held me until my wracking sobs finally quieted.

The comfort I found in his embrace was jarring. I didn't understand my new Master at all, but I was eager to do whatever he asked of me if it meant he would give me more of this.

Master only pulled away from me when someone cleared his throat loudly. He lowered me back down onto the hospital bed, but he kept one of my hands held firmly in his.

The stranger's imposing form filled the doorway. He wasn't quite as broad as Master, but he was a few inches taller. Although he held no appeal for me, he was undeniably handsome, with carefully-styled dark blond hair and striking blue eyes. They flashed as he frowned at Master censoriously, and I could sense the same forbidding power that emanated from Master pulsing around him.

I shivered and gripped Master's hand tightly, instinctively seeking his protection. The stranger didn't miss my small show of fear, and his eyes softened as they focused on me. I dropped my gaze, hoping he wouldn't be angry with me for openly studying him. My renewed interest in my surroundings that had returned with my mental clarity might get me into trouble.

"Can I help you with something, Vaughn?" Master asked the man coolly as his thumb traced small, soothing circles across the palm of my hand.

Vaughn. I recognized the name. This was the man who had argued with Master.

"I was just coming to check in on you, *James*." Vaughn's voice was cold as he emphasized Master's surname.

Master sighed, and his shoulders dropped slightly as the aggressive tension left him. He looked weary and a little apologetic. "Shit. Sorry, Clayton. Things are better." He smiled down at me gently and gave my hand a little squeeze. "She's through the worst of it. We were just laying a few ground rules."

Clayton leaned against the doorframe and crossed his arms over his chest, one eyebrow arched. "Ground rules?" He asked drily. "Do you mean to tell me you're giving her orders?"

Master's forehead creased, and I was amazed to find that he appeared slightly chagrined.

"It's not like that, Clayton," he said gruffly. "She responds better to rules. This is why she needs me here instead of some nurse. I told you they wouldn't understand."

They were talking about me as though I wasn't there, but it didn't bother me. I was used to that. And to be honest, I didn't want to be caught up in whatever tense exchange was passing between the two powerful men.

Clayton studied Master for a minute before sighing. His hard stance eased, his arms dropping to his sides. "Okay, Smith. I get it. I just don't want you to intimidate her." He turned his blue eyes on me. "Are you alright with Smith touching you? He'll leave if you want him to."

Master shot him a glare, but Clayton ignored him.

"No!" I said quickly, my hand tightening around his. "I mean yes. I'm okay. I want Master to stay." If Master wasn't there to tell me what to do, I would be lost. And if he wasn't there to maintain his claim over me, someone less kind might decide to take me.

Clayton scowled at Master.

"I've told her not to call me that," Master said defensively. He turned his hard gaze on me. "In fact, it's one of her rules."

I opened my mouth to apologize, but he continued on over me.

"She's only just woken up," he told Clayton. "I was just trying to explain what's happened to her."

"I guess I came at a good time, then," Clayton said smoothly. "Can I come in?"

I was startled to realize that he was addressing me. Was he actually asking for my permission? Bewildered, I stared at him for a full minute, but he just waited patiently for my response. I finally managed a single, jerky nod of my head. A part of me still feared this was some sort of elaborate trick the two men were playing on me. Or maybe I was still dreaming.

I was pulled from my tangled thoughts by Master's firm order.

"Drink."

I obeyed, parting my lips to accept the delicious drink that he offered to me once again. As I eagerly gulped it down, I did my best to ignore the uneasiness that stirred in my stomach at the sight of Clayton's furrowed brow. The frown he turned on Master was disapproving, but he said nothing as he pulled up a chair and gracefully settled his powerful frame down onto it.

His eyes were kind as he regarded me. They were so earnest and open that my suspicions that he was trying to trick me melted away.

"No one is going to hurt you."

I could definitely believe that Master's promise applied where Clayton was concerned.

"My name is Clayton Vaughn. I work with Smith at the FBI," he introduced himself. "Has Smith explained where you are?"

I glanced over at Master, waiting for his approval to speak to another man.

"You can talk to Clayton," he assured me. "You don't need permission to speak freely to anyone."

The latter statement was almost more than I could wrap my mind around. I hadn't spoken to anyone but my former master for so long, and even then I was told what to say. Words hadn't come of my own volition in a long time, and now my new Master was telling me I could do so. He was ordering me to express myself as I wished.

Only a short time ago, I wouldn't have been capable of even thinking of words without specific instructions, but now my mind was remarkably clear. If I could speak freely, then maybe I was also allowed to think for myself.

The idea was almost as terrifying as it was tempting.

After a moment, I nodded. "Yes. Ma- He told me I'm in a detox center."

Clayton's eyes clouded over at my near slip-up. He seemed disturbed, but he remained focused on me rather than turning his ire on Master again.

"We've been trying to locate your family so we can inform them of where you are. When we found you at Decadence, you didn't have any ID on you, and we couldn't track down the man who brought you there." His features tightened at the mention of my former master, but he quickly schooled his features to something non-threatening. "I can understand if you're… estranged from your family, but it's our job to get you back to them so they can support you in your recovery. We need to know your name so we can do that."

Panic unfurled in my chest like a choking vine, twining up around my windpipe and restricting my ability to breathe. I remembered how angry Master had been on the night he had found me. He had demanded to know my name, and none of my answers had satisfied him.

I made the mistake of shooting him a terrified glance, and I found myself caught in his steady silver stare.

"Tell me your name, girl."

It was an order. I had to answer. But my reply would be no different now than it had been before.

"Slave," I whispered tremulously.

Both men tensed, the force of their anger pressing against me like a lead weight on my chest. My hand twisted in the sheets anxiously.

"I'm sorry. What do you want to call me?" I asked desperately. Master had promised not to hurt me, but I still feared his retribution if I displeased him.

Master's voice was calm when he answered me, but his eyes were still commanding me to comply with his order.

"I want to call you by your real name."

I didn't have a name. *She* had a name once. But that was before she was abducted and broken. And now that I had come out of my delirium, I could scarcely recall the time before I had come into being. I certainly couldn't remember a time before she had been taken. That was too painful to face. That woman was gone now. I had buried her so deeply within me that she would never surface again. The very idea of it terrified me. If she returned, then I would cease to exist. And I didn't know how to be her anymore.

"She…" I swallowed hard against the lump in my throat. "I don't have a name. I'm sorry."

Master didn't look angry any longer; he looked profoundly sad. And more than a little disgusted.

"Okay," Clayton said gently. "That's okay. You just need time. St. Paul's has you listed as 'Jane Doe' for now. Is it all right with you if we call you Jane?"

The name meant nothing to me. I wasn't Jane. I wasn't even a person. But if allowing them to call me that made the painful questions stop, then I would happily agree. I took a deep, calming breath.

"Yes," I said, my voice small. "You can call me Jane if that's what you want."

Master frowned, dissatisfied with my reply, but he said nothing.

"Can you tell us the name of the man who brought you to Decadence, Jane?" Clayton asked gently.

I shook my head as the panic reared up once again. "Master. He was just Master."

My new Master's hand tightened around mine, his grip almost crushing. "Don't call him that," he bit out, fury bleeding into his tone.

"I'm sorry."

I seemed to be saying that a lot. It seemed a waste of my new capability of expressing myself. It suddenly bothered me that I was so contrite. My voice was a bit stronger as I elaborated, exploring my new range of vocabulary.

"He never allowed me to call him anything else."

Master's grip eased as he visibly reined himself in. "We'll figure out his real name, sweetheart," he promised me gruffly. "For now, if you have to refer to him, I want you to call him 'that Bastard.' Can you do that for me?"

"That Bastard." I tasted the crude word on my tongue, and I found that the flavor gave me immense satisfaction. I didn't belong to him any longer. My new Master wouldn't let him hurt me ever again, and I owed him no loyalty. The corners of my lips twitched upward in an unfamiliar way.

Master returned my smile, his grin both encouraging and vindictively satisfied. I was flooded with warmth at the sight of it. I had managed to genuinely please him. His lips weren't twisted in cruel satisfaction as my former master's – that Bastard's – had so often been.

"Unfortunately, there aren't any surveillance cameras around Decadence. The owner wanted to protect the patrons' privacy, so we don't have any leads on the Bastard so far," Clayton informed me. "Could you give us a description of him if we got a sketch artist in here?"

The Bastard's face flashed across my mind, his pleasant features spoiled by the sick, lustful light in his pond scum eyes. I blinked the image away, focusing instead on the strong line of Master's jaw and his mesmerizing molten silver eyes. There was nothing disturbing about the light in them.

"Yes," I said firmly. "I could do that."

Now Clayton was smiling at me too. My bewilderment at the men's approval was overshadowed by the warm glow in my chest.

There was a soft knock on the open door, and my attention turned to the short, slightly plump middle-aged woman who was standing at the threshold to my room. Her soft brown eyes were regarding Master warily, but when she addressed him, her voice was saturated with asperity.

"Am I allowed to come in now, Agent James?" Her words were tart, but her drawl called to mind slowly dripping honey. "I need to check Jane's vitals."

Clayton shot Master an exasperated look. "Of course you can," he told the woman apologetically. "Don't let James bully you out of doing your job. We all want Jane to get better." He spared Master a significant glance, but Master just shrugged.

The woman strode confidently into the room. "Agent James seems to think us incompetent in that regard. But far be it from me to question the FBI when it comes to treating a patient. I didn't realize that all agents were required to attend med school."

Clayton seemed to be torn between amusement at the woman's gumption and disapproval of Master. "I assure you we don't. James is here to protect her, not to treat her." He stood smoothly. "And now that Jane is awake and has answered our preliminary questions, it's time for him to leave." He looked at Master expectantly, but Master didn't move.

"I think I'll stay a while longer," he said assertively. "There's a lot more that we need to find out."

Clayton frowned at him. "We've got enough for today. Do you really want to push her further? You can come back tomorrow."

Master shook his head. "I'm staying one more night. She shouldn't be alone."

Clayton crossed his arms over his chest and stared at Master as though willing him to leave me.

But I didn't want him to leave. I wanted more of Master's kindness. Now that I was allowed to express my wishes, I intended to take full advantage of that capability. I looked Clayton squarely in the eye when I spoke.

"I want him to stay," I said, my voice clear and even.

Master smiled down at me, and my stomach did a little flip. I definitely didn't want him to go. He was so kind to me. He would take care of me. I didn't want to lose that.

Clayton sighed. "Okay. If you want him here, then he can stay." His brilliant blue eyes were as hard as sapphires when he turned them on Master. "But I expect to see you at work tomorrow. And let the nurses do their jobs, for god's sake." He addressed the woman who was now standing by my bedside. "If he keeps being rude, please let me know, and I'll haul him out of here."

Master glared at him. "I'd like to see you try."

Clayton returned his icy stare. "Don't think that I won't." Aggressive tension filled the space between the two men as their wills squared off against one another. After a moment, Clayton's tense stance eased. He wasn't capitulating so much as he was allowing reason to quell his alpha urges. "I just want Jane to get healthy. She can't fully recover until we've found her family and caught the man who hurt her. I know you want to help with that, Smith."

Some of the tension left Master as well. "Why do you always have to be so goddamn reasonable, Vaughn?" He asked.

Clayton shrugged and gave him a small smile. "One of us has to be. Besides, I like being right all the time. It knocks you down a few pegs and saves the rest of us from your frankly staggering ego."

Master snorted. "Right. *I'm* the one with the huge ego. Says the Golden Boy who can do no wrong. In his opinion."

Clayton clapped him on the shoulder. "Yep. And it's not just an opinion if I'm right."

Master brushed his friend's arm away. "Get out of here, jackass." The insult held no real malice. "We can pick up this pissing game tomorrow. I'll see you at the office in the morning."

Clayton nodded his agreement before turning his easy smile on me. "I'll see you soon, Jane. Promise me you'll tell James off if he's annoying you."

"I will," I lied.

"Goodbye, Vaughn," Master said pointedly.

Clayton ignored him, winking at me before he turned to leave the room. I decided that I liked him.

For the first time in a long time, thinking for myself didn't have painful consequences.

Chapter 4

"My name is Susan," the kindly-looking woman who was checking my blood pressure introduced herself. Now that she was closer to me, I could tell she was perhaps a bit older than I had first estimated. Streaks of pale grey mingled with the light blonde wisps of hair that escaped her loose bun. The defined lines around her eyes and mouth were creased from years of broad smiles. She addressed Master in a tone that brooked no nonsense, but her voice was warm when she spoke to me, her softly reassuring smile reaching her eyes.

"Hi," I said shyly. I felt a bit awkward not introducing myself as well. Half-remembered social conventions were flitting around at the corners of my mind. But I still didn't have a name. Everyone seemed to want to call me "Jane." The name didn't mean anything to me, but I would respond to it.

And I hadn't failed to notice that Master didn't address me as "Jane." He always called me "sweetheart" or "girl." I was accustomed to being spoken to as though I was less than a person. Honestly, the idea of having a real name had terrifying implications about my own autonomy and sense of responsibility for myself. It was much easier to put my trust in Master and follow his orders. And his terms were so much more affectionate that "whore," "slave," or "fucktoy."

I took it as a sign that he had accepted ownership of me. He really was going to take care of me. And he didn't seem to expect anything in return other than my obedience.

I could scarcely believe that this wonderful, beautiful man had decided to keep me. I was no longer afraid of my present or my future, and I would bury my painful past just as thoroughly as I had buried the woman I used to be.

Susan's hands were gentle as she took inventory of my body, and Master never let go of my hand. Although my muscles still ached, I couldn't recall feeling more pampered.

The bed I had been given was soft and warm, and the room was brightly lit. Even when Susan and Master weren't speaking, the world was still rich with the sounds of humanity. The hallway outside my room was peppered with the soft slaps of footfalls, rustling papers, and disjointed flashes of conversations. Nothing had ever felt so *real*. It might have been overwhelming if Master hadn't been there, his hold on my hand grounding me. Nothing could hurt me while he was with me. He had promised.

Once she had finished checking me over, Susan took down a clipboard that hung on the wall beside my bed and made a few notes.

"Everything looks good," she told me brightly. "You've gotten through the worst of it, Jane. Now we just need to get you healthy. I'm going to get you something to eat. You need to put some weight back on." She eyed Master. "I'm going to leave you with the caveman for a little while. Are you okay with that? I can stay with you if you would prefer."

"That's okay," I said quickly. "I want him to stay."

It was odd expressing my own wishes. The word *want* felt strange on my tongue. But I was bolstered by Master's approving smile. I was so entranced by it that I barely noticed that Susan's lips were pursed in disapproval.

"Alright," she conceded. "I'll be back to check on you later." She delivered the reassurance to Master like a warning. He just gave her a sardonic little wave, dismissing her. She rolled her eyes at him and planted her hands on her hips. "The call button is on the side of the bed, Jane. Don't hesitate to use it if you need me."

She left the room, muttering to herself. I definitely heard "Yankee men" and "should never have left Georgia" as she stalked out.

"I don't think she likes me very much," Master remarked casually. "But I have to give her credit; she's the only nurse who's come in here since I told them all to get the fuck out unless you needed immediate medical attention."

He was smiling at me softly. I was fairly certain I liked Susan, but I didn't care that Master had been rude to her. It wasn't my place to comment on it anyway. And it made me feel safer knowing that he had kept strangers away from me. Now that he had staked his claim, I was confident no one would dare to take me from him. I would fight anyone who tried.

That thought shocked me. Defiance never crossed my mind. But Master was kind to me, and I was tentatively beginning to enjoy the freedoms he had granted me. I wasn't going to give that up easily.

"Thank you," I said softly. I added on *Master* in my mind, but I didn't say it aloud. That was against the rules.

His smile faded, his expression taking on a new intensity. "You don't have to thank me," he told me, his voice low and rough. He cupped my cheek in his large hand. "I'm not going to let anything happen to you, little one."

Little one. He hadn't called me that before. I liked the sound of it. I felt so small in his grip, but there was no fear that he would use his strength against me. The way his deep, rich voice caressed the words made it an endearment rather than a belittling term. Without thinking, I leaned into his touch, pressing my cheek against his palm.

The depth of my trust in him might have been jarring to me once, but I didn't have the option of not trusting him. He was my Master now, and my fate was entirely in his hands. Even if he had been cruel to me, I wouldn't have questioned him.

But I also wouldn't have found comfort in his touch.

We sat in silence for a while, and I closed my eyes as I relished the feel of his fingers running through my hair.

"Don't you think you're being a bit overly-familiar with Jane, *Agent* James?" Susan emphasized his job title.

Master pulled away from me, and I was amazed to find that he was shifting uncomfortably in his chair, as though he had been caught doing something he oughtn't.

"I don't mind," I defended him quickly, reaching for his hand. I hated the coolness that hit my skin when he released me.

Susan pursed her lips again as she eyed the way he wrapped his fingers around mine. But then her eyes came to rest on my anxious expression, and her demeanor softened.

"Okay, sweetie. I just don't want Agent James doing anything *inappropriate.*"

Master bristled. "Is that an accusation?" He asked, his low tone holding a dangerous edge.

Susan squared her shoulders, meeting his challenge. "It's an observation," she countered.

"If you had any idea what she's been through, you would know just how disgusting that insinuation is."

"I do have an idea," she said sharply. "And that's why you shouldn't be touching her at all."

"Stop." I was shocked by the authority in my own voice. "I want him here."

Susan studied us for a minute, her gaze flicking to Master and back to me. My eyes were wide as I silently pleaded with her not to anger him. I needed him to stay by my side.

"I'm not going to let anything happen to you, little one."

"Please," I added softly. "He'll keep me safe."

Susan sighed. "No one here is going to hurt you, Jane."

Master squeezed my hand, calling my attention back to him. "She's right. No one will hurt you ever again. And you don't need me by your side to keep you safe from anyone here." His expression was strained, as though he had to force himself to make the admission.

I trusted him implicitly, but it was difficult to believe him.

Susan nodded her approval. "It seems you can be sensible after all, Agent James. You might just be hiding a decent person under all of that alpha male bullcrap."

I couldn't believe that she had dared to insult Master. I expected his anger, but I was stunned when his warm, rich laughter filled the room.

"I suspect that I might like you as well if you weren't so goddamn bossy."

Susan tried and failed to suppress a smile. "See? I knew that you could be reasonable."

Master chuckled again, smiling easily at Susan for the first time. I was relieved that his open hostility towards her had faded. Susan's presence was warm, non-threatening. And I didn't feel that I had to defer to her in the same way that I did to Clayton. Although he wasn't as fierce as Master, he was still a man, and an imposing one at that.

Susan briefly retreated into the hallway to retrieve the food she had brought for me. Once she had set the tray up before me, I looked up at Master imploringly. He stared back at me for a moment, his eyes appraising as he tried to puzzle out what I needed.

Anger flashed across his features when comprehension hit him. He quickly smoothed his taut expression, but his eyes still glinted like sunlight on cold steel.

"You can eat," he told me firmly. "You don't need permission."

Master granted me another freedom. I could speak as I wished and eat whenever I wanted. The concept of exercising so much free will was terrifying. I re-arranged his words in my mind so that they were orders.

Speak freely. Eat when you want to.

The knot of tension in my chest eased. Obedience was so much easier.

Susan turned her attention back to Master. "I don't suppose I could convince you that the staff here are more than capable of looking after Jane overnight, could I?"

Master regarded her levelly. "Will you be here tonight?"

Susan's cheeks flushed pink, and she looked slightly abashed. "No," she admitted. "I won't be back until tomorrow morning. And although I'm flattered that I've earned the hardass Agent James seal of approval, you have to believe me when I tell you that she's in good hands here."

Master dismissed her insistent words. "I'll stay here until your shift starts tomorrow."

Susan sighed. "All right then. But you have to allow the nurses to come check on her periodically. The worst of the withdrawals have passed, but Jane is a long way from being healthy."

Master gave her a short nod, allowing the small concession. "Okay. But I don't want any male nurses or orderlies in here."

"I think that's sensible," Susan agreed. She turned her warm smile back on me. "Goodnight, Jane. I'll see you in the morning."

"Thank you." I liked the words. I hadn't been allowed to express gratitude in a non-sexual way in so long. And even then I hadn't been truly grateful. I had been desperate for my fix, for the pain to end.

I fought back the urge to shudder at the brutal memories.

That part of my life was over. Just as I had forsaken the woman I had been before I had been broken, I would bury the slave who had lived to serve her former master. Now that I had my new Master, I could be a different person. I could find joy in serving him that was far greater than the hollow bliss I had received from that Bastard's rewards.

I didn't even realize Susan was gone. Master was my whole world now, and I watched him greedily. I would do whatever was required of me to convince him to keep me. He would see that I was a good slave, and he would never want to let me go.

He rubbed the pad of his thumb across the back of my hand in a slow, soothing rhythm.

"You should get some sleep, little one," he said gently. *Go to sleep.*

That was an order that was easy to obey. I closed my eyes and was quickly pulled under by my exhaustion. This time, I wasn't haunted by visions of torture as I slept. That version of myself no longer existed. And Master's firm grip on my hand reassured me that I would never have to be that abused, degraded slave ever again.

∙∙∙

Soft light filtered into my room, and I opened my eyes to behold the long-forgotten sight of dawn. The pale beams of the morning sun slanted through the half-closed blinds that obscured the window across from my bed. Hints of the outside world were visible through the gaps in the blinds, but the brilliant green of foliage and steely grey of distant buildings held little interest for me.

I much preferred to study the way the light played across Master's features, illuminating the planes of his face and creating shadows beneath his brows. I longed for him to open his eyes, to see their silvery light cutting through that darkness.

Although the stubble on his jaw had lengthened to darken his cheeks, there was a deeper shadow just to the right of his full lips where a dimple would appear when he smiled. I craved to please him so he would bestow that smile on me once again.

"Master," I whispered, awestruck. I relished the word as it left my lips. He was so breathtaking. And I was *his.*

The corners of his lips quirked up as he stirred from his sleep, his large body shifting in the too-small chair he had pulled up beside my bed. But to my dismay, when he opened his eyes, his lips twisted downward in a frown.

"Don't call me that," he said softly. He sounded almost pained.

My heart sank in my chest. I had disobeyed him.

"I'm sorry," I said anxiously. My fingers closed around his hand like a vise, as though I could keep him by my side if I just held on to him tightly enough.

His expression softened, but he still regarded me seriously. "This is one rule you cannot break, sweetheart. You can't call me 'Master.'"

I nodded vigorously before he could tell me he wasn't my Master at all. I couldn't allow him to reject me and leave me vulnerable.

"I promise I won't," I said fervently. "I'll do better. I'll be good."

His brow furrowed as he studied me carefully, as though he was considering what to do with me. Although I believed that he wouldn't hurt me for my transgression, I still feared he would rebuke me. And I didn't know how to earn his forgiveness if he didn't want me sexually.

"I'm sorry," I apologized desperately, using my words to express myself as he had instructed me to do. I could follow his rules. I could. I stared at him imploringly, willing him to believe that.

He touched his fingers to my cheek in an effort to calm me. "It's okay, girl," he reassured me. "I'm not angry with you."

"Thank you," I whispered gratefully.

Thank you for forgiving me, Master.

There was a knock at the door. Susan didn't wait for Master's permission to enter.

"Good morning, Agent James," she said cordially. "And goodbye." She glanced at our intertwined fingers. "I promise you Jane's hand won't fall off if you release it. It will still be firmly attached to her wrist when you return."

Master frowned at her. "You're here awfully early," he remarked.

Susan shrugged. "I came in early. You're not the only one who wants to see Jane get better, you know. And I was concerned you might have ignored my stipulations and kept the other nurses out of the room during the night."

"I wouldn't do that. As many people have pointed out, I don't have a medical degree," he said coolly.

Susan nodded curtly. "You're getting more and more sensible all the time," she said with approval. "If you're ready to admit that you're an FBI agent and not a doctor, then might I suggest you go back to your own job and allow me to do mine?"

I clutched Master's hand more tightly. I didn't want him to leave me. My heart twisted as I took in his regretful expression.

"As much as I hate to admit it, she's right," he told me. "I promised Clayton I would help him track down your family. Don't worry," he reassured me. "I'll come back as soon as my shift is over." He turned his attention back to Susan. "How late will you be here?"

"I'm here for twelve hours. I'm supposed to get off at six."

Master nodded. "I'll be here at five-thirty."

Susan sighed heavily. "I don't suppose I could persuade you to sleep at your own home tonight, could I? Jane needs some room to breathe."

"No, you couldn't," Master replied unequivocally.

Susan threw up her hands in exasperated defeat. "Fine. I'll see you at five-thirty."

Master's expression softened. "Thank you," he said quietly.

Susan blinked hard, taken aback. "I'll stay with Jane today," she promised, all signs of bossy disapproval gone. She placed a tentative hand on Master's arm. "I might not approve of your interference, but it's obvious that you have a big heart under all that machismo crap. I've seen law enforcement agents bring in addicts more times than I can count, and they leave as soon as they possibly can. It's nice to see that you're so invested in helping Jane. And so long as you allow me to treat her, I'll allow you to stay."

Master gave her a lopsided smile. "I would stay whether you allowed it or not. But I appreciate it."

He turned to me, his expression gentle and somewhat reluctant. "I have to go now, sweetheart."

I fought back the urge to protest, to beg him to stay. He had ordered me to express myself freely, but I knew that didn't extend to open defiance.

"It's okay," he said soothingly, sensing my distress. "I'll be back in a few hours."

I swallowed back my panic at the prospect of being without him. I had no option but to agree. Besides, he had appointed Susan to look after me, so I had to trust his judgment. I forced myself to nod, communicating my acceptance of his wishes.

"That's a good girl," he said gently before squeezing my hand one last time. The apprehension that gripped me at the prospect of his absence was burned away by the warm glow that pulsed to life in my chest in response to his tender praise.

He nodded once at Susan before leaving me. I wanted to cry out at the loss of his reassuring hold on my hand. His touch had been my anchor since I had awoken to my new life, and I wasn't sure how I was going to get through the day without it. But he had promised to come back. I had to trust him. I would be good.

"Are you sure Agent James isn't making you uncomfortable, Jane?" Susan was frowning slightly, disapproval etched in her soft features. "I understand if you're scared to tell him you don't want him to touch you. I'll keep him out if he's bothering you."

"No," I said firmly. "I'm not scared of him."

I'm only scared of him leaving me.

But I didn't dare say that aloud. It was Master's will that I remain in Susan's care until he returned, and I wasn't going to protest.

Susan still appeared slightly uncomfortable. "Well, if you're happy with the caveman being here, then I'll look the other way. I really do appreciate that he cares so deeply about helping you recover, but he *is* acting inappropriately."

I said nothing, and after a moment, Susan's easy smile returned. "How about we get you some breakfast?" She asked brightly. "We need to get your calorie count up."

I nodded my assent. Master had ordered me to eat without waiting for his permission, so I would comply with Susan's wishes.

But my compliance was soon tested. After breakfast, Susan tried to convince me to defy one of Master's orders. Even though he wasn't there to witness my transgression, I didn't want to break another one of his rules. He had been so disappointed in me when I had slipped up and called him "Master." I only ever wanted him to be perfectly happy with me. I had promised I would be good, and I fully intended to keep that promise.

Susan had brought me into the bathroom so I could use the toilet and take a shower. I was so weak that I couldn't walk the short distance to the bathroom without her assistance, and she insisted that I sit down while taking a shower.

But once I was seated, she began tugging on the laces that held the back of my hospital gown closed. I quickly twisted away from her.

"You don't have permission to remove your clothes."

"Don't," I said desperately.

Susan placed her hands on my shoulders, trying to steady me. "It's okay, Jane. I just need to take your gown off so you can get clean."

"No!" I protested sharply. "I can't do that."

Susan's soft brown eyes gazed into my own. "I'm not going to hurt you, Jane. You can trust me."

"I do," I assured her, my voice rough with my rising panic. I had to make her understand. "But I can't take off my clothes. He told me I wasn't allowed to."

"That man isn't going to hurt you anymore, Jane," she assured me firmly. "You don't have to do anything he told you to do."

She thought I was talking about that Bastard. "No. Not him. He wouldn't let me wear clothes."

I wasn't sure how to explain myself. I couldn't refer to Master as "Smith" or "Agent James." He hadn't given me permission to call him by his name. But I wasn't allowed to call him "Master" either. Tears began to form at the corners of my eyes as my frustration and fear overwhelmed me.

Susan's brows drew together in puzzlement.

"Please," I begged raggedly. "I know he left me with you, but I'm not supposed to take off my clothes."

Understanding dawned in Susan's eyes, and she scowled as she pulled her cell phone from her pocket along with a business card. Glancing at the card, she punched in the number and held the phone to her ear.

"Agent James," she said coldly into the receiver. "Could you please explain to me why Jane thinks she can't take off her clothes?"

I could hear Master's deep voice rumbling on the other end of the line, but I couldn't make out what he was saying. After a moment, Susan pulled the phone from her ear and held it out between us.

"You're on speakerphone," Susan informed Master, her voice a bit louder than was strictly necessary.

"Hi, sweetheart." Just the sound of his voice made most of the tension leave my muscles. Master would tell me what to do. And he would know I had been good. I hadn't allowed Susan to persuade me to break his rule.

"Hi," I answered softly.

"I need you to do what Susan says."

My stomach clenched. Had I done something wrong? I had thought my obedience would please him, but apparently I was supposed to obey Susan in his absence.

"I'm sorry," I apologized tremulously. I had already disappointed him once today. What would he do to me now that I had failed him twice in the space of a few hours?

"It's okay, sweetheart," he reassured me. "You didn't do anything wrong. But I need you to mind Susan when I'm not there. Can you do that for me?"

"Yes," I said fervently, clinging to the promise of his forgiveness like a lifeline.

Susan was scowling at the phone. "Thank you for your help, Agent James. But you and I will talk about this before I leave tonight." There was no trace of her usually sweet demeanor in her narrowed eyes.

But I was too jubilant to allow her anger to bother me. Master knew I hadn't broken his rule, and now he had given me a new order to follow.

Obey Susan until I return.

The prospect of getting through the day without him was suddenly far less terrifying.

Chapter 5

I caught snippets of Master and Susan's heated conversation as their harshly whispered words drifted in through my open doorway. Master wouldn't consent to retreating further than the hallway to speak privately with Susan, so I was able to puzzle out some of what they were saying.

"Totally inappropriate… Don't think I haven't noticed that you give her permission to do everything… No different than that man -"

"Don't you dare compare me to him," Master barked before lowering his voice back to a murmur. "…don't understand…"

"Then explain it so I can understand," Susan hissed.

I picked out the words "structure" and "rules" in the midst of Master's low rumbling.

"Is everything okay here?" Clayton's voice cut through their hushed conversation.

"Yes," Susan said slowly, her voice returning to a more normal volume. "I think so." All of the fire had left her tone. Whatever Master had told her must have placated her.

"What are you doing here, Vaughn?" Master asked.

"We need to ask Jane some more questions. You know that," Clayton replied calmly.

"That can wait until tomorrow." Master's voice was firm.

Clayton sighed. "We're going nowhere fast with her case. Without more to go on, we can't get any closer to locating her family or tracking down the Bastard who abused her. Do you really want to waste one more day before we find him? The longer we wait, the colder his trail gets."

"Fine." Master sounded resigned.

Susan poked her head through the door so she could address me. "I'll be back first thing in the morning, Jane," she assured me.

"Okay. Thank you." I truly was grateful that she had resolved whatever had made her angry with Master. I liked Susan, and Master trusted her to take care of me. I felt safe with her.

Then Master stepped into my room, and I forgot all about Susan. I had never really noticed how he moved before; he had spent most of his time with me sitting at my bedside. Although his body was imposing, he moved with the smooth, controlled grace of a predator. His eyes looked tired, but he had shaved since I had last seen him. It seemed he had a perpetual five o'clock shadow, but it only made him even more appealing, giving him a rough edge that belied the orderliness of his neatly tailored suit. And although he had straightened his appearance for work, his dark, wavy hair still fell haphazardly to curl just beneath his jawline.

Beneath his civilized veneer, there was a wildness to him that I relished. It was that ferocity that made me feel so safe with him. He would never turn it against me, but no one would dare to touch me while this powerful man claimed ownership of me.

"Hi, sweetheart." He beamed at me, and the sight of his dimple elicited a reciprocal smile from me. The upward tug of the muscles around my mouth was still only a vaguely familiar sensation.

Clayton followed Master into my room. "Hey, Jane." He was smiling at me too.

Everyone was so kind to me here. I never wanted to leave this place.

Master settled into the chair beside my bed again and covered my hand with his. I didn't realize just how keenly I had missed his presence there. Tension I didn't even know I had been holding in my muscles finally eased, and I felt safer than I had in hours.

Obeying Susan had been easy once Master had ordered me to do so, and we had followed a regimented schedule all day. I had eaten several small meals and even walked around for a short time to begin building up my strength. She explained that I would repeat the processes daily until I was healthy.

I couldn't contemplate what might come after they deemed me healthy. The prospect of more change terrified me. All I wanted was for Master to tell me what to do. Before he had taken me for himself, I had been imprisoned in the dark for most of the time. Back then, I didn't have to think about anything other than waiting for my ma – that Bastard, I corrected myself – to come and use me.

Now Master had burdened me with too many freedoms all at once. I would have been overwhelmed by them without his constant guidance. All of my senses were assailed by sights, sounds, and smells that were disturbingly familiar to me. I had forgotten about the world outside my dungeon, and now my recollections of such things threatened to call forth the woman I had once been.

She was the one who remembered these things, but I couldn't allow myself to remember *her*. If she existed, then the abused slave also existed. I couldn't face either of them. I had to stay in the present, had to focus on pleasing my new Master so I could remain in my new reality. I couldn't look back.

"I'm afraid we're going to have to ask you a few questions, Jane." Clayton's expression was slightly reluctant, regretful, even.

My gut clenched. I had gathered from their hushed conversation in the hallway that they wanted to question me about that Bastard. I didn't want to think about him. But Clayton hadn't asked whether or not I wanted to answer his questions; he had simply told me he would ask me.

Master squeezed my hand. "It's alright, sweetheart. I'll be right here with you."

I swallowed hard and nodded. Master wanted me to comply with Clayton's wishes. Even though it wasn't an order, I couldn't refuse.

"We want to track down the man who hurt you, Jane," Clayton said, his tone calm and even. "I know you can't remember his name, but we can't find him without more to go on. Can you tell us where he lives? Is he here in New York or did you travel to come to Decadence?"

I bit my lip. I didn't know the answer to his first question. The Bastard had kept me in the dark, blindfolding me before he took me from my prison. And I had been so desperate for my fix that I hadn't been able to focus on anything else. I had no concept of how much time had passed between leaving my dungeon and arriving at Decadence.

"I don't know," I whispered. "I'm sorry."

Clayton's brow furrowed. "Did you meet up with him at the club that night? Where do you live?"

"Here." This was my new home.

"Where *did* you live, Jane?" Clayton's voice was cajoling, but the question penetrated my new sense of safety like dozens of needles pricking at my brain. I didn't want to remember. I had resolved to bury the woman who had existed in that dungeon. I couldn't be her any longer. A fine tremor ran through me as the scent of damp concrete and coppery blood filled my nostrils.

"Answer him, girl," Master spoke softly, but it was an order.

"In the dark. I lived in the dark."

Clayton shot a worried glance at Master. "I know your addiction must make it difficult to recall, but I need for you to try to remember where you were before you came to Decadence."

Where was I before I had felt the sting of the needle for the first time?

My mind shied away from it. That was before I had been broken. There was nothing before the darkness.

But they wanted more from me. My answer didn't please them.

"Can you describe your home to me?" Clayton pressed.

Home.

That word meant little to me. It was laughably incongruous with the dank misery in which I had existed. But I had nothing else to give Clayton.

"It was cold," I whispered reluctantly, allowing the memory of that place to brush at the edges of my mind. "I think it was underground. It was always dark unless he was there."

The fury rolling off of Master was so powerful that I couldn't bear to look at him. Clayton's expression was carefully neutral, but his knuckles were white where his clenched fist rested on his knee. I was trying my best to give them what they wanted, but it still wasn't enough.

Answer him. Master had ordered me to answer Clayton's questions.

I willed myself to fully return to the dungeon. Behind my closed eyelids, the image of my prison bloomed to life. I shuddered as it solidified around me, and I was once again immersed in the horror of that place.

"The walls and floor were concrete. There was a cage. A cross. Chains."

Whips. Bruises. Tears. Blood.

I touched my fingers to my neck where I felt the phantom weight of my iron collar.

"Pain."

So much pain.

My lungs burned as I struggled to draw breath through my constricted windpipe.

Large hands cupped my cheeks, their warmth pushing back the cold that had seeped into my veins.

"Open your eyes, girl."

I did as ordered, and I found silver eyes staring down at me rather than muddy green ones.

"Stay here with me," Master commanded. "Breathe."

I complied, drawing air into my oxygen-starved lungs.

"How long were you there?" Clayton's voice drifted down to me.

I shook my head slightly. I didn't know. Time meant nothing to me. There was no time. There was only the pain. And that never ended.

"That's enough, Vaughn," Master said sharply.

"We need to know more, James," Clayton replied firmly. "It's August 26, 2013," he informed me. "When did you first go to that place?"

I had been there forever, for my entire existence. *She* had arrived there. She had a life before that place.

She awoke in a cage. She wanted to escape. He beat her. He raped her.

"He took her there. She tried to get out. He wouldn't let her go. He hurt her."

A sob ripped its way up my throat. I couldn't remember her. I couldn't.

Master's arms wrapped around me, their strength enfolding me, sheltering me. I buried my face against his chest, and my fingers twined into the fabric of his shirt as I clutched at him.

"Master," I whispered desperately, voicing his title aloud to reassure myself that he was real. I belonged to him now, and I would never be forced to go back to that place.

This time he didn't admonish me for saying the word.

"It's okay, little one. He can't hurt you anymore. You're safe with me." His deep voice rumbled over my skin like a soothing balm.

"James." Clayton's sharply spoken word was imbued with warning.

"Get out, Vaughn," Master growled.

"You can't let her call you 'Master.'" Heat colored Clayton's usually calm tone. "She doesn't understand what that means. Not in the same way you understand it."

"I know that," Master snapped. "But she needs this."

I clung to Master more tightly. I couldn't allow Clayton to convince him to leave me. I peeked up at Master's friend, staring into his blue eyes imploringly.

"Please. I'm sorry I said 'Master.' I know it's against the rules. I promise I'll do better. I'll be good."

The light in Clayton's eyes was deeply sad and more than a little horrified. "Okay," he conceded. "It's okay, Jane. No one is going to punish you. But you can't call Smith 'Master.' You're not a slave."

My mind couldn't comprehend his firm declaration. If I wasn't a slave, then I didn't know what I was. I didn't know how to exist as anything else. The concept of no longer belonging to Master terrified me. I brushed Clayton's words from my conscious mind.

He glanced over at Master. "I suppose you're going to stay here again tonight."

"Yes," Master replied roughly. "And don't you dare try to tell me not to."

Clayton shook his head. "No. I wouldn't do that. I think it's actually a good thing that you're staying."

Master's arms tightened around me. I turned my face into his chest, inhaling his comforting scent. It was warm and rich with a hint of a sharp edge, like a smooth whiskey that burns deliciously as it slides down your throat.

"I'll see you in the morning, then, Smith," Clayton said, weariness roughening his voice.

"Definitely," Master growled. "We're going to catch the Bastard. I thought he had taken advantage of her, but he fucking abducted her, Clayton."

"I know. We'll bring in the guys from NYPD Missing Persons."

"I won't turn down the extra manpower, but this is our collar, Clayton. We're going to be the ones who bring him in. I won't let the NYPD treat him gently."

"Agreed," Clayton said firmly. His chair scraped against the floor as he stood to leave. I didn't watch him as he walked away; I kept my face firmly pressed against Master's chest.

"Clayton," Master called after his friend. "Thanks."

I breathed Master's scent in greedily as Clayton's footsteps retreated, allowing him to claim all of my senses. No matter what Clayton said, I belonged to Master. And I wasn't ever going to let anyone take me from him.

●●●

Over the next four days, Master guided me through the challenges of my new life. My schedule was carefully regimented, and Master's orders for compliance with Susan's wishes made tackling the unfamiliar less terrifying.

The greatest difficulties came from the requests of the FBI agents who came to see me. A strange woman came to take my fingerprints. I would have been frightened of her touch if Master hadn't assured me that my compliance would please him.

It was much more difficult to obey the sketch artist. She wanted to know what that Bastard looked like, and recalling his appearance in detail had been traumatic. Master held me for hours afterward, stroking my hair and whispering words of comfort. He didn't say it aloud, but his touch and promise of safety reassured me that I belonged to him now.

Clayton came to check in on me frequently, but he didn't ask me any more painful questions. Truthfully, he seemed to watch Master just as carefully as he assessed my own well-being. I appreciated that he wanted to look out for Master, and I found his presence comforting. Clayton was always so kind and calm. He laughed easily, and even Master's more prickly comments seemed to roll right off him.

A psychologist came to see me once, but – much to Susan's disapproval – Master scared her off. Master and Susan had a heated argument about it in the hallway just outside my room, but Susan finally backed down. It was decided that I should recover my physical strength before facing therapy. I was immensely grateful to Master for protecting me from the pain of facing my past.

He was so good to me, and he never asked me to do anything for him in return. All of his rules were established for my own benefit rather than his pleasure. I was puzzled by this arrangement, but I knew better than to question my Master. I eagerly accepted my new life, fully committing myself to serving Master and pleasing him through my obedience.

I dreaded the rising sun; daylight meant Master's absence. He stayed with me every night, and the pang in my heart that accompanied his departure in the morning troubled me throughout the long hours until he returned.

Now that pang had sharpened to the cut of a twisting knife. Darkness had fallen hours earlier, but Master had yet to return to me. He had called around sunset to let me know that he was going to work late. He wanted so badly to track down the man who had hurt me, and apparently the FBI had found a promising lead. I didn't care about that, but it wasn't my place to question Master's wishes.

Susan had agreed to stay with me until Master could come back to me. She had been with me since the crack of dawn, and lines of exhaustion appeared around her eyes as midnight approached.

The clinic had gone quiet. Only minimal staff stayed on to cover the night shift, and the usual bustle in the hallway outside my room had lowered to intermittent hushed conversations. Laughter emanated from the TV in my room. Susan had put on some sitcom to help distract me from my growing anxiety, but the rapid-fire jokes exchanged by the beautiful people on the screen were lost on me.

Susan yawned widely and glanced at her watch. Sighing, she turned off the TV and stood, stretching her muscles.

"I'm going to get a cup of coffee, Jane," she informed me softly. "And don't worry. I'm going to call Agent James to find out where he is. I promise I'll make him come see you soon. In the meantime, close your eyes and try to get some sleep."

I knew it would be impossible to fall asleep without Master's warmth beside me, but Susan had given me an order.

Compliantly, I closed my eyes as she turned to leave my room. I did my best to brush off my uneasiness at being left completely alone. I knew Susan would be back soon, and she was going to call Master. She would convince him to return to me. I took several deep breaths and tried to push down my rising panic.

A hand clamped down on my mouth, long fingers digging harshly into my cheeks. Despite Susan's order, my eyes snapped open as fear shocked my system.

The sick light in his muddy green eyes made bile rise in the back of my throat along with choking terror.

"Don't make a sound, whore," my former master whispered menacingly.

Chapter 6

No.

He couldn't be here. Master had promised that the Bastard would never touch me again. But his cruel grip on my jaw and the savagely pleased smile that twisted his lips were all too real.

"You're going to come with me quietly, slave. If you resist me or try to call for help, your punishment will be even more severe."

His chilling words threatened to make my muscles freeze. But I had to fight him. I couldn't allow him to take me from Master. I didn't belong to him anymore, and I didn't have to obey him.

I struggled beneath him, clutching at his arm in an effort to free myself from his grip. His hand only left my mouth for an instant before it cracked across my cheek.

Pain and the taste of coppery blood ripped me from the present. The warmly-lit room that was my new reality swirled around me as my head spun.

It wasn't real. It had never been real. It was just a harsh trick that the Bastard – no, he was Master – had played on me to give me cruel hope that my life could be less painful. He had told me He was taking me to Decadence to test me. All of this had been a test. And I knew I had failed.

Agony awaited me in my cold prison. I didn't want to go back there. But I didn't dare fight my Master. The horror of the torture I would endure would only be that much more terrible if I did try to defy Him.

Tears rolled down my cheeks as His hand closed around my upper arm, but I swallowed back my despairing sobs. He had ordered me to be quiet.

He wrenched me upright, jerking me from the comfortable warmth of the bed. I stumbled as I struggled to find my feet.

"What are you doing in here?" Susan asked sharply from where she stood in the doorway, a steaming cup of coffee clutched in her small, wrinkled hand. Her stance was threatening, but she had never looked more slight and frail. Master would hurt her if she stood in His way.

"She fell, and I came in to help her up," Master replied smoothly.

Susan's eyes narrowed as she appraised Master, taking in His blue scrubs before studying the way that His hand gripped my arm. "All of the male staff members know to stay out of Jane's room. And you certainly shouldn't be touching her. What's your name, orderly?"

Master's fingers dug into my flesh as His muscles coiled. I couldn't let Him hurt Susan. I knew He would punish me if I spoke without permission, but I had to try to protect her.

"Please don't hurt her, Master," I whispered imploringly.

Susan's eyes widened, and she gasped as comprehension dawned. To my horror, she lunged towards us rather than turning and running as she should have. I clutched at Master's arm in a desperate attempt to hold Him back, but He had always been far stronger than I was.

My efforts allowed Susan a split-second to punch the nurse call button beside the bed before Master was on her. There was a sickening crack as He slammed her head against the wall. Her body slid to the floor, leaving a crimson streak on the white paint as she fell.

Master cursed as He grabbed me, His hand gripping my sex roughly.

"This cunt is mine, slave," He snarled. "You thought you could run from me? You'll always belong to me."

Approaching footsteps echoed down the hall. Master released me, shoving me away from Him with another curse. I dropped to my knees automatically, desperate to prove my supplication.

"No amount of groveling will save you," He told me furiously. His boot drove into my side, and the world flickered out of existence as agony ripped through me. "I'll be back for you, slave." His vicious promise drifted down to me where I lay on the floor, my body curled protectively around my injury. I heard Him walk quickly away from me, but I felt no sense of relief.

"I'll be back for you, slave."

He was going to return. He would come back to torment me, to use me. He always did. I had to do everything I could to appease Him. Maybe He wouldn't hurt me as badly if I pleased Him.

The t-shirt and sweatpants that I wore grated against my skin. I wasn't allowed to hide my body from Him.

Shoving back the pain that paralyzed me, I tore at the clothes. Once I was appropriately naked, I pushed myself up onto my knees and spread them wide, exposing my cunt for His use. My hands clasped at the small of my back, and I thrust out my breasts as I straightened my shoulders. I bowed my head, staring at a spot on the floor.

I had thought the abused slave no longer existed, but that was a lie. The agony that radiated outward from my side, the throbbing of my cheek, and the tang of blood in my mouth made that all too clear. My tears burned as they rolled over my frigid skin.

"What the-? Susan!" The woman's voice was panicked as she raced into the room.

I didn't look up. I barely breathed for fear that any movement would be taken as a sign of defiance.

"I need help in here!" The woman shouted. Shrill beeping filled the room when she pressed the Code Blue button. "Oh, shit, shit! Susan!" Her voice was tinged with hysteria.

Susan. Master had hurt Susan. But I couldn't go to her. The only way I could help her now was to prove to my Master that I could be good. If I pleased Him, then maybe I could convince Him not to hurt her again.

The room was suddenly cacophonous as several people stormed in. Sharp, quickly-spoken words punctuated the incessant beeping. All of the sounds swirled together to become a high, piercing whine.

"Jane!" A masculine hand reached out for me, but I didn't recognize it. I couldn't allow anyone but Master to touch me. He wouldn't like that. I cringed away from the man, but I didn't break from my submissive pose. "Someone get me a sedative," the man barked. Seconds later, a syringe appeared in his hand.

I shook my head vigorously. I didn't want the sting of the needle. I didn't want the oblivion that would come along with my reward. It hurt too badly when I was denied its kiss. I would rather endure the pain of the beating that was coming than return to that state.

"Get away from her." His voice boomed through the small space, and all of my attention honed in on him.

He was real. My new Master was real.

The whining quieted, and I realized that the sound had been issuing from my own throat.

He crouched down in front of me and placed his fingers beneath my chin, forcing my head up. His concerned eyes filled my vision, and a fresh flood of tears welled up. Only this time, they were tears of relief rather than despair.

"Tell me what happened, girl," he ordered evenly.

"Master came for me," I whispered. "He hurt Susan."

His eyes flashed. "What have I told you about calling him that?" He demanded harshly. "He's not your Master."

"I'm sorry," I sobbed. My mind was reeling, torn between my past and present. The pain and fear that gripped me threatened to pull me under, to return me to my deadened state where nothing existed by the need to please my former Master. But now my new Master had returned to me, and my heart yearned to accept him.

Master's gorgeous eyes regarded me carefully. "Address me properly, girl," he commanded evenly.

"I'm sorry, Master." The acknowledgement of his ownership centered me, and the paralyzing terror eased from my muscles. Master had claimed me. He would keep me safe.

"That's a good girl," he praised. "But if I'm your Master, then why are you following his rules? I ordered you not to take off your clothes without specific instructions to do so."

Oh, no. I had disobeyed him. I trembled as I braced myself for his anger.

His hand stroked up and down my arm in a soothing rhythm. "It's okay, girl. I forgive you. But know that there will be consequences if I ever hear you refer to him as 'Master' again. Is that clear?"

"Yes, Master," I said quickly. "I'm sorry, Master."

"That's enough apologizing," he told me steadily. "Get dressed."

He did most of the work for me, directing my limbs as he wanted them so he could more easily pull on my clothes. When he was finished, he hooked one arm under my knees and placed the other around my back, cradling me to his chest as he lifted me up.

I realized that the only person left in the room with us was the man who had been holding the syringe. Susan was gone. A pool of her blood mingled with her spilled coffee.

"Where's Susan?" I asked shrilly as panic threatened to claim me once again.

"They've taken her to ICU," the man replied. He eyed Master warily. "Where do you think you're taking Jane?"

"You people are obviously incapable of keeping her safe," Master said derisively. "I'm taking her into protective custody."

Without sparing the man a backwards glance, he strode from the room and carried me out into the unfamiliar outside world. The prospect would have terrified me, but I was calm in his arms. So long as I gave myself over to his will, he would keep me safe. I didn't have to think, didn't have to worry, didn't have to be afraid. Master would look after me and tell me what to do.

I stared up at him in order to avoid the overwhelming sights, sounds, and smells of the outside world. His ferocious scowl would have been terrible to behold, but I knew his ire wasn't directed at me.

The scent of damp asphalt filled my nostrils as we stepped out into the night, and the summer air hit my skin for the first time in longer than I could remember. The way the warm breeze played over my skin and ruffled my hair was both exquisite and disconcerting.

Master's eyes keenly surveyed the area before proceeding beyond the threshold of the building that housed the detox facility. When he deemed it safe to do so, we crossed the short span of sidewalk that separated us from a shiny black sedan. His movements were hurried but his hands were steady as he situated me in the passenger seat.

A pang of fear made my stomach twist when he released me to circle around the car, but it soon eased when he slid into the driver's seat and the car doors locked with a reassuring click. He wasted no time cranking the engine and slamming his foot down on the gas pedal. The speed of the moving car as we wove in and out of traffic made the lights of the city flash through the interior of the car in rapid starbursts.

Despite Master's comforting presence, my body was going into sensory overload. Since I had been freed from my prison, I had known nothing but the small room in the clinic. Adjusting to that radical change had been difficult enough. Now I was reminded of just how big the world was outside of those confined spaces. Memories that belonged to the woman I used to be stirred in the depths of my mind. *She* was the one who recognized this wide world, but I couldn't allow myself to access her awareness of it.

That woman was a wild thing, a real person with free will and independent thought. Those capabilities were beyond my realm of experience, and attempting to harness them would shatter me.

"Clayton," Master said abruptly. "I need you to get to St. Paul's ASAP."

I felt a moment of confusion, but then Master continued on. "That Bastard came back for her. Fuck!" He barked out. "I should have been there."

There was another brief pause. I realized Master was talking to his friend on the phone.

"No. She's with me. She's a little banged up and traumatized, but she'll be okay. I need you to get over to the clinic to see what you can find on that Bastard. And take Miller with you. I want him in on this."

Clayton's voice emanated from the phone in an unintelligible, distorted rumble.

"No." Master growled the word. "There was no sign of him. I would have searched the place, but I was more concerned with getting her out. Check the surveillance cameras and question the staff. Don't let anyone leave that building until they've been vetted. The fucker hurt Susan. It looked pretty bad, but she might be able to tell us more if she makes it through."

Pause.

"Of course I'm going to ask her what happened. But I'm not about to put her through that tonight. And no, you can't question her. I'm taking her to my apartment."

Pause.

"She's not going to a fucking safe house, Vaughn," Master snapped. "I don't trust anyone else to keep her safe. You can come by my place in the morning if you want to argue with me about it then."

Master didn't say anything else; he had ended the call.

Despite the horror of what I had been through in the last hour, a small smile played around the corners of my mouth. Master was going to keep me with him. He was going to protect me. Just like that, the last vestiges of my fear melted. So long as he was by my side, I would be safe.

A few minutes later, the car stopped, and Master was at the passenger side door. He gathered me up in his arms again, and I pressed my face into his chest as he carried me, honing all of my focus on him. His rich, amber-tinged whiskey scent enfolded me, anchoring me.

There was a *ping* and the sensation of upward movement. *Elevator.*

I shook off the recognition. Where I was didn't matter. All that mattered was that Master was taking me where he wanted to. There was only his will and my compliance. Nothing else mattered.

He laid my body down on something soft before he released me from his firm hold. My eyes snapped open at the absence of his reassuring strength.

I was lying on a bed in an unfamiliar room. It was smaller than my room at St. Paul's, and it smelled warm and slightly earthy. It was far preferable to the sharp, cold antiseptic scent of the clinic.

Master pulled the black duvet over my body, but my skin still felt uncomfortably cool without his heat surrounding me. He stroked his fingers through my hair soothingly.

"You'll be safe here with me, little one," he assured me, his voice gentle.

"I know, Master," I replied. I trusted him completely.

He smiled down at me softly. "I'll be in the next room. If you need anything, just call for me."

He started to pull away from me, and my hand shot out of its own accord to fist in his shirt. I didn't want him to leave me, but I was frightened to speak out of turn.

No. That was my former ma – that Bastard's – rule. My Master had ordered me to speak freely.

"Please don't leave me, Master," I begged, desperation roughening my words.

He stared down at me for a moment, his quicksilver eyes considering. Finally, he sighed. "Alright, little one. I'll stay with you."

I heaved in a relieved breath, and I couldn't hold back my smile. "Thank you, Master."

He smiled back at me, and my stomach did a little flip at the sight of his dimple. My request had pleased him. And he was happy for me to address him as "Master." I felt as though a weight had been lifted from me with his permission to verbally acknowledge that I belonged to him.

He removed his suit jacket and tie, peeling away his civilized veneer. I loved the untamed wildness that was only thinly veiled by his professional appearance. This was how he was meant to be: his innate power fully revealed, unrestrained.

I suddenly craved for him to unbutton his white collared shirt, to remove his belt and well-fitted slacks that concealed his strong body. I wanted to run my fingers, my tongue, over every inch of him, to demonstrate my reverence for him. I wanted him to claim me in every way possible, to mark me and fully declare his ownership.

But I didn't have permission to touch him in that way. He had told me he didn't want anything sexual from me. I bit back my disappointment, saying nothing.

I was consoled when he settled down on the bed beside me, and I pressed my body up against his. The long days of him sleeping in the chair beside my bed were over. I could finally cling to him as I had longed to do.

He stiffened beside me, but after a moment, he wrapped his arm around my shoulders, holding me against him. A warm glow pulsed to life at the center of my chest at the sign of his acceptance.

"Go to sleep, girl."

When I was touching him like this, I could feel his deep voice rumble through me. I sighed happily and eagerly obeyed his order.

Chapter 7

Master's warm, rough hands were running over my naked body, and something unfamiliar stirred low in my belly. His fingertips trailed over my abdomen, tracing their way upward. When they reached the undersides of my breasts, I gasped as pleasure raced over my skin, flooding my mind. I couldn't remember having ever felt anything this delicious.

He abandoned my breasts to trace a line around my throat. There was something heavy there. The weight of it pressed against my windpipe, restricting my breathing. Fear flashed through the pleasure that fogged my mind.

I stared up into Master's gorgeous eyes in order to ground myself. I trusted him. I didn't have anything to fear from him.

But the light in his eyes shifted, morphing into something lustful and disturbing. Muddy green bloomed to life amidst the silver, bleeding across it until the metallic shine was consumed. My former Master's fingers hooked through the ring at the front of the iron collar that encircled my throat, dragging my face to his.

"I told you I would come back for you, slave. You belong to me. Your cunt is mine."

Terror flooded my system, and I tried to lash out at him. Manacles were secured around my wrists and ankles, spreading my body wide for his use. My side and my cheek throbbed from where he had abused me earlier. He was going to hurt me again.

I screamed out my fear. I knew I should give in to him. Everything would be so much easier if I just accepted him.

I couldn't. He wasn't my master any longer. I wouldn't allow him to claim me.

But it hurt so much. His vicious hold on my iron collar was making it difficult to breathe. I gasped, but I couldn't draw in any air. I couldn't even beg him to stop.

"Wake up, girl." He ordered.

Instinct drove me to try to fight him off, but my efforts were useless. I was chained down. I couldn't move my arms.

"Wake up." The command was sharper this time. I couldn't refuse him.

I blinked hard.

Silver eyes stared down at me. Master's hands encircled my wrists, holding me down. I was lying on a bed, not on the cold, hard floor of my dungeon.

"Breathe."

I gasped in air, easing the burning in my lungs. When I exhaled, a relieved sob escaped me. It hadn't been real. The pain in my side and my cheek was still there, but my cruel metal collar was no longer choking me.

He released my wrists and wrapped his arms around me, pulling my body up against his. His hand stroked up and down my back in a soothing rhythm. I breathed him in, reassuring myself that *this* was real, and my torment had been the dream.

"Master." I whispered his title like a prayer.

"I'm here, little one," he murmured.

I snuggled into him as closely as I could. I didn't want any distance between us. I didn't want to leave him, not even for a second.

"You're okay, sweetheart," he reassured me. "You're safe." He tenderly kissed the top of my head. Pleasure washed over me in response, but it was different from the pleasure I had felt in my dream. This was a deeper sense of satisfaction. I wasn't simply Master's slave; I was a cherished possession.

"Thank you, Master," I mumbled against his chest.

He held me for a long time, petting me and whispering words of praise and reassurance. I gloried in it.

The shrill ringing of Master's phone punctuated my blissful state. He frowned and pulled it from his pocket, checking the number before answering.

"Clayton," he said into the receiver. "Did you find anything?"

His frown deepened.

"Fine. But she's not going anywhere. You can come over."

He hung up on his friend without saying goodbye. His harsh expression melted when he looked down at me, but his eyes were still troubled.

"Let's see if we can find you some breakfast, sweetheart," he said gently. "I'm sure I have something in other than coffee."

I hated the loss of his arms around me, but he still held my hand as he led me out of the small bedroom.

The morning sun illuminated Master's living room. The light shone in through one large window, which provided a stunning view of the New York City skyline. The room was made all the brighter for the stark décor. The walls and carpet were white, the blankness punctuated by black furniture. The space was sleek and minimalistic, unencumbered by frills or unnecessary adornment. It suited Master's powerful nature. And yet the simplicity of it held the barest suggestion of loneliness; there was no place here for sentiment.

I was suddenly filled with anticipation at the prospect of exploring Master's personal space. I wanted to know him better, to feel closer to him. The sensation of excitement was yet another vaguely remembered concept. Longing had claimed me when I had been desperate for my reward under that Bastard's ownership, but that yearning was an empty, pitiful thing.

Master led me through the living room to the bathroom. It was similarly decorated to the living room, with a black tile floor and white walls. It might have seemed coldly impersonal if it weren't for the fact that it reflected Master's personality.

Once I was in the bathroom, he released my hand and moved to shut the door behind me. Panic spiked through my gut, and I reached for him.

"Please don't leave me, Master."

Something I couldn't quite identify clouded his eyes. He seemed almost disturbed. And a bit pained. He blinked, and the lines of his face eased to a calm mask. His fingertips traced the line of my jaw, and I leaned into his touch, relishing the contact.

"I'm not going anywhere," he reassured me gently. "I'm going to be right outside that door. I want you to do this on your own." His voice turned firmer, authoritative. "And you'll do as you're told. Won't you?"

My stomach sank at the prospect of him leaving my side even for a minute, but I didn't have a choice. "Yes, Master," I replied meekly.

He watched me for the space of a few heartbeats, impressing his will upon me with his steady silver stare. I dropped my eyes, communicating my submission. Once he was sure of my compliance, he turned on the sink, adjusting the hot and cold water until he was satisfied with the temperature. Opening the mirrored medicine cabinet, he retrieved a toothbrush and removed it from its packaging before setting it down on the sink alongside a bar of soap.

"Wash your face, brush your teeth, and use the toilet," he ordered.

"Yes, Master," I replied hollowly, still staring at a spot on the floor. His fingers were beneath my chin, applying pressure so that I was forced to face him.

"It will make me very happy if you do this. You want to make me happy, don't you, girl?"

I nodded, swallowing hard against the lump forming in my throat.

"Good girl." He planted a gentle kiss on my forehead. The sign of affection gave me the strength I needed to let him go.

I *did* want to please him. I would prove to him that I was worthy of his care. The soft thud of the door closing behind him threatened to open the floodgates, but I ruthlessly held back the fear that arose when he left my sight.

Master had given me orders, and it was my job to comply. It was my sole purpose to obey him. My determination to please him tapped into a wellspring of strength within myself I hadn't known I possessed. Focusing only on him, I easily completed my tasks.

As soon as I turned off the sink, he returned to me, pulling me into his embrace.

"That was very good, sweetheart." I glowed at his rumbling praise.

All too soon, he released me so he could attend to his own needs. "Stay here," he ordered before disappearing into a room adjacent to the one where we had slept. He reappeared quickly, holding a black t-shirt and a fresh pair of slacks. I hated losing sight of him as he closed the door to the bathroom, but I stood patiently in the living room, not moving from the spot where he had ordered me to wait for him.

He emerged only minutes later, dressed in his fresh clothes. The t-shirt was tight, doing little to disguise his muscular chest and bulging arms. My mouth practically watered at the sight. I knew Master was strong enough to protect me, but his physical perfection had always been obscured by his professional suit. There was no doubt in my mind that Master was more than capable of keeping me safe.

He led me to the kitchen, where it quickly became apparent that he didn't have much other than coffee in stock. His fridge held little more than beer and an expired block of cheese, and his freezer was sparsely littered with a bottle of chilled vodka and a few frozen dinners.

I was shocked to find that he appeared slightly chagrined when he fished out a Toaster Strudel for my breakfast. "I'm afraid this is all I have to offer you," he said with a self-deprecating smile. "Unfortunately, I have fuck all in the way of culinary skills."

He gripped my waist so he could lift me up onto one of the barstools at his kitchen counter. Pain flared where his fingers dug into my bruised flesh where that Bastard had kicked me. The image of his twisted, cruel snarl flashed across my mind.

"No amount of groveling will save you. I'll be back for you, slave."

My whimper was a result of residual fear as well as pain.

Master released me instantly, concern etched in his handsome features. He reached for the hem of my shirt and pulled it up to examine my injury. A dark, purplish splotch stood in stark contrast to my pale skin. Master swore under his breath, his concern giving way to fury.

A buzzing sound broke through the tension that was radiating off of him. He blinked, his ire receding ever so slightly as he lowered my shirt to cover me once again.

"That'll be Clayton," he explained. "He's going to ask you some questions about what happened last night. I want you to answer him as thoroughly as possible. If you get scared, I'll be right here." He paused, studying me. "Don't call me 'Master' in front of him. If you do, he might try to take you from me."

"I won't, Master," I promised quickly. "I won't," I amended, omitting his appellation. I liked Clayton, but I would claw his eyes out if he tried to take me away from Master.

He nodded, satisfied, before leaving me briefly in order to let Clayton in. As always, Master's friend had a smile for me.

"Hi, Jane," Clayton beamed at me. He always seemed to radiate positivity, his bearing implacably lighthearted.

"Hi." My lips quirked up of their own accord in response to his levity.

"Jane, this is Agent Reed Miller. He works with Smith and me at the FBI," Clayton introduced the man who followed him into Master's apartment.

Agent Reed Miller was about the same height as Master, but he wasn't quite as broad. He was younger. His face didn't bear the same care-worn creases that crinkled at the corners of Master's eyes, and his skin was tanned and smooth. He was also tidier than Master, his carefully-styled black hair and clean-shaven jaw likening him more to Clayton, who ever looked the professional in his sharp suits.

"You can call me Reed," he told me.

He extended a hand towards me. Reflexively, I shrank back. I hadn't met any men other than Clayton and Master since Master had claimed me.

The boyish smile was instantly wiped from his face, his dark brown eyes suddenly uncertain as he pulled his hand back slowly.

"Shit. Sorry." He cut his eyes to Master when he apologized.

Master was instantly at my side, his warm hand splayed across my lower back in a show of support. I leaned into him, allowing his touch to ground me.

His eyes flashed as he frowned at Reed. I hated that he was angry with his friend because of me. If Reed worked with Master and Clayton, then he was safe. And even if he wasn't, he couldn't do anything to me with Master by my side. Gathering up my courage, I struggled to recall the mechanics of social niceties.

I was pleased that my hand barely trembled as I extended it towards Reed. "It's nice to meet you, Reed," I said, my voice a bit softer than I would have liked.

Reed glanced at Master briefly. He was clearly seeking some sign of approval before he acted. Master nodded once, the tension leaving him. Reed's deference to his ownership of me had placated him.

Reed smiled at me when he took my hand in his. Although his eyes were such a dark brown that they were almost black, they reflected the light rather than swallowing it, giving off a decidedly mischievous twinkle. "It's nice to meet you too, Jane," he said warmly. His grip was firm when he shook my hand, but he released me quickly, seeming to sense that I couldn't handle much more contact than that.

Master's hand rubbed my back, and I glanced up to find him smiling down at me with pride. My answering grin was wide and silly. What might have been otherwise challenging seemed laughably easy with Master's approval. If my actions pleased him, then I was fulfilling the purpose of my existence. I practically glowed with self-satisfaction. My world was rapidly changing, but I would be able to adapt to anything so long as he was there to guide me.

His eyes sharpened as he turned his attention back to Clayton and Reed. "Did you find anything at St. Paul's?"

Clayton's expression tightened, and he shook his head. "Nothing so far. The guy's good, Smith. And someone's helping him. There's nothing on the security cameras. Someone looped the feed just minutes before he went into the building, so we don't have any footage that we can plug into facial recognition. It's unlikely he was able to do that by himself and get into Jane's room when he did. He – and whoever his accomplice is – must have been watching the live surveillance feed so he could act as soon as Jane was left alone. It's the only way to explain how he got in at just the right time to find Jane on her own."

"Can you trace whoever hacked the feed?" Master asked, a muscle ticking in his jaw as he ground out the question.

"We're working on it," Reed said, "but this guy is good. It's federal level tech he's using."

"What about the lead we were working last night? The witness from Decadence who recognized the sketch. Has his information gotten us anywhere?"

"No," Clayton responded, a trace of bitterness in the word. "Turns out it was a dead end. The guy was just bullshitting to try to get out of the possession charges he's facing. He didn't know anything." His bright blue eyes shifted to me. "We were hoping to get some information that might lead us to his accomplice. Did you ever see anyone else while you were being held captive, Jane? Did the man who imprisoned you ever mention a friend?"

The Mentor.

I had first met him on the day that I broke.

Blood running down my thighs as the whip slashed across my back. The two men using my broken body.

Master's arm was around my shoulder, his fingers under my chin. He lifted my face up to his, and I clung to the sight of him like a lifeline.

"Stay here with me, girl," he ordered.

I drew in a deep, shuddering breath. I would obey him. I would be good.

"Answer Clayton's question." He spoke gently, but it was an order nonetheless. I preferred it that way. If it was an order, then it was something I had to do. Master would guide me through it. Clayton was kind in the way he requested information, but my dark memories threatened to suck me under if I was left on my own. My own will wasn't strong enough to overcome the terror of my past, but Master's will was.

"Yes," I breathed, staring resolutely up into Master's eyes. "There was another man."

"Do you know his name?" Clayton asked.

I shook my head. He didn't have a name. He didn't even have a face.

"Keep your eyes closed, whore. If you look at me, I'll make sure you never see anything again."

I couldn't suppress my shudder at the memory.

"He was just the Mentor," I whispered. "I didn't know his name."

"'The Mentor'?" Reed asked, puzzled. "Is that what he called himself?"

I shook my head again. "No. That's just how I thought of him. Ma- that Bastard called him 'Sir.'"

Master's brow furrowed. "Why did you think of him that way, girl?" He asked. "Why 'the Mentor'?"

I flinched as my skin crawled with remembered agony. Master waited, his hand squeezing my upper arm gently in encouragement.

"He…" I swallowed down the bile rising in the back of my throat. "He taught that Bastard how to hurt me. How to break me."

My mind shied away from that. It brought me far too close to brushing against the woman I used to be before I had become a slave. I touched my fingers to my throat, half-expecting to find the cool weight of my iron collar.

Master's handsome face was twisted into a furious mask. Once, I might have recoiled from that fierce expression, but now I understood that it wasn't directed at me.

"Can you tell us what he looked like, Jane?" Clayton asked. "We can get you to talk to a sketch artist again."

"I don't know," I replied softly, my voice strained. Nothing I said was of any use to them. I didn't know anything important. All I knew was pain and abuse. I had no knowledge of anything else. "I'm sorry. He told me he would blind me if I looked at him."

Despite Master's warm presence, a pervasive cold had pulsed to life in my bones, emanating out through my muscles to make my flesh pebble. A fine tremor raced across my skin, and a moment of tense silence passed as the men absorbed my gruesome explanation.

When Clayton finally spoke again, his voice was tight with suppressed anger. "Okay." He took a deep breath. "That's okay, Jane." His tone resumed most of its usual cool surety. "Can you tell us what happened last night?"

Last night.

Spilled coffee mingling with blood.

Oh, god.

"Is Susan okay?" I asked quickly, my voice high with panic. I had been so determined to avoid the dark memories that I had forgotten about Susan.

"She's going to be fine," Clayton reassured me. "She has a concussion, but she'll make a full recovery. But she doesn't remember what happened last night. I need you to tell me. Can you do that for me, Jane?"

Yes. I could do that. Master had ordered me to answer Clayton's questions.

"Susan left to get coffee," I began quietly.

I was waiting for Master to return to me. I was so anxious without him there to watch over me.

And I had been right to be afraid. I wasn't safe without Master by my side.

"She hadn't been gone more than a few minutes when he came. I tried to fight him. He hit me."

"You thought you could run from me?"

I wanted to bury the memory, but I closed my eyes, forcing myself to recall every detail. "He was wearing blue scrubs. When Susan came back and saw him, she thought he was an orderly. I begged him not to hurt her, and she realized who he was. She hit the nurse call button so help would come. I tried to hold him back, but he hit her. He realized people were coming, so he decided to leave me."

"This cunt is mine. You'll always belong to me."

"He said he would come back for me. He said I belonged to him," I finished in a whisper.

I touched my fingertips to my neck again, but Master caught my hand in his. I blinked and stared up into his eyes. They burned with possessive fury.

"You don't belong to him," he told me firmly. "He will never touch you again."

I knew I shouldn't contradict him, but fear of that Bastard overwhelmed my fear of displeasing my Master. I had to make him understand how important it was that I remain with him at all times.

"That's what you said before," I reminded him, my voice small.

Master frowned, and I held my breath, worried I had pushed too far.

"You're right. I did say that," he admitted. "I won't leave you again, little one. Not until we've found him."

"Smith," Clayton's voice was cautious as he addressed his friend. "You know that's not practical. We need to get Jane to a safe house, and you need to be at work helping us track this guy down."

Master's arms tightened around me. "She's not going to a safe house," he said firmly. "If that Bastard can get into the clinic when we had her under twenty-four hour surveillance, then I'm not trusting her safety to anyone but me. As of now, I'm taking my vacation days. I believe you'll find I have about twelve weeks stored up."

Clayton's brows rose in surprise. "You don't want to help us find the guy?" He asked incredulously.

"I'll do the desk jockey shit," Master said. "Just send me paperwork, and I'll do it. Miller can work in the field with you."

Clayton frowned at Master. "You suck at being a desk jockey."

"Just because I don't like it doesn't mean I'm incapable of doing it," Master fired back.

Clayton was more direct this time. "I don't think this is a good idea, James. It really isn't appropriate for Jane to be alone with you."

Master's expression darkened. "What are you insinuating, Vaughn?" He asked, his voice low and dangerous. "That I'll do something *inappropriate?* How could you even think-?"

"Of course I don't think that," Clayton cut him off firmly. "But this is totally against protocol."

Master raised a brow at his friend. "And when have you ever known me to give a shit about the rules?"

The lines of Clayton's handsome face hardened. "This is different, James. And you know it."

"Of course she's different," Master said hotly. "That's why we brought in Miller. That's why we're the ones taking care of this. That's why I'm taking care of her."

Reed seemed to have been deferring to the two senior agents, but at the mention of his name, he chimed into the heated conversation. "Why don't we ask Jane what she wants?" He suggested levelly.

"I want to stay here with him," I said in a rush, relieved someone had decided to include me in the decision. I couldn't bring myself to refer to Master as "Smith," so I clutched his hand firmly to communicate just who I meant when I said *him.* I wanted to gauge Master's reaction to my vehement outburst, but all of my attention was focused on Clayton as I stared at him imploringly. He couldn't make me leave. I couldn't allow him to convince Master to give me up.

Clayton's keen blue eyes studied me for a moment, his uncertainty plain on his face. "The idea of being alone with a man doesn't bother you?" He asked gently.

"No!" I insisted quickly. "I know he wouldn't hurt me. He'll keep me safe. Please don't make me leave." My desperation was starkly evident.

Clayton's eyes roved over my strained features once more, and he sighed. "If that's what you want, Jane, then you can stay." His gaze shifted sharply back to Master. "But if I'm going to smooth this over for you at the Bureau, I'm going to need you to promise me that you'll keep me in the loop about how she's doing, James."

Master nodded curtly. "Of course. I'll be in touch every day to check on the investigation anyway." The tense stance he had been holding finally eased. "Thanks, Clayton," he said earnestly. "Thanks for putting up with my shit."

Clayton shrugged, his easy smile returning. "It's no different than any other day."

Master inclined his head ever so slightly, allowing that. Then he jerked his chin in the direction of the door. "Now you can get the fuck out. I believe you have a shit-ton of work to get on with." His words were harsh, but his tone was light, and he was smiling slightly at his friend.

"Yes, we do. And I'll be sure to send you the most boring, tedious bits of it. After all, you did volunteer for the position of paperwork bitch."

Master growled, but there was no real menace in it. "Don't let the door hit you on your way out."

I noticed that Reed's smile was slightly forced as he observed the men's banter, and he shifted uncomfortably. It was obvious he didn't feel like he was part of the boys' club yet, and the deferential position that placed him in didn't suit him. Although he hadn't spoken enough for me to get a strong read on his personality, I liked the idea that he was helping Master and Clayton protect me. The men's powerful personalities might cause them to clash with one another, but they had each made it clear that my well-being was their priority. I could scarcely believe this was real. I don't think I could have believed it was real if it weren't for the visceral effect of Master's skin touching mine.

"Thank you," I said abruptly, before the men could leave. In the past, I would have used my body to demonstrate my gratitude, but Master had ordered me not to do that. He had commanded for me to say "thank you" when I was grateful. I much preferred it to degrading myself.

Clayton and Reed paused where they had half-turned to leave.

"You don't have to thank us, Jane," Clayton said kindly.

Once the two men left, I allowed myself to melt against Master as relief washed over me. I no longer had to pretend he wasn't my Master, and the lingering threat that Clayton might take me from him had been eliminated.

Master stood beside me where I sat on the stool, allowing me to press my face against his hard chest as he stroked my hair.

"That was very good, sweetheart," he told me approvingly. "I know talking about what happened to you was difficult. You were very brave."

I snuggled into him more closely, glowing at the praise. "Thank you, Master."

The taste of his title was sweet on my tongue.

Chapter 8

"I'm sorry I don't have anything better to offer you, sweetheart," Master said apologetically as he placed the warm Toaster Strudel in front of me. "I'll order some groceries online later."

I glanced down at the plate in front of me and then back up at Master. It would be wrong of me to take this when he had nothing for himself. I pushed the plate towards him.

Master frowned slightly and pushed it right back at me. "Eat."

"But you don't have anything, Master," I protested, trying to communicate how wrong it would be for me to take the food. My purpose was to make him happy, and he wasn't allowing me to do that by making him go hungry.

His expression was suddenly cool and remote, a single brow arched. His arms folded across his chest, and his already large body seemed to take up more space than usual. "I believe I gave you an order, girl," he said evenly.

I took in a sharp breath, horrified by what I had done. Although I only had service in mind, I had defied him. Balancing the new freedom of thought and speech that he had granted me with being a good slave was proving difficult.

Anxious to make it up to him, my hand darted out for the pastry. Steam rose from it, and the hot crust burned my fingertips. I winced slightly, but I wasn't about to set it back down. I started to lift it to my lips, bracing for the burn of the hot filling on my tongue and throat. That discomfort didn't matter. I had to rectify my mistake.

"Wait." I froze at the singular authoritative word, holding the pastry just inches from my mouth.

Master reached out and plucked it from my fingers. He let out a soft curse and flung it back down on the plate, sucking his overheated fingertips into his mouth. I suddenly longed for him to use my mouth to soothe the burn, to penetrate my lips with his long fingers, instructing me to lick and suck at him in the way he would like for me to taste his cock.

He had done so much for me. He had freed me from my agony and protected me. It seemed that his sole desire was to take care of me. All he asked for in return was my obedience, but obedience wasn't sufficient for expressing my gratitude towards him. I wanted to demonstrate how much I worshipped him. And the only way I knew how to do that was by using my body.

"You are not allowed to do anything for me that is sexual"

But he had given me that order days ago, when he wouldn't even allow me to acknowledge him as my Master. Now that he had fully asserted his ownership, that particular rule might have changed.

He tore off a corner of the pastry, holding it gingerly between his fingers as he blew air over it in order to cool it. When he was satisfied, he lifted it to my lips.

"Open."

I obeyed eagerly, welcoming him in. He popped the warm pastry into my waiting mouth, but some of the gooey filling had dripped onto his forefinger. Before he could draw back, I touched my tongue to his skin, savoring the unique flavor of his flesh even more so than the intense sweetness of the strawberry jam. He paused, his eyes darkening as I boldly closed my lips around the tip of his finger, sucking it clean.

His jaw clenched, and he abruptly jerked his hand back. For a moment, I feared he would rebuke me, but he just pushed the plate toward me again.

"Eat."

I suppressed a small sigh. It didn't seem Master would be feeding me my breakfast after all. Although he hadn't reprimanded me for my suggestive action, he hadn't invited more either. I decided not to push him further, but hope blossomed within me that he might accept me soon. I craved for him to claim me. I was utterly devoted to him, and I wanted to bind him to me as tightly as possible. If he wouldn't allow me to give him all of myself, then he wouldn't realize just how much I could please him. He wouldn't realize just how much he needed me.

I lowered my eyes, pulling my gaze away from his enigmatic expression as I focused on complying with his command.

"Eat."

Allowing the one simple order to consume my attention was a welcome reprieve from the frankly jarring autonomous thoughts that were spinning in my mind. Touching Reed and standing up for myself when Clayton tried to take me away had been exhausting enough, but actively scheming to test Master's order for me not to touch him sexually was especially taxing. I could hardly believe that I was daring to entertain such thoughts. My obedience to him was everything.

But perhaps that wasn't true. Ensuring he kept me was everything, and I was willing to do whatever I had to do to secure him as my Master. Even if that meant testing his authority.

"Eat."

Using his command to focus me, I quieted my disturbing thoughts. I went on autopilot, allowing Master's will to become my own as I mechanically ate the food he had provided for me. Out of the corner of my eye, I noticed him frowning slightly, but I didn't allow myself to contemplate what that meant. If he was displeased with me, then all I could do to change his feelings was comply with his order.

When I was finished, I lowered my hands to my lap, keeping my eyes downcast. My heart leapt into my throat when his fingers closed around mine, gently tugging me forward. I stepped down off the barstool, submissively avoiding his gaze as I followed docilely where he led.

He seated himself on the black leather couch in his living room. Automatically, my knees folded, the plush carpet cushioning the impact with the floor as I knelt beside him. My hands clasped behind me at the small of my back, and my thighs parted. His fingertips touched the top of my head, accepting my submission. I drew in a deep, even breath, utterly satisfied with his control. Things were so much easier this way.

His hand jerked back abruptly, and the leather of the sofa creaked as he shifted his weight away from me. A small whine escaped me at the loss of the heat of him, his rejection causing panic to spike in my chest. My arms jerked as I was tempted to clutch him to me. My fingers knotted, locking my hands together behind my back so I couldn't break from my proper position.

"Get up off your knees, sweetheart," Master ordered, his voice strained. "Sit on the couch beside me."

Beside him?

That couldn't be right. I wasn't his equal. My place was at his feet. I caught my lower lip between my teeth, uncertain.

"That's an order, girl." His tone was deep and authoritative this time.

I reacted instantly, again awash with horror that I had dared to defy him. I perched on the edge of the couch, my back ramrod straight as I kept my gaze trained on the carpet.

"I'm sorry, Master," I gasped out. "I didn't mean to -" I swallowed hard. My intentions didn't matter. "I'll be better. I'll be good. I promise."

Master sighed heavily. I wanted to sob from the intensity of my relief when he closed the distance between us, wrapping his arm around my shoulders and pulling me up against him. He touched his fingers to my cheek, turning my face so I was forced to look up into his eyes. Their quicksilver light was liquid comfort, flowing through my flesh and over my mind, calming me. I drew in a shuddering breath as he absently traced the line of my jaw.

"You've been very good today, little one," he assured me firmly. "I'm not angry. It's my job to take care of you, but I can't do that if you don't follow my rules. Whatever you were taught before -" His jaw clenched as he cut himself off. "Everything I ask of you is meant to help you. I will never hurt you, sweetheart, but I won't allow you to degrade yourself for me. Understood?"

Something about the order made my heart twist. He wouldn't allow me to properly demonstrate my devotion. But it was an order, and I wasn't about to defy him for a third time in one morning.

"Yes, Master," I said, my voice small. "I understand."

"Good girl." He planted a tender kiss in the center of my forehead. The warmth that flooded me at the intimate act helped to allay the disappointment that had gripped me.

"What would you like to do today, sweetheart?" He asked kindly.

"Whatever pleases you, Master," I said automatically. There was no other acceptable answer.

My heart sank when he frowned. I hated the downward twist of his full lips. I only ever wanted him to be perfectly happy with me, but I couldn't seem to get it right. The moment of silence seemed to stretch on for excruciating minutes as his disapproval made all of my muscles go taut with the strain of my distress.

"I'm sorry, Master," I apologized desperately. "I don't know... Please tell me what you want."

He touched his forefinger to my lips, silencing me. His expression had softened, but his eyes were studying me carefully, penetrating more than just skin-deep.

"I think we should establish more ground rules," he said finally. "I don't want you to feel uncomfortable around me, and I think having guidelines for your behavior will help with that."

"Yes, Master," I agreed quickly. I had already made so many mistakes since he had taken me into his home. If he told me what was acceptable, then I would know how to avoid his disapproval. I wanted that more than anything.

"Firstly," he began, "You can speak to me freely at any time, and you are to look me in the eye when we are talking." His tone was business-like as his steady stare fixed me in place, impressing his authority upon me. "You are to use the bathroom at any time you want. You don't need my permission. You will tell me if you are hungry. In fact, I'll make a schedule of when you will eat and how many calories you will consume every day." He paused to brush his thumb across my pronounced cheekbone. "I need you to put on some weight. You'll exercise every day. I'll make a schedule for that too. You're gorgeous, sweetheart, but we need to get you healthy."

I flushed pleasurably at the compliment. "Master is kind to say that," I said softly.

"I said it because I mean it," he said firmly. "I will never lie to you, little one. And I expect complete honesty from you as well. You will always tell me if you want something that I'm not giving you. I want to look after you, but I'm not a mind reader. It's your job to communicate your needs to me. Can you do that for me?"

It was a rhetorical question. Of course I would obey his rules.

Speak freely, and look Master in the eye.
Don't ask for permission to use the bathroom.
Eat what you're told, when you're told.
Exercise when you're told.
Don't lie to Master.
Tell Master when you need something.

The rules weren't difficult, and having them in place was immensely comforting. Now that I knew what was expected of me, I knew how best to please Master. The only rule I didn't care for was the one that was already in place.

Don't touch Master sexually.

I tamped down my rebellious thoughts as schemes for circumventing this rule began stirring in the depths of my mind. My compliance with his other commands would have to be sufficient for binding him to me, for ensuring him of my complete devotion.

"So, what do you want to do today, little one?" He asked again. I hesitated, still unsure of what to say. "I ordered you to tell me what you want," he reminded me sternly.

"I… I'm not sure," I admitted. The concept of having choices was baffling. I couldn't even begin to think up a desirable activity.

I want you to hold me, Master.

But I didn't dare say that. I didn't want him to think I was trying to manipulate him into bending his cardinal rule. Which, if I was honest with myself, would be my exact intention if I did give voice to that particular desire.

"Okay," he said gently. "That's okay. How about we put on a movie while I order some food online and check my emails."

I nodded eagerly. It was a suggestion, but the cadence of his voice let me know it wasn't really a question. The definitiveness was reassuring.

He reached for the remote that rested on his glass-and-wrought-iron coffee table. It was the only object on the table. There were no books or magazines with attractive pictures. I was again struck by the starkness of his home. But his hard body beside me and his reassuring scent were more than sufficient to fill the space with comforting warmth.

He pressed a few buttons on the remote, and sharply defined images appeared on the huge flat-screen TV mounted on the wall opposite the couch. He accessed Netflix and began scrolling through genre options.

"Do you like romantic comedies?" He asked.

I shrugged. I wasn't sure. I didn't have any memories of movies. All I knew was my new life with Master and the darkness that had come before him. Firmly suppressing those memories, I snuggled into him more closely, resting my head on his shoulder.

"I guess we'll find out, then," he said, selecting the first option that was sorted by popularity.

As cheerful music blared to life and beautiful people appeared on the screen, Master pulled his laptop from its case where it rested against the couch. Settling it on his lap, he proceeded to order groceries online. I didn't pay attention to the movie or his food selections; all of my focus honed on his large hands, his long fingers darting deftly across the keys. I wished they were roving over my flesh rather than the keyboard. I was addicted to his touch, craved the reassurance of his innate strength.

After a while, his sigh broke through my entranced state. "The groceries won't arrive till late this afternoon," he told me. "I can order a pizza for lunch. Would you like that?"

"If that's what you want, Master," I replied.

A shadow passed over his eyes, but it was gone as soon as it had come. "We'll figure out what you like soon enough, sweetheart. But I want you to tell me if you don't like it. You don't have to agree with everything I suggest. In fact, I don't want you to do that. You are always to be completely honest with me."

"Yes, Master," I agreed quickly. "I remember."

"Good girl." He brushed a swift kiss on the top of my head. I loved when he did that. If my truthfulness would ensure his continued affection, then I would never lie to him.

He sighed again, turning his attention back to his laptop. "Now. Let's see what tedious bullshit Clayton has sent me to do today." When he opened his email, he muttered a string of colorful curses.

Master cussed a lot, but I didn't mind. I loved his fierceness, the intensity of his emotions. I settled back into him; he was far more captivating than the insipid characters and their insignificant dramas that were playing out on the screen before me.

After a while, an annoyed growl emanated from Master's chest, and he snapped the laptop closed. "For someone who considers himself to be my best friend, Vaughn is a real bastard. Fucking spreadsheets."

The corners of my lips quirked up in a small smile. Now that I could read his moods better, Master's blustering was amusing. Just those few words were more entertaining than the entirety of the film that had been playing for the last hour.

Master stretched, his muscles shifting under my fingers where my hand rested on his stomach. I loved his strength. It made me feel safe, protected. My mind flitted to earlier that morning, when I had awoken to find his hands pinning my wrists to the bed, holding me down as he demanded that I return to my reality with him rather than being trapped in the horrors of my past.

That strange sensation stirred low in my belly once again. I didn't understand it, but it caused yearning to rise up within me. I craved to be closer to him, to further cleave myself to him. Acting on my desire, I drew my legs up onto the couch beside me and positioned myself on my side, my head resting in Master's lap.

My smile broadened as I felt his cock jerk beneath me in response.

Chapter 9

Unfortunately, Master's cock wasn't the only thing that stiffened beneath me. All of his muscles tensed as he froze.

"What do you think you're doing, girl?" He asked harshly.

My breath caught in my throat. Even though I was pleased that I had aroused him, it hadn't been my intention. Reluctantly, I turned my head slightly so I could look up at him while I spoke to him, as he had commanded me to do. His forbidding frown made me flinch, and I licked my lips nervously. His eyes watched the movement of my darting tongue, and his cock pulsed beneath my cheek again.

"I just wanted to be close to you, Master," I admitted breathily, my voice husky with anxiety and something darker that I didn't recognize. "Please. Did I do something wrong?"

My cheeks flushed. I knew I had done something wrong. But resting my head in his lap didn't really count as trying to do something sexual for him, did it? I hadn't been actively trying to manipulate him.

Or had I?

He hardened further as he brushed his fingers across my pinkened cheek, a hungry light making his predator's eyes gleam. My tremble was a result of eagerness, not fear. I was desperate to ease that hunger, to fall prey to him as he claimed my flesh and my spirit, consuming me and making me a part of himself.

His lips suddenly thinned, and he pulled his hand away from my face to close it around my shoulder. Although his expression was strained, his movements were gentle as he repositioned my body so that my head rested on his thighs rather than his groin. He drew in a deep breath, the lines of his face easing into something neutral and non-threatening. But I noticed that his hands were fisted where they rested on the couch on either side of him, no longer touching me.

"You didn't do anything wrong, sweetheart," he said, the tightness of his voice belying his calm façade. "I shouldn't have -"

He shook his head slightly, erasing the discomfiture that had flashed across his features. "Just don't do that again."

I swallowed hard against the lump that had formed in my throat, fighting back the distress that threatened to overwhelm me.

"It's okay, little one. I'm not angry."

But his hands didn't shift to comfort me; they remained resolutely at his sides.

"Are you sure?" I asked, my voice small.

He sighed and touched his fingers to my forehead, smoothing away the concern that had creased it. "I promised I wouldn't lie to you, sweetheart. I'm not angry with you. You can stay as close to me as you want. Just not there."

I nodded my understanding, leaning into his touch. Although residual disappointment lingered within me, the sweetness of the sensation of his skin against mine was far stronger.

The buzz that signaled the presence of someone at the door made me want to groan in frustration. I enjoyed the way Master was looking down at me, and I hated the interruption. He gripped my shoulders, carefully maneuvering me into a sitting position so he could stand.

"Wait here," he ordered as he went to retrieve the pizza from the deliveryman who was waiting in the hallway. He opened the door just wide enough for the man to pass the box through and then offered a perfunctory "thanks" as he shoved a tip at him. Master shut the door firmly in his face, sliding the lock back into place with a definitive *click*.

Master wasn't going to allow anyone to come near me who he didn't trust.

Safe.

When he turned back to me, his face was lit up with a grin. My heart skipped a beat. He was beautiful in his ferocity, but his smile was breathtaking.

"Come here," he ordered, gesturing at the barstool where I had eaten breakfast. "Let's see if you like pepperoni."

As it turned out, I loved pepperoni. The rich saltiness of it on my tongue, mingled with the subtly sweet marinara sauce, was incredible. The flavor was familiar, the simple pleasure of it eliciting pleasant emotions from some deep part of my brain. I suddenly realized I would prefer a thicker crust and more cheese. The construction of this pizza seemed all wrong to me. But I wasn't about to complain. It was too delicious.

Although he wanted to get my calorie count up, Master wouldn't allow me to eat more than two slices. He claimed that he didn't want me to get sick since I wasn't accustomed to such rich food. I wanted more, but I didn't argue with him. I loved that he was taking care of me, and I craved that much more fiercely than I wanted more pizza.

When we were finished with lunch, Master guided me back to the couch. I frowned when he set his laptop back on his thighs, blocking me from resting my head there. But I was thrilled to realize that his expression was as regretful as my own.

"I have to do more of this fucking paperwork," he told me. "Did you like the movie you were watching? I can put it back on."

I reflected back on the little bit of the film I had actually absorbed when I hadn't been completely focused on Master. "No," I said after a moment's consideration. "I don't think I did."

"What didn't you like about it?" Master pressed.

I searched my mind, sifting through the feelings I associated with it and sorting them into something that I could express. "The characters were... annoying." I rolled the word around in my mind, recalling what it meant. I hadn't had the luxury of being annoyed with someone in a long time. My dislike had been inconsequential, and I had learned to quash it. "The women claimed to be friends, but they did terrible things to each other. They were... bitchy."

Master laughed. I savored the way the rich sound boomed through the room, echoing in the large open space. "Sweetheart, it seems you might actually have good taste in movies," he said with approval. "Thank god. I was really not looking forward to filling my days with cheesy rom-coms." He gave a dramatic shudder. "The spreadsheets are torture enough."

My lips parted slightly; I was momentarily stunned. He was willing to endure something he disliked? For me? The enormity of the gesture was too much for me to contemplate. I shut it away, focusing on the fact that I had pleased him.

"Okay," he said definitively. "Let's try something else." He grabbed up the remote and scrolled to his recommendations.

Thumbnails of movie posters appeared on the screen. Judging by the tone of them, they were mostly action films or comedies, with a few old Westerns thrown in the mix.

"He glanced over at me. "Action or comedy?"

"What's your favorite?" I asked, genuinely not having a preference.

"Let's go with both," he grinned, an anticipatory light in his eyes. I was thrilled that he was about to share something he enjoyed with me. All of our interactions so far had been centered around my own behavior and well-being. I was eager to learn more about Master.

He selected a movie called *Hot Fuzz*, pressing play before turning his attention back to his laptop. But he kept glancing up at the screen, chuckling at the jokes that were obviously familiar to him. Barely fifteen minutes had passed before he closed his laptop.

"Fuck it," he muttered as he set it aside.

My smile had nothing to do with amusement at the film as he wrapped his arm around my shoulders, pulling me up against him. I was tempted to rest my head on his thighs again, but I quickly decided against it. I loved the way his laughter rumbled through me as his chest vibrated beneath my cheek. Every few minutes, I moved my eyes from the screen to sneak a glance up at him. I had never seen him so relaxed. His tousled dark hair and the flash of his white teeth as he smiled broadly made him appear almost boyish.

I was enamored with my serious, demanding Master. His control centered me, focused me. And I loved his ferocious, protective side. But seeing him like this touched something deeper within me. I suspected I was witnessing something precious, a part of himself he didn't often share. He was completely at ease with me by his side.

My trust in him was implicit, a requisite part of his ownership. But it seemed he trusted me as well, allowing me to see this side of him.

He glanced down at me, catching me staring. "Watch the movie, sweetheart. I promise you it's far more interesting than I am."

Not possible, I thought.

But he had given me an order, even if it was delivered lightheartedly. I turned my attention back to the screen, determined to absorb the humor that brought Master such pleasure. To my surprise, a giggle bubbled up my throat a few minutes later.

Master kissed the top of my head. "That's a beautiful sound, little one," he told me warmly.

I glowed at the praise. I allowed myself to become lost in the story, loving how my laughter mingled and danced with Master's, filling the room with joy. It was the sweetest sound I could ever recall.

We stayed like that all afternoon, Master seated on the couch with me cuddled up by his side. He didn't touch his laptop. Instead, he fired up the film *Bad Boys II* as soon as the credits started rolling on *Hot Fuzz*. Master evidently liked movies with over-the-top gunfights punctuated by well-timed jokes. They were cheesy, and they didn't take themselves too seriously. Master had always seemed so serious to me. I enjoyed his levity immensely.

The Netflix selection box was hovering over *Lethal Weapon* when the door buzzed again. Master grinned at me as he turned off the TV.

"We'll save that one for tomorrow, then," he told me. I nodded fervently.

The groceries Master had ordered were passed through the barely-open doorway. I remained on the couch once the deliveryman had left, watching Master put away the food in the fridge and various cabinets. I felt like I should help him, but he hadn't told me I could move from the spot where he had left me.

He glanced over at me as he placed two frying pans on the stove eyes. "I hope you're okay with breakfast food for dinner. It's about all I can manage." He waved me over towards the kitchen. "You don't have to stay all the way over there."

I leapt up with alacrity, eagerly closing the distance between us. He cocked his head at me. "You don't have to wait for my permission to move around the apartment, sweetheart," he told me. "Just don't go into the hallway. Or my bedroom." He gestured towards the closed door that he had retreated behind to retrieve his clothes that morning. My curiosity was instantly piqued. I wanted to explore the heart of Master's personal haven.

Don't go into Master's bedroom.

Ignoring my own wishes, I resolutely added it to my list of rules. I seated myself on the barstool, preferring to stay in a spot that Master had designated for me. Besides, from that vantage point I could watch the way his powerful shoulders flexed as he moved.

But my enthralled admiration soon shifted to concern as Master cursed over the smoking stove. The acrid scent of burning permeated the room.

I acted before I could think, drawn by the need to allay Master's distress. I crossed the short distance between us and gently placed my hand on his arm, stilling his furious scraping at the egg that had blackened and stuck to the bottom of the overheated pan. His brows rose in surprise as his eyes snapped up to meet mine.

"Can I help, Master?" I asked, somewhat shyly.

One corner of his mouth quirked up in a lopsided smile, and I was shocked to realize that he appeared slightly self-conscious. "Please do. I'm a clusterfuck in the kitchen. Let me clean this up and we can start again. Take a look at what we've got in the fridge and go to town."

We. I liked the sound of that, as though we were an inseparable entity.

Compliantly, I took inventory of the new food supply while Master scrubbed the burned pans clean. I decided to stick with the breakfast for dinner idea. I found that I liked it. Master already had the eggs and a pack of bacon out, so I selected a stick of butter and a bag of shredded cheddar cheese before taking an onion from the basket on the counter.

"So, what are we having?" Master asked as he placed the pans back on the stove.

"Omelets," I replied automatically. A part of me was shocked to recognize the term, and even more surprised to find that the knowledge of how to make one was readily available in my mind.

Master pulled out a cutting board and a large knife and began dicing the onion as I set the bacon in the pan. I enjoyed the way that we worked in tandem, both of us going about our tasks in companionable silence. Well, it was silent until Master cursed softly.

"Shit." He swiped the back of his hand under his watering eyes. "That burns like a motherfucker."

Although I didn't like the fact that he was in pain, I couldn't stifle my giggle. The idea of my fierce Master being brought to tears by a vegetable was undeniably funny. And his harsh expletives were laughably extreme.

He raised an eyebrow at me. "Something funny?" His tone was cool, but the corners of his lips twitched as though he was suppressing a smile.

"I think you've been watching too many action movies," I said, distantly amazed at the teasing note in my voice. "They've gotten you worked up. Sounds like you're pretty enraged with that onion."

Now he did smile, chuckling at me. "I'm glad to see you have a sense of humor, sweetheart. And I would invite you to come over here and see how you like it, but I wouldn't dream of subjecting you to the full horror of it."

"If you keep them in the fridge, they won't sting so much," I informed him.

He waved me back to my bacon imperiously. "Thanks for the tip, but that's enough mockery for now, thank you. My ego is very fragile."

I snorted. I highly doubted that. But I obediently returned to my task with a grin plastered across my face.

About twenty minutes later, I slid two perfect omelets stuffed with crispy bacon, cheddar cheese, and sautéed onions onto plates for Master and me. I watched him with rapt attention as he took his first bite.

"Holy shit, that's fantastic." He smiled at me with pride. "Okay, you're responsible for cooking all meals from now on."

"Yes, Master," I agreed brightly, nearly bursting from the joy that swelled in my chest at his approval.

From now on. He really was going to keep me. Bliss thrummed through my veins at the thought.

After dinner, we settled back down on the couch. I couldn't smother my frown when Master opened his laptop. He didn't fail to notice it, and he reached over to squeeze my hand.

"I'm not going to do any more work today, sweetheart," he reassured me. "We need to order some clothes for you. After you shower tonight, we'll see if anything of mine will remotely fit you. Amazon will do two-day delivery, so you won't have to be stuck in my stuff for too long."

"I don't mind, Master," I said. In fact, I rather liked the idea of wearing one of his t-shirts. His scent would cling to me. No, I wouldn't mind that at all.

"Well I do," he said, frowning slightly. "You need some things of your own." He opened up his web browser. "What would you like to get?"

I shrugged. "What would you like, Master?"

His frown deepened as he studied me for a moment. "I'll get you some sweats and t-shirts for now. But I want you to take the next two days to decide what you really want. Don't take my wishes into consideration. I want you to pick out what you like. Understood?"

I considered the daunting task he had set out for me. He wanted me to choose for myself? Without any rules or guidelines?

I swallowed hard and nodded my acquiescence. He had given me two days. Maybe I could ascertain what he would prefer in that time.

I was again shocked to realize that I was scheming ways to circumvent his orders. I shook off the disturbing thought. Master had indicated that he was going to keep me, and I wasn't going to give him a reason to change his mind.

"Okay," he said as he closed his laptop a few minutes later, his purchases completed. "You should get a shower before bed, little one." He took me by the hand and led me into the bathroom. "You can use my shower stuff." He gestured towards the singular large bottle of Old Spice that claimed to serve as shampoo, conditioner, and body wash. I wasn't surprised in the slightest to find Master's toiletries to be minimalistic; he didn't strike me as the sort of man who wasted time preening.

He adjusted the shower's water temperature and retrieved a fluffy black towel from beneath the sink for me. "Do you need anything else?" He asked me, his eyes quickly perusing the small space to ensure that he had provided me with everything I needed. I shook my head. He was so good to me. How could I possibly want for anything when he was by my side?

He pulled away from me, reaching for the doorknob. My hands shot out to clutch at his arm.

"Wait!" Panic lanced through me at the prospect of being alone. "I need you, Master."

I didn't want him to leave me. With his orders to guide me, I had been able to take care of myself on my own that morning. But this was different. I hadn't showered by myself since Master had rescued me. At the clinic, Susan had always stayed with me. The prospect of being naked and alone was terrifying.

My heart sank when Master's fingers closed around mine, carefully extricating himself from my grip. His expression was hard, reproving. "This is something that I can't help you with, girl," he told me firmly. "Get yourself cleaned up. When you're done showering, cover yourself with the towel. Then we'll see what we can find for you to wear to bed."

I bit my lower lip hard to hold back the desperate protests that were fighting to bubble forth. My head bowed, demonstrating my compliance with his wishes. The sound of the door clicking shut behind him made me flinch.

"Get yourself cleaned up."

Master had given me an order. I tried to focus on him, to give myself over to his will completely and quiet my resistant mind. Still, I couldn't stop my fingers from trembling as I gripped the hem of my camisole and slowly pulled it up over my torso. I paused when the cottony material bunched beneath my breasts.

Naked and alone in the dark.

Cold flashed across my skin. I gritted my teeth and shoved back the memories of my horrific past. I wasn't in my prison any longer. That Bastard couldn't hurt me anymore. He couldn't use me. I ripped the camisole over my head in a flash of defiance. The ghostly paleness of my skin reflected in the mirror over the sink, catching my eye.

It was the first time I had really looked at myself. And I looked... *wrong,*

My skin was supposed to be tanned. I hated when I got this pale. My hair was a wild, untamed mass of brunette waves that swirled down to cover my breasts. I brushed my fingertips against the rough untidiness of my split ends, and I grimaced. I loved my hair, and I never let it get so out of sorts.

As I regretfully touched the ragged strands, my gaze fell on my wrist.

A jolt of horror shocked through me when I took in the purple, slightly raised scar that ringed it. Trembling, I raised my other wrist to inspect it, only to find it identically marred. I took a step back, my stomach churning as I examined the way my skin rippled across my defined ribs at the movement. Another purple scar wrapped around the left side of my ribcage. Hardly breathing, I twisted my body so my back was reflected in the mirror.

It was a mess of crisscrossing, darkened lines. Some of them disappeared below the upper edge of my sweatpants. Incapable of wrenching my eyes from the horror, I shoved the pants down my legs. The terrible marks covered my bottom, extending down to my thighs.

The snap of the bullwhip. Blood running down my legs. My back flayed.

I screamed and I cried and I begged, but they wouldn't stop.

"Are you alright in there, sweetheart?" Master's deep voice floated through the closed door, cutting through the choking memories.

Master had ordered me to take a shower.

I had to focus on him. I tried desperately to clear my mind of everything but his order.

"Get yourself cleaned up."

But it wasn't enough. Without Master's physical presence to ground me, I was helpless to stop myself from being sucked under. The darkness of my prison closed in around me.

My former Master's lips were twisted in a savage, satisfied grin as he swiped his hand across my chest, smearing his hot seed that he had spilled across my breasts.

"Get cleaned up, you dirty whore."

The remembered heat of his disgusting mark burned into me, sinking through my skin, searing through my lungs to char my heart. I wrapped my arms around myself tightly, desperate to hold my scorched flesh together. While fire consumed my chest, ice encased the rest of my body, the freeze searing me just as cruelly as the blaze.

A rough, masculine hand touched my shoulder, and a scream ripped its way up my throat as I jerked back. My foot slipped on the slick tile, sending me sprawling. I braced for the bruising impact with the hard floor, but the man's hands caught me around the waist. My body was pulled up against a hard chest. I struggled against his iron hold, but my feral efforts were useless.

I sobbed. God, he was so strong. I wouldn't be able to stop him from using me, from hurting me. But I couldn't stop fighting. The days of hollowly accepting abuse were over. Even though I was powerless against him, I wouldn't meekly comply with his horrific demands any longer.

"Open your eyes, girl. Look at me." Master's harsh demand penetrated my panic with exquisite, brutal efficiency.

I realized I was inflicting the darkness of my dungeon upon myself. My eyes snapped open with eager obedience, searching for his glinting silvery gaze.

"Master." His title was a ragged whisper as tears of relief burned twin streams down my cheeks. I stopped fighting; I pressed against him so closely that my body was molded to his.

Keeping one arm firmly around my back, his other hand cupped my cheek, his thumb hooking under my jaw to tilt my face up to his. His intense stare, authoritative yet compassionate, rolled over and through me like a soothing balm, smothering the pain that had gripped my entire being.

"You're okay, sweetheart." His reassurance was firm, demanding that I believe him. "I've got you."

I melted into him as I allowed his control to take hold of me, to enthrall my mind so that there was no room for my torturous memories.

"What happened?" He asked. His tone was gentle, but his eyes brooked no resistance.

"I..." I heaved in a shuddering breath, wrestling back my remaining fear. "The scars." Those two words were all I could manage. I refused to revisit the horrors that had overcome me, to give voice to what had been done to me.

No. Not to me. That abused slave wasn't *me*. Not anymore. Not now that I was in Master's care. I touched my fingers to my neck, reassuring myself that my iron collar no longer encircled it. No, I didn't belong to that Bastard anymore.

The lines of Master's gorgeous face were taut as he grasped my hand, pulling it away from my neck and placing it on his chest. His heartbeat was strong and even beneath my palm, the regular rhythm calming me.

"You're mine now, little one." The ferocious, possessive edge to his voice made me quiver delightedly. "That Bastard can't hurt you anymore."

More tears welled up as joy soared through me.

"You're mine now."

His.

It was the first time Master had voiced his ownership.

"Thank you, Master." Again, the words were laughably insufficient to express the depth of my gratitude. I pressed my cheek against his chest in an attempt to physically demonstrate my devotion. A pleasurable sigh escaped me at the sensation of his heartbeat reverberating through me, my own heart slowing its frantic palpitations to match his even rhythm. His hand closed around the nape of my neck, holding me to him as his fingers stroked up and down my back, his touch seeming to erase the horror of my scars with every swipe of his palm across my damaged skin.

After a while, he pulled back from me slightly.

"Let's get you in the shower before the water goes cold," he said gently.

Anxiety instantly gripped me. I couldn't allow him to leave me again; I couldn't be left alone, naked and vulnerable to my dark memories.

Master read my expression before I could even begin to voice my protests.

"Don't worry, sweetheart. I'm not going to leave you alone again."

He guided me towards the shower, opening the glass door and encouraging me to step in with his hand on the small of my back. Once I was situated under the warm spray, he drew away from me, moving to close the door, to shut me in by myself.

I couldn't bite back my whine of distress. I was still deeply shaken by the sight of my scarred body, and even having his visage obscured by the frosted glass was too much for me to handle. I needed him to stay close, to keep me grounded in the present.

He studied me, his eyes clouded with uncertainty. After a moment, he blew out a long breath, the lines of his face heavy with resignation. He kicked off his shoes and then stepped into the cubicle with me, fully dressed.

"Just this once," he muttered. I wasn't sure if his words were meant for me or for himself. If they were meant for me, I chose to disregard them. I wouldn't even contemplate a time when I might have to be without him. I would figure out a way to keep him close.

He popped open the cap on the shampoo bottle and squeezed a liberal amount into his hand. The fresh, clean scent engulfed me as he worked it into my hair, his fingers massaging my scalp. A small moan slipped out with my pleased sigh, and I gripped his hips to steady myself. His eyes flashed and his lips thinned, but his strained expression wasn't one of anger. I understood that now. He desired me. A small, triumphant smile played around my lips.

"You're mine now."

I craved to touch him, to run my fingers over every sculpted inch of him; to worship him. I ruthlessly suppressed the urge.

"You are not allowed to do anything for me that is sexual."

I would have to wait until he chose to initiate our intimate contact. But I was confident now that it was just a matter of time. Heat flared between my legs as his hands began to rove over my body, sliding against my skin as he washed me. When he reached my chest, he was careful to avoid touching my breasts directly. But as his fingertips brushed just below the lower swell of them, I gasped as pleasure jolted through me, making my sex pulse. His gaze was suddenly riveted to my chest, and my eyes followed his to find that my nipples had tightened to firm peaks. My body was awakening for him in a way that was utterly foreign to me. But I wasn't frightened by it. It was only right that my body would crave to serve Master in a way that it never had welcomed that Bastard.

The water had soaked Master. Little glistening drops of it clung to the curling ends of his hair, dripping down his tanned neck to race in tiny rivulets down to his chest. His sodden t-shirt was molded to his muscles like a second skin, and for the first time

I could clearly see the hard, flawless lines of his body that had been obscured by his clothes. Helplessly drawn to his perfection, I leaned into him.

He hissed in a breath when I tentatively brushed my lips against his exposed collarbone. Emboldened by his reaction, I traced the line of it with my tongue, savoring his unique flavor that infused the water that was beaded on his skin.

He jerked away from me with a low curse.

"Don't do that."

The fear induced by his furious glare was tempered by his desire-roughened tone. Still, I knew I had pushed too far.

"I'm sorry, Master," I apologized.

But I wasn't sorry. I was thrilled that Master had allowed me to touch him, even if it had been cruelly brief.

His chest swelled as he heaved in several deep breaths, mastering his lust. "It's okay," he said, his tone clipped. "I know this must be confusing for you, but all I want is to take care of you. I don't want anything else from you."

"Don't you?" I asked softly, hardly believing my daring.

His brows drew together. "No," he bit out. His eyes assessed my body, clinically inspecting me. But I didn't fail to notice that they had shifted to a darker, steely shade. "I think we're done," he declared, his voice tight as he tore his gaze from me.

He reached around me to turn off the water, careful not to touch me. Then he opened the shower door and gestured for me to step out. I frowned at his sudden distance, but I said nothing.

Soon, I thought. Master would take me soon. And then I would be his completely, irrevocably.

As I compliantly covered my body with the towel Master offered me, I savored the taste of him that lingered on my tongue.

Chapter 10

I slept peacefully beside Master that night. Despite his evident discomfiture with what had passed between us in the shower, he kept his promise not to leave me alone. He had lain stiffly beside me on the bed for a long time, but he had allowed me to press my body up against his side. I kept my eyes closed and my breathing even, but I didn't allow myself to fall asleep until his muscles relaxed, his arm snaking around me to hold me close. The reassuring heat of him and the calming rhythm of his heartbeat beneath my cheek kept dreams of my dark past at bay.

Although the room was windowless, I was awakened by the pale sunlight that slanted under the door and filtered into the room. I remained perfectly still, savoring the strength of Master's arm wrapped around my back, his large hand gripping my hip.

My eyes greedily drank in his sleeping form, openly admiring every detail of him as I was unable to do when he was awake and watching me. He had changed out of his soaked clothes before joining me in bed, trading them for a t-shirt and sweatpants that matched my own. I relished the way his oversized clothes engulfed my body, encasing me in his comforting scent.

Then my eyes fell on the impressive bulge that tented his sweatpants, and my pulse ratcheted up to outpace his. He had ordered me not to touch him sexually, had said he didn't want that from me. But his body plainly told me what he wouldn't admit aloud. My mouth watered at the prospect of bringing him pleasure, of watching his handsome face as I gave him perfect ecstasy.

My fingers shook slightly as I reached for him, my concern for displeasing him with my defiance making me jittery. Steeling my resolve, I stilled my trembling and tentatively brushed my fingertips over the bulge. His cock jerked under my touch, straining towards me, inviting more. Encouraged, I stroked the length of him with greater surety. Even through the thick material of his sweatpants, I could feel him harden further in response to my ministrations.

The sound of his low groan made my heart soar, my gratification only increasing when his hips lifted, causing his cock to grind against my palm. My touch trailed higher, my fingers dipping beneath the hem of his shirt to trail through the line of dark hair that disappeared into his pants.

His savage growl and his sudden, fierce grip on my wrist elicited a small, shocked cry from my lips. He jerked my hand away from his skin and quickly shifted his body away from me. He was abruptly on his feet, his expressive eyes glaring down at me from where he towered over me, his teeth bared.

This time, my quivering had nothing to do with either excitement or hesitancy; I was terrified. I knew Master would never hurt me, but the fury etched into his features made me fear that I had done something unforgivable.

"Please, Master. I'm sorry. I thought…"

"You thought what?" He barked, livid. "That you could break a rule and there wouldn't be consequences?" I tried to shrink away from him, but his hand on my wrist held me fast.

The lines of his face softened ever so slightly in the wake of my distress. "What were you thinking? Tell me, girl."

"I thought you wanted me to." My voice was barely audible.

His brows drew together forbiddingly. "I've told you I don't want you to touch me like that. But you chose to defy me. Why?"

"I… I'm worried you won't keep me if I don't show you what I can do for you. I want to please you, Master. I want to give myself to you."

His frown deepened, but disquiet replaced the anger in his eyes. "You can't do that, sweetheart. I can't keep you forever. I'm just taking care of you until we can find your family."

His words hit me like a blow to the gut, making my insides writhe as agony tore through me. "But you… You said I was yours," I insisted faintly, unwilling to accept his words.

"I shouldn't have said that," he countered roughly. "I'm sorry. Shit." His hand clenched to a fist. "I'm just trying to help you, sweetheart. You're not my slave."

Oh, god. I had pushed him too far. I had disobeyed him, and now he was rejecting me.

"No!" The word was a wrenching sob. I flung myself off the bed, kneeling at his feet in a show of supplication. I couldn't allow him to let me go. "I'm sorry, Master. I'm sorry I'm sorry I'm sorry…" The words ran together, devolving into a pained whimpering as terror gripped me.

He knelt before me, his arms enfolding me. "Shhh. It's okay, girl. You can stay with me. But so long as you're here, you'll obey my rules. Can you do that for me?"

I stared up at him, clinging to his order like a lifeline. "Yes, Master. I'll be good. I'm sorry."

He pressed his finger to my lips, his eyes troubled. "That's enough apologizing," he told me. "*I* need to apologize to you."

My jaw dropped. What could Master possibly have to apologize for? He was my Master; he could do no wrong.

"I promised you I would always be honest with you, but I lied to you last night. You asked if I wanted anything more than to take care of you." He drew in a deep breath, his lips twisted as though he had bitten into something distasteful. "As much as I wish that were true, I can't help reacting to you. You're a beautiful woman, and my sexual tastes…" He shook his head slightly, grimacing. "My body is used to reacting certain ways to certain stimuli. But I can't act on those impulses when it comes to you. I won't take advantage of you like that." His glowing eyes speared me to the core, and I was shocked to find that the light in them was beseeching rather than demanding. "Don't touch me like that again, no matter what you think I want. My body might react to you, but I never want that from you. Understand?"

I was silent for a moment, my mind reeling as I struggled to process everything he had just said. He wanted me, but he didn't want me.

I shook my head, clearing it. I didn't have to understand. All I had to do was accept his order and cede to his will. It was my only chance of securing him as my Master.

"I won't do it again, Master."

Something twisted inside me as I made the promise. But my discontent was quickly chased away by the sweet sensation of his lips brushing the top of my head.

"Good girl."

I sighed into him, my muscles going limp with relief. He shifted my body so I was cradled in his arms where he knelt on the floor. We stayed there for a long time as he murmured reassuring words and held me tenderly.

When he finally helped me to my feet, my muscles were still watery from the terror that had taken hold of me at his rejection. He steadied me with his hands on my waist, guiding me to the bathroom. This time I took care of my business without begging him to remain with me. I would be stronger for him. I would be better.

Much of the morning's tension eased as I cooked breakfast for the two of us. Sweet memories of our laughter the day before buoyed my spirits, and the act of preparing something for Master calmed me. After breakfast, I resumed my place on the couch beside Master. He half-heartedly tapped away at his laptop, but most of his attention was focused on the films we watched.

In the afternoon, Master commanded that I exercise. He worked out alongside me, continuing long after my own muscles gave out. I leaned back against the wall, content to watch his muscles bulge and ripple as he toned his body. Afterward, he insisted that I shower on my own. The prospect made me anxious, but I focused solely on pleasing him, resolutely ignoring my scarred reflection as I went about my tasks.

When I emerged, he rewarded me by holding me close, stroking his fingers through my damp hair as he told me how proud he was. I glowed at the praise.

The next day was much the same. The only difficult part was when my clothes arrived in the mail in the late afternoon. The delivery prompted Master to follow through on his order that I pick out my own clothes. Mercifully, he helped me through the challenge by giving me options.

"What do you like?" He asked as he opened up his web browser. "Slacks or dresses?"

"Dresses," I answered automatically. Dresses were feminine and flirty. They made me feel pretty. And a cute dress made picking out an outfit ridiculously easy. One article of clothing and I was done.

His approving smile elicited an answering grin from me. Suddenly, I regarded my task with eager anticipation. I wanted to look pretty for Master. I became aware that I felt extremely frumpy in my shapeless sweatpants.

"We'll have to start at square one, sweetheart," Master said, his eyes twinkling. "Believe it or not, I don't often shop for women's clothing."

I couldn't hold back my giggle. Master smiled at the sound as he turned his attention to the computer. A quick Google search for "day dresses" brought up modcloth.com as the first hit. I was instantly in love. An hour later, there were ten items in the shopping cart. I cringed when my eyes fell on the total price.

"That's too much, Master," I protested.

He waved a dismissive hand at me. "You've been very good; you've earned it."

"But -"

He shot me a hard look, silencing me instantly. "I want you to have these. Are you questioning me?"

"No, Master," I said quickly. I wasn't about to defy him again.

Master also insisted on purchasing jeans and a few blouses for me. I was overwhelmed by his generosity, again struck by the disquieting feeling that I didn't deserve it; he did so much for me, but he allowed me to do so little for him.

Our shopping done, Master closed the laptop and selected a new movie for us to watch, and our pattern from the previous day resumed.

Two more days passed in what was rapidly becoming a predictable fashion: I prepared out meals, Master and I cuddled on the couch watching movies, we exercised together, and I showered afterward. The routine was comforting, providing my life with structure. Master would ask for my opinions about food and the films we watched, but I never had to make any important decisions about what we did for the day. And Master slept beside me every night, holding me close. His hard cock would nudge me awake in the morning, but I never tried to touch him again.

But on the third morning, I was awoken by the ringing of Master's phone. He retreated into the living room to take the call, but I didn't fail to notice the bulge of his erection as he quickly walked away from me. His tone was agitated as his muffled words drifted through the closed door.

"Who was that?" I asked when he finally returned to me.

"Just Clayton being an asshole," he said dismissively. "Apparently I'm not doing enough of his goddamn paperwork."

I said nothing. Master had agreed to do something he disliked immensely just so he could stay home and look after me. The thought made me realize the impermanence of my situation; Clayton assumed Master would return to work once they found my family.

But I didn't have a family. The woman who had been taken by that Bastard had a family, but she didn't exist anymore.

Besides, even if she did exist, I didn't *want* to be her. I wanted to be Master's.

It didn't matter. Clayton and Reed wouldn't find that woman, not without my help. And I had buried her too deeply for them to ever find her. I would stay with Master.

Later that day, my dresses arrived. I was eager to try on the new clothes, but I was distracted by the other delivery that came along with them. Master set a gorgeous bunch of deep purple irises in a crystal vase, placing it before me where I sat on my customary barstool. My fingers trembled slightly as I reached out to brush the soft petals, marveling at the cheerful, bright yellow heart nestled in the center of the flower.

"While you were picking out dresses, I noticed that you like purple," Master rumbled from behind me as I stared at the flowers reverently. "Do you like them?"

I turned to him, blinking away the tears that obscured his visage. "I love them," I said fervently. "Thank you, Master."

"You are more than welcome, little one."

His eyes burned with an intensity I didn't quite understand. Whatever it was entranced me completely; I couldn't have torn from his gaze even if I wanted to. And I definitely didn't want to. I barely breathed as I stared up at him, waiting. For what, I wasn't sure. But I wanted it desperately.

He blinked, breaking the intimate connection.

"I like seeing you happy, sweetheart," he said gruffly.

I bit back my instinct to protest when he put distance between us, returning to the couch to retrieve his laptop. I silently followed in his wake and settled down beside him in my usual spot.

After exercising that afternoon, I went to take my customary shower. As I washed myself, my fingers brushed over the fine hairs that covered my legs. I frowned. I was going to wear one of my pretty new dresses for the evening, and I didn't want to appear at all untidy.

My mind made up, I darted out of the shower, dripping wet, to search for a spare razor. I quickly found what I was looking for in one of the cabinets beneath the sink, and I tore the razor from its packaging before stepping back into the shower. I slicked soap over my legs and meticulously shaved them. I took care of my underarms as well, vaguely disgusted to realize I hadn't done so in a long time. How could Master have possibly called me "gorgeous" when I was so unkempt?

My gaze fell on the hair that covered my sex. That was all wrong as well. Even though I knew Master wouldn't see that particular part of my body, I couldn't resist the impulse to tidy it up.

When I emerged from the bathroom, I was pleased to see Master suck in a breath as his eyes fell on me. I was even more gratified when his gaze fell on my bare legs, roving slowly up my body until his eyes came to rest on my face. I was beaming at him, and he returned my smile easily.

Now it was my turn to inhale sharply. God, he was beautiful. And I finally felt like I might be worthy of him. I was still too thin, but the retro cut of my amethyst dress – tapered to the waist before flaring out to fall mid-thigh – gave a hint of the curves I used to possess.

Then my mind drifted to the ugly scars that marred my skin, and I realized I would never be good enough for him, no matter how much I preened.

He crossed the room in four long strides to gather me up in his arms. "What was that thought, little one?" He asked.

"My scars…" My gaze fell on my wrist, and I shuddered. I touched my fingers to my throat to reassure myself that the phantom weight of my iron collar was just that: a phantom.

Master grasped my fingers in his, pulling my hand towards his face. His lips brushed against the scar at the inside of my wrist, and my pulse jumped.

"You're beautiful, sweetheart." His voice was a low rumble. "That Bastard can never take that from you."

"Thank you, Master," I said breathily, stunned by his praise and his intimate touch.

He blinked hard, his expression falling with regret as he slowly lowered my hand from his lips. Still, he didn't release me even as he stepped away. Keeping his hold on my wrist, he gently guided me to the kitchen so he could help me prepare our dinner.

"We're running low on food," he told me after we had finished eating. "Why don't you make a list of what you want to cook, and I'll order it." It was worded as a question, but it was an order.

I happily complied, excited by the prospect of pleasing Master further. He took such good care of me; the only time that I could care for him was when I prepared his meals. While he grumbled over his laptop, I took up the paper and pencil he had set before me.

I paused, frowning. I hadn't written anything in so long. What if I didn't remember how?

No. I had to remember. Master had ordered me to do this, and I wasn't going to disappoint him. I touched the lead to the paper, and the word "eggs" flowed out in cursive. The form of the letters wasn't perfect, but it wasn't wrong either. I smiled to myself as I recognized the handwriting as my own personal scrawl. It was yet another thing I had lost that Master had given back to me. The pencil moved across the paper in assured, continuous strokes. I hummed softly to myself as I worked, contented by the scratch of the lead as it left bold charcoal lines in its wake.

"So you're a baseball fan, then?" Master's question cut through my reverie. I glanced up at him, my brow furrowed in confusion. "You're humming 'Take Me Out to the Ballgame,'" he informed me, his full lips quirked up in an amused smile.

"Oh," I said, a bit dumbly.

Was I a baseball fan?

Flashing signs emblazoned in blue, red, and white. The roar of the crowd. The scent of beer and hotdogs.

Joy.

"Yes," I said slowly. "I do like baseball."

Master grinned as he stood, crossing from the couch to join me in the kitchen. "We'll watch a game later," he told me as he approached. "You had better be an Orioles fan."

I grimaced, and Master laughed. "I guess that's a 'no,' then," he said. His gaze fell on the list I had been writing, and his eyebrows rose. "That's amazing, sweetheart."

"What?" I asked, confused. I glanced down at the paper to find a sketch of an eye staring back up at me. My fingertips were darkened with lead where I had smudged it to add shading to my drawing. I stared at it, bewildered. Had I really done that? I hadn't even realized it. I gazed up at Master and found the inspiration for my drawing glinting down at me. My sketch didn't even come close to capturing the multifaceted beauty of his eyes.

"Where did you learn to do that?" He asked, the curiosity in his tone colored by something more inquisitive, incisive.

An elderly woman sat beside me at the dining room table, her wrinkled hand moving with the surety of years of practice as she gave life to a sketch of a pretty little girl with dark, curling hair. A pencil was clutched awkwardly in my own tiny hand, and I tried to mimic her drawing. My efforts were laughably rough in comparison to her masterpiece, but she praised my work, altering my grip on the pencil as she instructed me on how to improve.

Granny.

I shook my head hard. No. Those weren't my memories. They were *hers.*

"I don't know."

It was the first time I had lied to Master. I knew I was breaking one of his rules, but I couldn't remember the woman who owned those memories. I wouldn't. Master wasn't a part of her life, and I refused to let go of him.

He studied my face carefully, but I schooled my expression to a blank mask. I hoped it would pass for genuine ignorance rather than deceit.

After a moment, the intensity of his stare eased, and I resisted the impulse to heave a sigh of relief at the reprieve. He smiled at me gently.

"Come on." He took me by the hand and tugged me towards the couch. "We'll watch a game while I order groceries."

His gaze turned hard, authoritative, but a smile was still playing around his lips. "You'll learn to root for the Orioles."

I snorted and rolled my eyes. "So long as you don't ask me to support the damn Cardinals, we'll be okay."

Master's booming laugh filled the room. "Sweetheart, I think that's the first time I've ever heard you cuss."

I smirked at him. "I wonder where I might have picked up that habit?" I asked pointedly.

His chuckle held a dark edge as he tugged my wrist hard, sending me tumbling down onto the couch beside him.

"Don't go getting bratty with me, girl. You won't like the consequences." I froze as he paused for a beat, fear and something darker stirring in my belly at the mention of *consequences.*

"I might have to cook dinner tomorrow," he threatened.

I laughed and gave a dramatic shudder. "You wouldn't."

"Watch me."

I made a show of pursing my lips, playfully letting him know he wouldn't get any more sass off me. For now.

He planted a swift kiss on my forehead. "Good girl. I really didn't want to put both of us through that."

"You are truly terrifying, Master," I quipped. "I am thoroughly intimidated."

He gave a playful growl and pinched my arm hard. He grinned at the sound of my surprised yelp. "Don't push your luck, girl. What kind of Master would I be if I can't follow through with my threats?"

My breath caught in my throat. It was the first time he had made reference to his ownership of me aloud since the morning that he had almost rejected me. Rather than quivering in fear at his threat, I flung myself into his arms, pressing my face into the crook between his neck and shoulder, breathing deeply and inhaling his intoxicating scent.

"I'm sorry, Master," I said, my tone low and husky. "I promise I'll be good."

He stiffened beneath me for a moment, but then he sighed, his arms wrapping around me as he tilted his head to rest it atop my own.

"You've been very good, sweetheart. I'm so proud of you."

Unable to help myself, I turned my head slightly so I could press my lips gently against his neck.

Instantly, I jerked away from him, horrified at my mistake. But he held me fast, refusing to release me.

"It's okay, girl." His warm breath tickled across my ear as he reassured me. "I'm not angry. Just don't do that again."

"I won't, Master," I agreed, my voice ragged with relief.

He cleared his throat abruptly, shifting so he could retrieve the remote from the coffee table.

"We'll watch an Orioles-Cardinals game," he told me. "That way you'll have to root for the Orioles."

I huffed out an annoyed breath, but I couldn't fully suppress my amused smile. "You're evil, Master," I informed him.

He pinched my arm again, laughing when I tried to squirm away from him. He held me firmly to his side. "Watch yourself, girl. You're on thin ice as it is."

I sighed happily and snuggled into him, ceding to his beautiful control. I enjoyed this playful side of Master almost as much as I relished his power over me.

Chapter 11

"I have something for you, sweetheart," Master told me the next day after we had finished putting the groceries away. I had noticed the two extra packages that had been passed through the door, but I hadn't asked about them. If Master wanted me to know what they were, he would tell me. Now my heart leapt at his words. Even though it made me feel even more unequal in what I gave to him in return for his generosity, I loved how he pampered me.

He opened the first, smaller cardboard box and proffered me the blue velvet-covered box that he retrieved from it. I hesitated. I knew that kind of box meant he had purchased something extravagant for me. He had already spent so much on me, and I was unsure if I should accept more.

"Open it," he ordered steadily.

I reached for it; I didn't have an option now. When I snapped open the box, I gasped. Nestled in the silken white lining was a simple tourmaline pendant set in silver. The stone was a gorgeous, vibrant green with a fiery blue heart that flashed elusively when the light played through the gem's facets.

The heat of Master's body suddenly washed over me as he entered my personal space. His fingers curled beneath my chin, guiding my face up to his. There was an intense light in his silver gaze. It shone through my flesh to illuminate my soul.

"It reminded me of your eyes," he said, his voice gruff with emotion.

My eyes?

I thought back to when I had studied my reflection in the mirror. I had taken inventory of my body, but I hadn't looked myself in the eye. I realized now that I was afraid to see the deadened, defeated flatness of them. The stone I held was vibrant, sparkling as it caught the light. Was that really what Master saw when he looked into my eyes?

He plucked the box from my fingers, carefully extricating the delicate silver chain that held the pendant.

"Turn around and lift your hair for me," he commanded.

I obeyed with alacrity, eager to accept Master's gift. It was so much more than just a pretty piece of jewelry.

"I've noticed how you touch your throat when you're anxious," he said, his breath fanning across the exposed skin at the nape of my neck. I shivered delightedly. "I know you're looking for that Bastard's collar." The silver was cool on my skin as he clicked the clasp closed. "Now you can touch this and think of me instead."

To my utter shock, his lips brushed against my neck where he had clasped the necklace. I leaned back into him, a small, pleasurable sigh escaping me.

The intimate contact was broken all too soon. Master stepped back from me with a grunt, his hands closing around my upper arms and pulling them down so that my hair cascaded down my back. He applied gentle pressure, turning my body so I was facing him once again. His predator's eyes shone with a hungry light, but his lips were pressed into a thin line. As though he couldn't help himself, he reached out to stroke his fingertips along the line of the silver chain.

"Beautiful," he said softly. But he wasn't looking at the pendant.

I touched my fingers to his, silently communicating that I welcomed the contact.

"Thank you, Master," I whispered fervently.

Shaking his head slightly, he cleared his throat. But his movements were hesitant, regretful, as he pulled away from me. My face fell as disappointment flooded me. Resolutely, I rolled the chain between my fingers, reminding myself that he had claimed me as his, even if he was fighting his desire for me. His jaw clenched as his eyes followed my gesture, and he tore his gaze away from me, his attention turning to the other package.

Moments later, he offered me a large sketchpad and a vibrant set of colored pencils. Again, I hesitated to accept his gift. My flash of memory the day before had unsettled me, and I wasn't at all sure that I wanted to tap into that part of myself further.

"I want you to draw something for me," Master said firmly.

I swallowed hard, knowing I couldn't refuse. Compliantly, I took the sketchpad from him, but I offered no words of thanks this time. Master studied my troubled expression.

"It would make me very happy if you would draw something for me," he told me gently.

A pang shot through my heart. Now I definitely couldn't refuse. If I could do anything to please him in the way that he had pleased me, then I had to do it.

"What would you like for me to draw?" I asked, my voice slightly tremulous.

"How about someplace that makes you happy?" He suggested. "And don't draw my apartment," he stipulated after a moment's consideration.

Uneasiness made my gut churn. I didn't know anyplace else that made me happy. I bit my lip, but I nodded to demonstrate my compliance. Master closed the short distance between us to kiss the top of my head sweetly.

"Good girl," he said with approval. "I'm going to sift through some of this goddamn paperwork. Otherwise Clayton might come by and demand that I return to the office."

No. I couldn't allow that to happen. If he needed me to draw so he could focus on his work rather than being distracted by a movie, then I would happily do so. I flipped open the sketchpad before he had even made it to the couch.

Closing my eyes, I took a deep breath.

I re-arranged his suggestion into an order, allowing his will to guide me rather than my own mind.

Draw someplace that makes you happy.

Taking up a pencil, I settled into a trance-like state, the sketch coming to life before me almost of its own accord. I had tapped into some contented part of my mind, where primal emotions ruled me rather than my own busy thoughts. I slipped out of time as I sank back into that deep part of myself, and I barely even noticed what I was drawing.

"Chicago, huh?" The sound of Master's voice just behind me made me jump. "That's really beautiful, sweetheart."

I blinked, pulling myself out of my trance to actually take in what I had drawn. The colors were muted, the scene softly illuminated by the early morning sun that shone weakly through the blanket of snow clouds above. The city rose up abruptly from the shore of Lake Michigan in the distance. A woman stood in the foreground, her face in profile as she stared out over the lake. She huddled in her purple pea coat as the wind caught up her light brown, wavy hair, lifting it so that it floated behind her, lending her an ethereal quality.

"When were you in Chicago?" Master asked.

I froze. Ice began to crystalize at the base of my spine, creeping upward to radiate a chill throughout my entire body.

"I wasn't," I said. But my voice wavered.

"Then why did you draw yourself there?" Master's voice rumbled through my skin, but it didn't bring the comfort that it usually did. It sank into my chest, filling the space until my lungs threatened to burst.

"I didn't," I insisted.

Master reached around me to point at the woman in the picture. "That's you," he told me firmly.

"No." I shook my head vigorously. "That's not me. That's Lydia."

My mouth snapped closed, and coppery blood spilled onto my tongue as I bit the inside of my cheek hard.

Master grasped my shoulders and forcibly swiveled my body on the barstool so that I was facing him. I wouldn't meet his eye. I couldn't face what he was saying.

"That's you, sweetheart," he said, more gently this time. "You're Lydia."

A small whimper slid up my throat as I shook my head again. I wasn't her. I wasn't her.

He gripped my chin between his thumb and forefinger, turning my head so that I was staring down at the drawing. I squeezed my eyes shut, unwilling to face it.

"Look at her, girl," he ordered.

Oh, god. Why was he doing this to me? Master was going to destroy me. I wasn't Lydia; I was his slave. And I didn't want to be anyone else.

"I won't tell you again." This time his words were a threatening growl.

Dread pooling in my stomach, I obeyed, forcing myself to study the woman in my drawing. Her skin was lightly tanned, and her cheekbones weren't as pronounced as mine. But she had my delicate, sloping nose and my pointed chin. Even though her gaze was directed towards the water, her eyes flashed a hint of blue-green.

"This is Lydia," Master said firmly from beside me. "She's been to Chicago. Judging by her hatred of the Cardinals, I'm guessing she's a Cubs fan. She's an artist and an excellent cook. She hates romantic comedies. She prefers dresses to jeans, and her favorite color is purple. Isn't that right, girl?"

My entire body trembled, and tears pooled in my eyes. "She doesn't exist anymore," I whispered desperately. "She died."

Master applied pressure beneath my chin, forcing my face back to his. His expression was hard, determined. But something akin to sadness flickered through his steely gaze.

"She's not dead. She's you. You're Lydia."

Panic tore through me, ripping my insides apart.

"NO!" I shrieked. My knees hit the tiled kitchen floor as I flung myself at his feet. I stared up at him with feverish desperation. "I'm yours, Master. I'm yours. I don't want to be her. Please…"

His features twisted with horror and disgust.

He didn't want me anymore.

I screamed as my entire world shattered, the shards of it ripping at my soul. My body collapsed to the floor, and I curled up in on myself, hugging my knees to my chest protectively. My fingers closed around the pendant at my throat with a vice-like grip as despairing sobs wracked my body.

I wasn't Master's slave. He didn't want me anymore.

But I wasn't Lydia either. I couldn't be Lydia. She would be disgusted by what my former master had reduced me to. She couldn't face that.

I was no one.

I was no one.

My mind went completely blank as I allowed the thought to claim me. If I didn't exist, then nothing could hurt me. The pain would stop.

God, I wanted the pain to stop.

My trembling ceased, and I went utterly silent as I embraced the nothingness. I was aware of the sound of his voice, but his words were meaningless. It was easier that way.

"Fuck!" His thumb traced the line of my cheekbone. I chose to ignore the almost painful sweetness of the sensation of his skin against mine. "Open your eyes, sweetheart. Look at me. I'm right here. I've got you." His voice was taut with anxiety, but I didn't respond. He didn't have any authority over me.

He grasped my shoulders, shaking me. "Look at me, girl," he almost snarled the demand.

But I wasn't his sweetheart and I wasn't his girl. I was no one.

"God damn it!" He shook me harder. "Lydia!"

I certainly wasn't *her*. I remained in my merciful blankness.

Curses dropped from his lips in a continuous stream. After a few minutes, he went quiet, and his touch left me. Dimly, I was disturbed by the loss of the heat of him. I shied away from the emotion. I was tired of hurting.

God, I was tired.

When he spoke again, his voice was deep and authoritative, his words even. All signs of his earlier kindness and concerned anxiety were gone.

"Open your eyes."

The clear, controlled tone frightened me. His iron will was almost strong enough to penetrate my sweet nothingness, and I flinched ever so slightly.

Stinging pain bloomed on my cheek as his palm cracked across it.

"I gave you an order, slave." The calmly-spoken words held a more serious threat than his ferocious snarl.

Slave.

Tears of joy spilled down my cheeks as my eyes snapped open. His expression was cool and remote as he stood, his arms folding across his chest as he towered over me. I scrambled up onto my knees, desperate to demonstrate my utter devotion and gratitude.

"Master." My voice broke on his title.

He brushed his fingers over the top of my head, accepting my submission. Unable to help myself, I leaned forward, pressing my cheek against his leg. This was where I wanted to be. This was where I belonged. Master owned me. He would take care of me, protect me.

He allowed me to stay there for a few minutes, my tears dampening his trousers as I clung to him.

After a while, he bent down and gathered me up in his arms, cradling my body against his chest. I stared up at his perfect face with open adoration. He caught my eye, but he quickly looked away, his jaw tightening as he resolutely gazed straight ahead. Once we were in the bedroom, he settled down on the bed, his back resting against the wall so that he was sitting upright.

My heart swelled when he didn't release me. Instead, he shifted me so one arm was supporting my back. His free hand brushed against my cheek. My skin pulsed with gentle heat where he had struck me.

"I'm sorry I had to do that, sweetheart," he said quietly. "I didn't know what else -"

He cut himself off, clearing his face of concern. His hard, impassive mask was back. I loved the sight of it. I didn't have to worry about anything when Master was in control.

"You're going to listen to me now," he told me coolly. "You're not going to protest and you're not going to cry. You'll take deep, even breaths while I'm talking to you, and you'll look me in the eye. You are not allowed to panic. You'll accept what I'm saying because you don't have the choice to do otherwise. I expect your complete obedience, or there will be consequences. Do you understand me, girl?"

I was utterly enthralled by him. I took a deep breath and stared up into his captivating metallic eyes. "Yes, Master."

He gave a short nod, acknowledging my compliance. "I don't want you to think about the woman in your drawing. You are not allowed to worry about who she was or what happened to her. But you will accept that she is a part of you."

I flinched.

"Breathe," he commanded sharply.

I obeyed. I would never refuse him anything.

"Your name is Lydia. And I'm going to call you by your name. You will answer to it. Understood?"

I could do that. He could call me whatever it pleased him to call me. I was his slave, and I would obey him in everything.

"Yes, Master." The tremulous note was gone from my voice; the words rang out clear and fervent.

His perfect smile hit me like a blow to the solar plexus, taking my breath away. "That's a good girl. I'm very proud of you, Lydia."

The praise sent joy bubbling through me. And I was distantly amazed to find that I liked the way the name sounded on his lips.

My name.

I was Lydia, and I belonged to Master.

I stared at those full lips that had formed my name so perfectly, and I licked my own as longing rose up in me. I wanted to be closer to Master, to somehow express the magnitude of what I felt for him. My gaze flicked up to his eyes, and a little thrill shot through me at the hunger that shone in them as he watched my tongue swipe across my lips.

Surrendering to my desire, I leaned up into him and softly pressed my mouth to his.

He had ordered me not to do anything sexual for him, but this wasn't sexual. This was pure, desperate *need,* a painful yearning to connect. I wasn't doing this to please him; I was doing this because my soul craved to brush against his.

He responded instantly, a low growl rumbling from somewhere deep inside of him. I caught it on a gasp, taking it into myself, relishing the way it reverberated through me. His tongue delved into my open mouth, stroking me with almost feverish intensity. The kiss wasn't sweet, and it wasn't gentle. The voraciousness with which Master claimed me let me know I wasn't the only one who had been longing for this intimate contact.

My hands closed around the back of his neck, holding him to me more tightly as I drank him in greedily. He nipped my lower lip in reprimand, and I moaned into him, savoring the sharp, sweet reminder of his dominance. My head spun as he consumed me, controlling my very breath. Just when my lungs began to burn from lack of oxygen, he jerked away from me. I gasped in air, panting as I stared up at him, wide-eyed.

My wide, silly grin melted instantly in the wake of his anguished expression. I touched my fingers to the creases in his forehead, trying to erase them. He flinched away from me, his eyes tormented.

"I can't do this," he said raggedly. He started to shift my body away from him, to put distance between us. I tightened my hold around the back of his neck, my fingernails pressing into his skin.

"Please," I begged hoarsely. I couldn't bear his distance. Not now. Not ever. "Just hold me, Master. Please."

Uncertainty clouded his expression, his inner turmoil etched clearly across his handsome features.

"Okay, sweetheart," he finally conceded on a sigh. His lips thinned. "Okay, Lydia," he corrected himself. He speared me with a significant look. "I'll hold you. You didn't do anything wrong. I shouldn't have… We can't do that again."

My heart sank in my chest. Master's kiss had been the singular most glorious experience of my entire existence. But as much as I hated the thought of never experiencing it again, the idea of him turning away from me was far more painful. I would do anything to stay close to him.

All I could do was hope that one day he might change his mind.

Chapter 12

Lydia,
Master's Slave

Three long days passed, and Master didn't so much as bring his lips close to mine. We returned to our regular schedule: I cooked our meals, Master and I exercised together in the afternoon, and he held me as I sat beside him on the couch. But something had changed between us, and now he spent more time being absorbed by his work than he did laughing with me. I longed to reestablish our closeness; I feared that I was losing him. Sometimes when I called him "Master," something shifted in his eyes, and I wasn't sure if it was desire or disgust.

True to his word, Master called me "Lydia." I missed the endearments "sweetheart" and "girl," and thrill shot through me every time he slipped up and used one of them. I couldn't deny that it was strangely fulfilling to hear the name "Lydia" fall from his lips, but I didn't want Lydia to fully replace who I had been before. Lydia and Master's slave were one in the same, and I longed for him to give equal acknowledgement to both sides of me.

I hadn't touched my sketchpad since I had brought Lydia back to life, but I decided it was time for me to try again. Butterflies fluttered in my stomach as I lifted the pencil, the result of both the fear that had gripped me after my first attempt at drawing and nervousness at my daring plan. But this time, I had a clear objective, and I wouldn't allow my subconscious to determine the image that flowed from my pencil strokes. This time, I wouldn't give form to something horrific that stirred unsettling memories.

Master glanced over at me curiously as I settled myself down at the kitchen counter. I was pleased to notice that he was frowning slightly at my distance from where he sat working on the couch.

"What are you doing, Lydia?" He asked. "I thought we were going to watch a game."

"I'd rather not," I said, my voice a touch incisive. Master had suggested we watch a Cubs game, but I had decided against it. It was the first time I had chosen to do something of my own volition since he had taken me into his home. But my purpose was more important than my reluctance to counter his wishes. He hadn't outright ordered me to sit beside him and watch TV, so I wasn't technically defying him.

I was surprised when he gave me an encouraging smile. "That's the first time you've told me what *you* want," he pointed out. "That's one rule you had yet to follow. I'm proud of you, sweetheart."

"You will always tell me if you want something that I'm not giving you."

I beamed at him, all reservations regarding my defiance melting in the wake of his wholehearted approval. And he had called me "sweetheart."

His expression turned more serious. "I want you to draw something that makes you happy, Lydia. I don't want you to get upset again."

My smile took on a sly, secretive edge. Oh, I fully intended to draw something that made me happy. "Yes, Master," I agreed sweetly.

He cocked his head at me, clearly trying to puzzle out my expression. I ducked my head before his suspicions could become further aroused, pointedly turning my attention towards my sketchpad. After a moment of silence, the clatter of Master's fingers darting across his laptop keys resumed. I was careful not to audibly heave a sigh of relief.

I chose a black pencil. I intended for my sketch to be stark, commanding Master's attention through rendering the image in bold black and white.

Considering the amount of time I had spent staring at him in wonder, capturing the perfection of Master's face was more difficult than I had anticipated. All of his features were accurately formed, but expressing his powerful, intoxicating aura was more elusive. Even if I were an artistic savant, I would have been incapable of depicting that intangible quality about him that I found so rapturously enticing.

I set him aside for a while, focusing instead on myself. I thought of the woman I saw when I looked in the mirror. She was thin, scarred; she was somehow lacking the completion of spirit that was evident in my drawing of Lydia standing at the edge of Lake Michigan.

But that damaged woman belonged to Master. And that made her far more beautiful than Lydia would ever be.

Contented with the image I had produced of myself, I returned to perfecting Master's visage. I hadn't come close to succeeding when his voice cut into my reverie.

"So, what are you working on, Lydia?" He asked.

Nervous apprehension threatened to grip me as he approached. I took a deep breath, shoving it back. I was determined to see my task through.

"Something that makes me happy," I said definitively, looking him squarely in the eye.

His curious frown deepened to a scowl when his gaze fell on my work. In my sketch, Master's lips were crushed to mine, his hand tangled in my hair as he held me to him. The lines of his face were harsh and hungry as he claimed me. My eyes were closed, my expression beatific in my blissful submission.

"What is this, girl?" His voice was low and dangerous, holding a rough, threatening edge.

But rather than being intimidated, I was emboldened by his reaction. My fierce Master was back, and I thrilled at the sight of him, even if he was disapproving.

"Something that I want, Master," I told him, my voice clear and steady.

His brows drew together, his eyes sparking as he turned his glare on me.

I didn't flinch; I met his stare, lifting my chin in a silent challenge. His lips twisted into a fearsome snarl as his dominant side took over, unable to permit my flagrant defiance. His movements were harsh in his ferocity, lacking the fluidity of purpose that usually imbued his careful control. This was a different sort of power. I had tapped into the wild, untamed side of him that acted on his most primal urges.

My sharp gasp was one of delight when his hand fisted in my hair at the nape of my neck. The small pain as he sharply maneuvered my body off of the barstool was exquisite. The direction of his harsh guidance changed abruptly, pulling downward so that my head dropped back. But the pressure didn't relent, and I was forced to my knees before him.

"What have I told you about this, girl?" He demanded roughly. "That won't happen again."

He gave another sharp tug on my hair, reinforcing his control with the zing of pain that tingled across my scalp. My lips parted, and a low moan was released from deep within me. Heat pulsed to life between my thighs as I stared up at him, relishing his power over me. This was what I had craved so fiercely: for Master to fully stake his claim, to allow me to slake his need. A defined bulge appeared at his groin as his rapidly hardening cock strained against the material of his pants. I longed for him to remove that barrier between us, and my fingers itched to caress him. My mouth watered at the idea of tasting him.

Abruptly, he stepped back from me with a curse, releasing my hair. I whined at the sudden distance between us, and I reached for him.

"Stay," he commanded sharply.

His order connected with something deep within me, and a desire that had been perverted and tainted blossomed back to life.

I groaned as I finally realized what the almost painful pulsing between my legs meant: lust. Automatically, I settled back onto my heels, parting my thighs and twining my fingers together behind my back. For the first time I could remember, the action wasn't driven by fear of abuse or a desire to please; this was for me. This was what *I* wanted.

An answering lust flared in Master's eyes as he admired my position. He was clearly affected by the sight of me on my knees before him, inviting him to take control of my body. Begging him to do so.

His fists clenched at his sides as he visibly restrained himself.

"Fuck!" He barked out. His silver glare was resentful, pained. "What am I supposed to do with you, girl?" His tone was roughened with frustration, and I knew I wasn't supposed to answer his question. "I should turn you over my knee for this."

I sucked in a breath, but the flames that licked my skin were borne of desire, not fear. I craved the contact he threatened me with.

His eyes glinted at my reaction. Then his brows drew together, and he took another step back from me, a growl easing its way up his throat. The sound made me shiver delightedly.

"Stay here," he ground out. "Don't move until I give you permission to do so."

He began to turn from me, and disappointment lanced through me.

"Master, please -"

He paused, and his glower made my words instantly die in my throat. "If I hear one word out of your mouth that isn't 'Yes, Master,' I'll leave you here all afternoon," he threatened.

I swallowed hard, staving off the tears that stung at the corners of my eyes. He had devised the worst possible punishment for me: denying me his presence.

"Yes, Master," I whispered meekly, dropping my eyes.

I watched his boots as he quickly retreated from me. The *bang* of his bedroom door slamming shut reverberated throughout the apartment.

I couldn't stop the tears that flowed silently down my cheeks. I hated his distance, his anger.

But did I regret what I had done?

No. I didn't think I did. I had forced him to acknowledge that his desire for me was just as fierce as mine was for him. And I had come to a shocking realization about myself as well. All this time, I had thought I wanted to give Master my body so I could please him. If I just pleased him enough, then he would never let go of me. I still craved for him to stake a permanent claim; I feared one day the FBI might find Lydia's family and force me to leave him.

But even more fiercely, I wanted him to take me because my body burned for him to do so. I had thought that Bastard had robbed me of my capacity for lust. His torment had been so cruel that I had forgotten what lust was. Master had reawakened that within me. It was another gift he had given me.

Even if I didn't want to return to Lydia's life before she had been abducted and broken, I found I did want to possess some of the characteristics that made her uniquely *her*. Master had been right: we both loved art and cooking; we were Cubs fanatics; we preferred action films to insipid romances; our personal style was flirty and feminine. And we both harbored dark, unfulfilled sexual desires. I wouldn't access her memories, but these qualities, these wants and yearnings, resonated with me. I embraced them, accepting them as a part of me.

I was the version of Lydia that belonged to Master. And I wasn't going to deny my needs any longer.

My cheeks were dry by the time Master returned to me. His eyes widened slightly in surprise when he took in my calm demeanor. All of the furious tension had left him, and I wondered what he had been doing in his room that had siphoned it off. A decidedly wicked conclusion flashed across my mind, and I flushed at the idea of Master stroking himself as he thought of me.

He bent and clasped his hands around my waist, helping me stand. He steadied me as I bent my knees slightly and wiggled my toes, easing my stiff muscles. When he was satisfied that my discomfiture had abated, he lifted me up in his arms and carried me to the sofa. To my surprise, he situated my body beside his, placing my head on his thighs. He kept one hand curled around my hip while his other tenderly stroked my hair. I sighed happily, closing my eyes as I melted against him.

Despite his anger, Master was comforting me after my punishment. There had been a consequence for my defiant behavior, but it hadn't damaged our relationship. If anything, I felt closer to him than I had in days. He had fully accepted his role as my Master, had re-committed himself to taking care of me. My daring action had brought about a good outcome, even if Master hadn't kissed me again.

He held me long into the afternoon, and although his touch was tender rather than demanding, the insistent throbbing in my loins didn't abate. My need was keen to the point of being painful, my newly re-discovered lust tormenting me. But I didn't dare push Master further that day. As much as I relished his control, I didn't want him to exert that control by leaving me alone again.

When I found myself in the solitude of the shower later that day, I surrendered to instinct.

Master fully commanded all of my thoughts, and memories of our more intimate encounters played through my mind on a loop: Master's cock jerking beneath my cheek as I rested my head in his lap; the feel of his hardness beneath my fingers as I tentatively stroked him through his sweatpants; the heady beauty of his scorching kiss; the wild gleam in his eyes as he forced me to my knees before him.

I whimpered as my clit pulsed relentlessly. My mind flicked to Master sating himself in the privacy of his bedroom, bringing himself to completion with wicked thoughts of what he might do to my body. It occurred to me that I could do the same for myself.

Tentatively, I brushed two fingers over my hardened bud. A small, sharp cry escaped me as pleasure shot through my body. I had forgotten about this part of myself, about the bliss that certain parts of my body could give me. I explored my erogenous zones, old patterns of touching myself clicking back into place with each area I aroused. My fingers found the wet heat inside of me, gathering it up as I stroked myself. I trailed the wetness up to my clit, rubbing in steady, practiced circles. My nipples throbbed, begging for attention. Air was sucked into my lungs on a delighted gasp as I pinched them, sending answering lines of pleasure sizzling down to my clit.

Twining the silvery chain of the necklace that Master had given me around my hand, I closed my eyes and thought of him. I imagined that it was his fingers that were pinching me, stroking me. He would watch me with those hypnotic eyes, a twisted, pleased smile on his lips as he manipulated my body, wringing pleasure from me as he desired. His mouth would come down on mine, taking possession of my bliss as I moaned into him. He would drink in my ecstatic scream as I came completely undone.

My cry of pleasure echoed through the bathroom, the acoustics magnifying the lustful sound. I leaned back against the cool tiles, panting. The warm spray of the water pinging against my skin made me shudder as it continued to stimulate my sensitized flesh.

Concern flashed across my mind as I wondered if Master had heard me. I hastily shook it away. I hoped he had heard. I wanted him to realize what he had awoken within me, how I had so desperately needed release after the intensity of what had passed between us that day.

A sly, slightly devious smile played across my lips. I was manipulating Master. The beast within him wouldn't like that.

"I should turn you over my knee for this."

My lower lip caught between my teeth at the thought. Again, the idea tapped into deeply-buried desires that I thought had been extinguished completely by perverted abuse. Master would help me reclaim that part of myself, just as he had helped me rebuild who I truly was. My pussy pulsed back to life at the thought of him bringing me perfect pleasure as he possessed me completely.

I hoped that my next punishment would be more interesting than waiting on my knees.

Chapter 13

Master's disapproving frown let me know that he had heard my cry of pleasure. Was he angry with me for touching myself or was he displeased because he hadn't been the one to touch me? I sincerely hoped it was the latter.

But other than his disgruntled expression, he gave no indication that he was aware of my actions. In fact, he spoke little that evening, and his taciturnity continued into the following day. Mercifully, he kept me close, but some of the discomfited tension had returned to his muscles. I wanted so desperately to ease it. I couldn't bear it if he retreated from me again, not after I had come so close to goading him into touching me.

For the first time ever, I allowed my own wants to supersede Master's wishes. At one time, I had found thoughts of manipulating him into changing his rules to be disturbing. Now I went about formulating such schemes with willful determination. I didn't want to anger or disappoint him, but I couldn't allow him to continue denying what we both wanted.

I can't allow him?

I was shocked at the idea that I would demand anything of Master. But although I was utterly devoted to him, I wouldn't back down on this. Once, I might have feared that my deliberate disobedience would cause him to reject me. Now I was certain he couldn't release me any more than I could willingly leave him. And that bond would only be further strengthened once we had joined in the most intimate way possible.

Master was in the shower, giving me a rare moment of privacy in the apartment. I usually dreaded the loss of his presence, but now I was grateful of the opportunity it presented me.

My fingers stilled when they touched the doorknob to his bedroom. Master had forbidden me to enter his private space. But if I wanted to prevent him from drifting away from me, then I needed to learn everything about him that I could. Steeling myself,

I turned the knob and pushed open the door, darting across the threshold before I could talk myself out of carrying out my plan.

My eyes roved over the room, greedily drinking in the secrets of the place Master had forbidden me to enter. Unlike the stark, sparse living room, this space pulsed with a definitive emotive aura. If the rest of the apartment reflected Master's cool control, his bedroom housed his primal essence.

A king size, four-poster bed crafted of wrought iron commanded most of the space. It had a severe beauty to it, the elegantly curling lines of dark metal rendered harsher by their inherent rigidity. An image of lying atop the black sheets with Master, our naked bodies entwined, flitted across my mind.

I tore my eyes from the bed. I didn't have much time, and I needed to explore as much of the room as possible before Master emerged from the bathroom. I estimated I had about ten more minutes. There were two large chests of drawers crafted in polished ebony that sat flush with the red-painted wall across from the bed. I hastily opened the top drawer on one of them.

My lips pursed in a small frown.

Socks.

I wasn't sure what I had been expecting, but it hadn't been anything so ordinary. Shaking off my disappointment, I rapidly inspected the rest of the drawers, making my way down from top to bottom. All I found were Master's clothes. And while I loved the unique scent that infused them, it wasn't anything I hadn't seen before.

When I moved to the second dresser, I jerked the top drawer open almost irritably. At the sight of its contents, I froze. While the other drawers had been unremarkable, this one was jarringly exceptional.

No. Not exceptional. Terrifying.

Instruments that I associated with torture were carefully, lovingly, arranged in a horrifically perfect pattern. The precision with which they were laid out might have been almost artistic if the materials hadn't been so disturbing. Amongst the array were a leather cat o' nine tails, a cane, and – most upsetting of all – a coiled black bullwhip.

I stumbled away from the drawer in horror, reeling backwards until my knees hit the edge of the bed. They folded, and I sank down on the mattress. I had contemplated punishments that Master might mete out, had even excitedly anticipated the administration of a spanking to enforce his control. But I had never imagined he would own such cruel implements.

Memories of torture inflicted by those instruments assailed my mind, making my body go weak as tremors wracked me. I caught myself on my palms before I could fall back on the mattress. As I did so, my fingers brushed against something cold and hard, a tactile sensation that I recognized all too well. I was touching a heavy link in a chain. Perversely compelled to examine the full horror of it, I grasped the metal in my shaking hand, lifting it. The steel clanked against the iron bedframe as the length of chain came free from where it had been hidden. Attached to the end was a padded leather cuff.

My stomach churned, and I flung the chain away from me, my palm suddenly burning as though the metal had been sitting in a forge fire. I braced my head between my knees, fighting the urge to be sick. How could Master possess such things? He was kind, caring; nothing at all like the Bastard who had gloried in my agony.

Nothing at all like him.

That Bastard hadn't wanted to take care of me. He had wanted to break me. He had taken pleasure from my pain and found joy in violating my unwilling body.

My fingers found the reassuring coolness of the tourmaline gem that hung around my neck. Master had only ever tried to ensure my well-being. His rules and commands were all meant for my own benefit, not his own pleasure. I thought of his proud smiles, his words of praise as I reclaimed myself little by little. He had found his pleasure in helping me, in guiding me. As a true Master should.

A true Master.

I had wanted a Master, once. After years of secretly yearning, I had boldly pursued my desires.

My gaze fell back on the chain that was pooled on the bed beside me. Hesitantly, I brushed my fingertips over it. Once, this sight would have made lust stir within me.

"You want to be beaten, whore. I've seen how much you enjoy it. This is your fantasy. That's why I chose you."

I flinched at the memory of that Bastard's hated voice, the sick light in his eyes. He had taken me precisely because I had once enjoyed BDSM.

BDSM. Bondage and Discipline; Domination and Submission; Sadism and Masochism.

I had only just begun to explore that world that I had secretly longed to experience when he had abducted me. He turned my desires against me, twisting them and tainting them. One by one, he had robbed me of all of the dark pleasures I had once craved, chipping away at the foundations of my very self as he destroyed them.

Master had already returned my lust to me. He had claimed that all he wanted was to take care of me. If that was true, then he would help me recover the other precious things that I had lost, that had been cruelly ripped away from me.

A dreamlike calm washed over me. One of Master's rules mandated that I tell him if he wasn't giving me something I wanted. And I wanted this. I *needed* this. More than anything. I wasn't going to give up until I could make him see that.

Grasping the hem of my dress, I pulled the cottony material over my head and tossed it aside. My underwear quickly followed. I sank to the floor, my knees cushioned by the thick carpet as I spread them wide. My hands clasped together at the small of my back, and I squared my shoulders, thrusting my breasts out.

While the position demonstrated that I offered by body to Master, it was primarily intended to be a show of supplication. My bare skin and the exposure of my most vulnerable places would communicate my raw need. Torture had stripped me of everything that made me *me*, and I needed Master to help me rebuild myself from the basest level.

My posture was submissive, but rather than keeping my eyes downcast, I stared straight ahead, ready to face Master. My breaths were deep and even as I waited patiently for him to come to me. I sensed that I was on the cusp of something significant, something beautiful. Master had freed me when he had first rescued me, but now he would heal me.

"Lydia?" Master's voice was touched by a hint of concern as it rang out through the apartment. He usually found me eagerly waiting for him to emerge from the bathroom.

"I'm in here, Master," I called out calmly.

His quick footsteps pounded across the living room as he approached, his anger at realizing my location apparent in the string of muttered curse words that floated into the room. The door banged against the wall with the force of Master's entry. He froze when he saw me, his huge frame filling the doorway. The fury rolling off him should have terrified me, but I was too captivated by the sight of him for it to register.

In his haste to find me, he hadn't taken the time to get dressed. My breath caught in my throat as the magnitude of his perfection struck me like a palpable thing. Every muscle was precisely sculpted and defined, and they bulged and rippled as he flexed threateningly. His nostrils flared, and his usually-full lips were pressed together in a thin line. His strong jaw was clenched.

I watched in rapt fascination as a bead of water rolled along it, dripping down onto his bare chest to race in a wicked trail over his abs, only to be absorbed into the white towel that was slung low around his hips. The bulge of his erect cock tented the material as he hardened at the sight of me. I couldn't help licking my lips hungrily.

"Do you have any idea how much trouble you're in, girl?" He hissed. "Get up off your knees and get dressed. Now."

Taking a deep breath to brace myself, I tore my eyes from the sight of his arousal to boldly meet his steely gaze.

"No." The word was clear, definitive. "I don't want to."

His lip curled up in a snarl. "I'm going to give you one chance to reconsider your answer, girl," he warned.

"I already have considered my answer," I responded steadily. "I've considered it very carefully. You ordered me to tell you when I want something that you're not giving me, Master. I've been disobeying that rule for days. I want this. I *need* this. I need *you.*"

Master drew a deep, shuddering breath in a visible effort to calm himself. "You don't understand what you need," he told me firmly. "I know how that Bastard hurt you. I know he made you feel like the only way you can demonstrate your submission is by offering your body. I don't want that from you."

My expression hardened. "Now you're the one who's breaking a rule, Master," I informed him hotly. "You promised you wouldn't lie to me."

"Fine!" He snapped. "I want you, Lydia. I want to spank your gorgeous ass until it's glowing red. I want to sink my cock between your perfect lips. I want to chain you down and fuck you while you call me 'Master.' I want to make you come again and again until you beg me to stop, until you're weeping from excruciating pleasure. Is that what you want to hear?" His eyes took on a feverish light as he gave voice to his secret longings, but his lips were twisted in self-loathing.

"Yes," I said, a bit breathlessly. "That's what I want to hear. That's what I want, Master."

Something between a groan and a growl slipped through his lips at my words. "Can't you see that's the worst thing I could possibly do to you? You're confused, vulnerable. You barely remember your own goddamn name. You can't make a decision like this right now. So I'm going to have to make the decision for both of us." His hands clenched at his sides. "And my decision is that you are going to stand up, get dressed, and never try something like this again."

"Please, Master." I decided further defiance wouldn't get me where I wanted. "Please, just listen to me. You're wrong; I'm not confused. Not anymore. Being with you, seeing all this," I gestured towards the open drawer and the chain on the bed, "made me realize just how badly I need this from you. I remember…" I shied away from the wealth of Lydia's memories that were threatening to bubble to the surface, resolutely focusing only on the facts I needed. "I used to want this. I wanted to explore BDSM. That's why he… That's why that Bastard chose me. He thought I would survive longer because I liked pain. He took my greatest pleasures and turned them against me. He stole everything from me."

The lines of Master's face were taut with rage and disgust, but it was no longer directed at me or at himself.

Pressing my advantage, I plowed on. "You've helped me reclaim so much of myself, Master. I was nothing, no one, when you found me. You say all you want is to take care of me, to help me. I know it's greedy of me to ask you to give me more than you already have, but *this* is what I need. Please don't let him keep this from me. Help me take back this part of myself, Master. Please." The final word was a broken, desperate whisper.

I realized my cheeks were wet with tears. I had exposed myself completely, had risked the pain of Lydia's memories to prove to Master just how badly I needed this. It was essential to my healing, to my survival. If he denied me, I might just die inside again. I held my breath, my body trembling as I waited for his response. It would save me or shatter me.

He grimaced, the lines around his eyes tight with pain as he stared down at me. When he finally acted, his movements were almost violent in their desperate intensity.

"Fuck," he muttered as he gathered me up in his arms, his expression twisted with yearning and regret. "Do you have any idea how goddamn badly I've wanted this? I'm probably going to hell."

"Then I'll go with you, Master." My whisper was a fervent promise as my fingers curled around his biceps. I would follow him anywhere; I would never allow him to release me.

My blood sang through my veins when his lips came down on mine, harsh and hungry. He possessed my mouth, claiming it with hot, firm strokes of his tongue. His hand sank into my hair, wrapping the silken strands around his fist so he could angle me as he wanted. I opened for him, silently begging him not to relent, to consume all of me.

His fingers splayed across my lower back, pressing my belly against his erection. My hands fisted in the towel that still separated him from me. With a sharp, demanding jerk, I pulled the fabric free and flung it away from us. He swallowed my moan as his flesh touched mine for the first time. I ground into him, relishing the hard evidence of his desire for me.

A low, disapproving rumble vibrated against my lips before his hands closed around my shoulders, shoving me hard. Ripped from him, I tumbled backwards, the air knocked from my lungs at the soft impact with the mattress. He didn't give me so much as a moment to draw breath before he was on me again, the weight of his body trapping me beneath him. I was helpless to resist his vastly superior strength.

Trapped. Helpless.

My former Master's sneer flashed before my eyes, his laughter as he held me down and used me echoing in my ears. I cried out as terror spiked through me, and my fingers stiffened to claws, lashing out at my attacker. His hands encircled my wrists, halting my frantic efforts.

"Breathe, girl," he ordered evenly. "Look at me."

I obediently took a deep breath, blinking hard. Master's striking eyes were staring down at me, commanding my attention.

"Who am I, girl? Tell me."

"Master," I answered shakily. My gaze roved over his perfect face, drinking him in. The sight of him grounded me in my present reality. My voice was firmer, more assured, when I spoke again. "You're my Master."

"That's right." His voice was gentler this time, and he brushed a whisper-soft kiss against my lips. "Stay here with me, sweetheart." His eyes roved over my face, studying me carefully. His expression was hesitant, but when he spoke his voice was strained with longing. "I'm not sure if this is a good idea, little one. I don't want to upset you."

"No!" I cried quickly. "Please, Master. I don't want to see *him* in my head anymore. Help me."

The lines of his face softened. "Okay, sweetheart."

He paused, his lips pressing together as he wrestled with something internally. After a moment, he blew out a long breath. "I want you to enjoy this. And I can't have you screaming and trying to fight me off. I can't do this if I feel like I'm forcing myself on you. I won't do that to you."

Anguish flitted across his features, but it was quickly replaced by determination. His thumbs brushed across the insides of my wrists, and a small, satisfied smile played around his lips when my pulse jumped, my skin pebbling in response to the stimulation of the vulnerable area. "I'm going to restrain you, sweetheart. You won't have the option of fighting me; you'll have to accept that I'm in control. I'm going to remind you of what a beautiful instrument your body can be. You need to trust that I won't hurt you. Do you trust me, little one?"

The tightness around his eyes let me know just how crucial my answer was to him.

"Yes," I breathed. "I trust you, Master. Completely."

That predatory light that I loved so much illuminated his silver eyes, and he dipped his head so that his hot breath rippled across my neck. He caught my earlobe between his teeth, nipping at it sharply before sucking the pain away.

"Good girl," he rumbled against me, nuzzling the hollow beneath my ear. I shuddered as his lips traced a hot trail of kisses down my neck. His grip shifted from its hold on my wrists to twine his fingers through mine, applying gentle pressure as he slid my hands up the mattress, drawing my arms apart until they were stretched above my head.

He pulled away from me and straddled my hips, his weight pinning me in place. His eyes bored into me, piercing my soul as his power infused me, burning away fear as his control flooded my entire being. All of my muscles relaxed as I surrendered, fully ceding to his dominance. My lips parted as I stared up at him with rapt adoration. I trusted him implicitly.

He brushed another soft kiss across my lips.

"Don't move. Don't fight me."

He extricated his hands from mine and reached towards one of the bedposts. The clanking of the chain as he pulled it free made me shiver, but I resolutely held my fear at bay.

My determination wavered when the supple leather of the cuff touched my wrist. A low whine worked its way up my throat as memories assaulted me.

He had preferred to use soft cuffs so he wouldn't damage my skin. He didn't want to mar the beauty of his slave.

"Stop," I begged. "Please don't."

"Breathe," Master ordered. "Who am I, girl?" He repeated his earlier question, his hard tone commanding my attention.

I focused on him. "Master," I replied shakily.

"Am I going to hurt you?"

"No, Master."

"Do you want me to stop?"

"No, Master."

He returned his attention to his task, softly kissing the inside of my wrist before he buckled the cuff around it. I jerked slightly, testing the restraint.

"Don't fight me. Stay here with me."

"Yes, Master," I whispered, my voice ragged with the depth of my gratitude, not anxiety.

He was giving me exactly what I needed. He wasn't going to relent until he had given me what I had begged for. He would help me heal, and he wasn't going to allow that Bastard to take this from me. As Master claimed me, he would help me reclaim myself.

By the time he had secured my other wrist to the opposite bedpost, tears were leaking from the corners of my eyes. He gently brushed them away.

"Are you alright, sweetheart?" He asked tenderly.

"Yes, Master. I… I'm happy. Thank you."

He claimed my lips again, the strokes of his tongue gentler this time but no less assured. The kiss was thorough, demanding, and he didn't let up until my head was spinning from the need to draw breath. Despite my growing dizziness, I didn't so much as tug against my restraints. I welcomed the heady release, allowing Master to take me to the edge. My trust in him made what might have been terrifying incredibly freeing. And decidedly erotic.

By the time he allowed me to gasp for air, the spike of oxygen returning to my brain sent me soaring high.

I was still flying when Master's lips returned to my throat, his soft kisses alternating with sharp nips of his teeth. Under his ministrations, my flesh came alive in a way that was utterly foreign to me, and I gloried in the beautiful shudder that wracked my body.

When his teeth caught the sensitive skin where my neck met my shoulder, I moaned in wild abandon. He licked away the sting, his low sound of approval sinking through my skin to reverberate through my body. It reached my core, and my inner muscles contracted, craving Master's touch. I rocked my hips up into him. His cock jerked against my belly, but his weight still kept my body firmly pinned.

"I thought I told you not to move," he remarked almost casually before abruptly sinking his teeth into my nipple, giving me sharp pain in reprimand.

My shocked cry was laced with ecstasy as a hot line of pleasure sizzled from the tight, trapped bud to my clit, and my hips surged upward again of their own accord, my body begging him for more. He chuckled darkly against my skin as his tongue left a burning trail across my flesh, moving to my other breast.

"You'll have to learn quicker than that, girl," he warned. His bite was harder this time as he punished my other nipple. I whimpered as my pussy pulsed, coating my thighs with my wet arousal. I gritted my teeth as I forced back the urge to writhe beneath him. In reward, his tongue swirled around the tight peak, flicking across the tip as he sucked it into his mouth.

I had never experienced anything so excruciatingly wonderful in my entire life.

"Please, Master," I begged hoarsely.

His smile was a touch twisted as he stared down at me. "Please, what? Please stop?"

"Please. More. Please touch me, Master."

His fingertips traced the curve beneath the lower swell of my breasts, and I gasped as pleasure shot through me.

"I am touching you, girl," he informed me, his tone colored with amusement.

"No," I insisted huskily. "I want you to touch my..." I stumbled over the words, struggling to express what I so keenly desired. I was uncertain if Master would welcome a demand, even if it was worded as a request. He had commanded that I give him complete control, but his denial was making me ache. He had promised he would show me the incredible gifts my body could give me, but I was coming to realize those pleasures could be wielded as torment. Sweet, glorious torment.

"Tell me what you want," he ordered.

"I want... I want you to touch my pussy, Master," I said the crass words in a rush. "I want your cock inside of me. I want you to claim me." My last request was a desperate utterance as I finally gave voice to what I had craved from him for so long.

His lips returned to my breasts, kissing them softly. Too softly.

"I'm not finished with you yet," he told me, his voice holding a rougher edge this time. "Do you know how long I've ached to explore your body, girl? I'm not going to stop until I've devoured every inch of you. I *am* claiming you. Your body is mine. And I get to toy with it and play with it as long as I like."

His eyes glowed with a feverish, possessive light as he fixed me in his silver gaze. "Who am I, girl? Who do you belong to?"

I groaned as his words sent flames licking across my skin, branding me. "You're my Master. I belong to you, Master."

"That's right. So you'll accept the pleasure that I give you. You have my permission to beg. I like the sound of your begging. But you're not going to move against my cock again. You're going to wait for me like a good girl. If you want my cock inside you, you'll take it on my terms."

My moan was pure lust as my entire body quaked for him. I belonged to him. I would revel in this new form of torment because he willed me to do so. Because the throbbing, insistent ache within me was the most exquisite pain I had ever known.

He took his time with my breasts, languorously sampling them as he savored my every gasp and whimper. Finally, he shifted above me, his weight settling on my knees as his fingers slowly stroked their way down my sides. His tongue followed a similar path, leaving a line of searing heat in its wake as it traced down my sternum, trailing over my abdomen until his lips came to rest just above my soft curls. His thumbs hooked over my hips, his long fingers curling around them to grip my ass.

"I'm going to be merciful with you this time, girl."

My brow furrowed in my confusion. In the next instant, I understood his cryptic words.

His tongue licked the crease between my desire-slicked thigh and my swollen, pulsing pussy lips. No amount of determination could have stopped me from jerking beneath him as a ragged shout was torn from my chest. He firmly held me in place, not giving me the option of disobedience as his tongue continued its wicked exploration. He licked and suckled and nipped, but he carefully avoided the areas where I most desired his touch. My hardened clit was burning, my core contracting with such rapid insistency that my inner muscles ached from the cruel compulsion.

"Please, Master." I repeated the words in a desperate litany until I was nearly sobbing with need, but he just chuckled against me, glorying in his utter control over my body, over my pleasure. And despite the cruel denial, I gloried in it as well. His brand of torture wasn't accompanied by abuse or fear. He was demonstrating his complete ownership, forcing me to realize the depth of my trust in him. It was the most wonderful gift anyone had ever given me.

Just when I thought I would shatter from the intensity of the trembling that had possessed my entire body, Master abruptly sucked my clit into his mouth, his teeth closing around the swollen bud. I screamed as I blew apart, my vision going white as the ecstasy ripped through me with vicious force. His tongue stroked away the pain of his bite, circling my clit as little bolts of electricity sizzled through me.

I gasped for breath as I came back to reality, my vision returning. Master's entrancing eyes filled my whole world. The mischievous light in them made delighted apprehension bloom within me. His wicked strokes didn't stop, and what had elicited the most exquisite pleasure now turned to stinging pain. I tried to buck my hips away from him, to escape the discomfort, but Master held me fast.

"Please, Master," my voice was a hoarse croak. "I can't take anymore."

His lips left me only long enough for him to issue his command. "You can and you will. Your pleasure is mine, and I fully intend to feast on it."

Something between a moan and a sob ripped its way up my throat as his torment resumed. How could something so wonderful be so torturous? And how could that torture be so rapturous?

I lost track of the number of times he wrung ecstasy from me. He didn't relent until my body had stopped trying to fight him. All of my muscles went limp from exhaustion, incapable of doing anything more than trembling as raw, incoherent sounds issued from my lips.

His fingers entered me abruptly, easily sliding between my swollen folds. I was soaking wet and ready to receive him. He growled his pleasure and quickly retrieved a condom from the nightstand beside the bed. I stared up at him, and I was amazed to see that his fingers shook slightly as he quickly rolled it on. Despite the fact that my body had been utterly spent only moments before, my sex throbbed, desperate to accept him. I had craved for him to mark me for so long.

He settled his body over me, his palms pressing against my own as our fingers twined together. He crushed his lips against mine and drank me in like a man dying of thirst. As soon as his mouth touched mine, he drove into me with one jarring thrust. He swallowed my cry of pleasure/pain. His size stretched me ruthlessly, demanding that I accept all of him.

He took me with the ferocity that I loved so much, the primal side of him that had been denied for far too long taking over completely. His strokes were rough, almost frenzied. All of the careful control he had exhibited while he toyed with my body had been obliterated. He altered the angle of his thrusts, and the head of his cock hit a secret spot inside of me that I had forgotten existed.

"I want one more," he ground out. "Come for me, girl."

I had no option but to obey. I would give him anything he asked of me. My muscles fluttered around him as my ragged cry clawed its way up my throat. He pulsed within me, his own harsh shout drowning out the sound of my bliss. The world fell away as his pleasure washed through me, and I was possessed by a sense of completion I had never known before. We were joined inextricably now; Master had finally claimed me as fully as I had devoted myself to him long ago.

My mouth blindly searched for his, and I sighed into him when his lips softly caressed mine. His weight pressed down on me as he collapsed atop me, sated and spent. All of my muscles were limp and useless, but I managed to keep my fingers wound tightly though his. I would never let him go.

Chapter 14

Master held me for a long time after freeing me from the restraints. He ran his hands over my skin and tenderly kissed my cheeks, my nose, my eyelids, my lips. It felt as though he was worshipping me with a fervor that equaled my reverence for him.

"Thank you, Master," I whispered hoarsely when I finally found my voice again.

His fingertips traced the line of my cheekbone as he stared down at me, his lips quirked up in amusement. "It was my pleasure, sweetheart."

I didn't fail to catch the deeper meaning of his words. He wasn't just sardonically utilizing the social nicety. My pleasure *was* his pleasure. He owned my body, and the bliss that he gave me belonged to him.

"I've never..." The words caught in my throat as emotion welled up within me. I was elated by what he had given me; he had returned the pleasures of my body that had been robbed from me. He had returned them a dozen times over. But the reminder of what I had lost for so long filled me with grief. I swallowed hard, forcing myself to continue, to express just how much Master meant to me. "I've never felt anything like that. I forgot what -"

He pressed his lips to mine, silencing me. He kissed me thoroughly, sweetly, driving away the sorrow that threatened to grip me. I sighed into him, relaxing. The past didn't matter. Master would care for me from now on, and he would help me to remember everything I had forgotten about carnal pleasure. I suspected he would teach me far more than I had ever known. I eagerly anticipated his lessons.

After a while, Master gently pulled away from me. "It's time for you to eat. We've got to replenish those calories you just burned off."

I grinned, pleased that Master was joking about our coupling rather than returning to his earlier broodiness over his desire to touch me.

Stretching, he pulled himself up into a sitting position. For the first time, I could see his bare back. For days I had marveled at its defined musculature that had been hinted at through his tight t-shirts, but now I was absolutely transfixed.

A black tattoo covered his entire back, starting at the base of his spine. Long, curling tendrils expanded from it as it spread upward over his shoulder blades. It resembled a stylized rendering of a willow tree in winter, its thin, curved branches stripped bare by the bitter elements. Drawn to its harsh, hypnotic beauty, my fingertips brushed along it, tracing the broad black line that extended all the way up his spine. He shuddered at my touch.

"What's this?" I asked softly. "A tree?"

His shoulders stiffened. "It's a reminder."

"A reminder of what?"

"A fuckup," he responded shortly.

I withdrew my fingers, nervous I had pushed too far. This was something private, something painful. I longed for Master to share it with me, to allow me to help ease his pain as he had helped me ease mine.

He blew out a long breath, twisting his body so that he was facing me. "It's the Tree of Knowledge."

"You're religious?" I asked, curious.

"Not particularly," he admitted. "The tree of knowledge represents the inseparable nature of good and evil and the birth of free will. Good and evil live inside all of us, and our choices have the power to manifest either one or the other. The tattoo is a reminder of a time I chose wrong." He paused for a beat, his gaze turned inward. "But it's also a reminder that I can choose differently. I can choose the good in myself."

For several long moments, I could only stare at him. Master had just revealed more of himself to me than he ever had before. During our time together, I had slowly learned his likes and dislikes, had gotten a general sense of his nature. But this was something deeper. This was the root of who he was, the philosophy that drove his every action. I craved to know more. What terrible mistake had he made in the past? I wanted to know all of him, body and soul. I bit my lip, uncertain if I should question him further.

My moment of opportunity passed before I could work up the courage to press him for more information. His hands closed around my waist, and he pulled me up against him. I melted into him, allowing my lips to comfort him in a way my words couldn't accomplish. This would be enough for now. Master had claimed me, and I had forever to learn his secrets, to earn his trust as completely as he had earned mine.

Our bodies hardly broke contact that evening. Now that our long-denied hunger for one another had finally been fulfilled, neither of us was willing to stop touching the other. He dressed me in one of his huge t-shirts, and he wore nothing but his boxers. I was thrilled that he kept his body exposed to my greedy eyes.

For the first time, we went to his bed for the night. The iron structure that had briefly elicited the most horrific memories was now a thing of beauty. This was where Master had claimed me fully, had taken complete ownership of my body. As he held me against his chest, I reached out to touch a cool link in the chain he had used to bind me. I was no longer afraid of it or the cuffs that had restrained me, but my mind flashed back to the more disturbing items I had discovered in Master's drawer.

"Master…" I began hesitantly. He responded instantly to the hint of anxiety that colored my tone, turning my body so I was facing him.

"What's wrong, sweetheart?"

My mouth opened and closed as my mind struggled to find the right words.

"Tell me."

His command eased some of my nervousness. "Earlier. When I saw what was in your drawer. Some of those things…" I swallowed hard. "Why do you have those? I know you won't hurt me. But… Do you want to?" My final words were barely audible.

His grip on me tightened, pulling me closer against his chest as he kissed the top of my head. "No, little one. I might have lied about not wanting your body, but I would never lie about this. I don't want to hurt you. Everything I have in those drawers is ultimately meant to bring pleasure. I get off on control, not pain. But some people want to receive pain in order to give up control.

None of those things will ever touch you, sweetheart. I promise I will never hurt you."

I touched my fingers to the silver chain that Master had placed around my throat.

"Thank you, Master," I said earnestly.

His hand touched mine where it gripped the necklace, closing my fingers around it tightly. He kissed me firmly, his tongue tangling with mine, taming it. I relaxed against him, welcoming his dominance.

He held me to him throughout the night, and I gloried in the fact that no clothes separated our skin. I slept more peacefully than I could ever recall.

I awoke the following morning to the familiar sensation of Master's cock nudging my ass. A wicked smile spread over my lips when I realized that this time I wasn't forbidden to touch it.

Twisting my body so it was facing his, I pressed my lips to his neck while I boldly stroked him. I groaned at the silken feel of him, no longer separated from me by his clothing. When he had taken me the day before, his cock had rubbed against my belly and ravaged my pussy, but I had yet to caress it with my hand.

His eyes snapped open, and he jerked away from me. I reached for him insistently.

"It's okay, Master," I assured him, reminding him that he no longer had to resist touching me.

He grasped my wrist before I could make contact, stopping me short. His expression was cool, one eyebrow arched.

"'It's okay'?" He parroted my words a touch reprovingly. "I believe I'm the one who determines what's okay and what isn't, girl. And I didn't give you permission to touch me."

"Oh," I breathed, more aroused by his show of dominance than intimidated by his disapproval. "I'm sorry, Master."

He kissed the tip of my nose. "You're forgiven. But we're going to take a shower."

"'We'?" I asked huskily.

A wolfish grin was his response. With that as my only warning, he scooped me up in his arms. I squealed in shocked delight as he swung me up over his shoulder, his large hand gripping my ass as he carried me across the apartment in a fireman's lift. He only set me back down on my feet when he had turned on the shower and deemed it be the right temperature.

But the warmth of the water was nothing compared to the heat rolling off Master. His cock was still rock hard, pressing into me where he held me against him.

"I want to sink my cock between your perfect lips."

Master had given me so much pleasure. What I had given him in return hadn't been nearly sufficient.

"May I touch you, please, Master?" I asked, my lust evident in my low tone.

He grinned at me. "Seeing as you asked so nicely, I can't possibly refuse you."

I beamed at him. This was the way it was meant to be between us: beautifully simple, the two of us so at ease that we could be playful with one another. No more tense uncertainty, no more painful denial.

Gripping his hips for support, I eased myself down onto my knees, sliding my water-slicked skin across his on the way down. Tentatively, I stroked my forefinger along his cock, tracing the line of the vein that pulsed through it. He hissed in a breath as it jerked in response. I glanced up at him, and my breath hitched at the intensity of his expression. His nostrils flared like a predator that had scented his prey, and his muscles were taut as he restrained himself from giving in to the instinct for pursuit, for capture. His fists clenched at his sides as he resolutely kept his ferocity leashed, sensing that I would panic if he grabbed me and took my mouth as he wanted.

My lips parted, and I slowly opened for him, rubbing the underside of his cock with the flat of my tongue as I eased him into my mouth. He was impressively large, but I had been taught how to accept all of a man. My progress stilled as my mind flashed to the ruthless lessons that had taught me that.

Master's hand touched the top of my head, calling me back to him. When my gaze flicked up to his, he groaned at the sight of me staring up at him with his cock in my mouth.

"You are so fucking beautiful," he ground out, his voice tight from the effort of holding himself back.

I moaned around him as his words sent me flying as high as the orgasms he had given me. Relaxing my throat, I welcomed him all the way in.

His iron control snapped, and his fingers fisted in my hair. I clasped my hands together at the small of my back, offering full use of my mouth to him. A fierce growl escaped him at the sight of my utter submission, and he tugged on my hair, directing my movements so I sucked him at the pace he desired. With a grunt, he grasped either side of my head in his hands, holding me in place as he began to fuck my mouth.

I gave it to him eagerly, loving the way his will completely overwhelmed me. He possessed my mouth, my entire body. I couldn't panic when he touched it in even the roughest manner, because it belonged to him to use as he pleased. I trusted him not to hurt me. The knowledge that he could do whatever he liked with me but he wouldn't push me further than I could handle was heady. It demonstrated the depth of his devotion to taking care of me.

"Master."

The word was unintelligible as his cock slid in and out of my mouth, but the vibrations of his title as it wrapped around his length pushed him over the edge. His hot cum filled my mouth as he bellowed out his pleasure. I swallowed everything he gave me, not allowing even one precious drop to pass through my lips.

He held me there, running his fingers through my hair as he softened in my mouth. The satisfaction at having brought him pleasure, at having served him, aroused my own desire. I relished the sensation of the water trailing warm streams down my body, some of the rivulets tracing their way down my breasts, over my abdomen, to fall into the soft curls that covered my pulsing clit.

When he finally eased himself free from my mouth, he bent down and grasped my shoulders, helping me back to my feet. My knees were shaky, but he easily supported my bodyweight as he turned me so my back was pressed against his chest, holding me in place with one arm locked around my waist.

"That was very good, girl." His praise was gravelly after his rough shout. "I think someone's earned a reward."

My nipples pebbled at his words, and the spray of the water on my breasts was suddenly an erotic delight. With his free hand, he tweaked the straining peaks, pinching and pulling and rolling them deftly between his fingers. My head fell back against his chest as I arched my back so that my breasts pressed up into his touch.

His lips sampled my neck, the sensation of his tongue catching the water droplets on my skin making me shudder. He shifted his grip so he could continue tweaking my nipples with the hand that was supporting my weight. His other hand sank into my wet hair, wrenching my head back so that he had clear access to my vulnerable throat.

Sharp pain made me cry out as he gripped my flesh in his teeth with a possessive growl. The pain turned to a delicious throb that radiated outward from his bite, rippling through my body in waves of pleasure. The bliss washed across my mind as well, and my knees went weak, my body sagging against him.

His teeth remained sunk into my flesh as his tongue played across the skin that was trapped between them. My raw moan blossomed into a delighted scream when he abruptly shoved two fingers through my slick folds. He stroked the secret spot inside me, his thumb grinding against my clit in firm, merciless circles at the same time. The shock of my sudden explosion made my ecstasy all the more visceral, and the sensation of being trapped by his teeth and his possessive hold on my pussy as I writhed in his arms only heightened my pleasure.

He held my limp body as I came floating back down, shaking and gasping for breath. He released me from his bite, and the tip of his tongue tenderly stroked the indentations his teeth had left in my skin. I knew I would bear a mark there, and my sex shuddered around his fingers one last time at the thought.

When he removed his fingers from me, he lifted them to his own lips, groaning as he sucked them clean.

"Fuck, you taste sweet, girl."

I craned my head back, smiling at him weakly. "You're not so bad yourself, Master."

A strangled cry escaped me when he lightly slapped his palm against my sensitive clit. "Don't get flippant with me, girl." It was meant to be a warning, but his playful tone belied the seriousness of his expression.

"Sorry, Master." My apology wasn't in the least bit contrite.

His grin held a savage edge. "No, you're not. But you will be."

My clit was suddenly caught between his fingers, and his mouth swallowed my shocked shout of protest at the zinging pain. As he had done the night before, he mercilessly wrung pleasure from my body, the sweet sting of his touch on my over-sensitized flesh making me whimper against his lips even as bliss took me once again.

When my body finally stilled in his arms, he released me from his exquisite torment.

"Do you have anything you want to say to me, little one?" His breath tickled across my lips as I stared up into his lust-darkened eyes.

I nodded weakly. "I'm sorry, Master." This time I meant it. "Thank you." I meant that too. With every fiber of my being.

"My pleasure," he rumbled, brushing a sweet kiss on my forehead. Then he sighed, a touch regretfully. "Come on, sweetheart. Let's get cleaned up so you can have some breakfast. We'll have to double your calorie count at this rate."

"I don't mind, Master."

He chuckled. "I'll bet you don't." He grinned down at me as he rubbed soap between his hands. His lips were at my ear when his slick hands caressed my breasts. "I don't mind, either, sweetheart. I can do this all fucking day."

The renewed hardness of his cock pressing against my thigh let me know it wasn't an empty boast.

Despite his arousal, Master didn't take me in the shower. Instead, he carefully, almost reverently, washed every inch of me. And I returned the favor, silently worshipping his body with my hands, my lips.

Afterwards, I cooked breakfast for the two of us, and Master insisted I eat three extra strips of bacon. That was one order I definitely wouldn't protest. I had discovered that I loved all things pork. Master had grinned and declared me "a woman after his own heart." The phrase made my own heart soar.

"Why don't we hang these up?" Master said after breakfast, gesturing towards my sketchpad.

I bit my lip as he flipped it open, revealing the drawing of Lydia standing by Lake Michigan.

Noticing my hesitancy, he reached for me, cupping my cheek and easing my face close to his. "Your drawings are beautiful, Lydia," he told me, firmly emphasizing my name. "It would make me very happy if they were on display where I can admire them." He flipped the page, revealing the sketch of the two of us kissing.

Joy welled in my chest. He wanted to admire the image that had once caused him such discomfort? I wasn't about to refuse that request.

"Okay, Master," I agreed breathily. "I would like that too."

"Good girl." He touched his lips to mine briefly. "I'm afraid all I have is tape for now, but I'll order some frames for them online."

He wanted to frame my work to display in his home? I glanced covetously at the blank white wall in his living room, and I suddenly longed to hang my drawings there, to leave my stamp on his personal space.

Our personal space.

I beamed up at him, perfectly content. "Thank you, Master."

Minutes later, I had carefully arranged minimal strips of tape on the back of my sketches, using just enough to stick them firmly to the wall without causing too much damage when I removed it. I hummed happily to myself while I worked.

"Is that Miley Cyrus?" Master asked, sounding slightly horrified.

I paused, considering the tune. "Party in the USA." A giggle bubbled up from my chest.

"And how would you know that, Master?" I asked pointedly.

He grimaced dramatically. "Just because I have good taste in music doesn't mean I live under a rock. I couldn't escape that fucking song for months. That was what, 2009?"

The light in his eyes was suddenly keener. I realized he was trying to puzzle out when I had last been exposed to the outside world before being taken. Inwardly, I shrank away from that thought.

"Maybe," I shrugged, as casually as I could manage.

Master's small frown was quickly replaced by a look of alarm as the front door to the apartment rattled. He spun, positioning his body in front of mine, the exposed muscles of his torso bulging as he flexed. My heart stopped when the lock sprung back with a definitive *click*. It didn't start beating again until I registered the familiar face of the man standing in the open doorway.

But the tension didn't leave Master. "What the fuck are you doing here, Vaughn?" He snarled.

Chapter 15

Clayton's blue eyes were glacial as he studied us, his gaze taking in Master's bare chest and my exposed legs that weren't covered by Master's huge t-shirt.

"You haven't called me in days, and I haven't even gotten an email from you since yesterday afternoon. I came to check in on you," he said coldly. "Clearly, I should have done it sooner."

Master's face darkened to a thunderhead. "So you just thought you could use my spare key and barge in uninvited?"

"Yes," Clayton replied levelly. He gestured at our state of undress, the movement jerky with anger. "What the fuck is this, James?"

A muscle ticked in Master's jaw as he gnashed his teeth. "Nothing you would understand, Vaughn," he ground out.

"The hell I don't," Clayton countered darkly as he advanced towards us. "It's not too difficult to figure out."

Master shifted his body as his friend approached, careful to keep himself between Clayton and me. Clayton stopped short, his own jaw tensing.

"What the fuck are you thinking, James?" His eyes skirted around Master, searching for me. Instead, they found the drawings behind me. His face twisted to a mask of fury and disgust as he pointed at the image of Master kissing me. "I trusted you to take care of Jane. I covered for you at the Bureau. And all this time, you've been holed up here, taking advantage of her? Who the fuck are you?" He was looking at his friend as though he didn't recognize him at all.

Master opened his mouth to snap a response, but Clayton plowed on over him as his attention turned to the drawing of Lydia. "Chicago? She was in Chicago?" His glare returned to Master. "How long have you known this? You know we've gotten exactly nowhere with her case, and you've been keeping this from me?"

I stepped forward to come to Master's defense, but he placed a restraining hand in front of me.

"I didn't want him to tell you," I insisted. "Master is helping me. He's taking care of me."

Clayton reeled back a step, blanching. "Master?" He repeated faintly, incredulous. He shook his head hard, his lips twisting in a snarl. "What the hell is wrong with the guys in our department? First Santiago, now you? How many times will I have to say this to an agent? *You can't keep a woman locked up in your home as a slave.*"

Now it was Master's face that paled. He glanced back at me, and my heart sank at the uncertainty that flickered in his eyes. I clutched at his arm, desperate for the fierce, possessive light to return to them.

"Please, Master," I beseeched. "Don't listen to him. You didn't do anything wrong." I tried to reassure him as he had reassured me so many times. "Please. I want to be with you."

The lines around Master's eyes tightened with anguish. "Shit," he muttered. "Lydia, I -"

"Lydia?" Clayton's booming voice ripped through our intense moment with the force of a bullet. "You know her name, James?"

Master's attention was torn from mine, and my heart twisted in my chest at the pained expression he turned on his friend. His shoulders slumped, all of the violent tension leaving him. "Fuck. Vaughn, I…" He trailed off. I had never seen Master so unsure. Something akin to shame began to tug his features downward.

I clutched at him more tightly, my fingernails digging into his skin. "No!" I cried, my voice shrill with panic. "I'm not leaving you, Master." I turned a glare on Clayton. "Leave us alone."

"Jane," Clayton began, his calm tone marred by the note of strain that colored it. He shook his head sharply. "Lydia," he corrected. "You have to come with me. Now." He took a step towards me, and – to my horror – Master didn't shift to block his advance.

"NO!" This time the word was a piercing shriek as terror flooded my system. I dropped to my knees beside Master, keeping my fierce grip on his arm as I stared up at him imploringly. "Please don't let him take me, Master. You promised you would take care of me. Please, Master. Please..." My words were choked off as my fear wound its way up my throat, constricting my breath. Black spots danced before my eyes as I gasped for air, my lips silently forming his title.

"Breathe, girl. Look at me."

Just as it had done so many times before, Master's commanding voice penetrated my panic, reaching for me and pulling me out of its cruel claws. Obediently, I drew in a deep, shuddering breath, blinking hard so I could focus on his gorgeous eyes. He touched his fingers to the top of my head, reassuring me of his ownership.

"Don't worry, sweetheart. You don't have to go with him."

My next breath left me on a relieved sob, and I chose to ignore the horror that churned in the depths of his eyes.

"James," Clayton said sharply, warningly.

Master's handsome face was twisted as though he was suffering acute pain, but there was determination in the gaze that he fixed on his friend. "Do you understand now, Clayton?"

A long moment of silence passed. When Clayton finally answered, his voice shook slightly. "Yes. I understand. But that doesn't make it right, Smith."

"I know." Master's words were a low rumble, barely above a whisper. "I'll see you later, Clayton." His voice was stronger this time, holding a significant edge. I chose not to contemplate what it meant. Instead, I stared up at Master, all of my focus honing on his perfection.

I was his. He had claimed me. He had marked me. And he wasn't going to let Clayton take me away. I wrapped my arms around his leg, my tears of relief wetting his sweatpants as I pressed myself into him.

I heard Clayton draw in a sharp breath, but I kept my attention focused on Master.

"Fuck," Master swore softly. "Clayton..." His friend's name was a beseeching utterance.

"I'll see you later, Smith," Clayton said, his voice heavy with disgust. I didn't watch him as he left, and I sighed into Master at the sound of the door closing behind him.

Master allowed me to remain at his feet for a while after Clayton left, his fingers trembling slightly as they stroked through my hair. I nuzzled into him more closely, seeking to comfort him by demonstrating my devotion and gratitude. My stomach churned when he shifted uneasily in response.

"Are you angry with me, Master?" I asked quietly.

He sighed heavily, and his knees folded so that he was crouching beside me. His fingers curled beneath my chin, lifting my face to his.

"No, sweetheart," he said softly. "I'm not angry. You did nothing wrong. I shouldn't have -"

I quickly pressed my lips to his, cutting him off before he could say something I feared would break me. He was still beneath me for a few seconds, but I anxiously shaped my lips around his, tugging them into my mouth in a cruel parody of a kiss. A pained whimper eased up my throat at his unresponsiveness, but I couldn't stop my efforts.

The sound of my distress broke him. His hand closed around the nape of my neck, holding me so I was helpless to resist the feverish, ravenous onslaught of his possessive mouth. I eagerly gave him everything he demanded of me, pouring my longing and love into him, inviting him to feast on it.

Love. I loved my Master. What I felt for him was more than gratitude, more than devotion. He was everything to me, my reason for being.

A soft, regretful groan arose from deep in his chest, and he slowly pulled away from me. His expression was clouded with so many emotions that I couldn't even begin to separate one from the other. The sight of it pained me, and dread settled heavy in the pit of my stomach.

"Master?" I murmured his title questioningly, hesitantly.

He pressed a sweet kiss on the top of my head. "Come sit on the couch with me, sweetheart." The hollowness in his voice made my anxiety ratchet up a notch.

I pursed my lips against the flood of desperate pleas that were fighting to stream from my lips. Something had happened to Master; Clayton's words had changed something between us. And I feared I might not be able to make things go back to the way they had been.

I squared my shoulders, steeling my resolve. I wasn't the same weak, broken woman Master had found at Decadence. He had guided me, healed me, made me strong. He was the one who was hurting now, so I would have to be strong for both of us.

Compliantly, I settled down beside him on the couch, resting my head on his lap. After a moment, his fingers began their usual practice of trailing across my skin, petting me and comforting me. I closed my eyes and sighed happily, letting him know how contented I was in his arms. He had to realize how much his touch meant to me. Clayton had reacted as though our physical connection was something disgusting, horrific. I was determined to remind Master of how his touch had healed me.

There was a soft series of rapid *clicks* above me as Master composed an email on his phone. I was reassured that we were falling back into our regular pattern: Master holding me while he made a half-hearted effort at getting work done.

Still, he was unnervingly taciturn throughout the day; he hardly uttered two sentences during lunch, and he allowed a movie to fill the silence of the apartment in the afternoon. I had to fight back my distress when he ordered me to change out of his t-shirt and put on one of my less-revealing dresses. There was nothing I could do but swallow back my worry and comfort Master as best I could. Surely this would blow over in time.

I reminded myself that Master had fully committed himself to me, and we had forever ahead of us. A few hours or even a few days of tension were nothing we couldn't work through.

The waning light of the setting sun had flooded the apartment with a musty orange glow when the buzzer sounded. Someone was here to see Master. I glanced up at him, and the careful blankness of his expression sent a chill dancing across my skin.

"That'll be Clayton," he told me, his tone neutrally informative.

"Why is he back so soon?" I asked, my voice several octaves higher than usual.

Master didn't answer me as he stood and crossed to the door. He only slipped it open a crack, his body blocking my view of the hallway.

"Who's he?" Master asked, his chin jutting towards someone I couldn't see.

"I think I should come in first and explain a few things," Clayton's voice replied. "Would you mind waiting out here for a few minutes?"

"I... Yeah. Okay. Sure."

My gut clenched painfully. I knew that voice. I knew the person standing out in the hallway with Clayton.

Butterflies beat against the inside of my ribcage, and my grip tightened on my father's arm. He shot me a reassuring smile as he guided me through the chapel doors. The long train of my white dress pulled heavily behind me with the first step up the aisle. Then my eyes fell on him where he stood at the altar, and all of the nervousness flowed out of me at the sight of his wide, boyish grin.

I shook my head vigorously, clearing it. I didn't *want* to know that man. And I didn't want to know the woman in the white dress.

Master stepped back slightly, and Clayton slipped through the barely-open door, closing it behind him. Fissures of strain were crackling across Master's blank mask, and the pained reluctance in Clayton's eyes belied his soft smile. Reflexively, I shrank back into the couch.

"What's wrong, Master?" I asked anxiously.

He took a step towards me, drawn to my distress. Then his fists clenched at his sides, and he stilled his progress. He took a deep breath and closed his eyes briefly.

When they opened again, my cool, remote Master had me fixed firmly in his steady silver gaze. I scrambled upright, preparing to drop to my knees in response to the powerful aura that pulsed off of him.

"Stay," he said sharply.

I froze, my body teetering on the edge of the couch. Out of the corner of my eye, I noticed Clayton tense, his plastered-on smile slipping to a disgusted twist of his lips. But I didn't care about him; nothing mattered but Master and whatever he willed me to do.

"Clayton has something to tell you," he informed me coolly. "You're going to listen to him. You'll remain silent and accept what he says. You're going to take deep, even breaths. You are not allowed to panic. Do you understand me, girl?"

The dread that had been gathering in my stomach all day condensed to a massive block of ice. I shuddered as it radiated frigidity throughout my body, sending a fine tremor racing across my flesh. I was terrified of what was coming, but I had no option but to obey Master. Things were rocky enough between us as it was. What further damage might I inflict if I defied him?

"Yes, Master." My words were barely audible, but he nodded his acceptance.

"After I left here this morning, I processed the new information I had gained about your case." Clayton's business-like voice snapped my attention to him. Master had ordered me to listen to his friend. I would obey. I would show Master that I could be good, that all I ever wanted was to please him.

"Narrowing our search to women named Lydia around the Chicago area reported as missing after 2009 led me straight to your case file."

My eyes cut over to Master. Clayton hadn't overheard Master and me discussing the year 2009 that morning.

Oh, god. My mind flashed back to the sound of Master busily typing on his phone that morning. How much had he told Clayton?

"Stop shaking your head, girl," Master ordered sharply. "Listen."

My neck instantly stiffened, and my gaze riveted back to Clayton.

"Your name is Lydia Chase," he said firmly. "You were reported missing on June 10, 2012. We've contacted your family to let them know you're alive. They've missed you, Lydia. You need to go back home to them." His last statements were gentler, but they still had the ring of command to them.

Lydia Chase. Lydia Chase.

The name was so familiar and yet so heinous.

No. I wasn't Lydia Chase. I was Lydia, Master's slave. Lydia Chase was dead.

"There's someone here to see you, Lydia," Clayton continued, as though he was oblivious to the agony that his calmly-spoken words were wreaking on my entire being

I wanted so desperately to protest. But Master had ordered me to remain silent and still.

I clung to his commands, immersing myself in his will. If I was good for him, if I followed his orders perfectly, then he would make all of this go away. Clayton would leave, and Master would hold me again.

Clayton opened the door to admit the man who had been waiting in the hallway. I jerked my eyes away, unwilling to face him. I fixed my gaze on Master, silently pleading with him to make all the awfulness disappear.

"This is Tucker Chase," Clayton introduced the man to Master. "Lydia's husband."

Master sucked in a breath, his eyes widening in shock as he broke from my gaze to stare at the man. "Her husband." The words were awash with horror.

I couldn't help it; I defied Master's commands. My fingers shook as they reached for him imploringly. "Master. Please…" My hoarse whisper trailed off when he turned his stunning eyes back on me. They sliced into me, the cruel steel sinking through my flesh to pierce my soul.

"I'm not your Master."

All the air was sucked from my lungs, and a strangled gagging sound issued from my throat.

Breathe. Don't shake your head. Don't panic.

I would be good. Master didn't mean that. If I was just good enough, he would take back his impossible words.

"Lydia," the horribly familiar voice said weakly. "Baby, it's me. It's Tuck."

My gaze was drawn to him inexorably; he was a gory accident I just couldn't help but study. Only, when I saw him, I realized that the bloody mess was *me*. I was the tortured remnants of the woman he loved. The broken remnants of Lydia Chase.

Chapter 16

Lydia Chase

His sweet blue eyes were wide behind his black half-rimmed, rectangular glasses, and his mop of curly brown hair was just as untidy as ever. He looked exactly as I remembered, and yet not. The lines of his face were sharper, somehow, and faint wrinkles creased his forehead.

The face that had once elicited such joy now held nothing for me but horror. The memories I had kept at bay for so long surged forth, erupting from a place deep inside my mind with the destructive force of a volcano. The contented Lydia who was Master's slave was charred by the heat of it, her mouth filling with burning, choking ash.

Lydia Chase had a life. She had a spirit of her own that wasn't simply an extension of a Master's will. She hadn't been as beautifully, blissfully happy as Master's slave was, but the burdens of a complex life rich with wants and dreams and petty arguments held their own beauty.

And Lydia Chase's stomach rebelled at the sudden, vicious knowledge of what had happened to her, at what she had been reduced to.

I forced myself up onto my feet, stumbling in my haste to reach the bathroom. I flung myself over the toilet just in time to heave up the contents of my stomach. My eyes fell on my hands where they were braced on the toilet seat before me, and the sight of the scars that ringed them made me retch again. Convulsive dry heaves wracked my body, and my vision blurred with tears.

"Lydia." It wasn't the deep, commanding voice that I craved to hear. Tucker's hand gently touched my shoulder, and I cringed away from him with a panicked shriek. No man had touched me but Master since I had been rescued.

The realization of the depth of my dependence on him only heightened my distress. Even as I was horrified by memories of my slavish behavior, I still craved for him to hold me and tell me that everything was okay, that I had been good.

My fingers tangled in my hair as I clutched my hands to both sides of my head, desperate to crush the cruelly unrelenting memories from my skull. Everything hurt so much: the knowledge of what that I had lost; the recollections of my torture; the image of kneeling meekly at that Bastard's feet that was burned into my brain.

But most agonizing of all was Master's rejection. And the sick, twisted nature of that internal torment held its own pain. Lydia Chase had longed for a Master, but she never would have wanted to be a slave, to live to serve the whims of a man.

I never would have wanted that.

But then why did the prospect of leaving him cause my soul to scream?

"Lydia. Baby…" Tucker's voice trailed off, at a loss.

I was suddenly gripped by a desperate need to escape the place where I had been contented to surrender all of myself in return for simple human kindness. That Bastard had brought me so low that one gentle touch of Master's hand had earned my utter infatuation and unwavering devotion.

Wrong. Everything was so disgustingly *wrong.*

Angrily, I swiped the back of my hand across my eyes to staunch the flood of my tears. My vision cleared, and I turned my gaze on Tucker. He stood several feet away from me, his arm half-outstretched in a desire to touch me, to comfort me. The gold band that encircled his left ring finger glinted in the light. His expression was contorted with horror and longing.

"Tucker." His name was a ragged whisper on my lips. A watery smile split his features, and tears slipped from his eyes.

"God, Lydia," he said hoarsely. "I can't believe it's you. I thought…" His throat tightened, cutting off his words.

I just stared up at him as numbness began to claim me. I wasn't shutting down as I had when Master had forced me to acknowledge Lydia, but my mind couldn't bear to process anything further.

As Lydia Chase so often did – no, as *I* so often did – I put a pin in it, setting my problems aside until I could face them later. This was of much greater magnitude than what I usually tucked away for later examination, but the old coping mechanism was there, readily available to me.

It occurred to me that this tendency was what had kept me going for so long; this was what had kept me from shattering completely. I had set Lydia Chase aside. Rather than allowing her to be destroyed, I had buried her so deeply that she couldn't trouble me until I was ready to deal with her.

I still wasn't ready to deal with her. I wasn't ready to deal with what had happened to me.

But I also couldn't bear to keep living the half-life I had known under Master's care.

"I want to go home, Tuck." My voice was heavy, weary.

He just nodded, still incapable of speech. He approached me slowly, cautiously, before offering a hand to help me up. I bit my lip, hesitating.

I shook my head sharply. This was Tucker. I had never known anyone more non-threatening in my entire life. Still, my hand trembled slightly as I closed my fingers around his. As soon as he had pulled me to my feet, I jerked free of his hold. His face fell slightly, but he said nothing as he carefully put a few inches of distance between us.

Steeling myself, I stepped out of the bathroom. I stared resolutely at a spot just above Clayton's shoulder. Despite my disgust with my enslavement, I knew Master's silver eyes would break me if I dared to so much as glance at him. As it was, his potent aura threatened to wrap around me and drive me to my knees. I stumbled slightly as I collided with the force of it, but I gritted my teeth and quickly righted myself.

"Lydia wants to come home with me," Tucker told Clayton.

The words elicited a low sound of disapproval from Master, but he quickly stifled it. I couldn't help shuddering as the possessive rumble washed over and through me, and I wasn't sure if my reaction was a result of lust or disquiet. The small flare of heat between my legs told me it was the former.

God, my responses to him were so ingrained. It was sick. It was wrong. I had to get away from him before I threw myself at his feet and begged him to keep me.

"Okay," Clayton said with his usual calmness. "We've got you booked on a flight back to Chicago in two hours. I'll escort you to JFK, and then officers from CPD will meet you at O'Hare Airport. Lydia will have a twenty-four/seven protective detail until we track down the man who abducted her. We've referred her to a psychologist to help her work through what's happened to her. Dr. Stanger will consult with Lydia and determine what comes next."

I frowned slightly, suddenly bothered by the fact that Clayton was speaking to Tucker about me in the third-person, as though I was incapable of absorbing the information for myself. The idea that he thought I was completely dependent on Tucker grated on me. Tuck and I had been partners for years. If anything, *I* took care of *him.*

"Come on, baby." Tucker's soft voice nudged through my consternation. "Let's go home."

My legs were leaden as I followed him towards the door, my body protesting leaving the home I shared with Master.

No. He wasn't my Master. Not anymore. Had he ever been? Or had he only allowed me to call him that in the interest of helping me to function on a daily basis?

"I'm not your Master."

Today hadn't been the first time he had told me that. Only, I hadn't been able to face that terrible truth until now. A part of me still didn't *want* to face it, but the memory of Lydia Chase that had entered the apartment alongside Tucker made it impossible to deny any longer.

It was time for me to leave the man I had called Master behind me.

I didn't look back at Agent Smith James as I walked out of his apartment.
∎∎

Dr. Rachel Stanger's sharp features were framed by straight black hair, which was styled in a bob with bangs. She would have seemed almost severe if it weren't for the soft set of her mouth and the gentleness of her eyes. They somehow conveyed kind understanding and incisive acuity at the same time.

"I've read the file that the FBI has compiled regarding what happened to you, Lydia," she began after the general introductions were out of the way. Her voice was a touch deeper than it had been at first. The sound was richer, warmer. Although I knew she was about to lead me through something that would be extremely upsetting, her voice eased some of the tension from my muscles.

"Based on Agent Vaughn's and Agent James' reports, it seems you suffered what is known as a psychogenic fugue state," she continued. "Do you know what that is?"

I shook my head. My high school education didn't include a background in Psychology.

"To put it in simple terms, you completely disassociated from memories of your life before you were taken because facing them was too traumatic. You created a new identity for yourself and forgot who you were before."

"So you're saying I had amnesia?" I couldn't keep the speculative note from my tone. To my knowledge, amnesia was something that only happened in fiction.

"Dissociative amnesia is supported by numerous case studies, Lydia. Spontaneous recovery from this state can be triggered by a range of stimuli, and it is usually rapid." She glanced at the open file that rested in her lap. "According to Agent James' reports, you remembered very little about your life before today. You only recently recalled your name. I believe that seeing your husband triggered the end of your fugue state."

I couldn't dispute her assessment of what had happened to me. The arrival of Tucker in Master's apartment had brought my memories of Lydia Chase roiling back to the forefront of my mind. I had been "Slave" for so long, and even under Master's care I had refused to let go of that identity. My desire to stay with him had been stronger than my desire to recall my former self.

Now everything I had known, the woman I had been, had taken up residence in my mind once again. The swiftness of her return when I had laid eyes on Tucker had been brutal and inexorable.

Slave was a lie, an identity my brain had fashioned for me in order to shield me from the horror of Lydia's abuse.

I pressed my hands to either side of my skull, seeking to suppress the pounding that was making my head ache. I didn't want to be here. I didn't want to be Lydia Chase. I wanted to go back to Master.

But that was wrong. That was disgusting. Lydia Chase wouldn't stand for that. *I* wouldn't stand for that.

"I know this must be hard, Lydia," Dr. Stanger's gentle voice penetrated the pain of my churning thoughts. "I want to keep you here under observation for a few days. Once I'm sure you're stable, you can go back to your family. You can go back to your life. You'll still come see me to work through your trauma, but you'll be able to go home."

I nodded my acquiescence numbly. She wanted me to stay in the psych ward. At least that gave me a few more hours before I had to face my old reality.

But the isolation wouldn't be enough to keep the painful knowledge of what I had been reduced to at bay. Lydia Chase was back, and there was no hiding from her any longer.

Chapter 17

"Lydia!" My name left my mother's lips on a disbelieving sob. She stood beside my father on the front stoop of Tucker's townhouse. She seemed shorter than I remembered; her shoulders had taken on a definitive slump in the year since I had last seen her. When she threw her arms around me, her body felt shockingly fragile. My mother had always been slightly doughy in a warm, maternal way. Even her now-fully-grey hair felt brittle as it brushed across my cheek.

She pulled back from me just long enough to clasp my cheeks in both of her hands, and her shining blue-green eyes studied my face hungrily. "My baby," she whispered wonderingly before enfolding me in her arms again. "Thank you, Lord! Thank you, Lord!" She cried out her prayer of gratitude.

I was stiff in her hold for a moment, stunned by the loving contact. But then her familiar scent suffused the air around me: lavender and baby powder. I buried my face in her hair as I breathed her in deeply, clinging to her like I was a child again.

"Mom," I sighed, my own tears flooding forth.

How could I have forgotten Mom? How could I have ever wanted to deny her existence? She was a story before bed and a snowball fight in the park and a homemade lemon merengue pie. She was a cup of tea and a kiss on the cheek. She was unconditional love.

My jubilation shattered when a pair of masculine arms closed around both of us. I cried out, jerking away from the restraining hold.

I was released instantly, and I took a hasty step back, my body shaking slightly from the adrenaline that had spiked through me along with my panic.

The fresh wrinkles around my father's brown eyes deepened with confusion and hurt, and his frown was visible through his close-cropped salt-and-pepper beard. Only it was more salt than pepper now, and it didn't disguise his slightly sunken cheeks.

"Di, honey…" He said my nickname weakly.

I took a deep breath. This was my father. He had never so much as spanked me as a child. Carefully, warily, I took a step towards him. He stood perfectly still, hardly breathing as I wrapped my arms around him gingerly. After a moment, he placed a tentative hand on my back.

"Dad." My arms tightened, squeezing him to me.

He returned my embrace fully. "Di." He wept as openly as my mother. It was the first time I had ever seen him cry.

I don't know how long we stood outside in the dimming twilight, holding one another. As though if we just held on tightly enough, it would make up for all of the times the opportunity had been taken from us.

Eventually, we moved inside the small townhouse, my mother fussing over me needing rest. I never wanted to take my eyes off my parents ever again, but her suggestion made me suddenly, acutely aware of the depth of my exhaustion. Just three days ago, I had awoken as Master's blissful slave, ebullient at my triumph in finally convincing him to claim me. Now I found myself thrust back into my old life, where everything and everyone wasn't quite as I remembered. The challenges facing Lydia Chase were daunting, and there would be no Master to help guide her through them, to tell her he was proud of her when she made small steps of progress.

The longing and sadness that arose in me at the thought made my stomach twist in disgust.

Put it away. Deal with it later.

Tucker hastily tidied my old bedroom as best he could, rearranging a year's worth of accumulated junk so the bed was clear. I pressed my lips together in disapproval. He had clearly fallen back on old habits in my absence, shoving his mess into a room where he couldn't see it rather than actually cleaning up.

He didn't try to stay in the room with me. I wasn't sure if he was hesitant to stay close to me given my skittishness or if he thought he might be unwelcome for other reasons; we hadn't shared a bed for nearly two years even before I was abducted.

My mother rummaged through the chest of drawers and found a ragged old pair of pajamas for me to sleep in. I hadn't seen those in quite a while. I wondered what had happened to my clothes that I had kept at my old place. The studio apartment hadn't had the storage space to accommodate all of my clothes, so the items I didn't really want anymore were still stored at Tucker's.

"What happened to my apartment?" I asked my mom.

She pursed her lips. She had never approved of my separation from Tucker. In her mind, falling out of love with someone wasn't legitimate grounds for divorce. Tucker had felt the same, so we had simply lived apart for the six months before my abduction.

"Your lease period ended," she explained. "All of your things are at home."

Home. My parents' house. I longed to return there, to bustle around the kitchen and laugh at my dad's terrible puns while my mom and I whipped up a culinary masterpiece.

"I'd like to go home," I said quietly.

She hugged me tightly. "We'll go tomorrow," she promised. "Tonight, I'm staying here with you."

I held her close, more grateful for her presence than I could ever recall. "I love you, Mom."

"Oh, my sweet baby. I love you too."

I was careful to face my mother while I got changed so she couldn't see my scarred back.

I wasn't sure how much the FBI had told my family, but I sincerely hoped they didn't have more than the barest inkling of what had actually happened to me. Not only did I never want them to know how I had been degraded, but I was afraid for them to learn that I had been abducted from a BDSM club. My conservative family would never understand why I had been there, and I didn't want any bitter disapproval to mar our reunion.

Terrible dreams tormented me through the night, but Mom held me as I cried after each one. Although the warmth of her familiar embrace was incredibly soothing, I found the coolness of the tourmaline pendant around my throat to be even more comforting.

I was still clutching the necklace tightly when I awoke the next morning. When I realized what I was doing, I had to force myself to pry my fingers loose from where they were twined around the silver chain. Briefly, I considered ripping it from my neck and flinging it away from me. The memories it elicited were painfully bittersweet, and the fact that I was still holding it to find succor from my fear was upsetting in and of itself.

But I couldn't bring myself to do it; the very idea of not having it encircling my throat made me feel naked and vulnerable.

Put it away. Deal with it later.

I would process my disturbing reluctance to rid myself of the pendant after I had made it through the debriefing I faced that morning. When Dr. Stanger had signed off on my release from the hospital the day before, she had informed me that I would have to meet with Agent Katherine Byrd to go over the details of my abduction. I shuddered at the prospect, and I resolutely turned my attention to getting showered and dressed rather than lingering on my apprehension.

Going about a morning routine in the house I had once shared with Tucker was eerily familiar. Unsurprisingly, one of the light bulbs over the bathroom sink was out. I wondered how long Tucker had been shaving under the dim lighting without bothering to fix it. The hot water handle in the shower squeaked exactly as I remembered, but the cleanliness of the tub left something to be desired. Tucker was a great guy, but he always had needed a mother more than he needed a wife.

I frowned at the scent of his shampoo. It certainly wasn't Old Spice. Sighing, I lathered it into my hair. I would buy my own toiletries at the first opportunity. I was done smelling like a man.

The thought sent anxiety shooting through my system as the scent of Tucker's Arctic Ice shampoo made me acutely aware of the loss of lingering notes of amber and whiskey. I barely took the time to rinse the soap from my hair before darting back to the bedroom, where I frantically gathered up the dress I had been wearing on the day I had left Master's apartment. I buried my face in it, inhaling deeply. Miraculously, it still smelled like him.

Safe.

"What are you doing, honey? You can't wear that dress again without washing it."

I jolted at the sound of my mother's voice, dropping the dress as though it had bitten me. A heartbeat later, I released my hold on my pendant as well.

When I craned my head back to look at my mom, I found her staring at me wide-eyed, the back of her hand pressed against her mouth as though she was fighting the urge to be sick.

Too late, I realized that I hadn't taken time to do more than wrap a towel around myself before moving from the bathroom to the bedroom. The scars on my upper back and lower down on my thighs were visible. My stomach sank. I hadn't wanted her to see this. I quickly turned so the marks were hidden from her, but the damage was done.

"Mom…" I said weakly, a hint of pleading laced into her name. Her expression of abject horror at the sight of my damaged body was eliciting a similar feeling from deep within me.

Master hadn't flinched at the sight of my scars. His assurances that I was still beautiful had all but erased the distress I had associated with them. Now, each one seemed to burn into me, the scars leaving an imprint that was more than just skin-deep.

Recognizing my mounting distress, Mom took a deep, shuddering breath. She swallowed hard. Once. Twice. Her hand lowered slowly, but it trembled at her side.

"Let's find something else for you to wear, honey." She made a brave effort to sound casual, but it was ruined by the way her voice shook.

I let out the breath I didn't realize I was holding. It wasn't like Mom to avoid a difficult discussion; usually she badgered me until I cracked and told her what was bothering me. Then she would impart what she considered to be sage advice and the situation would be dealt with. She meant well, but her advice wasn't usually suited to me at all. She had a very clear – very conservative – view of how the world should work, and I had stopped trying to contradict her years ago. Besides, talking to her about my problems was soothing in and of itself. I didn't begrudge her her maternal right to dole out advice.

But this… This was nothing so insignificant as dealing with an annoying co-worker or a domestic spat. The magnitude of what I had suffered could never be fully expressed through words, and I had the feeling voicing it aloud would be destructive rather than healing. I wasn't ready to deal with that right now. Possibly not ever. And I certainly wasn't going to let Mom deal with it.

What advice could she possibly give that would erase the marks on my skin, on my soul?

She seemed to realize the same thing, and her cheeks colored with shame as she tore her eyes away from me.

I found an old dress in the closet. I had left it behind because it was too small for me at the time I moved out, but now it hung loosely on my too-thin frame. Thankfully, the wrap-around design allowed me to cinch it tightly enough that the effect wasn't too noticeable. As I studied myself in the full-length mirror, I took in anew the shocking changes my period of enslavement had wrought on my body. I touched the dark lines that encircled my wrists, and I resolved to dig my bangle bracelets out of storage as soon as possible. I was also going to trim the ragged ends of my hair and go to a tanning bed. Usually, I would have disapproved of the cancer box, but I was desperate to return some of the usual color to my pale skin.

My eyes fell on the gem that flashed at my throat. The deep green was perfectly complemented by my purple dress.

Beautiful.

Then I noticed an unfamiliar, purplish mark on my neck. Confused, I examined the half-moon shape more closely. I quickly averted my gaze with a small gasp.

Master's mark. My heart twisted painfully.

Jerkily, I drew my hair over my shoulder, effectively hiding the bruise. But even though it was no longer visible, I felt it like a brand on my skin. And I didn't entirely hate the idea of being branded by him.

I shuddered.

No. I would deal with it later. In fact, if I just put off dealing with it for long enough, the mark would fade, and it wouldn't trouble me anymore.

When I emerged from the bedroom, a delicious scent drew me towards the dining room table. Well, I thought of it as the "dining room." In reality, it was the same space as the "living room," but the furniture was arranged in a pattern that made each area distinctive.

My parents were already seated around the table, and Tucker was shifting food from a to-go box onto a plate. His smile was tentative, almost sheepish.

"I went out to Southport Grocery and got you the sweet and savory French toast."

My heart swelled with affection. He must have gotten up very early to get from Pilsen to downtown and back by this hour. "Thank you."

I resisted the urge to inhale the ham-and-swiss-covered French toast, instead savoring every unbelievably delicious bite. I was only just finishing up when a knock on the door made me jump. Reflexively, I shrank back into my chair. Master usually answered the door, keeping his body firmly between me and whoever waited outside.

I shook my head to clear away the memory. I had thought that Master had made me strong, but in many ways he had kept my weakness firmly ingrained.

Tucker had already crossed to open the door by the time I got to my feet. A CPD officer greeted him, then informed us it was time for me to see Agent Byrd for my official debriefing.

I found myself regretting my delicious breakfast as my stomach churned at the prospect.

Chapter 18

Agent Katherine Byrd was younger than I expected, maybe a year or two younger than me. Although after studying my reflection that morning, I felt like I looked far older than my twenty-eight years. I certainly appeared to have aged more than a year in the time I had spent imprisoned by that Bastard.

Instinctively, I shied away from the thought of him. I wouldn't have the luxury of doing so for much longer. In a few minutes, Agent Byrd was going to force me to think of him, to recount what he had done to me.

Tucker had offered to sit with me during the debriefing, and a part of me had been sorely tempted to accept. Although our romantic relationship had ended a long time ago, our friendship never had. The warm grip of his hand around mine would have been comforting. But the idea of him knowing what I had been through was abhorrent. I had always been the assertive one in our relationship, the strong one. Having him see my vulnerability, to know just how low I had sunk, would be unbearable. I had to protect him from that.

So I found myself alone with the pretty, copper-haired woman in the small, warmly-lit office. Her bright green eyes were kind, her soft features open and sensitive. But the strong set of her shoulders as she sat with perfect posture on the chair across from me gave off an air of confidence. I tried to straighten my own back in response, to harness the confidence that I used to possess. My efforts were a pale mimicry of her bearing.

"I'm Agent Byrd," she needlessly introduced herself, "but you can call me Kate."

Unable to return her soft smile, I just nodded in acknowledgement.

"I'm going to have to ask you some difficult questions, Lydia," she told me gently. "If you need a break, you can tell me. I know this will be hard, but we want to find the man who abducted you. We have to make sure he can never do that to anyone ever again."

Her last statement made me go cold. Since I had been freed, the thought of that Bastard taking another woman had never crossed my mind. I had been so absorbed in my own determination to forget him that I hadn't allowed myself to contemplate what he might be doing now.

"Oh, god," I breathed shakily. "I hadn't even thought…" I swallowed. "He said there had been others before me. He said they… He said they didn't last long." Mustering my courage, I met Agent Byrd – Kate – squarely in the eye. "I'll do whatever I can to help you. I can't let him… What do you need to know?"

Kate regarded me with a new respect before beginning her questioning.

"You were officially reported as missing on June 10, 2012, but your husband said he hadn't heard from you in two days before that. It seems your friend Rebecca Thomas was the last person to see you. She said you had lunch together on the ninth. Your mother became concerned when she couldn't get through to you on your cell phone on the tenth. Your parents and your husband filed an official report that day." She paused, allowing me to absorb the information. "Can you tell me where and when you were abducted?"

I took a deep breath, steeling myself. I hadn't realized how little the FBI knew. It occurred to me that I had hardly uttered two sentences to Master and Clayton regarding the circumstances of my imprisonment before they had relented with their questioning. After that, Master hadn't actively pressed me for more information, and neither had he allowed anyone else to do so. He had kept me isolated, slowly working bits of information from me. I realized now that he had been trying to protect me from the trauma of facing what had happened to me. But in doing so, he had kept the FBI's hands tied when it came to tracking down that Bastard.

I wasn't sure if I was grateful or resentful.

"I was at Dusk on the night of the ninth," I began, struggling to keep my voice even as I accessed the now-readily-available memories. Kate's brows drew together in confusion. She didn't recognize the name of the club. Of course she didn't. "It's a BDSM club," I explained reluctantly.

"Oh." Her face was carefully blank.

"I had been going there every weekend for almost two months. My family and friends didn't know. They... They wouldn't have approved." My cheeks heated, but I pressed on. "Tucker and I had been officially separated for four months when I first started going," I explained, almost defensively. "But things had been over between us for a long time before that. I wanted a divorce, but he wouldn't agree. I couldn't afford to fight him on it."

"So he was angry about you moving out on your own?" Kate asked, suspicion regarding Tucker's character stirring in her eyes.

"No," I said quickly. "The separation was amicable. We got along just fine. But Tucker doesn't believe in divorce. And neither do either of our families. He thought we should stick together because it was the right thing to do."

Kate nodded, her suspicious expression clearing. I was relieved. The last thing I wanted was for Tucker to suffer over my abduction any more than he already had.

"So you were at Dusk on the night of the ninth," Kate prompted. "What happened that night?"

"I..." My mouth instantly went dry as *his* face materialized in my mind, studying me with lustful interest from across the bar area. "I noticed him in the club at the beginning of the night. He gave me the creeps, but I didn't think much of it. There's always a creepy guy or two on the scene. Usually, they leave after getting the cold shoulder from people in the community, or someone sets them straight. I figured he would get filtered out soon, so I ignored him. I went to... play with my friend Mark." I stumbled over the word.

"So you had sex?"

"No!" I said quickly. "It wasn't like that. I didn't have sex with anyone in the community. I've never slept with anyone but Tucker."

No one else except Master.

I went cold.

No one else except Master and that Bastard.

No. I didn't *sleep with* that Bastard; he *raped* me.

I had willingly, eagerly, given myself to Master. And that had been so much more than just sex.

I shook off the thought, returning my focus to the night I had been taken. The amount of effort it took for me to tear my mind away from the memory of Master's beautifully fierce expression as he claimed me was almost painful. Especially because I was replacing the image of him with the leering face of that Bastard.

"Anyway, that Bastard told me later that he had watched me with Mark."

Kate's brows rose at the moniker that Master had given me for the man who had tortured me, but she didn't have to ask me who I was talking about.

"And what was it, exactly, that he saw you doing?"

My cheeks burned, and I pursed my lips.

"I need to know, Lydia. And I won't judge you for anything you say."

I was hesitant to believe her, but her emerald eyes seemed sincere.

"Mark and I... We went to the dungeon together. He tied me down and hit me with a crop." I said the words in a rush, unable to suppress a cringe as I did so. I had never spoken to anyone outside the community about my proclivities. Well, I had hinted at them to Tucker, but I had quickly decided to keep them secret from him after his uneasy reaction.

But, true to her word, Kate's expression wasn't judgmental in the least. "Why was it important to him – to that Bastard – that he watched?"

The sound of the derisive name on her lips bolstered my courage. And I needed every shred of courage to make my next admission.

"He said... He told me that was why he chose me. The other women he had taken before me, they... They died. He thought I would survive longer because I liked pain." My voice got quieter, shakier, as I forced out the words.

The permanent pink flush that colored Kate's alabaster cheeks paled a shade. She cleared her throat delicately. "What happened after you played with Mark?"

The ease with which she absorbed "played" into her pertinent vocabulary bolstered me once again, reassuring me that she truly didn't judge me for my unconventional sexual tastes.

"I decided to go home early. My work week hadn't been great, and I was pretty worn out."

My job as a receptionist at Real Listings, a small local real estate firm, had been thankless. Most of the women I worked with were catty, and my boss had been a chauvinistic ass. But it had paid the bills, and I couldn't quit and devote myself to art if I was going to afford the rent on my studio apartment.

I hadn't thought about my job until that moment. My complaints about the trials of working there now seemed laughably trivial.

I turned my attention back to what was important.

"Usually, I would have asked Mark to walk me out to my car. But he was talking to a sub – a submissive – who he had been interested in for a while. Romantically interested. I didn't want to interrupt, so I slipped out on my own. I had almost gotten to my car when…"

When my life ended.

"When that Bastard took me. I didn't see him coming. He grabbed me from behind and injected me with some drug. When I woke up, I… I was in the dungeon where he kept me."

"The dungeon?" Kate asked, her voice slightly fainter than it had been before.

I couldn't bring myself to look at her. As coldly and clinically as I could, I described my prison. Any detail might help the FBI figure out its location. Determinedly, I divulged every aspect of the room that I could recall.

"Good," Kate said when I had finished. "That's good, Lydia. We'll see what we can turn up with that information." I glanced up at her to find that all of the color had drained from her cheeks. "Tell me about the heroin. We have the sketch you helped us create. We'll circulate it through the proper channels. If we can connect him to a dealer in the area, we might be able to get a lead on him."

I nodded, clinging to the possibility that any of my information might save another woman from suffering at his hands. "I'm not sure how long I was there when he first gave it to me. Maybe a few weeks. I gathered that he hadn't tried giving any of the women before me heroin. He was frustrated with me.

He planned to get me addicted so that I would do… *things* for him more willingly."

My gut twisted. It hadn't been the drug that had broken me, but it had certainly kept me compliant after I had broken. No. Not just compliant. Eager. Desperate.

Kate gently placed a comforting hand on my knee, calling me back to the present. "That's good," she told me encouragingly. "That gives us a timeline to work with." Her eyes appraised me carefully before continuing her line of questioning. "Agent Vaughn told me you mentioned another man. 'The Mentor'? What can you tell me about him?"

The crack of the whip. Blood. Agony.
"Please make it stop, Master."
Broken.

"If that Bastard had an accomplice, we need to track him down as well," Kate told me carefully.

"That Bastard." Not "Master". He's not my Master. He never truly was.

I gritted my teeth, pulling myself away from the visceral memories, struggling to study them from a distance. I wasn't Slave any longer. That identity had never been real, it had never been *me*. I clung to that knowledge, denying the weakness of Slave and drawing on the quiet strength possessed by Lydia Chase.

"The Bastard deferred to him. He seemed almost scared of him. The Mentor said something about having taught him to channel his urges. He said he would kill the Bastard if the cops linked his victims to him and came after him. The Bastard asked the Mentor for help so that he wouldn't have to risk drawing attention to himself by taking another woman."

I stopped talking. Nausea had rolled over me, and my head started spinning. The front of my skull pounded as though a jackhammer was drilling away at it from the inside.

"What did the Mentor help him with?"

I dropped my head into my hands, clutching at my skull in an effort to hold it together, to keep it from shattering.

"Breaking me," I said on a whimper.

For all my self-reassurances that Lydia was a separate entity from Slave, the memories of what had happened to her, to *me*, were still crippling.

The couch dipped slightly beside me, and Kate placed a tentative arm around my shoulder. The simple act of human kindness wrenched a sob from my chest, and I leaned into her slightly, welcoming the comfort. Her hand brushed up and down my back soothingly as she let me cry.

I was trembling when the flow of my tears finally abated. Shyly, I glanced up at Kate. Her complexion was still wan, but her expression was nothing but compassionate. She wasn't judging me, and she wasn't pitying me.

"Thank you," I said shakily.

She gave me a weak smile. "No problem. It's the least I can do. The information you gave me might be what we need to catch the Bastard. He won't be able to hurt anyone else."

I nodded, but I didn't share her confidence. In truth, I had very little valuable information to offer. I didn't know the Bastard's name, I didn't know where he had held me prisoner, and I didn't even know what the Mentor looked like. Still, I had given Kate everything I knew. I could only hope it would be enough.

"Dr. Stanger will help you work through what happened," Kate reassured me. "You'll be able to rebuild your life, Lydia."

Again, I wasn't nearly as confident as she sounded. Despite the return of my memories, I would never be the same woman I had been before I was taken. And I wasn't at all sure if I was capable of finding the strength within me to rebuild. My life had been shattered, and even the tiny shards of it seemed to weigh a ton. I wasn't strong enough to wrestle them back together. Not on my own.

I realized that my fingers were fiddling with the silver chain around my neck.

Yes. I *definitely* needed to see Dr. Stanger. I had to get my head back on straight. And I couldn't do that while Master still had a hold on my heart. I needed someone to help me deal with my disturbing obsession with him.

But the idea of purging him from me made my soul ache.

• •

That afternoon, I found myself sifting through boxes of too-big clothes alongside my mom. She had stored everything from my apartment in my childhood bedroom. While every other aspect of my former life seemed subtly different than it had been before I was taken, this room was exactly as I remembered. My twin bed was still made up with the girly, garish purple-and-green duvet that I had chosen long ago, and my beloved autographed Dave Matthews Band poster still hung above my dresser.

"I found this in your chest of drawers when I was cleaning out your apartment."

I looked up to see that my mom was holding a small, red velvet-covered box. My throat constricted at the jumble of emotions that arose within me at the sight of it.

"Mom..." Her name was a weak protest.

She reached out and gently took me by the hand, pressing the box into my palm and closing my fingers around it. Her eyes were sharp, significant. I knew that look all too well. Mom was about to put her foot down.

"Tucker has been a wreck since you... Since you went missing. He loves you, Lydia."

My left ring finger burned with the memory of the simple gold band that the box concealed. As though angered by the sensation, Master's mark on my neck flared even hotter, insistently reminding me of its presence.

"I know," I said quietly. "I love him too. But I'm not *in* love with him, Mom. And he's not in love with me."

Her eyes softened, but the set of her jaw was still determined. "You might feel like that now, honey. But marriage is forever. The all-consuming love you feel when you first get married grows and changes. It feels different, but it becomes something deeper. Everyone goes through rough patches. Stick through it, and you'll come out the other side stronger than ever."

I sighed. I really didn't want to have this conversation right now. "Tuck and I did grow and change, Mom. We grew into different people. We got married so young. We didn't even know who we were then. I tried to make it work, but the people we grew to be just aren't right for one another. I know you think divorce is wrong, but do you really want me to spend the rest of my life in a loveless marriage when I could be happier with someone else?"

She touched her hand to my shoulder, a caring gesture. "Of course I want you to be happy, honey. But I think you could be happy with Tucker, if you just open up your heart to him again. When you were... Tucker has had a year to realize what he lost. I know he'll want to make your marriage work. He doesn't want to lose you. Not again."

Anguish gripped my heart. I didn't want to hurt Tuck. Especially considering all of the hurt I had already caused him. Was he really in love with me? And even if he was, would that love be enough to sustain us forever? Or would we grow bitter over the long years of passionless companionship?

The affection I felt for Tucker filled my chest to the point of aching. I *did* love him. He would always own a piece of my heart. And the thought of having him out of my life completely, permanently, was almost too painful to bear. If he was in love with me, it would be disgustingly selfish of me to expect him to be in my life while not allowing him to be with me as he truly desired.

I sat down on my bed heavily. "Can I have a minute, Mom?"

She squeezed my shoulder. "Of course, honey. I'll be in the kitchen. Come down when you're ready."

Once she had softly closed the door behind her, I took a deep breath and opened the small box that was still nestled in my palm. The gold band glinted dully in the afternoon light. Nearly eight years of wear had left light scratches across its surface. I thought back to the day Tuck had first slipped it on my finger. Despite the way we had drifted apart, the memory was still sweet.

I had been so nervous that day. I knew beyond a shadow of a doubt that I loved Tucker Chase, but we were so young. Marrying at nineteen had never been part of my plan.

I smiled wryly to myself. If Tuck and I hadn't both had a rebellious streak a mile wide at the time, we might have dated for years before the beautiful wildness of first love had finally run its course. Our conservative families were proponents of prudence, of abstinence. And Tucker and I were both artistic types with decidedly imprudent dreams. We read Jack Kerouac and Hunter S. Thompson, and we snuck the occasional joint when our parents were out of the house. Tuck would jam on his guitar and I would draw. And we would make love.

But we were careless in our passion, and two months after high school graduation, I found out I was pregnant. Tuck did the "right" thing by me and proposed. He hadn't even thought twice.

I had been crying for hours. The little blue plus signs on the pregnancy tests mocked me. They told me I was stupid and irresponsible and had ruined my life.

I touched my hand to my belly. I didn't feel any different. My body wasn't telling me that something beautiful and horrific had blossomed inside of me. But all five of those little white sticks yelled it loud and clear.

All of those small plus signs added up to one thing: the destruction of all of my plans and dreams. I wouldn't be able to go to college. My parents loved me, but once they found out, there was no way they would pay my tuition. What if they kicked me out of the house? Where would I go? What if they didn't love me anymore?

There was an insistent knock on my bedroom door.

"Lydia, baby, let me in."

I couldn't hold back my raw sob at the sound of Tucker's voice. I had been avoiding his calls all day. I had no idea what I was going to say to him. What if he didn't love me anymore, either?

Tuck didn't wait for an invitation; he burst through the door at the sound of my distress. He crossed the room in an instant, joining me where I was sprawled out on my bed and holding me to him tightly. His expression was alarmed, his sweet blue eyes filled with concern. I had fallen in love with those eyes on the first day he had arrived at school during my junior year. They were a deep, dusky blue, soft like well-worn denim.

"What's wrong, baby? Talk to me."

"Tuck, I..." I choked on the words. "I'm pregnant."

I dropped my gaze, unable to face the horror that would swirl in his eyes. I couldn't bear to see the light of love in them extinguished.

His fingers were instantly beneath my chin, lifting my face up to his. The raw love in his expression took my breath away.

"Marry me, Lydia."

"Wh-What?"

He pushed himself upright, settling himself on one knee on the bed beside me. He tugged off his class ring and gently took my left hand in his.

"Will you marry me, Lydia?"

"Tuck. You don't have to -"

"I've known that I want to spend the rest of my life with you since I saw you in Art class on my first day at Jones Prep. You're passionate, Lydia. You're beautiful and smart. And you have great taste in music." He grinned, that wide, boyish grin that held the joy of innocence untainted by the trials of the real world. "I love you. I know I always will. What's the difference if we make it official now or four years from now? Marry me, Lydia. Please."

A mad giggle bubbled up from my throat. Tucker Chase loved me. And I loved him. Of course I wanted to spend my forever with him. There would never be anyone else.

"Yes!" I said emphatically, suddenly giddy. "Yes, of course I'll marry you, Tuck!"

Beaming, he slid his class ring onto my finger. It was far too big for me. Laughing, he slipped it onto my thumb instead.

"I love you so much, Lydia."

"I love you too, Tuck."

Our kiss was a sweet promise of our devotion to one another. It turned feverish as we poured all of our love and longing and joy for our life together into one another. There was a sense of urgency as well, an anxiety that neither of us would openly acknowledge, not even to ourselves.

We made love, our bodies desperate to join, to convince ourselves that our union was all that mattered in the world.

Tuck held me afterward, and the slight trembling of my fingers wasn't the product of residual passion. My future, so secure and assured only a day before, was suddenly a terrifying unknown.

"I'm scared, Tuck," I whispered.

"I'm not."

I studied him skeptically, but all I found was surety in his beautiful eyes.

"I want to have a family with you, Lydia. I'll get a job. We'll get a place of our own. I'll take care of you, baby."

"But what about Notre Dame?" Tuck was supposed to study for a Music major, and I was going to study Studio Art for my BFA.

"We'll put it on hold," he said firmly. "I'll support us. Once our baby's born and we're settled, we can think about school. We're going to be happy, Lydia. I swear I'll make you happy."

Our *baby.*

Suddenly, the idea of being pregnant wasn't so terrifying. This was Tuck's baby. Tuck's and mine.

A new future unfolded before me. It wasn't so different from the one I had harbored the day before. Tuck and I would attain our dreams. It would just take a few years longer than we had originally planned. And our baby would be a part of those dreams.

But that beautiful, blissful picture of our little family that Tuck painted for me never existed. I lost the baby only a few weeks after the wedding. We never tried again. And neither of our dreams ever came to fruition.

Chapter 19

Officers Santino and Johnson – the CPD officers who had been assigned to my protective detail that day – drove me from my parents' house back to Tucker's.

My parents' house. Tucker's house.

I didn't have a place to call my own anymore. I didn't belong anywhere.

My mind flashed to a starkly black-and-white apartment. Bare of sentiment but for my drawings hanging on the wall. A pang shot through my heart at the memory of my unbridled joy on the morning Master had asked me to put them on display.

I wondered what had happened to them. Had Master kept them? Had they ever really meant anything to him? Or were they simply a means to an end, his interest sprung from his desire to help me recover rather than true emotion?

I jerked my fingers away from the silver chain around my neck. My head was enough of a mess without thinking about Master. I had to deal with Tucker now.

I had to try to make things work with him. After everything he had given up for me – his dreams, his freedom – I owed him that. I stared down at the gold band on my finger as I unlocked the front door to the townhouse.

"Lydia!" Tucker sounded slightly alarmed when I opened the door. He practically leapt to his feet from where he had been sitting on the couch. The woman sitting beside him drew away from him hastily as well, her cheeks flushing slightly.

"Becs?" I said her name questioningly, but I recognized my best friend instantly.

Rebecca Thomas was as beautiful as ever: short and busty with olive skin and a silky curtain of black hair. Her soulful dark brown eyes widened at the sight of me.

"L," she breathed my nickname.

She quickly blinked away her moment of shock at my altered appearance and rushed over to me. She was already crying by the time her arms closed around me.

"Oh my god, Lydia!" She sobbed into my shoulder. I returned her hug with equal fierceness. Becs had been in my life since I was nine years old. We knew one another better than I even knew Tucker. She had held my hand through the pregnancy, the miscarriage. She had let me crash at her apartment when my marriage started to fall apart.

As soon as the familiar scent of her Coco Mademoiselle perfume enfolded me, I was transported back three years.

The wind buffeted my hair into wild tangles around my head as I drove down I-94 at sixty miles per hour with the windows down. Rebecca rode in the passenger seat, practically bouncing with giddy excitement.

"Come on, L!" Becs insisted. "Punch it!"

We were road-tripping to Detroit for a Ben Folds Five concert, and in her mind, we couldn't get there soon enough. But I wasn't going to break the speed limit. Especially not in my dad's old Buick sedan. For some unfathomable reason, he was obsessed with the beast of a car, and I wasn't about to risk damaging it.

I shook my head and shot her an imperious smile

"Sorry, B. Driver's rules."

She rolled her eyes at me, scoffing. "Well, if you get to control the speed, I get to control the music."

She reached forward and fiddled with the audio controls, switching from my Guster CD to a Top 40 radio station. Miley Cyrus' nasal voice instantly filled the car. I groaned in protest.

"God, B. Put Guster back on."

She just grinned at me evilly and proceeded to "put her hands up" because they were "playing her song."

"Speed up, and I'll make it stop," she stipulated before throwing herself full-force in to tormenting me.

She sang shrilly, nodding her head "like yeah" and moving her hips "like yeah."

What the hell did that even mean, anyway?

It meant my best friend appeared to be having some sort of fit in my passenger seat.

"Okay!" I capitulated loudly as I pressed down on the gas pedal. "Okay, you win!"

I tried and failed to hold a glare. We both burst into a fit of giggles as Becs followed through with her end of the bargain. I

heaved a dramatic sigh of relief when "What You Call Love"
blared from the speakers once again.

The little exchange had seemed so insignificant at the time;
I hadn't even realized I had filed it away in my lexicon of
memories. But there it was, sharp and sweet.

My humming "Party in the USA" so happily when I had
hung my drawings in Master's living room suddenly made more
sense. I hated pop music, but I associated that particular song with
joy.

Even when I had been keeping Lydia Chase resolutely
locked away, denying her existence, Becs had still been there with
me.

And that was Becs all over: insistent to the point of being
irritating. Usually intentionally so. She was teasing and bluntly
assertive and annoying as hell.

She was the best friend a girl could ask for.

I don't know how long we stood there, holding each other,
reassuring ourselves that the other was real. Eventually, Becs
pulled away from me with a watery laugh.

"Don't let the tears fool you. I'm really happy to see you,
L."

Laughter burst forth from me as well, the sound of it almost
shocking me. It was the first time I had laughed since I had left
Master.

God. He couldn't keep popping into my brain like this. I
was constantly comparing everything in my newly re-discovered
life to the life I had known with him. But that wasn't really a life
at all, was it? I had been a shadow of a person, a mere extension of
Master's soul.

But being a part of him had brought me bliss more pure
than I had ever known in my entire existence as Lydia Chase.

And that was *wrong.* So very, very wrong.

I shook it off.

Later. I would deal with him later.

"Can I stay with you tonight?" Becs asked eagerly, her
hand still clutching my arm as though she couldn't bring herself to
stop touching me.

I didn't want her to stop. She was the sister I never had,
and I never wanted to lose her again. A small part of me feared

that if she left my sight, I would forget her again. I couldn't do that to her. I couldn't do that to myself.

But I also couldn't stand the idea that she might bear witness to the nightmares that I knew would torment me in the night. It was one thing to allow my mother to hold me as I thrashed and cried; she had been taking care of me since I was I child, and I couldn't deny myself the temptation of her maternal embrace on that first night back in my old life.

Becs and I were equals. We had leaned on one another throughout the years, but this was something different, something deeper. I never wanted her to know the extremes of the trauma I had gone through, just as I couldn't bear it if Tucker suspected just how torturous my existence had been over the last year. It was jarring to return to my old life; the subtle changes in everyone I had loved were difficult to take in. I didn't want our relationships to change, as they inevitably would if they discovered just how messed up I was inside. If I was ever going to re-assimilate myself into their lives, their hearts, I couldn't allow them to see me as the broken victim that I was.

"B, I… I think I need some time alone."

I need some time to fall to pieces without you witnessing, without you realizing just how shattered I am.

Her face fell, and I squeezed her hand reassuringly.

"Let's have coffee together tomorrow afternoon. Please?"

She smiled at me weakly, her eyes filling with sad understanding. That understanding didn't quite erase the hurt that lurked within them.

"Okay, Lydia. I'll see you tomorrow." She pulled me into another fierce hug. "I'm so glad to have you back, L. A part of me still can't believe you're real. You have no idea how much I missed you."

I swallowed hard, trying my best not to shift uncomfortably in her embrace.

No. I didn't know how much she had missed me. Because I hadn't missed *her.* I hadn't even thought of her in months. I had forgotten her, just like I had forgotten everyone else. Just like I had forgotten myself. Missing them had been too painful to face.

Shame flooded me. I had surrendered them to *him.* I had given the people I loved to that Bastard on the day I broke.

I stepped away from Becs, no longer able to resist the urge.

"I'll see you tomorrow, B," I said, trying to make the words come out evenly.

Tucker ushered her to the door, laying a reassuring hand on her arm. His touch drew her gaze to his, and I could see that her eyes were shining, the lines around them betraying anguish.

Her pained expression reassured me of my decision not to allow her to stay. I had managed to deeply upset her after exchanging only a few sentences. She would have been unfathomably more distraught by the sound of my despairing sobs in the night.

Once the door had locked behind her, I turned to retreat to my bedroom. I was more than ready to put this day behind me.

"Wait," Tuck called me back. "Will you sit with me?"

I didn't want to sit with Tuck. I wanted to crawl into my bed and huddle under the covers like a child hiding from the monsters in her closet.

The gold band weighed heavy on my finger, reminding me of the choice I had made. Tucker was my husband. Our marriage would never work if I shut him out completely.

My feet dragged as though the soles of my shoes were made of concrete, but I managed to walk to the couch. Tucker settled down beside me, his expression troubled. I knew whatever he had to say to me wouldn't be pleasant. I stared at him expectantly, waiting.

"Agent Scott came by to ask me some questions this afternoon," he said carefully.

"Agent Scott?" I didn't recognize the name.

"He's Agent Byrd's partner," he explained. "He wanted to know how I felt about… About where you were when you were abducted."

I sucked in a breath.

No. I didn't want him to know about that. Kate's suspicions about Tucker seemed to have been eased during the course of my debriefing. Why did they have to tell Tuck my dark secret? Even Becs didn't know about what I had been up to in those last months before I was taken.

Just when I had decided to work things out with Tucker, the FBI had gone and complicated things further for me. He would never understand this. He never had.

"I'm not upset, baby," Tucker said quickly. "But why… Why would you go to a place like that? Is that why things fell apart between us? If I had just given you that -"

I shook my head sharply, and he stopped speaking instantly.

"I don't want to talk about it, Tuck," I said firmly. "I don't want that. Not anymore."

Not with anyone but Master.

Master had given me that part of myself back. He had returned an essential part of my soul to me through helping me reclaim my lusts from that Bastard.

I shoved him from my mind almost angrily. I was going to be with Tucker, and Tucker didn't want that kind of sexual relationship. I would learn not to want it, either.

"I want to make things work between us, Tuck," I forced the words to form on my tongue. "I married you, for better or worse. Things couldn't be much worse. The problems that we had before… They were nothing in comparison. Even after everything, I… I still love you, Tuck."

It was true. I loved Tucker fiercely. I just wasn't *in* love with him.

But maybe that didn't matter anymore. Maybe I wasn't capable of loving anyone like that anymore.

You loved Master.

No. No, that wasn't love. That was slavish devotion. Obsession.

Tucker's hand tenderly cupped my cheek. I had to fight the urge to flinch away.

"I love you, too, Lydia. I always have. I always will."

I studied his face. Although there were fresh lines at the corners of his soft blue eyes, he was just as handsome as he had been on the day I first saw him. His cheekbones were sharply defined, his mouth full and sensitive. I remembered staring at him in wonder as he strummed his guitar in my bedroom, singing the first song he had ever written for me. We had been so young then, so naïve.

My heart swelled at the memory, aching to recall that time of perfect innocence, our love just blossoming, untainted by years of pain and resentment at all that we had lost when we had committed to eternity together.

Tuck and I were supposed to go to college together. I was going to be an artist, and he was going to be a singer-songwriter. We weren't supposed to have spent our early twenties working jobs we hated just to scrape by. And all for a family that had never come to fruition.

I glanced down at Tucker's crisp blue button-down shirt and khakis. He looked like he had stepped out of a J. Crew catalogue now; all signs of his youthful, carefree style were gone. It had been stamped out of him by years of struggling in the corporate machine so that he could support us. He hadn't even picked up his guitar in years.

Tucker had sacrificed the life he should have had for me. He had sacrificed *himself* for me. I would do everything I could to give him as much of myself as possible in return. He deserved nothing less. Focusing on supporting Tucker and making my family happy was a welcome distraction from thoughts of what I had suffered. That distraction would help me survive the re-integration into my old life.

Still, I couldn't stop myself from shrinking away from Tucker when he leaned in to kiss me.

His hand dropped from my face, turmoil flickering across his features.

"I'm sorry, Tuck. I'm just... I'm not ready for that yet. Can we take it slow?"

"Of course," he said softly. His voice was so earnest and understanding that it made my heart twinge. "Of course we can."

I took a deep breath. Would I ever be able to accept his intimate touch? Would I be able to allow his lips to caress mine without stiffening beneath him? Would I be able to accept him into my body again without wanting to cry?

I came to the disturbing realization that it wouldn't be memories of that Bastard that caused my tears to flow. It would be because the man moving inside me wasn't Master.

The possession which I had once so desperately craved, which I had demanded from him, had proven to be my destruction as well as my salvation. Master had shown me the pleasure that I had always dreamed of – no, my dreams hadn't even been capable of conjuring up such a perfect fantasy – and in doing so, he had ruined me for anyone else.

"Do you know how long I've ached to explore your body, girl? I'm not going to stop until I've devoured every inch of you. I am claiming you. Your body is mine. And I get to toy with it and play with it as long as I like."

Even though I would never see him again, he would own my body, my pleasure, for the rest of my life. And although the comprehension of that fact pained me like a knife twisting in my gut, I couldn't regret our coupling.

My time as Lydia, Master's slave, was something I would never bury, would never forget. I would tuck it away, but I would pull it out from time to time, savoring it.

That night, I replayed the memories of my time with Master in my mind in lurid detail, burning all of them deep into my psyche so they could never be erased.

Those memories would help me preserve my sanity when I wanted to fall apart. Master was the bridge between my time as that Bastard's plaything and who I truly was: Lydia Chase. He had gently coaxed my soul out of hiding without me even realizing what he was doing.

I idly stroked the tourmaline gem at my throat until I finally fell into sleep.

Chapter 20

The following morning, my stomach was doing somersaults as I settled down on the couch in Dr. Rachael Stanger's office. Only a day had passed since she had released me from observation after deeming me stable enough to function outside the hospital. I wasn't so sure her assertion was correct. I didn't feel at all stable.

I had made it through the reunion with my family without completely breaking down, but that was only because of my determination not to distress them any further than I already had. My concern for them had given me the strength to hide just how broken I was inside.

But as soon as I was no longer in the presence of my family, I was assailed by memories of my torture at that Bastard's hands. Without Master's reassuring strength and guidance, I had no one to lean on, no one to hold me and tell me I was okay. Even if I had let my mom, Becs, or Tucker see that ravaged side of me, I wouldn't have believed those words from anyone else's lips.

That realization was almost as disturbing as my dark memories. How could I ever heal if I couldn't learn to function without Master? Because I knew I would never see him again. He wouldn't allow it even if I returned to him on my knees, begging him to take me in.

"I'm not your Master."

I turned imploring eyes on Dr. Stanger. She had to help me learn how to live again without him. If I was to have any chance of being whole again, I would have to learn to let him go. I knew she would force me to face what I had endured in my dank prison, but my eagerness to end the pain and terror that plagued me overcame my fear of recalling my torture in lurid detail.

"You don't have to tell me anything in detail, Lydia" Dr. Stanger began. "We'll be dealing with your trauma through EMDR – Eye Movement Desensitization and Reprocessing. Right now, all of the memories of what you went through are stored away in your mind. Since you came out of your fugue state, I'm sure you've actively tried to put them away in order to avoid them."

I nodded. The accuracy with which she already understood how my mind operated in relation to my trauma helped to further calm my anxiety. Dr. Stanger knew what she was doing. She was going to be able to help me.

"Even though you're free now, you're susceptible to the pain of those memories if they're triggered by some stimuli surrounding you. EMDR allows us to access those memories one by one and deal with each of them. We'll do this style of intensive therapy for several weeks until your memories are no longer debilitating. Then we'll begin more introspective therapies to help you stabilize and rebuild your life. EMDR is meant to lessen the most extreme effects of PTSD, but this is only the beginning of the healing process."

I nodded my understanding. I hadn't expected a quick cure, but I was determined to take my life back. The debilitating fear that always hovered at the edges of my mind had to be dispelled. I couldn't live like that anymore.

"Facing your memories in detail will be very difficult, Lydia," Dr. Stanger continued, "but afterward you'll be able to put them away again. Only then, they'll be organized in a way that you control, and they won't be able to cause you further trauma if they do surface. We'll begin by establishing a positive memory for you to focus on if you become distressed during the course of the exercises. It should be something you associate with being safe and calm. Take however much time you need to select your positive memory. When you're ready, I'd like for you to share it with me."

My mind instantly flashed to Master's face.

His steady silver eyes stared down at me from where he loomed above me. He touched the top of my head affectionately as I knelt at his feet. Master was in control, and I didn't have to worry about anything. He would take care of me.

Safe. Calm.

But now that memory held its own edge of distress. I couldn't be his mindless slave any longer, couldn't live my life in the pursuit of pleasing him.

It was wrong that I ever had been his possession.

My mind turned to a different memory, but it was still about him. Only, it didn't hold the same imbalance of power as my first thought.

Master held me in his arms as my body slowly stilled its blissful quivering. Nothing separated our naked flesh, not even air. I was his, but he was finally mine as well. We were irrevocably bound, and his claiming of me granted me my own sort of claim over him.

I had demanded that Master join with me in that way. I had come to him from a position of supplication, but I hadn't relented when he tried to deny me. Even while he dominated my body, I felt empowered as I never had before. Not only was I taking my lusts back from that Bastard, but I had also asserted myself with Master. I hadn't begged him to use my body because I wanted to please him; I had begged him to touch me because it was what *I* wanted.

I couldn't recall another memory that came close to that perfection, not even from my life before I had been taken. Even though I knew relying on a memory of Master during my healing process was probably a very bad idea if I wanted to regain my independence, I couldn't resist the temptation of his strength. I wasn't at all sure if I could get through this without him.

I'll just think of him to get through this. Just for a little while, I rationalized.

I would deal with the ramifications later. Dr. Stanger said she could teach me to control my memories of what that Bastard had done to me. She would be able to help me overcome the enticing allure of memories of Master as well. Eventually.

But I might get Master into trouble if I told Dr. Stanger what had happened between him and me. She wanted me to share my safe memory with her. I had to make sure my admission wouldn't hurt him in some way.

"Do you work for the FBI?" I asked her warily.

"Yes," she said evenly. "But nothing you share with me will leave this room."

I wavered for a moment, unsure if I should believe her.

"You can trust me, Lydia," she reassured me. "This is solely about helping you heal. That's all that I'm concerned with."

I decided to take the leap. I needed advice on how to deal with what had happened with Master almost as badly as I needed help dealing with what that Bastard had done to me.

"If you've read my file, then you know that three weeks passed between when the FBI found me and when I was reunited with my family. Did it... Did it say where I was during that time?"

Dr. Stanger nodded. "After you were attacked at St. Paul's, you were taken to an FBI safe house at an undisclosed location."

A small sigh of relief escaped me. What Master had done wasn't part of the official record. Clayton must have kept his secret.

Even though I was discomfited by how I had behaved while I was with him, I didn't want Master to suffer any consequences. He had only ever tried to help me. And he had tried so hard to do the right thing, the decent thing. I was the one who finally broke him down and convinced him to touch me sexually.

And I didn't regret that, either.

"I wasn't at a safe house. I stayed at Ma- at Agent Smith James' apartment."

The sound of his real name issuing from my lips was strange; it was the first time I had ever voiced it aloud.

"And how did you end up there?"

"He was the one who found me at Decadence," I explained. "He was very disturbed by what had happened to me, and he stayed with me every day while I was at St. Paul's. He became invested in my recovery, and... And he understood a kind of treatment I needed that the doctors didn't."

I watched Dr. Stanger carefully as I made my next admission.

"He's a Dominant in the BDSM lifestyle, and he recognized that I needed very specific rules and structure in order to function in the state I was in. It wasn't his intention, but I immediately identified him as my new Master."

Dr. Stanger's expression didn't change one iota, but still I plowed on quickly, rushing to defend his actions.

"He wouldn't allow me to call him that, but I never stopped thinking it. It was only after that Bastard came back for me and I almost slipped back into the place where I had been when he found me that Ma- that Smith told me to call him 'Master.' He insisted on personally ensuring my safety after that, and he took me to his apartment."

A note of pleading entered my voice as I pressed on. Dr. Stanger had to understand that Master had done nothing wrong.

"All he wanted was to help me. He allowed the power dynamic because I wouldn't have been able to function on my own. A few times, he tried to tell me that he wasn't really my Master, but I couldn't handle his rejection. Everything just sort of... happened."

Dr. Stanger allowed me a moment of silence before she asked the question I had been dreading.

"Did your Master/slave relationship become sexual?"

"Yes," I admitted, but I shook my head at the same time. "But it wasn't like that. In the beginning, he just held me, comforted me. *I* was the one who tried to seduce *him.* I could tell he wanted me too, but he never allowed me to touch him like that."

"Why did that change?"

"Because I begged him to." It was a quiet utterance, and I forced my voice to be clearer. I might have been disturbed by my shocking level of dependence on him, but I wasn't ashamed of the fact that I had stood up for myself and reclaimed my sexual identity. "During my time with him, he slowly helped me remember who I was, who I had been before I was taken. I remembered that I had wanted a BDSM relationship, but the way that Bastard tortured me destroyed that. I asked – I insisted – that Master help me reclaim that part of myself. And he did."

I looked at Dr. Stanger steadily, significantly.

"He *did* help me. I wasn't even a person when he took me in. He helped me find myself again. And I... I loved him for that."

"So that's your safe memory, then? Being with him?"

"Yes," I said, my tone colored with uncertainty. "But that's wrong, isn't it? I thought of myself as his slave. Those memories... They shouldn't comfort me."

"You just referred to Agent James as 'Master.' Do you still think of yourself as his slave?"

I rolled the question around in my mind. *Did* I still think of myself as his slave? I certainly still thought of him as "Master."

My mind raced through my memories of my time with him, of how he had treated me.

"You're mine now."

His.

But not his slave. He had only called me "slave" once, when he had been desperate to snap me out of my catatonic state. Even that had been about helping me rather than degrading me. The whole time I had been with him, he encouraged me to make my own choices, to speak my own mind.

He hadn't been training a slave; he had been teaching me how to be myself again.

But he *had* been my Master. He had guided me and cared for me as a Dominant would care for his submissive.

"No," I said finally. "He never wanted me to think of myself as his slave. I understand that now."

"But you still think of him as 'Master'?"

"I've never known him as anything else."

No. That wasn't true. I called him "Master" because that was his title, his name. But I hadn't spent every minute mindlessly serving him. While I always had his pleasure in mind, there was more to our relationship than that. He wasn't simply some remote entity that I worshipped; he was a man. A wonderful, achingly beautiful man, but a man nonetheless.

He cussed worse than a sailor, he couldn't cook to save his life, and he had an almost unhealthy knowledge of every single action-comedy movie that had ever been filmed.

His body reacted like a man's, even when he didn't want it to.

He had made a mistake years ago, a mistake so terrible that he had permanently marked his body as a reminder not to do it again, to choose to be better.

He was fallible, flawed.

He was *real.*

That man was Smith James, I just hadn't known him by that name.

"That's not right," I corrected myself. "I think of 'Master' as his name, but I know him better than that. I… I miss him. And I'll never see him again."

My heart twisted agonizingly as I whispered the last words.

"The relationship you formed with him must be confusing, and I think it's something we should revisit after we deal with your trauma," Dr. Stanger said gently. "Do you want to pick a different memory for your safe memory?"

I considered for a moment. Yes, the memory of Master – of Smith – was upsetting in its own way. But now it was bittersweet rather than disturbing. And despite the pang that shot through my chest at the loss of him, no other memory came close to the bliss I had felt in his arms that day.

"No. I don't want to choose another memory."

Dr. Stanger nodded her agreement. If she thought my decision a poor one, she made no sign.

"I'm going to ask you to access a memory of your trauma now," she told me. "What we're going to do is called bilateral stimulation. I want you to pick a memory, and for thirty seconds, you'll focus on the negative thoughts, associations, and body sensations that memory elicits. During that time, you're going to follow the movements of my finger with your eyes. We'll repeat the process until the memory no longer causes those negative feelings. If you get upset, I want you to go to your positive memory."

I fixed the image of Master's face in my mind, focused on the feel of his heated, sweat-slicked body against mine. I savored the recollection of the pure joy that had flooded my system at the knowledge that we were inextricably bound.

The idea of facing the horrific things that had been done to me was terrifying, but – as he had done for me so many times before – Master would help me through it.

"Is there a recurring memory from your trauma that bothers you most often?"

I glanced down at the purple rings around my wrists and shuddered.

The day I was broken.

"Yes."

"Okay, Lydia. I want you to focus on that memory completely, every aspect of it. While you do, I want you to follow my finger with your eyes. This will only last for thirty seconds. Are you ready?"

I pictured Master's silver eyes one last time before I nodded.

Dr. Stanger began to move her finger from side to side, and my eyes followed it obediently as I forced myself to become immersed in my most horrifying memory.

The crack of the whip. The coppery smell of my own blood. The agony of my skin being sliced repeatedly, mercilessly.

Alone. Helpless. Hopeless.

I was gasping for air by the time Dr. Stanger's finger stopped its steady movements.

"Focus on your good memory, Lydia."

Ecstasy. Beauty. Completion. Joy.

Safe.

I didn't even realize that my fingers were locked around the silver chain that encircled my neck.

"Okay, Lydia. That was good. We're going to do it again. Are you ready?"

We repeated the process over and over again, until I lost count of the number of times I had been forced to relive what had happened to me. It was horrible, and several times I thought I was going to be sick.

But every time I thought I was about to be overwhelmed, Master calmed me.

I'm not sure how much time passed before Dr. Stanger broke our pattern.

"How did you feel that time?" She asked after she lowered her finger. "How do you feel when you think of that memory now?"

My mind instantly accessed it, but it didn't elicit the horror, the panic, that it once had. What had been done to me was still heinous, but now I controlled the memory rather than allowing it to control me.

"I feel... Well, not okay. But I don't want to throw up, either."

Dr. Stanger gave me a small smile.

"That's good. Now, we're going to apply a positive belief to the memory. Can you think of something good that came of it?"

I almost laughed.

Something good?

That Bastard and the Mentor had taken everything from me that day. They had taken my defiance, my free will, my soul. I had died that day.

No. That wasn't right. I still existed. Lydia Chase was still alive.

They hadn't broken me, after all.

I had saved myself. I had put Lydia Chase away somewhere out of their reach. They hadn't shattered my soul; I had protected it from them.

I was stronger than them. Stronger than their chains, their whips, their wills.

I nodded definitively, my back straightening as a new confidence and pride fortified my being. "Yes. There is something good: I survived."

We resumed the same therapeutic process, but this time I focused on the positive belief as I replayed the images of their torment in my mind.

By the time I walked out of Dr. Stanger's office, I felt more centered, more at peace, more powerful than I had in longer than I could recall.

And I had achieved that because of Master. Without the beautiful memory of our perfect night together, I wasn't at all sure if I could have overcome the terror of the day I thought I had been broken.

I toyed with my pendant as Officer Santino drove me back to Tucker's house.

Master.

Throughout the session, I had thought of him as "Master." That was the comforting memory, the safe memory. When I was in his care, nothing could hurt me.

But now he was "Smith" as well. And that imperfect man was every bit as wonderful as Master. In truth, one bled into the other; they were indivisibly intertwined.

I wouldn't want it any other way.

My soul screamed in protest of the idea that I would never see him again. I ached to return to him, to tell him that I didn't hold anything he had done against him. That he hadn't done anything wrong by me.

But I couldn't do that. I had committed to Tucker. I couldn't abandon him now, not when he was so relieved to have me back. Not when he so earnestly professed his love for me.

I was exhausted by the time I stepped up onto Tucker's front stoop. I paused for a moment before putting the key in the lock. Becs would be inside, waiting to have coffee with me. All I wanted to do was go to my bed and pass out, but I owed it to her to spend some time with her.

How had all of my cherished relationships become obligations?

Movement inside the townhouse caught my eye. I peered through one of the small windows that framed either side of the front door.

My mind temporarily went blank with shock.

Becs was waiting for me, all right. But she appeared to have decided to pass the time waiting by shoving her tongue down Tucker's throat. Her arms were twined around his neck, her body molded to his as she kissed him fiercely.

And he was kissing her back. Kissing her with a passion I hadn't seen in him in years.

Betrayal coiled in my gut, and my hand flew to the doorknob as I prepared to burst in on them and tell them just what shitty human beings they were.

Then they shifted, and I could see the tears that were streaming from Becs' closed eyes. Tucker's brows were drawn, the lines of his face strained as he hungrily, desperately, devoured her mouth.

I recalled how Tucker had leapt up from the couch when I had arrived home the night before, how Becs had blushed. How the touch of Tuck's hand on her arm as she left seemed to cause her physical pain.

Tuck had meant it when he said he loved me. And Becs had meant it when she said how much she had missed me, how glad she was to have me back.

But something had obviously happened between them in my absence. The raw need evident in the way they clung to each other was something I recognized: love.

My best friend and my husband had fallen in love with one another while I was being tortured and raped.

A strange mixture of conflicting emotions swirled within me. Before I could even begin to sort through them, Officer Santino's voice cut through my turmoil.

"Mrs. Chase?" He said my name questioningly. "You really should go inside. It's not safe for you to stay out here."

"Right," I said shakily. "Okay. Thanks."

He tipped his hat at me and headed back to his patrol car that would remain stationed outside the townhouse for the night.

I was careful to make a lot of noise while I unlocked the door, jiggling my key in the lock as though I was having difficulty with it.

Seconds later, Tucker opened the door for me. His cheeks were flushed, his eyes shining.

I pretended not to notice.

"Thanks," I said, as casually as I could manage. "The lock was sticking."

I stepped past him to find Becs in a similar state. She had managed to dry her cheeks, but her eyes were red-rimmed from crying. And her lips were swollen from the ferocity of Tucker's kiss.

That ugly, unpleasant sensation curled in my gut again, but I ruthlessly tamped it down. I had been through too much today; I had already gone through enough emotional turmoil to last a lifetime.

I plastered on my best attempt at a smile and tucked the upsetting situation away.

I would deal with it later.

Chapter 21

Nearly four weeks had passed since I had witnessed Tucker and Becs' betrayal, and I hadn't said a word about it to anyone. Becs might have suspected that something was up; I had ben dodging her at every opportunity. Once, she had come to the townhouse to hang out with me. And Tucker. The longing glances they shot each other from time to time set off that sick churning in my stomach. I couldn't help feeling jealous and angry at what they had done, but I also felt terrible for making them unhappy. They had already suffered so much because of me. Causing them further anguish only doubled the illness that gripped me when I was in their presence.

I had settled into a routine over that time. Routines were reassuring, providing a stability that I craved. Every morning, I worked with Dr. Stanger to overcome the horror associated with my memories of imprisonment. I would spend the afternoon with my parents – usually baking with my mom – and then I would go back to Tucker in the evening. Surrounding myself with my family helped me find the strength to overcome the exhaustion from my sessions with Dr. Stanger. My determination not to worry my family forced me to learn to master the residual trauma.

Between the intensive therapy and the presence of my loved ones, I was able to heal my mind a little more every day, re-claiming the identity of the strong, independent woman I had been before I was taken.

Memories of Master's calming aura helped me most of all. I still hadn't even begun to deal with the twisted nature of my feelings for him. I wasn't ready yet; I needed him too desperately to let him go.

My reliance on him was making my recommitment to Tucker that much more difficult. The atmosphere between us was awkward, our conversations stilted, but we both made an effort to communicate. Mostly, we talked about the past; we never touched on what had happened to me or what I had been doing in the months before I was abducted. Instead, we reminisced about the early years of our relationship, when we were still in love and the world had seemed so full of opportunity. It was as though we felt if we could just cling on to those memories tightly enough, we could re-create the love we had once known.

The futility of our efforts made me profoundly sad. But if we just kept at it, if we just tried hard enough, maybe we could come to accept our life together without bitterness.

Still, we slept separately every night – Tucker in his room and me in mine – and Tuck didn't try to kiss me again.

When the tension between us became too much to bear, I would retreat into my room and draw.

Dr. Stanger had recommended that I focus on my art every day. She told me the familiar habit that had once brought me such joy would help to calm me after our difficult sessions. Creating would also give me a sense of accomplishment and self-sufficiency.

While drawing did empower me, it also caused me pain. Whenever I touched pencil to paper, I couldn't help drawing *him.* When I flipped through my sketchbook, Smith's eyes stared back at me from every page.

There was something not quite right with the images; I never could manage to capture that elusive sense of power that emanated from him. All of my drawings were of Smith, and while he was beautiful, he didn't embody that sense of "Master."

It made me anxious. If I couldn't commit his image to paper, would I forget that side of him? Were my memories of him dulling already, slipping away from me?

Sometimes, I told myself it was for the best. My life with Tucker would be so much easier if I could allow Master to fade away.

But like the masochist I was, I couldn't stop indulging in my self-inflicted torment.

It took me twenty-six days, but I finally worked up the courage to talk to Dr. Stanger about it. I had tucked away the upsetting emotions elicited by the idea of Becs and Tucker together, had tried to suppress the painful thought of never seeing Master again, but they were insistently surfacing at every opportunity. Now that I had dulled the power that my memories of torture wielded over me, I recognized the need to also take control of the anguish-inducing memories I had formed since I had returned to my old life.

Dr. Stanger had moved on from employing EMDR as a treatment five days earlier, having determined that I was ready to talk about what had happened to me without curling into a ball and sobbing on her couch. Our conversations were still difficult, but I felt incredibly empowered by the realization that I could give voice to what had happened to me without succumbing to terror and despair. I felt more like myself than I had since my abduction, and yet I wasn't my old self in so many ways. Everything was different now, and I needed to learn how to exist in this new version of my world.

"Can I talk to you about something different today?" I asked Dr. Stanger as I settled down in my usual spot on the plush couch in her office.

"Of course," she said kindly. "You can talk to me about anything, Lydia."

I nodded my thanks. Dr. Stanger had already helped me so much. Surely she could help me with this, too.

"What we've been doing… It's made things so much better. I'm still having nightmares, but when I wake up I know that I'm okay. I don't completely fall apart anymore every time I think of that Bastard." I hesitated. "But now that I'm back, I feel like there isn't a place for me in my old life anymore. Everyone I love is different now; my disappearance changed them. I don't know how to erase that pain. I don't know how to make things right."

"Of course losing you affected your loved ones deeply, Lydia, but the pain that they suffered isn't your fault. The man who hurt you is also responsible for their hurt."

I shook my head. "I don't want to let him take anything from them. I'm taking myself back from him. How can I make things go back to the way they were?"

"You can't, Lydia," Dr. Stanger told me levelly. "And it's not good for you to take on their problems as well as your own. Everyone will adapt in time. Your relationships will never be exactly the same as they were, but that doesn't mean they can't be healed."

"But what if their relationship with me is hurting them?" I asked quietly.

"What do you mean, Lydia? Who do you think is hurting because of you?"

"My parents… I know they're happy to have me back. But thinking about what happened to me upsets them. Sometimes, my mom sees the scars around my wrists, and she looks like she's going to be sick. I don't want them to know everything I went through, but I can't shield them from that when… When he marked my body."

I couldn't suppress a shudder when my eyes riveted on the purple lines that ringed my wrists. I hated that the Bastard and the Mentor had done that to me. I could smooth the debilitating scars they had left on my mind, but I could never remove the marks they had left on my skin. They would serve as a constant reminder of the pain of my disappearance every time my loved ones saw them.

"If your parents would agree, I would like to have them come in with you for a joint session. It would be helpful for them if they understand how you're healing mentally. You won't have to tell them details of what happened to you, but they need to know that you want them to heal as well."

"Yes," I agreed. "I would like that."

"And what about your husband? Are the scars upsetting him as well? We could do a joint session with him."

I swallowed hard.

"Yes. Yes, they upset him. But… It's so much more complicated than that with Tuck. We were separated at the time I was abducted. We had been essentially living separate lives for two years before that. We were like very good friends who happened to live together. I wanted a divorce; I knew that being tied to me was holding him back. Neither of us was happy with what our lives had become, and I wanted him to be free just as much as I wanted freedom for myself. But Tucker doesn't believe in divorce, and there was a lot of pressure from our families to stick it out."

"So now that you're back, you don't know if it's right for you to abandon him again," Dr. Stanger concluded perceptively.

"Yes." I traced the curve of my wedding ring with my thumb. "I decided I owed it to him, to my parents, to make things work with him. But then I found out… I saw him kissing my best friend. And I can tell they're in love."

I paused, staring at Dr. Stanger beseechingly. I needed her to help me sort through the myriad emotions that wracked me at the memory of their passionate kiss.

"It's not uncommon for people to come together over a loss," she said gently.

"But now I'm keeping them apart. I'm making them unhappy," I said anxiously. "But it's not right for me to leave Tucker. Not when he doesn't want a divorce. Not when a part of him still loves me."

"Do you love him?"

"I always will. He's been a huge part of my life, and he's never done anything wrong towards me. We just grew up and we grew apart. I feel like being tied to me, having to provide for us, has kept him from being the person he was supposed to be. It kept both of us from the lives we wanted."

I drew in a shaky breath before making my next admission.

"And… And I can't stop thinking about Smith. I know it's wrong, and what I thought was love was actually obsession. But the idea of never seeing him again is tearing me apart. How can I commit to Tucker when I'll always want someone else? When I know he'll always want someone else?"

"You just referred to Agent James as 'Smith,' not 'Master,'" Dr. Stanger pointed out. "It's undeniable that your relationship with him stemmed from a very unhealthy place. But you've recognized that you're not his slave, and that he's a man rather than an infallible entity to be blindly obeyed."

"So you think it would be okay for me to go back to him?" I asked disbelievingly, hopefully.

"I think you need to deal with your feelings for him if you're going to heal fully. I think you should be happy, and you can't do that until you confront what happened between the two of you."

She speared me with a significant look.

"After everything you've been through, don't you think you deserve happiness, Lydia? It seems to me that you've been chronically concerned with pleasing the people around you for your entire adult life. You need to live for yourself. Your loved ones will be happy to see you happy, even if they aren't entirely comfortable with your choices."

I bit my lip, unsure.

"So you think I should divorce Tuck and try to work things out with Smith?"

"Even now you're more concerned with how your actions will affect other people than you are with doing what *you* want to do. What I think doesn't matter, Lydia. What matters is that you do whatever will make you happiest. You said you feel like your marriage has kept you from having the life you wanted for yourself. Now that you have your life back, don't you think you owe it to yourself to live it as you want to?"

"I… Don't I owe it to the people I love to ensure their happiness after I've caused them so much grief?"

"You can't ensure anyone's happiness but your own, and the grief they suffered is not your fault," Dr. Stanger said firmly. "You can't allow your own happiness to hinge upon theirs, because it's not within your power to change the people around you. It's time for you to live for yourself, Lydia."

I was still turning Dr. Stanger's words over in my mind that afternoon as I pulled the cherry pie that my mom and I had baked out of the oven. She was seated at the island countertop in the center of the kitchen, knitting a scarf for me while watching me all too perceptively. I could sense some motherly advice coming, and I decided to duck out before the barrage of questioning could begin.

"Is Dad in his office?" I asked quickly as I removed the oven mitts from my hands. "I should let him know that the pie will be cool enough to eat soon."

Mom snorted. "If you tell him, good luck getting a piece for yourself. You know he'll devour the whole thing if you don't fight him off with a fork."

My grin was genuine. Dad could put away pastries. I had no idea how he stayed as trim as he did. I had always lamented the fact that I hadn't inherited his metabolism, but now I was glad of it. Thanks to the copious amounts of baked goods I had been consuming, I was putting some weight back on. My clothes still didn't fit quite right, but they weren't hanging off me either.

"Well, you'd better go ahead and arm yourself, then," I warned my mom as I headed towards Dad's office. "I'm telling him it's ready."

As was typical, I found Dad frowning at his computer screen, his brow creased with concentration as he worked on his latest article for the *Chicago Tribune*.

"What are we working on today?" I asked, a teasing note in my voice. "A serious critique of our corrupt politicians or a snappy piece on a local art fair?"

I knew it was likely more in the vein of the latter. Dad didn't do serious. He took great pride in peppering his articles on cultural events with groan-inducing puns.

"Neither," he replied, his tone a touch embarrassed. "I'm working on Flip Words."

"Well, I caught you at a good time then. You can come eat some cherry pie while you're taking a break."

He sighed heavily, and his eyes were sad when they found mine.

"I'm not taking a break, Di. I'm retired now."

"Retired?" I was shocked. "You've always said you would probably die at your keyboard. What about your last words being a truly amazing pun?"

His gaze dropped from mine.

"I haven't felt much like joking over the past year," he said quietly.

A lump instantly formed in my throat as grief swelled within me. What had happened to me had caused so much damage.

Dr. Stanger was right: I wasn't responsible for their unhappiness. It wasn't my fault that I had been abducted. But I wasn't about to let that Bastard keep pieces of the people I loved. If I was going to take back my own life from him, then they would reclaim what they had lost as well.

I skirted around Dad's desk and wrapped my arm around his shoulders.

"It's over now, Dad," I reassured him softly. "I'm back, and I'm rebuilding my life. I'm not going to let what he did to me ruin me. And I won't let him hurt you, either. Not anymore. You should go back to work, Dad. You love what you do."

He stood, pulling me into a tight embrace. His tears wet my hair as he leaned into me.

"Di," he said hoarsely. "It's so good to hear you bossing me around again."

A shaky laugh escaped me. "I guess I really am getting better. I just want you to be happy, Dad."

He pulled back from me slightly, but he still kept his hands around my shoulders. His eyes searched my face.

"That's all I want for you, too, honey. That's all any of us want for you. Your mother and I, Tucker…"

He paused at the sight of my pained expression.

"Your mother told me how you feel about Tuck," he said quietly. "I know she convinced you to stay with him. But is that what *you* want?"

It was the same question Dr. Stanger had asked me. And I knew my answer all too well.

"It's the right thing to do," I said, but I couldn't fully conceal the resignation, the regret, in my tone.

"Honey, the only 'right' thing to do is the thing that makes you happiest. If you want to move to Nebraska and dig ditches, I'll support you. Of course, I would follow you to make sure you didn't dig yourself into too deep a hole."

I couldn't hold back my laugh. "That was terrible, Dad. One of the weakest puns I've ever heard from you. In fact, I'm not sure if that even qualifies as a pun. You'll have to step up your game if you're going to start writing again."

He chuckled at me. "I guess I'll just have to get in some practice."

I gave a dramatic groan. "Practice on your keyboard, please, and save the rest of us the pain. I'll make you a deal: you can eat the entire cherry pie if I don't have to hear one pun for the rest of the afternoon."

His lips pursed in mock-consideration. "You drive a hard bargain, Di. I suppose I could do that, if you can keep your mother from pestering me about it."

"Agreed," I said quickly. "Once I tell her the terms, I'm sure you won't hear a peep out of her."

He clapped me on the shoulder, smiling.

Then his eyes turned serious again.

"I meant what I said, Di. Do what makes you happy. I'll deal with your mother if she flies off the handle. She'll come around eventually."

I hugged him again, breathing in his peppermint and tweed scent as I rested my head on his shoulder.

"Thanks, Dad," I whispered. "I needed to hear that."

■■■

Tears of wonder and sentiment welled in my eyes as I stared hungrily at Georges Seurat's *Seated Woman with a Parasol*. It was my favorite work of art housed at the Art Institute of Chicago. The century-old black Conté crayon-on-ivory paper drawing had been a conceptual effort in preparation for Seurat's *A Sunday on La Grande Jatte*, but for me it held every bit as much majesty as that famous work.

Granny had brought me to the Institute to study it when she was teaching me about shading. I was eleven years old at the time. After her death four years later, I had come here often to visit the drawing, to remember her.

Tucker's fingers touched my hand tentatively, closing around mine when I didn't flinch away.

I turned my watering eyes on him. "Tuck…" I swallowed against the tightness in my throat and squeezed his hand. "Thanks for bringing me here."

As soon as I had returned to his townhouse that evening, he had insisted that we come here. He knew me so well. He knew how much this place meant to me.

"I have something I want to tell you, baby," he said seriously, his own eyes clouded with emotion. "I want you to go to Notre Dame and get your BFA. After what happened… You should have everything you've always wanted. You should pursue your art."

My heart swelled with affection even as it ached to recognize that what he was saying was impossible. "You know we can't afford that, Tuck. You must have cut in to a lot of your savings covering the rent on the townhouse by yourself. In a few weeks, I'm going to see if I can get my job at Real Listings back."

"No, Lydia," he said firmly. "You hated it there. I've put out some applications for a second job. You can go to school full time, and we'll be able to squeak by without having to take out any loans." He gave me a small smile. "Then, when you're a famous artist, you can share your millions with me."

"I can't let you do that, Tuck. I *won't* let you do that."

I took a deep breath. It was time to stop Tucker before he gave up even more of his life, more of his self, for me.

"I know about you and Becs," I said quietly.

Panic flashed across his features.

"Lydia, I… We spent so much time together after you… It just sort of happened." His eyes were tight with desperation, with anguish. "But it's over now. You and I are going to be together. I promised you forever, and -"

I pressed two fingers to his lips, stopping him short.

"It's okay, Tuck. I'm not angry. I… I want you to be happy. You said I should have everything I've ever wanted. I want the same for you." I regarded him seriously. "Do you love me, Tucker?"

"Of course," he breathed. "Always."

"Are you in love with me?"

His soft blue eyes searched my face. They were filled with both longing and regret. He wanted so badly to be able to answer in the affirmative. But we both knew it would be a lie.

"No."

He blinked, as though surprised to hear the word fall from his lips.

"So, I guess that's it, then," he said, his voice trembling slightly. "This is the end of us."

I touched my hand to his cheek. "No, Tuck. There'll never be an end for us. We'll always be a part of each other. But this is the beginning of our lives. The lives we never got to have together."

He leaned into me, and his mouth softly touched mine. We poured the last of our love into the kiss. Every tug of our lips pulled the pain of years wasted from our souls, purging the bitterness that had weighed us down for so long.

When we went back to the townhouse for the night, we had a long talk about our respective futures. It was the most comfortable, genuine conversation we had shared since my return. The eager excitement that pulsed around us filled the living room with a shared joy that had been absent for years.

I was going to find a part time job and take out student loans so I could finally get my BFA. My parents had always told me it was irresponsible to have debts, but I was following my own heart now. My father had given me his blessing. Even if I never made a dime off my drawings, I would have achieved one of my biggest dreams. A dream that had seemed unattainable only that morning.

And I was going to go back to Smith. I didn't tell Tucker that part of my plan, though. There was a chance – a very big one – that Smith would reject me. He was obviously deeply disturbed by what had happened between us. I wasn't going to tell anyone in my life about Smith until I was sure of his response.

I spoke openly with Tucker about his romantic life. I gave him my blessing to be with Becs. It would be awkward to see them together, but I wanted both of them in my life, no matter what.

Tucker was going to start writing music again. Like me with my art, he wasn't sure if anything would come of it, but success didn't matter. Music was at the core of Tuck's being, and he had shut that part of himself off for far too long.

We shared a bed that night, for the first time in years and for the last time ever. There was nothing sexual about the way we held one another; it was an expression of intimacy that was deeper than physical passion.

Our joy was undiminished in the morning. There was no sense of reluctance or regret over our decision.

I grinned when Tucker met me in the living room for breakfast. He was wearing a red flannel shirt and light-wash jeans. The shirt was unbuttoned, hanging open to reveal his green Jimmy Eat World t-shirt. Everything clashed horribly.

"What are you smiling about?" He asked suspiciously.

I stepped towards him, meeting him in the center of the room so I could smooth out his rumpled collar.

"You look like Tucker."

He laughed. "Thanks?"

"Don't worry. It's definitely a compliment. You don't look like a nondescript cog in the corporate wheel anymore."

Tuck was reclaiming his identity, just as I had reclaimed my own. We were ready to go our own ways, but we would never truly be parted from one another.

I took his left hand in my right, lifting it up between us. My fingers touched his wedding band. I gave him a soft smile as I said my loving goodbye.

"I, Lydia Chase, take you, Tucker Chase, to be my constant friend. I offer you my solemn vow to be your faithful partner in sickness and in health, in good times and in bad, and in joy as well as in sorrow. I promise to love you unconditionally, to support you in your goals, to honor and respect you, to laugh with you and cry with you, and to cherish you for as long as we both shall live."

Tucker mirrored my movements, taking my other hand in his and echoing my altered recitation of our wedding vows. He smiled down at me gently as we both removed the gold bands from each other's fingers at the same time. He pressed his own into my palm and closed my hand around it, raising my fist to softly brush his lips over my knuckles.

A gratingly familiar scream tore through our tender moment. We both jumped, our attention whipping to the TV, which had suddenly turned on of its own accord.

For a few seconds, my mind rejected the horror of what I was seeing.

A thin, wasted version of me filled the screen, her face contorted in pain as her tormentor ruthlessly held her down, tearing her unwilling body as he pounded into her.

Then *his* voice, clear and matter-of-fact, overrode the sounds of my agony.

"I don't share my toys."

The screen went black.

The sounds of glass shattering and Tucker's grunt were almost simultaneous.

Tucker looked down at his own chest, a shocked expression on his face. A crimson stain was blooming on his t-shirt.

He collapsed to the floor, and I followed him down.

"Tucker!"

My hands fluttered around him uselessly as the gory stain grew, widening outward from a neatly circular little hole in the center of his chest.

His body jerked. Once. Twice.

He drew in a shuddering breath. His eyes stared in abject terror at something I couldn't see.

The air left his lungs with a horrible rattle.

The taut lines of his face eased, his eyes drooping half-closed.

"Tuck!" I shrieked his name as I gripped his shoulders, shaking him hard.

He didn't respond.

I threw my body atop his, hugging him to me with the same fierce desperation that we had held each other on the night he had proposed to me. If I just held him tightly enough, everything would be okay. Everything would work out.

There were loud voices behind me. The wails of sirens screeched their way into the townhouse through the broken window.

I ignored them. I couldn't let go of Tuck.

Hands closed around my shoulders, prying me away from him. I screamed and twisted and fought.

Didn't they understand that I couldn't let Tuck go? I had to hold him. If I didn't, everything would fall apart.

Something sharp pierced my upper arm. Darkness swirled at the edges of my vision, and my muscles turned watery.

No!

I couldn't lose sight of Tucker.

My fingers loosened as I lost control of my limbs, and Tucker's ring bounced against the hardwood floor.

I struggled against my darkening vision, willing my eyes to remain focused on Tucker. His face – oddly slack, but his mouth still open in a silent scream of shocked protest – was the last thing I saw before I was pulled under.

It was the last time I would ever see him.

Chapter 22

Agent Byrd's face was fuzzy when it appeared above me. I blinked several times to clear the fog from my eyes, but it still lingered in my mind. I glanced around, gauging my surroundings. I was lying on a bed in a small, sparsely decorated bedroom. Frowning, I returned my gaze to Kate.

The lines of her face were concerned, sympathetic.

I didn't understand what was happening.

"Where am I?" My voice was little more than a croak. Why did my throat feel so raw?

"You're at a safe house," she told me gently. "The medics had to sedate you. You were very... distressed."

Sedate me?

I just blinked at her, nonplussed.

"We're looking for the sniper now," she continued carefully. "Can you tell me what happened from your perspective? The more time passes, the harder it will be for us to track the guy who shot Tucker."

Glass shattering. Tuck's soft blue eyes, wide and terrified. A gory red stain spreading across his t-shirt.

I shook my head sharply, shoving the memories away. It was a practice with which I was all too familiar. My mind couldn't acknowledge the full horror of what had happened.

Tucker and I were going to be happy. We had vowed to love and support one another for the rest of our lives.

The rest of our lives.

"Lydia?" Kate prompted me.

No. It hadn't happened. I couldn't exist if Tucker didn't. I didn't know how to exist in a world without him.

I turned away from Kate, curling up on my side as I hugged my knees to my chest.

"If you get upset, I want you to go to your positive memory."

This time my mind didn't select the recollection of being held by Master after we had joined for the first and only time. I turned to the memory of kneeling at his feet instead, his fingers brushing the top of my head as I clung to his leg.

Safe. Calm.

I didn't have to worry about anything, because I wasn't in control. My wishes, my thoughts, didn't matter.

Closing my eyes, I sank into the memory.

I was dimly aware of Kate speaking to me, her hand touching my shoulder insistently.

I ignored her.

I would stay with Master. Master would keep me safe. He would take care of me.

* * * *

"Hey, Lydia." I instantly recognized Clayton's kind, rumbling voice as it drifted down to me. "You should get up and eat something."

I ignored him, too. He wanted me to return to the present. He wanted to ask me questions.

But I wasn't going anywhere. I was going to stay with Master.

Several beats of silence passed before Clayton sighed resignedly.

"Lydia." His voice was deep, commanding. "Sit up. Now."

My limbs jerked, instinctively moving to obey the order of a Dominant. I squeezed my eyes shut tighter and resolutely resisted the urge.

"I won't tell you again." This time, a hint of a threat darkened his hard tone.

Stiffly, I unfurled my arms from around my knees and stretched out my legs from where they had been curled up to my chest. Even once I had pushed myself into a sitting position at the edge of the bed, I didn't look up at Clayton. I didn't allow my vision to focus on anything so that I could remain in some sort of blank limbo where nothing was real. If nothing was real, then nothing could hurt me.

A foil wrapper crinkled, and a half-unwrapped protein bar appeared in front of my face.

"Eat."

Mechanically, I opened my mouth and bit into it. The strawberry and oatmeal flavors tasted like ashes in my mouth. I gagged as my body rebelled against the sustenance.

"Swallow."

The order helped give me the resolve to force my tongue and throat to work.

"Again. Finish it."

I blindly obeyed. Following orders was easy. I didn't have to think. I fell further into my fantasy, a blissfully simple reality in which I had no responsibilities, no cares, no will of my own.

A small, round blue pill appeared in Clayton's large hand.

"Take it."

My fingers shook slightly, but I popped it into my mouth. Clayton held a glass of water to my lips, and I drank.

His heat withdrew from me. I didn't move.

He cursed under his breath.

"Lie down."

I settled back down on my side, closing my eyes as I resumed my earlier protective position.

Clayton began murmuring, but his words weren't aimed at me.

"You need to get your ass here. Now."

Pause.

"No. She's a mess. And I don't know how to deal with this."

Pause.

"I tried topping her. I don't know how you did it, but I just can't. It feels so wrong."

A part of my mind registered that Clayton was talking to someone on the phone. I couldn't summon up any curiosity over whom he was speaking to. What he was doing didn't concern me. What I thought didn't matter.

"Stop angsting like a teenage girl and get your ass to Chicago. She needs you right now. You can go back to beating yourself up about it later."

Clayton stopped talking. His conversation was finished. The chair in the corner of the room creaked slightly as he settled down onto it with a sigh.

I went back to ignoring him. Whatever pill he had given me made that even easier as it further cushioned my mind in fluffy clouds.

* * * *

The door clicked open. One pair of footsteps entered, another exited. The door thudded closed softly.

"Open your eyes, Lydia."

My fantasy was becoming remarkably vivid. Or maybe it wasn't a fantasy after all. I wasn't sure anymore.

The sense of power that always pulsed around Master enfolded me like a tangible thing. I reveled in it, mentally drawing it closer, welcoming it to smother me and put an end to everything that wasn't him.

"Look at me, girl." The command was sharper this time, cutting through my haze with painfully sweet clarity.

My eyes snapped open. His steady silver stare was the most beautiful thing I could ever recall.

"Master." His name was a relieved, ragged whisper as it clawed its way up my ravaged throat.

I was instantly on my knees before him. The scent of amber and whiskey washed over me, bringing with it a wave of calm.

God, this was so much better than any fantasy.

Tears of joy sprang to my eyes when his large, warm hand settled on the top of my head, his fingers working through my hair. Sighing happily, I leaned against him, giving myself to him completely.

"You're okay, sweetheart. I've got you."

For a few glorious minutes, the world was exactly as it should be: blissfully calm, perfectly simple.

But a dull sense of panic began pulsing insistently at the back of my mind. For some reason I couldn't quite grasp, Master's presence was inducing a sharp fear within me.

My eyes darted around the room of their own accord, searching for a window. I found nothing but blank, pale yellow walls. But my terror only increased as the worry ratcheted up another notch.

Master's hand stilled its steady stroking.

"What's wrong, sweetheart?"

I scrambled away from him with a gasp. Something was wrong. Master couldn't be here. He couldn't be with me.

"You have to leave," I insisted shakily.

His expression tightened, and pain flashed across his gorgeous eyes. He gave me a short nod.

"Fair enough," he bit out.

He turned to leave, and I couldn't bear the sight of the tension in his shoulders as he clenched his fists at his sides.

"Wait!"

He pivoted, raising a cool eyebrow at me.

"I don't want you to go."

His lips thinned to a dangerous line. "You really should make up your mind, girl. I won't tolerate this much longer." His nostrils flared angrily, but the tight lines around his eyes betrayed hurt.

I shook my head against the increasing pain of my dawning realization.

"I don't want you to leave. But if he knows you're with me… He'll kill you. Just like… He killed Tucker. Oh, god, he killed Tucker!" I shrieked the last words, tangling my fingers in my hair as I tried to physically rip the image of his terrified eyes from my mind.

Master's hands closed around my wrists, firmly halting my efforts to tear out my hair. He crouched down beside me where I was sprawled on the floor and wrapped his arms around me, lifting me up and cradling me against his chest.

He murmured a stream of soothing words as I cried against him, my punishing sobs ripping their way up my abused throat. I realized it was raw from my screaming as I had fought the people who pried me away from Tucker's body.

His body.

The soulless shell I had left bleeding on the living room floor hadn't been Tucker anymore.

Tucker was dead. My first love, my one-time partner, my lifelong friend, was gone.

I had taken back the parts of myself that the Bastard had stolen from me, and in retaliation, he had taken Tucker.

When my ribs felt like they would crack if my chest convulsed one more time, my body finally gave up on sobbing. I heaved in deep, shuddering breaths. My lungs burned in protest of the sudden overdose of oxygen.

"That's it, sweetheart," Master said softly. "Breathe."

He touched his lips to my forehead, and a delighted shiver raced across my skin, through my soul. The pure comfort elicited by the gesture gave me the courage to speak again, to face the horror of my current reality.

"What..." I swallowed. "What's happening now?"

His hand cupped my jaw, angling my face so I was staring up at him. I drank in the sight of him hungrily now that my lucidity had fully returned to me.

"CPD is working with the Chicago branch of the FBI to track the sniper." He wasn't cautious or careful in the way he delivered the information. He spoke to me calmly, steadily. It helped quiet my own mind as I absorbed what he was saying.

"Based on the bullet's trajectory, the shooter was situated on the roof of the apartment block across the street from Tucker's townhouse. We've been going through traffic cameras in the area to see if we can get an ID on the guy, but the feed was looped on every camera in the area within an hour window of the shooting."

His expression was grim, angry.

"We still don't have any leads on the Bastard's identity. Whoever the fuck he is, he's got way too much knowledge of how to cover up the evidence that would help our investigation. He can't be an ordinary civilian." His eyes were regretful as they focused back on me. "I'm sorry, Lydia. Can you tell me what happened from your perspective? Anything you saw, no matter how insignificant it seems, might help us."

I shuddered. What I had seen wasn't remotely insignificant. Now that I was no longer shutting it away, I found the memory readily available in sharp, horrible detail. It was burned into my brain as though by a brand.

"Tuck-" His name stuck in my throat. "We were in the living room."

The image of Tucker's soft, fond smile as he placed his wedding ring in my hand and kissed my knuckles made me flinch.

Master's thumb traced the line of my jaw soothingly, his touch keeping me tethered to him.

"The TV turned on, and…" I swallowed against the metallic tang in the back of my throat. "There was a video of me. And *him*." I cringed. I hadn't realized he had been filming me. The idea of that Bastard having those days of my torment readily available for him to enjoy again and again made my gut clench painfully. I had thought I was free from him, but he still owned pieces of me.

"What was happening in the video?" Master's voice was tight as he pressed me. He didn't want to hear it any more than I wanted to say it. But if it could help the FBI catch the man who had taken Tuck from me, I would tell him.

"He was raping me." My voice was barely audible. Master's muscles flexed around me as he fought to physically contain his fury. I forced myself to continue on. "Then his voice… He said, *'I don't share my toys.'* And then… Then he shot Tucker."

I stared up at Master – at Smith – imploringly.

"Please leave," I rasped. "He'll kill you too if he knows I've been with you." I couldn't live with it if anything happened to him because of me. My mind had refused to function in the face of Tucker's death. It would shatter completely if Smith was taken from me as well. No amount of therapy would be able to heal my broken soul if I lost both of them.

Smith's arms tightened around me as his eyes glinted steel.

"If you think for one second that I'm going to leave you because I'm afraid of that Bastard, you really have lost your goddamn mind, sweetheart."

"*I'm* afraid," I countered softly. "Please, Master. Please go." I used his title in a show of supplication, praying he would listen to the respectful request. I suspected an outright demand would only make him dig in his heels further.

But my tactic made no difference.

"I'm not going anywhere." His firm promise filled me with despair. "You'll accept that, girl."

But I wasn't his slave anymore. I never had been. The right to refuse him, to defy him, had always been mine. I just hadn't realized it before.

"No. I won't accept it," I declared staunchly. "Leave, Smith." I pushed against his chest in order to free myself from his hold. He didn't even seem aware of my efforts.

His brows rose in surprise as he drew in a shocked breath at the sound of his name on my tongue. Then his lips curved into a smile, and he chuckled.

"Nice try, sweetheart. But I don't follow orders."

"But -"

Smith gently covered my mouth with his hand, smothering my protest.

"I'm not saying this as your Master. You have every right to tell me what to do. But that doesn't mean I have to listen. And I won't. As Clayton will happily tell you, I'm a pigheaded asshole." His jaw firmed, and the amusement left his eyes. "I'm going to find the fucker who hurt you, Lydia. So I'll only be leaving you when I'm not out hunting him. Is that clear?"

His hand left my mouth, his questioning eyes demanding my affirmative answer. Anger swelled within me.

"The only thing that's clear to me is that you're a goddamn idiot as well as a pigheaded asshole," I hissed.

There was a sharp edge to his pleased grin.

"I don't know where you picked up that kind of language, sweetheart, but it really doesn't suit you."

My anger flared at his lighthearted reaction to my fearful demands. Couldn't he understand I needed to keep him safe?

"Listen to me, Sm-"

My heated words melted into a groan when he brought his mouth down on mine, and something darker than anger flared deep within me. He took advantage of my parted lips, penetrating them with his tongue, moving it against mine in firm, dominant strokes. I shivered in his grip, instantly relaxing into his arms as my body eagerly ceded to his control. His low, approving growl reverberated through my mind and rumbled through my flesh, concentrating at the heated place between my legs.

The release brought on by my submission to him was heady. His lips drew my grief and my fear from me and took them into himself, helping me shoulder their seemingly insurmountable weight.

My hands fisted in his shirt, clinging to him more tightly. His fingers sank into my hair in response, holding me in place so I couldn't escape him even if I wanted to.

And I didn't want to. I never wanted to.

When he finally pulled away from me, I was gasping for breath, my head spinning from the high of his kiss. I was shocked to realize that his chest was rising and falling rapidly as he drew in ragged breaths of his own

"God, I've missed you, Lydia," he said, his voice rough with longing and regret.

I touched my fingers to his brow, trying to smooth the creases that had appeared there. He was obviously still unsure about what had happened between us. But I wasn't. I would help him to see that he had done nothing wrong.

"I've missed you too, Smith," I said softly.

One corner of his lips quirked up in a lopsided smile, and his eyes glowed molten silver.

"Do you have any idea how goddamn sweet my name sounds on your lips?"

My breath caught in my throat at the intensity of his words. Before I could remember how to breathe again, he crushed his lips to mine, devouring the sweetness there.

Suddenly, breathing didn't matter anymore. The twisted nature of the beginning of our relationship didn't matter. The fact that there was a sadistic man stalking me didn't matter.

Nothing mattered but the sensation of his tongue moving against mine, the comfort of his powerful arms holding me.

Safe.

Chapter 23

The loss of Smith's heat roused me instantly. His body had remained shaped around mine throughout the night, his presence the only thing keeping my sanity intact when I awoke from nightmares of Tucker's lifeless eyes.

The weak light of dawn filtered through the crack at the bottom of the door, the only source of illumination in the windowless room. Even though Smith was no more than a darker shadow in the indigo gloom, my eyes found him straightaway.

He bent to silently retrieve his belt, tie, and shoes, the only articles of clothing he had removed before climbing into bed with me. I had craved the sweet sensation of his skin against mine, but he had refused.

Master had demanded that I relent. I knew my protests were useless when he called upon that side of himself.

It seemed I had more protests to voice this morning.

"Where are you going?" I asked, my voice not in the least bit meek.

Smith paused.

"That bossy tone is going to take some getting used to," he said, evidently amused. "But I don't mind. I like a challenge."

"This isn't a game, Smith."

My hot words only elicited a laugh. "You sound like Clayton. Minus the expletives."

"Fine. Where the fuck do you think you're going?"

I had never been one to cuss, but if that was what it took to get his attention, I would gladly curse up a storm.

He just laughed again. "Nice try, little one, but I don't listen to Clayton, either. Besides, I thought I told you that sort of language doesn't suit you."

His voice had taken on a huskier edge, and he slowly, languidly approached me. I should have been thrilled with my small victory; my crass words had kept him from leaving me. But all I could think of was how badly I wanted him to touch me. I sat stock still where I had pushed myself up on my elbows, my breaths turning shallow as the predator slinked toward me.

More soft light had filtered into the room with the rising sun, and all of it seemed to have been absorbed by his gleaming metallic eyes. Despite the fact that everything about his demeanor communicated an approaching threat, my body remained frozen, trapped in rapt fascination as I watched his graceful movements.

His forefinger stroked a feather-light line down my vulnerable neck, pausing on my carotid artery. His teeth flashed white in a pleased, hard edged-grin as he enjoyed the feel of my racing pulse under his touch. I hardly breathed when his hand gently cupped my neck, his thumb resting across my throat in a silent threat. A shiver raced across my skin at the ultimate show of dominance, and my body compliantly eased back onto the pillows as he guided me down with only the barest pressure.

His thumb brushed up and down over my artery as his lips softly caressed mine, reinforcing my utter helplessness in his grip. He caught my raw, animalistic whimper in his mouth, savoring it. His tongue demanded more of the sweet flavor of the sound of his victory over me, and he stroked into my mouth in teasing forays.

When he had consumed his fill, he pulled back from me just enough so that his lips still teased across mine as he spoke.

"I'm going to work for the day. You're going to stay here and mind Clayton like a good girl."

His fingers squeezed ever so slightly around my neck as he nipped at my lower lip, reinforcing his order.

I found myself nodding my acquiescence automatically. "Yes, Master."

I shook my head sharply, struggling to shake off his intoxicating power. "I mean no." My protest was laughably weak. I cleared my throat and tried again. "If you refuse to leave Chicago and insist on staying with me, then you're going to stay with me in the safe house."

He growled in disapproval at my demand, and he moved to press his lips against mine again, to further drug me with his kiss. I wrenched my head to the side, desperate to keep my wits about me.

"Please, listen to me. I know you're not afraid of him, but you can't stop a bullet. I can't let him take you from me. He already… He already took Tuck. Please don't go after him, Master."

The shadows that were retreating in the wake of the sunlight pooled beneath the suddenly taut lines of his face as he pulled away from me.

"I'm not your Master, Lydia," he said, his efforts at a cool tone ruined by the jagged edge to his words. "What I did was wrong. What I'm doing now is wrong. Fuck," he muttered. "All I wanted was to help you, to keep you safe. But I kept you from your life. I kept you from your husband." His lips twisted bitterly.

I touched my hand to his forearm. His muscles were tense beneath my fingers.

"You did nothing wrong," I insisted softly.

Self-loathing bled into his features. "The fact that you think that just proves how thoroughly I fucked things up. I knew how vulnerable you were, and instead of helping you find yourself again, I kept you in your slave mindset. I didn't want that for you, but that doesn't change the fact that I did it. It doesn't change the fact that I took advantage of you."

"You're wrong," I said firmly. "I've thought about this a lot. I won't deny that my mind was warped when you found me. I won't deny that I was obsessed with you from the very beginning, when you showed me kindness. I had forgotten kindness existed. What you did for me – providing me with rules and structure – *was* a kindness. I wasn't even a person then, much less Lydia Chase. I couldn't face how far I had fallen, how I had been degraded. If she had been thrust back on me all at once, I wouldn't have been able to handle it. I might have rejected her forever. You made me feel safe enough that I slowly re-discovered myself without even realizing it."

The yearning that stirred in his eyes communicated that he was desperate to believe me, but it didn't fully drive away the anguish that flooded their silvery depths.

"I'm glad to hear that, Lydia. That's what I wanted, what I had hoped to do for you. But I took things too far. I fell into the illusion I had created for you. You were so sweet, so trusting. And when you said you needed me… Fuck, Lydia. The Dom in me couldn't help but respond to that."

"I did need you."

He shook his head, his shoulders slumping slightly. "You thought you did because of the roles I allowed us to slip into. If I hadn't allowed you to see me as your Master, you wouldn't have felt the need to interact with me sexually. That's all you knew then. You had been abused into thinking that the only way you could demonstrate your submission was by giving your body. I should have controlled myself. Hell, I shouldn't have let things get that far. As soon as I found out about Chicago, as soon as I learned your name, I should have gone to the Bureau and tracked down your family."

"But I didn't want to go. I wasn't ready to face my old life then. You just honored my wishes. You respected what I needed."

"No, Lydia," he said harshly. "I didn't *want* to let you go. Don't make excuses for what I did. I've played them through my own head thousands of times. I'm sick to death of them. Because none of them justify what I allowed to happen between us. None of them justify my selfish decision to keep you."

"I don't regret what happened between us, Smith," I said quietly. "Please don't say that you do."

His brows drew together, and he shifted uncomfortably. "Lydia, I..."

"Don't say it." This time it was a desperate demand. "You swore you wouldn't lie to me. So don't you dare say you regret it."

He pursed his lips together, choosing to say nothing rather than admit aloud that he wouldn't go back and change what he had done if he could.

"I wouldn't have healed at all if it weren't for you," I continued in the wake of his silence. "Everything I told you that day was true: that Bastard chose me because I liked pain. I had only just begun exploring BDSM when he abducted me. He took everything I had secretly desired for so long and twisted it until it became something foul and wrong."

Fury flashed across Smith's features at the mention of the man who had tortured me. Bolstered by his response, I pressed on. The Dom in him hadn't been able to resist my plea for help on that day, hadn't been able to resist rectifying the wrongs that had been perpetrated against me. Appealing to that side of him would be the key to forcing him to understand just how much he had done for me.

"You helped me reclaim those desires. Without you, I never would have been able to allow a man to touch me like that ever again. That Bastard would have kept that part of me forever. You helped me take it back from him."

I paused for a beat before making my next admission. I wasn't sure if he would approve of my enduring dependence on him. But he had to know just how much he had done for me, how he had returned my sanity to me.

"Being with you that day… You did more than return my sexuality to me. I begged you as my Master to touch me, and you respected my wishes. I didn't ask for that out of a desire to please you; it was what *I* wanted. You held me as a woman who desired to be touched, not as a slave you used to sate yourself." My lips quirked up in a wry smile. "You gave me a dozen orgasms, for god's sake. And you only had one. I can't imagine anything more unselfish."

He let out a low growl. "This isn't something to joke about. This is serious, Lydia."

"I'm being completely serious," I said evenly. "I was more empowered that day than I had been since I was taken. Possibly more so than I had been in my entire life. You showed me that my body, my desires, aren't something to be ashamed of. That they're something beautiful. You made *me* feel beautiful."

My gaze was drawn to the scars around my wrists.

"*He* made me feel disgusting, like something that was less than human. Like something that wasn't worthy of humanity."

Smith placed his fingers beneath my chin, lifting my face to his. I didn't even realize I was crying until he wiped the warm tears from my cheeks. His touch was tender, but ire swirled in his eyes.

"You *are* beautiful, sweetheart. In every way a person can be beautiful. Why do you think I lost all control when it came to you? My mind rationalized my actions because I couldn't help myself. You're right: I don't regret what happened. I wanted you then, and I still want you now."

"Then take me," I whispered. "Please, Master. Please, Smith."

He groaned softly. "I can't, Lydia. You have to be free of me. You'll never recover if I don't let you go."

"I'll never be free of you," I declared fiercely. "Because I don't want to be. This is my choice, Smith. I'm choosing you. You can choose not to accept me, but that won't change the way I feel. I wouldn't be sane right now if it weren't for you. The whole time I was going through therapy, when I was... When I was re-living what was done to me. Whenever everything became too much and I thought I couldn't do it anymore, the thought of you kept me going. Thinking of you made me feel safe. I could put my fear aside because I trusted you to keep me safe. I *do* trust you, Smith," I amended.

"How can you possibly trust me?" He asked, his expression torn between wonder and longing. "I kept you from your life. I kept you from your family. From your husband. If I had known -"

"Don't, Smith," I said softly. The mention of Tucker made my heart squeeze painfully. A part of me felt wrong discussing our divorce with Smith in an effort to win his affections, but I had to convince Smith to stay with me. If he went out to hunt that Bastard, he would end up dead, too. I couldn't let that happen. I couldn't survive that.

"I loved -" I choked on the past tense. "I will always love Tucker. But our marriage was over a long time before I was abducted. We had just agreed to divorce when..." I shied away from the torturous memory of his terrified eyes. "I was coming back to you, Smith. Would you... Would you have taken me back?"

"I don't know, Lydia. I don't know what's right anymore." He sounded exhausted.

I touched my fingers to his cheek, calling his full attention to me.

"I don't care what's right. I just know what I want. I've worried what other people think my whole adult life. I've allowed my concern for their reactions to my choices to rule my actions. I have my life back now, Smith. And I'm not wasting a single day of it. I'm living for me now. I don't care what anyone else thinks."

His lips parted slightly, and I was amazed to recognize awe, reverence, in his expression.

"You are the strongest woman I've ever known, Lydia."

I gave him a small, slightly embarrassed smile; I didn't know how to deal with such an overwhelming compliment.

"I wouldn't be if it weren't for you," I insisted softly. "I need you, Smith. I need you, Master. Please."

"Fuck," he breathed.

Then his fist tangled in my hair, tugging sharply so that my head dropped back, offering my lips up for his use. His silver eyes burned down into mine.

"Are you still prepared to go to hell with me, Lydia?" He asked roughly.

"Of course, Master," I promised huskily. "So long as you take me to heaven and back first."

He shot me a wicked grin. "Sweetheart, I can promise you're not coming back down to earth for a long time." His hot breath played across my lips as he brought his mouth teasingly close to mine. "I can do this all fucking day."

It was a promise he had made before. One he had never gotten to keep.

I arched up into him, my lips straining to touch his. His grip on my hair kept me firmly in place, and his darkly amused chuckle danced across my skin as he denied me.

"That's not how this works, girl. If you want me to be your Master, then you have to play by my rules."

I moaned as his words sent my pulse racing. It pumped through my body in double time and made my core throb.

"I'm sorry, Master. I'll be good."

This time, there was no trace of fear behind the promise, only pure, unrestrained lust. This was what I had craved for so long, what I had been so cruelly denied when I was ripped from Master's presence.

His fingertips traced the line of my lips.

"I know you will be," he said cockily. "Now. You're going to be very quiet, girl. We aren't the only ones in this apartment. And while I usually wouldn't mind making you scream for everyone to hear, this isn't the time or place for that."

Before I could whisper my compliance, he pressed two fingers through my parted lips. The tactile sensation of his rough fingertips brushing across my tongue elicited a groan from deep within me.

"I thought I told you to be quiet," he remarked. His fingers penetrated further, touching the back of my throat. He stared down at me censoriously as he maintained the uncomfortable pressure, trapping me in place with his hold on my hair. It took all of my concentration to relax my muscles, so much concentration that I could hardly remember to breathe. His message was clear: he could control me with very little effort. I could comply with his orders willingly, or he would find a different way to get what he wanted.

My nipples and clit hardened in response, but I held in my desperate whimper. I went completely limp in his hold, silently demonstrating my total submission to his will.

"Good girl," he whispered in my ear. His fingers retreated to brush over my tongue once again. I closed my lips around them, sucking them as I would his cock. He pumped in and out as he pressed me back down into the mattress, settling his body over mine.

His hand left my hair to find the hem of my camisole. Slowly, he worked the cottony material up my body as his hand glided across my bare skin, teasing over my abdomen before sweeping up between my breasts. My back arched when the air hit my tightened nipples, but his palm pressed me back down firmly. At the same time, his fingers pressed deeper into my mouth, a silent warning for my compliance. He didn't withdraw until I managed to relax completely beneath him once again.

He rewarded me by pinching and pulling at my nipples while grazing his teeth across my neck. I wanted so badly to lean into his touch, to cry out my pleasure. It was even more difficult to resist the urge to grind my hips up against his rock hard cock in an effort to alleviate the painful pulsing of my clit. The power-play was a torturous pleasure of its own, adding another dimension to the eroticism of his touch while further tormenting me by heightening my aching need.

In my motionless silence, my entire world became focused on him: the feel of his teeth teasing my flesh; the slightly salty taste of his fingers; the intoxicating smell that was uniquely his.

He abandoned my breasts, and I resolutely swallowed my cry of protest. Mercifully, his touch moved to the upper edge of my sweatpants. His fingers left my mouth so that both of his hands were fisted in the material. Hooking his thumbs into my panties, he jerked them down my thighs along with my sweats. The sudden exposure made me whimper in a mix of delight and thrilling fear.

I realized my mistake half a second too late.

His grin was downright evil, as though he had been waiting for me to slip up and was pleased at the opportunity to further discipline me.

His palm abruptly clamped down over my mouth, and he pinched my clit hard. My eyes flew wide as a shocked scream tore its way up my throat, mercifully muffled by his grip on my face.

He *tutted* at me for my second show of disobedience, knowing full well that it would have been impossible for me to hold back my cry.

I glared at him.

My Master was a bastard. A cruel, evil, manipulative –

I gasped when he abruptly drove two fingers into me. They found the sweet spot at the front of my inner walls and stroked against it.

My brow furrowed, and I looked down at him in confusion. He was rewarding me when I had disobeyed him?

I didn't trust the glint in his eyes, but I could no longer summon up the will to wonder what it meant or why he was giving me pleasure. All I knew was there was a storm gathering deep within me, and I was desperate for the lighting to strike. The electricity crackled inside me, setting the fine hairs at the back of my neck on end as my flesh tingled. My thighs trembled in anticipation. Almost there. Almost.

His fingers withdrew from me abruptly.

My whine of protest was smothered by his palm.

His smile was twisted. He was taking immense pleasure in toying with me. If his grin hadn't been enough to communicate that, his hard cock certainly was. It jerked against my thigh, separated from me only by the thin fabric of his trousers.

In a burst of defiance, I reached for his zipper. The element of surprise gave me enough time to snake my hand into his boxers before his fingers found my clit again. This time the pain of his pinch was made even worse by my increased sensitivity. But after his cruel denial, it also brought a spike of pleasure that sent me hurtling over the edge. Even as I screamed out my orgasm against his hand, his voice penetrated my mind from where he whispered at my ear.

"You have a lot to learn, girl," he told me roughly. "And I can promise I will thoroughly enjoy teaching you."

His fingers left my clit to grip his cock, drawing it out fully so he could drive into me. His flesh entered mine with beautiful ruthlessness, stretching and filling me. His harsh thrusts punished me for each sharp cry that escaped me, even as the shocking pleasure of him moving roughly inside me elicited more.

He reached between us to pinch my nipples in further reprimand for my disobedience. All of his efforts to correct my behavior only made me helpless to prevent my own defiance of his command. If it weren't for his firm hold on my mouth, my delighted screams would have echoed throughout the room.

The lustful light in his dancing eyes let me know that was his exact intention. He controlled me completely, even in my disobedience. He took possession of my defiance, harnessing it and using it as a weapon against me, fashioning it into a toy he could play with.

With that realization, I gave him everything: my body, my will, my soul.

He would have settled for nothing less. I had demanded that he be my Master, and he was showing me exactly what that meant.

The complete release brought on by my acknowledgement of his mastery of my entire being sent me soaring. My cry of pleasure was magnified for the space of a moment when he removed his hand from me, only to replace it with his lips. His groan and my scream mingled in our mouths, an echo of our inextricable joining in our shared ecstasy.

Heat lashed into me as he spent himself deep inside me, marking his possession. The sensation only heightened my pleasure as I reveled in his ownership.

Master couldn't leave me now; he was mine just as much as I was his.

Chapter 24

Master shifted his weight off me, pulling me with him as he rolled onto his side. He kept one arm locked around my back, his other hand brushing my hair off my sweat-dampened brow. I hated the clothing that still separated our skin, but my muscles were too watery to do anything about it. Besides, I didn't mind that Master hadn't wasted the time to undress before taking me.

Concern suddenly clouded his eyes. "Fuck. I didn't use a condom. Are you -"

"It's okay," I assured him quickly, before his worry could ruin the perfect moment. "I was tested after... I'm clean. And I'm on the shot."

I flinched at the thought of when I had received the shot. It hadn't been my choice.

Master pressed his lips to the top of my head. "I'm sorry, little one. I didn't mean to upset you."

"It's alright. I'd rather he gave me the shot than..." I locked the thought away where it belonged. Those memories didn't rule me anymore. Master had helped me take control of them.

I looked up into those gorgeous eyes that had kept me grounded through the last weeks. "I'm glad you didn't use a condom. I like the feel of you inside me. Nothing separating us."

He smiled at me gently. "I like it too, sweetheart. But I'm sorry I lost control."

I gave a very unladylike snort. "You seemed pretty in control to me," I remarked.

His lips took on an arrogant twist. "That's because controlling you is easy. Controlling myself is more difficult."

I rolled my eyes at him. "Could you be any cockier?"

He just shrugged. "This is what you signed on for, sweetheart." His eyes suddenly turned serious, burning into me. "And it's too late to turn back. You're mine now."

I shivered in the wake of his intense stare, thrilling at his possessive words. He had said them before, but it was different now. He wasn't claiming the frightened slave he had rescued; he was claiming Lydia Chase. He was claiming *me*.

His fierce devotion was baffling. Yes, our mutual need had always bordered on obsession. Hell, it had crossed that border a long time ago. Had he been struck by the same desire for me that I had felt for him from the very beginning? Why had he chosen to take me in, to commit himself to taking care of me?

"Why did you help me?" I asked softly. "You stayed with me through the withdrawals. You spent every night by my bedside. Why?"

His expression tightened with remembered anger. "When I found you at Decadence… I was furious that your so-called 'Master' had allowed you to use. It's a Dom's responsibility to take care of his submissive, and the thought that the man who was supposed to have been caring for you had let you succumb to addiction made me sick. Then I spoke to you, and I realized he had been using your addiction to ensure your obedience. The fact that he had used BDSM as a guise for abuse disgusted me. The marks he had left on you…"

His arms tensed around me, and he made a visible effort to rein in his ire. When his gaze focused on me once again, his eyes were disturbed.

"I understand how to use pain to earn a woman's submission. I understand how to play mind games to manipulate her into doing what I want. I saw the man who had abused you reflected in myself, and that sickened me. BDSM saved my life, and the knowledge that I was like him, that my mind worked in the same way, shook me to my core. I felt I had to prove it to myself that I could use that part of me to help you."

I regarded him seriously, touching my fingers to his cheek to call him back to me. "You are nothing like him," I said firmly. "Don't even begin to compare yourself to him. You *did* help me. You are helping me. I've told you that."

He blew out a long breath. "I know. If I didn't believe that, I wouldn't be here right now."

"What do you mean when you say BDSM saved your life?" I asked tentatively. Master's brand of BDSM had certainly saved *my* life. I burned to understand this shared bond, to learn more about Master. To learn more about Smith James.

"I made mistakes when I was younger," he said earnestly, openly. "Hell, 'mistakes' doesn't even begin to cover it. I fucked up in so many ways. *I* was fucked up in so many ways." His eyes searched mine. "You want to know why I was so intent on helping you? I didn't just see myself in that Bastard; I saw myself in *you.* I used to suffer from an addiction of my own." His lips thinned in a grim, self-effacing smile. "No. I didn't 'suffer' from it. I chose it. But I suffered because of it. And so did the people I loved."

He paused as his gaze turned inward.

"You don't have to tell me about it if you don't want to," I said softly. He had already revealed so much more of himself than he ever had before. I didn't want to upset him by pressing him.

"No," he said. "I want to. You deserve to know. When I was eighteen, I said to hell with all of my family's expectations and didn't show up to college for my first semester. I wasn't very good at taking orders back then, either." He shot me an uneven smile. "My parents didn't even realize it until they received a letter from Johns Hopkins saying I had never attended a single class. I was an ungrateful, obnoxious little shit. I took all of my savings and the money my dad had given me to live for the year and bought a used Harley Road King. I had always loved bikes, and I liked the idea of being a rebel. College and a corporate career were beneath me.

"Since I had blown all of my money in the course of a day, I started working at Slim's Garage, where I had bought the bike. The guys asked me to ride with them, and I ended up joining their gang. I thought I was so badass."

He shook his head, as though he could admonish his teenage self. "The Pagans, a one-percenter outlaw motorcycle gang, were affiliated with my gang, and we dealt meth for them. It was an easy way for me to make more money, and meth was a hell of a rush. I spent my days dealing, fucking, and using."

He hesitated, his eyes turning haunted as he became lost in memories of his own darkness. I ran my fingers through his hair, lightly scraping his scalp. He leaned into my comforting touch without seeming to realize it.

"One day, my father showed up at Slim's. He had received the letter from Johns Hopkins, and he had tracked me down. He was furious, and he tried to drag me out of there. But I was a hard man then, and I wasn't about to let my daddy boss me around in front of my gang. I threw the first punch. I just wanted to make him leave me alone; I didn't want to actually hurt him. My father had never done anything wrong by me, other than being a strict tight-ass. But my boys got involved. They beat the shit out of him. And I didn't stop them. I just sat back and watched."

He drew in a shaky breath. For all of his boldness in recounting his sins, he was obviously still deeply disturbed by what he had done.

"A month later, my mom showed up at the garage. She was a wasted wreck, and when I tried to calm her down, she just slapped me. She told me that my father had died from cerebral edema – brain swelling – following head trauma from the beating. He had been dead for a month, and I hadn't known. I had missed the funeral, had left my mother alone to deal with the grief. And I was responsible for his death."

His jaw tightened. "I never saw my mother again after that day. I thought if I made things right, I could somehow make amends for what I had done. But how can you ever make something like that right? I turned on the Pagans, gave them up to the feds. Getting clean was harder than turning them in; fixing myself seemed almost as impossible as fixing what I had done."

I remained silent, allowing him to take the time he needed to continue on. He was sharing a deep part of himself with me, and I wasn't going to cut him off with unnecessary words. He wanted me to know this, to know his deepest sins now that I had committed to him. I had come to him at my worst, and he was sharing the worst of himself with me. Despite the nature of our sexual relationship, we were finally coming together as equals.

"That's when I found BDSM," he said. "My cravings for meth ruled me; I felt powerless to my addiction. I had thought I was taking control of my own life by rebelling against what my family had wanted for me, but my life was a chaotic, meaningless mess. Taking control sexually gave me the sense of power I needed to resist my cravings. It wasn't just about controlling a submissive; I had to exert control over myself. They placed their pleasure, their safety, completely in my hands. It was incredibly heady, a rush better than any drug. But even more importantly, it was my responsibility to take care of them, and I couldn't uphold that responsibility without complete mental clarity."

He tenderly cupped my cheek in his large hand. "The trust of a submissive is the most beautiful gift that can be given, and to betray that trust would be unforgivable. And when it came to you... You had no choice but to trust me when I took you in. You were completely dependent on me. In a twisted way, I relished that. Caring for you, watching you blossom back to life because of my guidance... I've never felt a sense of satisfaction deeper than that. The realization that what gave me so much pleasure had actually led to me take advantage of you was horrible to face. I've been a fucking mess since you left."

I smoothed the creases in his forehead with a gentle brush of my fingertips.

"You didn't take advantage of me," I said quietly.

"Just because you're happy with the way things turned out doesn't make what I did right. But I meant what I said before: I don't regret it. God knows I should, but I don't. I'm glad you had time to get your head on straight without me, though. I don't think I could have ever forgiven myself if I didn't at least try to let you go."

I gave him a small smile. "Nice try. Too bad I'm not letting *you* go."

He returned my smile and kissed the tip of my nose. "You're a feisty little sub, aren't you?"

Sub. Not slave.

"I like that word," I breathed.

His grin was wolfish. "So do I. It suits you."

"Speaking of suits," I said lightly, plucking at the buttons on his rumpled white shirt, "you are wearing far too many clothes, Master."

He caught my wrists in his hand, chuckling as he stilled my efforts. "You're definitely too demanding for your own good. Do you know what happens to demanding subs?"

My grin was wicked as I gave a dramatic shudder. "I suspect they're punished with multiple orgasms."

He barked a laugh. "I think I like Lydia Chase. She's awfully cute when she's trying to be flippant." He leaned into me, and his teeth grazed the shell of my ear. "Too bad for her, flippant subs don't get to choose their punishments."

His lips came down on mine, drugging me with his kiss once again. With only a few strokes of his tongue, I went soft and pliant beneath him, my body moving under his silent direction as he removed our clothes.

His cock was fully hard when it pressed into my naked thigh. I shifted towards it, my pussy instinctively seeking to be filled. He suddenly gripped my sex hard, pinning me in place with his fingers inside me and his palm on my clit. His rough, possessive touch made my core throb, and I pulsed around him greedily. But he just held me firmly, his hand unmoving as he brought his lips, his teeth, down on my nipples. With each sharp nip and swirl of his wicked tongue, my muscles spasmed around his fingers, desperately seeking further stimulation.

A violent trembling claimed my entire body as he took me to the edge and held me there, torturing me with pleasure that was both too much and not enough.

"Please, Master." The whispered words were so ragged, I wasn't sure if I had managed to form words at all.

His lips left my nipples, and he cocked his head at me. Before I could release my sigh of relief at the end to his torture of my breasts, he brushed his forefinger against my g-spot. A little zing of bliss sizzled through me, but it wasn't enough. The tease of pleasure had only been meant to punish me further, to prolong my suffering.

"Did you have something you wanted to say to me, sub?" Master asked casually, as though he had missed a passing remark rather than a desperate plea for release.

"Please, Master. Please let me come."

Another little jolt struck as he moved in me again, and I whined at the sweet torment.

"'Please'?" He repeated the word a touch condescendingly. "Is that all you have to say?"

What more did he want from me?

Instinct drove me to roll my hips up against him in a desperate bid for further stimulation, but he held me fast.

"I'm sorry!" I gasped, realizing what I was supposed to say. "I'm sorry for being demanding, Master."

His smile was proud and perversely pleased. He touched his lips to mine in a doting kiss. "You're forgiven, girl. Now, are you going to be flippant with me in the future?"

I bit the inside of my cheek. I knew the answer he wanted, the answer that would allow me to come. He wanted me to say 'no.' But that would be a lie, and lying was against the rules.

"If I tell you the truth, may I please come, Master?"

Confusion entered his cocky expression, but he nodded.

"Yes," I admitted quickly, breathlessly. "I probably will be flippant in the future. I'm sorry, Master. Please..."

He laughed as he released me from his cruelly restraining hold, replacing his fingers with his cock. My raw moan was caught between his lips, and he swallowed all of my cries as I rode out my release. He kept me in that heightened, enraptured state as he found his own pleasure in my body, taking me back over the brink with him when he spent himself inside of me.

He held me to him as we both came down, our breathing finding a more normal rhythm until our chests were rising and falling in tandem.

"Thank you, Master," I said quietly.

"You're welcome, little one. You earned it."

"No," I corrected him. "I mean, yes. Thank you for the orgasms. But thank you for sharing your past with me." I stroked my forefinger up his spine, tracing the line of his tattoo. "Is that what this is about? Is that the mistake you made?"

He leaned his forehead against mine. "Yes, Lydia. But like I said, nothing can make what I did right. The tattoo reminds me of that, and it reminds me that I can choose better. When it came to you, I chose wrong again. I let my feelings for you control my actions." He smiled at me wryly and trailed his fingertips along my jawline. "You're a far more compulsive addiction than any drug, Lydia."

I caught his hand in mine, pressing his palm against my cheek. "Maybe it was wrong. But you told me free will is about making the choices that will manifest either good or evil. And what you did, what *we* did, was good. It was the good choice, even if it wasn't the right one."

Master smiled at me gently as he hugged me closer. "You are full of surprises, little one. Lord knows I didn't do anything to deserve you. But I'm keeping you."

"The feeling's mutual. I'm keeping you, too, Master."

He laughed, a full, rich sound that warmed me to my core. "Such a demanding little sub. What have I gotten myself into?"

I smirked at him. "This is what you signed on for," I mirrored his earlier words. "It's too late to go back now."

He grinned at me, his eyes dancing with delight. "I guess I have no choice but to accept my fate, then."

I nodded with mock-solemnity. "That really is for the best. Things will be so much easier for you if you just surrender."

His low growl was playful as he swept me up in another intoxicating kiss.

"I recommend you reconsider your position," he advised softly when he finally allowed me to draw breath again. "Who's surrendering to whom, here?"

"I am," I replied, my voice meekly contrite. "I surrender, Master."

His grin was smugly triumphant. "Good girl."

I rested my head against his chest, melting into his strength, his power. We laid in contented silence for a while as he stroked my hair, my skin, as though he couldn't bring himself to stop touching my body.

"How did you become an FBI agent?" I asked, my curiosity still aflame, craving to know more about the man who held me so tenderly. "If the Bureau knew about the meth, wouldn't that bar you from working for the government?"

"That was all Ken's doing." Smith's voice was affectionate when he spoke the man's name. "Agent Kennedy Carver was the man I worked with when I turned in the Pagans. I don't know why he decided to help a little shit like me, but he took an interest in getting me back on my feet. He's actually the one who suggested I look into BDSM to help beat my addiction. Once I got clean, he convinced me to go through college. I worked at a garage – a reputable one – part time and managed to pay my way through in five years. Afterward, Ken asked if I wanted to apply for the FBI Academy. I never should have been accepted to Quantico after what I'd been involved in, but he stuck out his neck for me. That gave me a pretty good incentive not to fuck up. I've been a pain in his ass for seven years now, and he hasn't fired me yet."

"Wait," I said, catching upon one detail as I digested everything he had said. "You're telling me that your boss is in the lifestyle too? And Clayton? And… Wait. Reed's a Dom too, isn't he? Is it a prerequisite to be kinky if you're going to be in the FBI?"

Master laughed in surprise, as though he had never really thought about it before. "Well, Reed was brought in precisely *because* he's familiar with the lifestyle." He shrugged. "Maybe Ken has a hiring bias. Or maybe there's a commonality in our psychological makeup that makes us suited to the job. In any case, Clayton's newly converted, so he barely counts."

My brows rose. "How would Clayton feel if he heard you say that he 'barely counts'?"

Master grinned. "Please don't tell him I said that. It took me years to get him to come out of the vanilla closet. I'd hate to scare him back into it. He's so much more fun now."

"What do you mean, 'came out of the vanilla closet'?"

"Clayton was uneasy with the idea of hitting a woman. His obsession with being the good guy held him back."

"What changed?"

Smith smirked. "He fell in love with a woman who wanted him to hit her. It's amazing how quickly he took to it once he realized that he could use BDSM to help Rose. His White Knight Syndrome ended up corrupting him. It was extremely satisfying to watch."

The uneven tilt of my lips mirrored his. "You're a little bit evil, you know."

"I know," he said unapologetically. "And you like it that way."

"Yes," I agreed, just as easily. "I don't at all mind that you suffer from Dark Knight Syndrome."

His low chuckle held a threatening edge. "And I don't at all mind your flippancy. By all means, continue giving me reasons to punish you. You're making this very easy for me, girl."

His hand splayed across my lower back, pressing my hips against his hardening cock.

I gasped. "Already?"

"I promised I wouldn't lie to you, didn't I?" He ground his erection against me, his voice roughening. "All fucking day, sweetheart."

Chapter 25

"James. Can I speak to you privately?" Clayton's voice was clipped, barely clinging on to his usual calm.

Smith and I had just emerged from the bedroom, our hair still wet from the shower. If that weren't enough to suggest our intimacy, the glow that I could practically feel pulsing around me told Clayton all he needed to know about what we had been up to that morning. I also suspected we hadn't been all that quiet, despite Master's intentions.

Smith shifted uncomfortably, but I boldly laced my fingers through his.

"Whatever you want to say to him, you can say in front of me," I told Clayton firmly.

Clayton's brows lifted slightly at my assertive bearing. I wasn't surprised; the last time he had seen me, I had been practically catatonic with shock and grief. And before that, I had been shaking at the prospect of returning home with Tucker.

Tucker.

I flinched at the thought of him.

Smith's thumb pressed firm, soothing circles across the back of my hand. I took a deep breath, returning to him. I would cry about Tucker later. Right now, I had to convince Clayton to make Smith stay with me. Otherwise, I wouldn't be able to face what had happened to Tucker at all. I needed Smith; I needed my Master. I needed his soothing voice, his confident assurances that everything was going to be okay.

Now it was Clayton's turn to appear uncomfortable. "Fine," he said, eying me uneasily before turning his attention back on Smith. "You can't do this, James. I asked you to come here to help Lydia, not..." He trailed off, his lips thinning in distaste.

Smith tensed aggressively beside me.

"Smith and I are going to be together," I said before Smith could snap back at his friend.

My bearing was confident, self-assured. Memories of my Master had sustained me through the last month of my healing process, but his physical presence at my side gave me more strength than I would have thought possible. I had thought I would never be whole again if I couldn't learn to let him go, but now I knew that I couldn't be whole without him. He completed me in a way I had never known; he was everything I had always needed, even before I had been abducted.

I wouldn't allow Clayton to force him to leave me. Smith was essential to my survival. Maybe some people would call that unhealthy. I preferred to call it love.

Clayton's brows rose further at the sound of Smith's real name on my lips. Then they drew together in disapproval of my declaration.

"Lydia," he said my name slowly, as though trying to reason with a child. "That's really not appropriate. I know you've been through a lot, and, given the circumstances," he shot a censorious glace at Smith, "you think you have to stay with him."

"I don't give a damn about the circumstances," I said sharply. "I don't *have* to do anything. I'm doing what I want. And I want to be with Smith. You can choose to disapprove, if that's what you want. But honestly, I don't think you do want that. You seem like a nice guy, Clayton. You wouldn't want your friend to be unhappy. And – as you said – I've been through a lot. Do you really want me to be unhappy?"

Clayton stared at me, dumbfounded, his jaw working as he struggled to process my words. I could practically see him weighing our happiness against what he thought was right.

Smith chuckled and wrapped his arm around my shoulders, pulling me close. "I think you broke Clayton's moral compass, sweetheart. Fascinating." He turned his grin on his friend. "Isn't she great?"

In the wake of Smith's pleased, proud smile, Clayton's eyes cleared, his decision made. "Of course I want you to be happy, Lydia." His lips quirked up as he studied me, assessing my new-found assertiveness. "And watching you put Smith through the wringer will definitely make *me* very happy."

"Thank you, Clayton. For everything." My voice lowered, turning more serious. "I know you might have thought you did the wrong thing in letting me stay with Smith, but it was the best thing that could have happened to me. I couldn't have found myself again without him, even if the FBI had figured out my identity and reunited me with my family. What he did for me – what you both did for me – was exactly what I needed. You weren't wrong in recognizing that I needed a form of treatment the doctors couldn't give me."

Clayton nodded in solemn acknowledgment, his expression grateful. "Thanks, Lydia. I needed to hear that. Smith here's not the only one who's been beating himself up about what happened with you."

I shot him a teasing smile. "Well, now you can both – How did you put it? – stop angsting like teenage girls."

Smith's laughter filled the room, joined by Clayton's half a second later.

And just like that, the tension was gone. Clayton had needed my assurance that he had done the right thing almost as badly as Smith had needed to hear it.

Smith seated me on a stool at the kitchen counter while he and Clayton shuffled around the small, combined living room/kitchen space getting breakfast together. Now that I could take inventory of the safe house, I realized just how minimal and insulated the space was. There were no windows in the living room, and the only other rooms were the ensuite bedroom where Smith and I had stayed and a second bathroom close to the entrance of the apartment. The only point of entry was the front door. I might have felt claustrophobic, if it weren't for the sense of relief at not being within the sights of a single window. So long as I kept Smith here with me, he would be safe.

With that, my thoughts returned to Tucker, and my stomach twisted painfully. I set my spoon back into my cereal bowl without taking a single bite.

"Lydia?" Smith said my name questioningly as he came to stand beside me. His arm was instantly around my waist, and I automatically leaned into him.

"What will happen now?" I asked quietly. "About… About Tucker?"

"We're still looking for leads on the sniper," Clayton told me gently.

My eyes burned up into his as my rage tore through me. "'The sniper'?" I repeated hotly, accusatorily. "You know who it was."

"Lydia, we have to consider this from all angles," Clayton told me calmly. "Otherwise, we might miss something."

"You might miss something if you waste time looking for anyone else!" I snapped.

Smith's hand rubbed up and down my arm, calming me. "She's right," he told Clayton evenly. "It was him. The fucker hacked her TV right before Tucker was shot."

Clayton's brows drew together. "Hacked? How? How do you know it was the man who abducted you, Lydia?"

"I don't share my toys."

I shuddered and leaned into Master more closely. He cupped my head in his hand, holding me against his chest. He turned a glare on his friend.

"We're not having a goddamn debriefing right now, Vaughn. Suffice it to say, it was footage only he would have. It's not particularly difficult to hack a Smart TV, but we already know he's good with tech. We'll keep pursuing that angle and see if we can trace the hack."

We?

I couldn't allow him to leave the safe house.

"Please stay here, Smith," I begged, fisting my hands in his shirt.

The firm, determined set to his jaw told me he didn't have the slightest intention of hiding out from that Bastard. He wanted him dead. By his hand.

Well, I wasn't above using underhanded tactics. I turned my beseeching gaze on Clayton.

"The recording…" The words stuck in my throat as my mind refused to verbalize what I had seen. "The bullet wasn't meant for me. He killed Tuck for being with me. He'll kill Smith if you let him out in the field. Smith has to stay here with me."

Master's low growl rumbled against my ear where it was pressed to his chest. "Don't even try it, girl. I don't take orders from Vaughn."

"No," Clayton agreed coolly. "You don't." He shot a pointed glance at me. "But do you really think the field is where you're needed most right now, James?"

Master stiffened beside me, but he made the mistake of looking down into my terrified eyes.

He let out a long breath, the tension leaving him as his fingers began to work through my damp hair.

"Goddamn it, Vaughn," he grumbled. "Fine. I'll stay here today. But we're going to discuss this later."

His stern expression wasn't meant for his friend.

One day. I had one day to convince him to stay away from the investigation. I clung to him more tightly, physically demonstrating my need for his nearness.

He tore his gaze from mine.

"Goddamn it."

I could practically feel his *need* to hunt the man who had abused me thrumming through his body. But he was my Master, and according to his philosophy that meant my needs came before his own. His most important job was to take care of me, mentally as well as physically. Right now, I needed him to keep me sane far more than I needed that Bastard to be brought to justice. Especially if Master's involvement in the latter put him at risk.

Master glanced down at my untouched breakfast.

"Eat," he ordered shortly.

I meekly complied, deciding it was best not to show any further defiance after daring to collude with Clayton to keep Master out of the field.

Clayton made a quick exit, and I wasn't sure if it was because he needed to get to the office or because it seemed likelier with every passing minute that Smith would take out his frustrations on his friend.

"For someone who's happy, you're sure doing a great impression of being a miserable asshole, Smith," Clayton remarked as he stepped out of the apartment.

He was gone before Smith could snap a retort. His jaw ticked as he ground his teeth together. Smith evidently didn't like it when Clayton got in the last dig.

The man I had chosen as my Master could be extremely ornery. But he was a good man, and I loved his ferocity. As always, his fierceness made me feel safe when I was with him. And now that I knew him better, I could tell when his anger was genuine and when it was actually affectionate grumbling.

"What's so funny, girl?" He asked suspiciously when he caught me smiling at him.

"You're cute when you're blustering," I told him coquettishly.

The shocked expression on his face was priceless, and my smile widened. I had managed to render Master speechless.

My self-satisfied smile slipped as his own hard-edged grin cut into me. He closed the short distance between us faster than I could process, and I gasped as his hand closed around my throat. He didn't squeeze, but his grip was firm. Rather than being angered by my flippancy, he seemed thoroughly amused.

"So my sub thinks she can be a little brat, does she?" He asked softly. My breath was suddenly coming in shallow pants as his sparking eyes became my whole world. He sighed as though he was very put-upon. "I can't allow that kind of behavior, girl. But I think you already knew that."

I shivered as I automatically ceded everything to him in the space of a second. When I was caught by him like this, my mind ensnared by his power just as thoroughly as he trapped my throat in his firm hold, everything else could fall away. I didn't have to be worried or sad or scared. I *couldn't* be any of those things, because Master would take them all upon himself. He demanded that I give him all of myself in my submission, and that included all of the ugly things as well as the beautiful.

But imparting them to him necessitated that they surface within me, and a warm tear slid from the corner of my eye as I stared up at him, unblinking.

His hungry smile faded, but his grip on my neck didn't ease. He tenderly brushed the wetness from my cheek as he kept me firmly fixed in his power.

"Talk to me, sweetheart." The words were gently spoken, but it was a command.

"I…" All of the bad things tangled together, a knotted mess of ugliness that had become rooted in my being. "Tucker." His name left my lips before my mind could even recognize the source of the pain that was flaying my soul.

Master's grip shifted so that he was cupping the nape of my neck, and his other arm hooked under my knees. He lifted me from the hard wooden stool and carried me to the couch. His eyes never once broke from mine as he settled down, keeping me cradled against his chest. I burrowed into his warmth, my own skin suddenly pebbled from the chill that had sunk into my flesh.

"Tell me about Tucker."

His tone was low, soothing. The cadence of his even breathing against me as I stared into his eyes was almost hypnotic. Master wanted to know about Tucker. Obediently, I fell into the memories. Words left me in a steady, quiet stream as my lips gave shape to the images in my head.

I re-lived my history with Tucker: the day we first met, the hours spent with him jamming on his guitar while I drew, his proposal, the wedding, the miscarriage, the bitterness, the resentment. It was like when I had accessed my memories of torture during therapy, but this time Master was real, solid. I didn't have to close my eyes to remember the comfort of his embrace, because he was right there with me. He held me while I faced the love and the joy and the pain that had been my life with Tucker, fully acknowledging all that I had shared with my husband, all that I had lost when the life had left his eyes as he lay bleeding on the living room floor.

I told Master about my conflicted feelings when I had caught Tucker kissing Becs, about our last kiss in front of Seurat's *Seated Woman with a Parasol*, about the morning we had released one another with a pledge of lifelong friendship.

My chest was heaving by the time I recounted the memory of his death in vivid detail, and Master held me as I choked out Tucker's final moments. Even once I finished speaking, Master remained silent, allowing me to pour out my grief in a flood of tears. He siphoned off what I couldn't bear to hold within me, and he took it into himself.

"Thank you for sharing with me, sweetheart," Master said as the heaving of my chest subsided. "Tucker sounds like a really great guy."

I didn't miss his use of the present tense. He was acknowledging that Tucker would always be a wonderful person, and that Bastard could never take that legacy away from him. I nodded against Master's chest in quiet thanks.

"What do you think you'll do now?" He asked gently. "You said you were going to apply to get your BFA. Is that still something you want?"

I hesitated. Yes, it was still my dream to pursue my art. And I wasn't about to let that Bastard take anything else from me. But at the same time, I didn't think I could bear to be in Chicago. Not for a while, at least. I needed to rebuild my life, to start the life that had never been mine. Maybe that life had never been meant to be lived in Chicago.

"Yes. I still want to study art. But not at Notre Dame. Maybe I'll apply to Pratt or the School of Visual Arts in New York. See if I can get in."

I met Smith's eyes, anxious to judge his reaction. Fleeing the darkness of my past in Chicago wasn't the only reason I wanted to live in New York. I wanted to be close to him.

My heart leapt when he grinned. "Excellent. Saves me the trouble of requesting a transfer to the Chicago office. And I won't have to rebuild my reputation on the BDSM scene from scratch. The subs of New York would be devastated if Master S moved away."

I would have frowned at his mention of other adoring submissives – of which I was sure there were many. But that little flare of jealousy was completely overridden by the shock of his casual mention that he had planned to move to Chicago.

"You..." I began incredulously. "You were thinking of moving to Chicago? Why?"

He shot me an admonishing look. "You're a smart girl, Lydia. I'm sure you can figure it out."

My mouth opened and closed, my mind still struggling to comprehend the enormity of what he was saying.

He sighed, shaking his head at me slightly. "I've told you, Lydia: I'm keeping you. And that means I'm keeping you close. So," he switched gears, as though that part of the conversation was settled. "We'll have to arrange to get your stuff shipped to New York."

"But I don't have a place yet," I protested. "I don't even know if any of the schools in New York will accept me."

Master looked at me as though I was being very slow on the uptake. "You're moving in with me, sub. There's more than one art school in the City. Hell, with your talent, you don't need to take classes." He shrugged. "If they don't accept you, it's their loss."

"Just like that?" I asked faintly. "I'm moving in with you?"

"Yes." Then he blinked, his brows drawing together. "I'm sorry. That's not an order, sweetheart. Of course it's your choice. Do you want to live with me?"

"Yes!" I answered quickly, before he could change his mind.

He beamed at me. "Good. It would have been terribly tedious for me to pretend to let you get your way."

"What?" I asked, confused.

He raised his brows at me. "Do you really think I would have let you spend one night away from my bed? It has some very handy built-in restraints for keeping rebellious subs where I want them, in case you don't recall."

I raised my hands in a dramatic show of capitulation. "Okay. You've charmed me into it. I surrender."

His hand suddenly fisted in my hair. "Damn right you do."

His lips claimed mine as he began to harden beneath me.

Master obviously intended to continue making the most of our day together.

Chapter 26

I had been confined to the safe house for three days, but I didn't mind being imprisoned one bit. Not with Smith as my cellmate. To my great relief, he had consented to stay with me rather than returning to the field. After many, many muttered expletives.

Smith insisted that I continue talking with Dr. Stanger about my trauma and my feelings about what had happened to Tucker. I might draw strength from his presence, but there were still a lot of things I had to work through that he didn't have the training to deal with.

"As many people have pointed out, I don't have a goddamn medical degree," he had admitted in a reluctant rumble.

My therapy sessions took place over Skype, because the FBI had declared that having Dr. Stanger travel to the safe house might tip off my location if the Bastard was still looking for me. Our daily talks were difficult, but I always felt better afterward. Especially with Smith there to hold me. I didn't have to hide my emotional exhaustion from him as I did from my family; it was okay to be vulnerable around him. It was just one more way he was helping me to heal more fully than I had been able to do when I was deprived of his presence.

Clayton checked in with us every evening, and it was always reassuring to see his broad, easy smile, even if he didn't bring news that the investigation was getting somewhere. The Bastard was as elusive as ever.

Today, I was less pleased to see Clayton. The reason for his presence beside me now made me ache inside. He and Smith were escorting me to Tucker's funeral.

Spending hours in Master's arms had helped distract me from my pain, had even helped me begin to heal the gaping hole in my heart where Tucker had once been. It was still raw and tender, but it was no longer hemorrhaging my life's blood. So long as Smith was there to support me, I could make it through.

I was nervous at the prospect of exposing Smith at the graveside service, but he had insisted on accompanying me. And despite my worry for him, I wasn't going to let fear of that Bastard keep me from honoring Tuck's life. My mind was eased by Clayton's assurances that the FBI would be closely monitoring the area, ensuring that no one could get close to the graveyard without them noticing.

The black sedan in which I was riding was rapidly approaching the graveyard. In a few minutes, I would face my parents and Becs for the first time since the shooting. I would have to face Tucker's parents. Did they know their son was dead because of me? They must at least suspect. Why would anyone have a reason to murder sweet Tucker?

I shuddered, and Smith's arm tightened around my shoulder. I was wedged between him and Clayton in the back seat. To my surprise, Clayton's hand covered mine, giving it a reassuring squeeze.

I glanced up to find his bright blue eyes regarding me with uncharacteristic solemnity.

"We'll be right beside you the whole time, Lydia," he told me firmly.

"Thank you," I whispered, blinking back the haze at the corners of my eyes. I wasn't ready to cry yet. There would be plenty of that in a little while.

When we stepped out of the car, Smith kept his hand firmly pressed against my lower back, and Clayton stuck close to my other side. Neither man was tense, but their eyes carefully surveyed our surroundings, scanning the faces of the grief-stricken people who were gathering beneath a tent by an open grave.

The sight of the dark, damp earth piled high, waiting to trap Tucker beneath its weight, made my stomach turn. I jerked my eyes away, taking a deep breath through my nose to push back my nausea.

My gaze fell on Becs, who was crying into her father's shoulder. In the wake of her raw pain, all of my conflicted feelings regarding her relationship with Tucker fell away. I made my way over to her; years of holding each other through difficult times led me to her by instinct more than conscious choice.

"Becs." I said her name weakly as I approached her.

At the sound of my voice, she stiffened against her father. She didn't look at me. Automatically, I reached out to touch her shoulder comfortingly. My fingertips had barely brushed her when she whirled on me.

I took an involuntary step back in the wake of her furious snarl.

"Becs…" I trailed off, the words shriveling in my throat at the hateful light that darkened her eyes.

"Don't you dare touch me, you whore," she hissed.

My mouth fell open on a pained gasp. I felt as though my best friend had punched me in the gut. A part of me knew I should turn and run, but shock rooted me in place.

"It's your fault! Tuck -" She choked on his name. "He told me about that place, that *club* you went to."

My lungs seemed to stop working as she hurled out the information like an accusation.

"That's why you were kidnapped. Because you're a perverted freak! You should have stayed gone! It's your fault he's dead! It's your fault, Lydia!"

She was shrieking now. Time slowed down as her words sliced into me like tiny shards of ice, melding together and crystalizing in my heart, transforming it into a jagged, frozen lump in my chest.

I could feel the needle pricks of everyone's eyes on me, judging me, blaming me.

Master's arm tightened around my waist, and his rage slapped up against me like a palpable thing. Becs' eyes widened as it hit her as well, and she shrank back against her father.

"James!" Clayton said sharply, warningly. "Don't."

His voice lowered as he addressed me gently. "Do you want to leave, Lydia?"

I managed a jerky nod.

Becs was right. How dare I sit with the rest of Tuck's loved ones and mourn him when I was the reason he had been taken from them? Of course they wouldn't welcome his killer to cry alongside them as he was lowered into the ground.

I wanted the world to blur around me, to sink into the numbness of shock. But everything was mercilessly sharp, my senses taking in the angry buzz of the mourners' whispered words of disapproval, registering the disgust in their eyes.

I stared resolutely down at my feet as Master and Clayton steered me back towards the parking lot. The slow, mournful drumbeats of Jimmy Eat World's "Hear You Me" started up behind me. They followed me even once I was ensconced in the black sedan, reverberating in my head with their torturously melancholy rhythm.

∎∎

We flew back to New York that night. There was nothing left for me in Chicago. Nothing but tears and death and betrayal. And a sadistic man lurking in the shadows, waiting to hurt more of the people I loved. Even if they didn't love *me* anymore.

Smith did his best to calm me, to comfort me. His hands never stopped touching me from the time we left the funeral to when we entered his apartment hours later.

Despite the emptiness of my ravaged insides, warmth weakly sparked in my belly at the sight of the stark space. Rather than being left cold by its severity, its simplicity was calming. Everything was as I remembered, as I had obsessively committed to memory so that it would never fade away. Only a month ago, I had thought I would never see this place again. Now, being here felt more *right* than being in Tucker's townhouse or even my parents' house.

I breathed in amber and whiskey.

Home.

This was where I belonged.

My frozen heart thawed slightly when my eyes fell on the white wall in the living room. It was no longer blank; Smith had left my drawings where I had hung them on the day I left him. Upon closer inspection, I could tell that the paper was slightly crinkled, as though it had been crushed into a tight ball and then carefully, lovingly smoothed back out.

"I never did get those frames," he said gruffly, almost apologetically, as he noticed the direction of my gaze.

I turned to him, my eyes wide with wonder. "You kept them," I breathed.

His expression was almost harsh in its intensity as he gently tucked a lock of stray hair behind my ear.

"I told you, Lydia: I'm not letting you go. I never let you go."

"I love you."

It was an essential truth that had lived inside of me for weeks, lingering deep within my soul since the moment I had first opened my eyes to find him staring down at me from my bedside. The love I had felt for him in those first days had been borne of gratitude, of slavish devotion. But it had grown to something all-encompassing, something *real*. It had swelled to a powerful force that was too much for my soul to contain. The intensity of it pulsed in a blissful ache in the center of my being.

Smith – Master – grabbed me up in his arms, crushing me to him. His eyes burned into me, twin stars falling to Earth to sear into my soul.

"I love you too, Lydia. So fucking much it hurts."

His lips captured mine with bruising force, imparting the pain of his love to me. I gave it right back, for once meeting the ferocity of his kiss rather than surrendering. My hands cupped the nape of his neck, my fingernails pressing into his skin as I held him to me. He growled into my mouth, his teeth catching my lower lip sharply.

His hands were at the hem of my dress, hastily working it up my body to wrench it over my head. My fingers made quick work of the buttons on his shirt, making their way to his belt as he shrugged it off.

I had barely managed to unzip his trousers when he gripped my shoulders, taking me tumbling down onto the thick carpet along with him. He didn't bother to finish undressing; the white-blue flames blazing in his eyes spoke of obsessive hunger that bordered on madness, and all of his focus honed on taking what he wanted.

He gripped my panties in both hands, ripping them off me with one jerk of his powerful arms. Without hesitation, his cock impaled me, driving in so fast and deep that fireworks popped across my vision. I welcomed the edge of pain that accompanied the pleasure that permeated deeper than just my flesh. My legs wrapped around his hips as I rocked up into him, taking him further into myself.

Our coupling was frenzied, all of his careful control gone. The possessive, ravenous beast inside of him had taken over, and it would have what it wanted.

It wanted to consume me.

No words passed between us, no commands or meekly-spoken acquiescent utterances. There were only the raw, animalistic sounds that filled the space around us. Our love surpassed the capacity of human articulation, so we expressed it in the only way our bodies knew how: joining so closely that I wasn't sure where I ended and he began.

We climaxed together, our bodies in perfect sync. As we came down, our sharp pants were the only sounds as we held one another. We lingered in that primal state, the heat of our flushed skin bleeding into one another communicating more than our words ever could. He rained soft kisses down on me, marking every part of my face, my neck, my chest. I returned the same reverent attention to him, marking him in kind.

After a while, he scooped me up and carried me to the shower, where we tenderly washed each other's bodies with loving, worshipful attention. Despite all of the terrible things that had transpired that day, I fell into sleep as soon as he laid me on his bed. He didn't need to use his restraints to keep me there; the tender touch of his skin against mine tethered me to him more securely than chains ever could.

- -

"Do you want to talk about what happened yesterday?" Smith asked gently as we lay in bed the next morning, his fingers stroking down my naked back. I knew he wasn't asking about the sex or the "I love yous" we had exchanged.

The funeral.

A cold knot formed in the pit of my stomach at the memory of Becs' hate-filled glare, of her venomous words.

"I… She was right," I whispered. "It is my fault."

Deep down, I had already known it, but having my best friend shriek the words at me in front of all of Tucker's loved ones had laid it out before me with stark, cutting clarity.

His fingers curled beneath my chin, forcing my gaze up to his. I looked up into his eyes to find my Master staring back at me reprovingly.

"No. It's not. Nothing that Bastard has done is your fault."

"But if I hadn't left Tuck, if I hadn't decided to pursue BDSM, that Bastard never would have taken me. If I weren't a *perverted freak,* he wouldn't have known me at all. And Tucker would still be alive."

Becs' cruel words were bitter on my tongue. But that didn't stop them from being true.

Master softly brushed a tear from my cheek, but his hard expression didn't waver with his tender touch.

"You're not a freak, Lydia. And you're not a whore." His jaw ticked as he ground out the last word. Becs' accusations were obviously sharp in his mind as well. "Tell me what drew you to BDSM. Why did you decide to explore the lifestyle?"

I blinked, thrown off by the question. I hadn't thought about it in so long. All of my memories of my early days at Dusk had seemed so insignificant in the wake of what had happened. They only mattered so far as being the impetus for my abduction, and for that, they were better left in the recesses of my mind. I hadn't realized that I had tucked them away until that moment. I hadn't accessed them while I was trying to make things work with Tucker, and then I had become so absorbed in my dynamic with Master that I hadn't bothered to recall the pale imitations of D/s I had dabbled in at Dusk.

I thought back to my early discussions with my friends on the scene as I had struggled to make sense of my need for BDSM.

"It wasn't something I really thought about until my early twenties," I began slowly. "I was happy with what Tucker and I had when we first got together. Maybe there had always been a latent interest there. I'm not sure. But it wasn't until after the wedding and the miscarriage that I became curious about it."

I turned introspective, my thoughts flashing through the disappointments that had followed those fateful events. "I used to think I was a bit of a rebel; I liked thinking of myself as a free-spirited artistic type. But then I got pregnant. I was reckless and irresponsible, and I let down everyone I loved: my parents, Tucker, myself. Two years into my marriage, I found myself trapped in a life I had never envisioned for myself, but I didn't dare break free and go back to school as I wanted to do so badly. That would be irresponsible, and I would let everyone down again. I lost control of my own life because I couldn't bring myself to disappoint the people I loved. I craved for someone to take that control for me, to lift that feeling of chaos just for a little while by taking the responsibility out of my hands."

I searched his face intently as I arrived at the root of my desires. "I was so *tired* of worrying all the time about how my actions might affect other people. I needed someone who I could trust to take away that worry."

Master traced his thumb across my furrowed brow.

"And you couldn't ask your loved ones for help because you couldn't burden them with your worries. You thought you had put them through enough worry because of you, and you took responsibility for ensuring their happiness at the cost of your own."

"Yes."

How could he see me so clearly? He easily understood my deepest needs, needs that had taken me years to sort through and comprehend.

He fixed me with a serious stare. "Do you think wanting to trust someone deeply enough to allow him to help and support you makes you a whore?"

"Well... No. Not when you put it that way. But -"

He touched his fingers to my lips, silencing me.

"There is nothing wrong with your desires, Lydia. You're a strong woman, and you need someone with a firm hand to challenge that strength in order for you to allow yourself to let go." He gave me a lopsided smile. "Luckily for you, helping and supporting you suits my kinks; I definitely don't mind taking you in hand. Accept it: you were made for me, sweetheart. And there's nothing perverted about that."

"No," I agreed fervently. "And even if it were, I'm too happy to care. I like being yours, Master. I love you."

"You see?" He said with a cocky grin. "It's so much easier when you just accept that I'm right."

I scoffed at him, my voice dripping with sarcasm. "Please forgive me for daring to question your wisdom, Master. I'll blindly accept whatever you say from now on. Won't that make for stimulating conversations."

He laughed. "You have a smart mouth, sub. By all means, feel free to question me whenever you like. If I feel you're being deliberately impertinent, I can always gag you."

My gasp was a mixture of shock and arousal. His fingers traced around my parted lips.

"Well, isn't that sweet? Open and eager. I think a pretty red ball gag would suit you nicely, girl."

My mouth closed with an audible snap, barring entry. I glared up at him in warning, unwilling to open my lips again to deliver a snappy retort.

He just chuckled at my threatening frown. "I think a blindfold will be in order, too. I can't risk your eyes burning a hole in my head."

Even as my scowl intensified, I couldn't stop my body from pressing up against him more closely, my pulsing clit seeking stimulation against his hard thigh.

It really shouldn't be legal for a man to look so arrogantly amused.

My disappointed whine was involuntary when he rolled away from me and got to his feet. At the sound of my protest, he cocked his head at me with a condescending grin.

"Did you want something, sweetheart?"

My jaw clenched, anger and something darker burning in my gut. He was toying with me. Did he really expect me to *ask* him to blindfold and gag me?

Hell no. It was one thing to melt under his touch, to cede everything to him at the power of his drugging kiss. Well, I wasn't about to beg him to *take me in hand* while he was being such a cocky ass.

Even if he was a devastatingly sexy cocky ass whose smug expression and glinting eyes did funny things to my insides. That expression messed with my brain, and for a second I actually considered falling to my knees and begging him to use me as he desired.

I shook my head at myself and straightened my shoulders as I got to my feet as well.

If anything, my show of bravado only appeared to please him further. I pursed my lips and resolutely ignored the gathering heat between my legs.

"Breakfast?" I asked pointedly. I had hoped to sound cool and unruffled, but he didn't miss the fact that I couldn't manage to force out more than one word.

He stepped to the side with a gentlemanly gesture towards the door. "After you," he prompted me to walk ahead of him. I couldn't hold back my disappointed frown when he didn't touch me as I passed. His grin widened in response. I didn't trust the playful light in his eyes at all.

His strategy became all too clear as I cooked breakfast: he wasn't going to touch me in any way until I asked him to fulfill the little fantasy he had spun for me. Well, I wasn't going to give in so easily.

We began a silent battle of wills as I did everything I could to tempt him with my body. I wore nothing but an apron in the kitchen, and I made sure to sway my hips as I worked around the small space. I even made a show of dropping a fork just so I could slowly bend to retrieve it from the floor before arching over the sink as I washed it. Out of the corner of my eye, I noticed that his hand was fisted on the countertop, belying his carefully calm expression. I quickly turned to hide my smirk.

Our game continued through mid-morning, by which time we were both thoroughly frustrated.

"This is stupid!" I finally burst out. "Just fuck me already."

He arched a cool eyebrow at me from where he was seated at the opposite end of the couch. I waited for his mocking reply, for his sharp admonishment. I couldn't predict how he would react, but I fully expected some sort of reaction.

But he just stared at me, fixing me in place with his suddenly icy eyes. I found I couldn't break away, and his power began to pulse over me. I sank under its weight, my mind giving way to its irresistible force. He didn't move until my breath was coming in short, shallow pants and my body was trembling.

He stood slowly, and my eyes remained riveted on his as he stepped towards my end of the couch. Within seconds, he was towering above me, his implacable gaze boring into my soul.

And still he said nothing. Instead, he merely pointed at the floor.

I was on my knees instantly. There was no hesitation, no thought. He had me completely under his power, my mind utterly in his grasp.

He kept his gaze trained on me, and I could practically feel myself melting into him, my will eagerly surrendering to his control. My body was suddenly incredibly light, and my mind went blissfully blank.

"Was there something you wanted to ask me, girl?" He asked coolly.

"Will you please fuck me, Master?" My voice was soft, docile. I didn't even think about what I was saying, didn't consciously formulate the words. Master had asked me a question, and I gave him the proper answer.

"Tell me what you want me to do to you."

"I want you to cuff me to the bed and blindfold and gag me. Then I want you to fuck me. Please."

He smiled and touched his fingers to my hair, working though it slowly. I practically mewled in pleasure at the renewed contact.

"The cuffs are a nice touch, little one. And you did ask for your punishment so sweetly."

In my normal frame of mind, I would have been galled to realize that I had indeed asked him to carry out my punishment. But in that moment, I felt nothing but pure joy at having pleased him.

His hand fisted in my hair and tugged me forward, guiding me onto my hands and knees. I expected him to take me from behind, but to my intense embarrassment and incredible arousal, he began to walk towards the bedroom, forcing me to crawl beside him. Other than my shocked gasp, I let out no words of protest. The insistent pulsing of my core commanded too much of my attention for me to formulate coherent thoughts. My thighs were increasingly slick as they rubbed together, my wetness coating them. By the time we reached the bedroom, my limbs were trembling. I was grateful for his physical guidance as he silently directed me up onto the bed.

He positioned me in the center of the mattress, facing the headboard. He released my hair and pressed his hand firmly between my shoulder blades, pushing me down so that my cheek rested on the bed. Still on my knees, my ass was raised flagrantly.

His grip around my wrists was gentle, but he inexorably guided my hands so that my arms extended out towards the bedposts. As my upper body was forced lower, my tight, aching nipples brushed against the duvet, and I couldn't suppress the urge to writhe, seeking further stimulation. Master chuckled at the sound of my low moan, allowing me to continue my desperate quest for sensual release as he secured my wrists with the cuffs that were attached to the bed.

Once he was satisfied with my bonds, he clicked his tongue at me as he guided my thighs apart, and cool air hit my exposed pussy. I was open, offered up for his use. My writhing had regulated to a steady rocking motion as my body begged for sex. I didn't even realize that I was begging aloud as well, repeatedly echoing the request that I had made of him, that I had so rudely issued as a demand only minutes earlier.

"Please, Master. Please fuck me. Please fuck me. Please..."

My conscious mind had been obliterated by his power over me. His skillful manipulation reduced me to my basest state, where there was only instinctive need, and my soul had recognized that his will was my only means of attaining release. I was beautifully, blissfully lost in him.

A drawer opened and closed.

"Shhh," he softly quieted my pleas. Something hard and smooth pressed against my lips, which were already slightly parted from my panting breaths. "Open."

Obediently, I relaxed my jaw, and the round sphere of the gag eased into my mouth. The rubbery tang was a scent in my nostrils and a taste on my tongue. My teeth sank into it slightly as Master fastened the buckle around the back of my head, forcing it to further invade my mouth. I drew in deep breaths through my nose as my breathing was suddenly restricted.

I was only just becoming accustomed to the unfamiliar intrusion when the soft, silky blindfold fell over my eyes. They had already been closed, but the thick material blocked out all light that had shone through my lids.

For the space of an unbearably long minute, there was nothing; no sight, no sounds, no tactile sensations. Then my senses began to heighten. The musky scent of my own arousal and Master's heady masculine smell mingled with the rubber of the gag and the salty leather of the cuffs, flooding my nose with the scent of darkly perverse sensuality. The sound of his even breaths beneath my increasingly staccato ones reinforced the sense of his control over my entire being. The heat of him beside me danced with the cool air on my naked flesh, causing the fine hairs on my body to stand on end.

My strangled cry was muffled by the gag when Master's fingernails lightly scraped down the length of my back. The rush elicited by his touch went straight to my head, sending pleasure swirling through my mind. I arched, my muscles tensing for a moment before melting completely.

Straps encircled my upper thighs. As Master pulled them tight to secure them, the slightly ridged nylon material rubbed against the skin where my inner thighs met my pussy lips. My body twisted in response to the sensation, and the clanking of chains as I tugged against my restraints made me whimper in delighted helplessness.

Something hard pressed against my clit, secured there by the tautly-drawn straps. Puzzlement stirred across the surface of my subconscious, but it was quickly eradicated when the object began to buzz softly. Moaning, I jerked harder against my restraints, grinding my hips in a circular motion as though I could press myself more closely to the maddeningly teasing vibrator.

Master's low chuckle danced across my skin.

"Such a greedy girl," he remarked with pleasure. "She'll have to learn patience."

My whine morphed to a shocked cry as his lube-slicked finger abruptly pressed against my asshole, pushing in steadily until he was fully seated within me. My clit pulsed madly against the vibrator, but it still wasn't enough to sate me. He pressed in a second finger, pumping gently as my body welcomed more in my need. My inner muscles began to contract around him as my orgasm neared, and he stopped his movements completely. I sobbed into the gag.

"You don't get to come until I allow it, sub," he informed me.

My entire body was quivering, teetering torturously on the edge of ecstasy.

His fingers withdrew, leaving me feeling achingly empty. I craved to be filled, for Master to fuck me. I didn't care how; I just needed him.

He obliged me, his lubricated cock pressing against my dark entrance. Despite my craving, I couldn't help moving away from him as he penetrated me. He was far too big; I would never be able to take all of him.

His hands closed around my hips, holding me in place with a warning growl.

"Relax, girl. Don't fight your Master."

Drawing in several deep breaths, I struggled to obey. His fingers trailed down my back, stroking me in approval.

"Good girl. Just like that. Breathe."

I shuddered beneath his praising touch. Despite my acquiescence, the burning sensation inside me increased as Master continued his progress. After a few more seconds of discomfort, the head of his cock fully breached the ring of tight muscles with a small popping sensation. He stayed there for a moment, his own breaths turning ragged with the effort of holding himself back so that I could adjust to the intrusion.

With the pause, my attention was again captured by the vibrations against my clit. They were still too light to allow release, but focusing on the teasing stimulation caused the burning in my ass to morph into a heated, erotic tingling.

At the sound of my lustful moan, Master's hands closed around my hips once again, slowly guiding me back onto his hard cock until he was in me to the hilt. My muscles tightened around him again as my orgasm neared, and he stilled.

"Not yet, girl," he ground out.

His hand cracked across my sensitive upper thigh, giving me enough pain to draw me back from the brink. When he was satisfied that I wasn't going to come, he began to ease in and out of me, pumping in slow, shallow thrusts. The tingling within me shot up my spine, exploding outward to flood my entire body. I bit into the gag with the effort of holding myself back. I wouldn't disobey Master. I wouldn't disappoint him.

With a satisfied grunt, he began to increase his speed until he was taking me in earnest, taking full possession of the only part of my body he had yet to fully claim. Sharp cries escaped me with every jarring thrust, my ecstasy pulsing insistently within me. My own will wouldn't have been strong enough to contain it, but Master's was.

He grew impossibly harder within me, and his hand left my hip to press against the vibrator, grinding it against my clit as his cock began to pulse.

"Come for me," he ordered, his voice harsh with his own release.

With his permission, my bliss erupted within me, bursting free of the bonds with which Master's will had contained it. The gag caught my scream, making it reverberate through my head as I came completely undone. It went on and on as my orgasm shattered me with exquisite force.

Nothing existed in the world but Master and the pleasure he gave me.

Chapter 27

Master toyed with the tourmaline gem that rested at the hollow of my throat, idly flicking it as he watched the colors shift in its blue-green depths. It caught the light, sending a small spark dancing across his face. I watched in hazy fascination as my brain slowly re-formed. When I realized that my wrists were no longer restrained, I touched my fingers to his, shaping them around the pendant.

"This kept me sane, you know," I told him quietly. "Whenever things became too much and I thought I was going to fall apart, I would touch this and feel safe. I would think of you. Just like you told me to do."

I thought back to the day he had given it to me, how he had kissed the nape of my neck as he had closed the clasp, how he had lovingly stroked the chain against my skin, as though he couldn't help himself.

It had always been so much more than just a pretty piece of jewelry, but now that I better understood Smith's nature, I came to a startling realization.

"You gave this to me to replace that Bastard's collar. Did you... Were you collaring me that day? Is that what this is?"

He blew out a long breath, and his eyes searched mine. "I told myself that wasn't my intention. But I was too far down the rabbit hole by that point to see the truth of it. Yes, Lydia. I put this around your neck to mark you as mine. I can understand if -"

"Thank you," I cut over him before he could apologize for his actions. "I love it, Master."

His lips quirked up, and he traced a line across the front of my neck.

"I suppose it's time I got you a proper collar then."

My breath caught in my throat. "Really?"

His eyebrows rose. "You've moved in with me, I've claimed you as my submissive, I've told you I love you, and I've just admitted that I collared you weeks ago. Is it really such a stretch for me to get you a proper collar?"

"I… No." I swallowed against the lump rising in my throat as intense joy overwhelmed me. "Can I still keep my necklace?"

"Of course, sweetheart. You don't think I would let you go walking around without any sort of collar at all, do you? You'll wear it outside the apartment at all times. That's an order."

I threw my arms around him, burying my face in his chest.

"Thank you, Master."

He returned my fierce embrace and kissed the top of my head.

"You're more than welcome, little one. I'm glad to see you so eager to follow an order."

I gave a watery laugh and pulled back from him slightly, wiping the wet evidence of my happiness from my cheeks as I did so.

"Don't get used to it."

He tweaked my nose affectionately. "You are such a little brat. I'm going to enjoy coming up with some more creative punishments for you."

Punishments.

My gaze strayed to his toy drawer that held the harsh implements that had terrified me on the day I first saw them. I realized Master had never once threatened to use pain as a punishment. He had used little sparks of pain to tease and torment, but nothing more. He hadn't even spanked me. Not properly.

"You haven't used pain as a punishment." I said the words aloud, letting him know I had come to the realization.

"I thought that was for the best, sweetheart," he told me kindly.

"But… You have all of that fancy gear." I gestured towards the chest of drawers. "Don't you want to use it?"

He eyed me appraisingly. "Do you?"

I bit my lip, considering. The array of Master's collection would have been intimidating even before my abduction. Many of those implements had never come close to my flesh. Some of them fell within my hard limits.

But that was before I had been tortured. During my imprisonment, I hadn't had the luxury of safe words or limits. Every boundary I might have once held had been shattered.

I lifted my chin, defiant in the face of those memories.

"Yes," I said firmly.

"Aren't you afraid of being hurt?" He asked carefully. "You're doing so well, sweetheart. I don't want to take you back to a place that's traumatic."

"I trust you not to hurt me, Smith. There's a difference between receiving pain and being hurt. I used to understand that. I used to enjoy it. I want that back."

He grinned at me. "I love how fierce you are, but there is a nicer way to ask for what you want, little one." He sighed as though he was very put-upon. "I thought we had just finished that lesson. Will you ever learn to be a good little sub?"

I giggled and slapped his chest playfully. "Probably not."

He did his best to arrange his features into a forbidding mask, but he wasn't fully successful in concealing his amusement. I shrugged. "Well, that's the truth. I'm not allowed to lie to you, Master. See? I can follow orders."

The corners of his lips twitched. "You seem to be under the impression that you can follow orders selectively. The choice is yours, of course. You can choose to be good, or you can choose to be punished for disobedience." It was his turn to shrug. "I'll enjoy myself either way."

Temptation tugged at my gut. I had enjoyed all of the punishments Master had meted out thus far. They had all involved mind-melting orgasms. But the taunting light in his eyes told me my next punishment wouldn't be so pleasant now that pain was back on the table. There was a difference between pain administered for my pleasure and pain wielded as a reprimand.

"Sorry, Master. I'll be good." I shot him a sly smile. "For now."

His hard expression finally cracked, and the sight of his dimple deepening in his cheek made my heart give a funny little flutter. God, he was gorgeous when he smiled.

"I wouldn't have it any other way, sweetheart." He brushed a kiss across my lips, communicating his pleasure with my irrepressible impertinence. I sighed into him happily, elated that the resurfacing of my defiant side only seemed to further endear me to him. He had been fascinated with me when I was in my unquestioning slave mindset, but he loved my true personality. He loved *me*.

■■

Decadence was eerily silent when we entered the club that evening. Our footfalls echoed loudly throughout the bar area with no pulsing music to swallow the sound. Smith tucked the key he had used to get us into the club back into his pocket.

"Why are we here?" I couldn't keep the nervous quaver from my voice. "It's closed."

"The owner is in the process of re-applying for all of his operations licenses. The club was shut down after the drugs bust. I agreed to help make the process smother for him if he loaned me the space for the night."

Smith's arms wrapped around my waist, pulling my body up against his. "I know this is scary, Lydia, but I want to replace your ugly memories. You said you want to take the pain aspects of BDSM back, and I want to give that to you. We're going to face it head on, sweetheart. Your safe word is 'red.' Say it, and we'll walk out of here right now."

His eyes were like twin moons in the night sky: calming and peaceful, yet powerful enough to control the ocean's waves.

"I don't want to use a safe word," I said softly.

He smiled as his thumb brushed across the stubborn set of my chin.

"That's my brave girl," he said proudly.

After kissing me swiftly on the lips, he led me deeper into the club, towards the theme rooms in the back. He watched me carefully as he opened the door to the room at the end of the hall.

A chill swept over my skin when he flipped on the light, and I froze in the threshold. The room was far too familiar. It held a St. Andrew's Cross, a spanking bench, and a bondage table. Chains hung from the ceiling. Although the walls were a grey stone façade rather than concrete, they gave the same oppressive sense of impenetrability.

No one would hear me scream. There would be no hope for rescue, for escape.

I didn't even realize I was backing up until Master's hand ensnared my wrist, stopping me short. Reflexively, I jerked against his hold, but he resolutely pulled me into him, caging me in his strong arms.

"It's me, sweetheart. I'm right here with you." He cupped my chin, lifting my gaze to his. "Breathe."

I drew in a shaky breath and nodded. Master would help me through this, just like he had helped me get through all of the seemingly insurmountable challenges I had faced since he had found me in this club. I had been a wasted, shattered wreck, but he had taken me in and forced me back together. Master would never do anything to harm me. Even if he did give me pain, it would only be meant to help me.

"I trust you, Master. I love you."

"I love you too, little one."

He set his gear bag down and led me to the center of the room, never releasing me from his calming gaze as we walked. When he was satisfied with where I was positioned, he pressed his lips to mine. His kiss was soft, coaxing, as his hands found the hem of my dress and eased it up over my body. All of his movements were careful and controlled, yet fluid. His easy grace was hypnotic. I allowed myself to sink into him, surrendering to his touch, his will.

By the time he was sliding my dampened panties down my legs, my breaths were calm and even, my mind going blissfully quiet as all of my worries evaporated.

Master still held me trapped in his gaze as he crouched before me. Whatever he saw in my own eyes elicited a small, pleased smile, and he planted a soft kiss low on my belly. My clit pulsed as though his lips had brushed against it instead. Master's smile widened at my gasp, and he dipped two fingers between my labia, swirling them in the wetness he found there.

"Good girl," he rumbled as he played through my soft folds, teasing, exploring. At the sound of his approval, I sank a little deeper into his power, longing to give him more of myself.

He stood, shifting away from me. I followed automatically, not wanting any distance between my body and his. His hands closed around my waist, directing me back to where he had originally positioned me.

"Stay."

I hated the loss of his heat, but I didn't protest when he stepped behind me. A brief rustling sound let me know that Master was retrieving something from his bag, followed by a metallic clanking that I didn't quite understand. Despite the disconcerting setting, the flutter in my stomach had nothing to do with fear.

"Give me your wrists, girl," Master commanded as he re-appeared before me. The familiar leather cuffs were buttery soft against my skin, the buckles clinking faintly as he secured them around my wrists.

He reached up, and the metallic sound rang out again as he pulled down a length of chain. Fear sparked in my chest when he clipped the end of it to the rings on my cuffs.

"Breathe, girl. Look at me."

As always, his commands grounded me and kept me firmly tethered to the present. God, I loved him so much. He gave me everything I needed. The Lydia Chase he had helped bring back to life was even more complete than the woman I had been before I was abducted.

Something soft touched my belly, trailing upward to tease across my breasts. My nipples tightened as the supple falls of the suede deerskin flogger brushed across my flesh.

"We'll start slowly, sweetheart. If it becomes too much, I want you to say 'yellow.' If you want to stop altogether, say 'red.' Tell me you understand."

His tone was gentle, yet deep and authoritative. He didn't want me to simply take anything he chose to give me; he wanted me to honestly communicate my needs to him.

"I understand, Master."

Satisfied that I was calm and unafraid, Master kissed me fleetingly and disappeared behind me once again. My chest tightened briefly as the chain began to slowly draw my arms up above my head, the metal clanking as it passed through the ringbolt in the ceiling.

Breathe.

I forced my lungs to expand as my body was stretched taut, forcing me up onto the balls of my feet. The position was horrifically familiar, and I couldn't help flinching when something touched my back.

The flogger.

My mind quickly processed that the man standing behind me was Master.

Safe.

His hands brushed the nape of my neck as he moved my hair so it hung over my shoulders, ensuring it wouldn't obstruct his access to my back. Cool air filled the space behind me as he stepped away, but the shiver that ran through me was the result of anticipation, not cold.

The flat of the flogger's falls lightly hit my upper back with a sound like pattering rain. Automatically, I arched away from the blow. But Master didn't back off. A few seconds passed as he gauged my breathing, and then the flogger hit again, with a bit more force this time. His pace steadily increased in speed and intensity. A warm, wonderful tingling arose on my upper back, spreading further throughout my body with each *thwap* of the flogger. By the time the delightful little sparks had reached my fingertips, the falls thudded across my flesh with definitive force.

Master began to work his way down my back. When the soft tendrils hit my ass, I registered the hits as light pain. He hadn't warmed up this area, and my skin smarted at the impact. My answering moan begged for more. I completely embraced my trust in Master. I craved to ride the edge of pain, welcoming it as I reveled in the resultant endorphins.

Encouraged by my lustful reaction, Master altered his style, and just the tips of the falls kissed the sensitive flesh at the lower curve of my ass, raking burning lines across my upper thighs. It took a heartbeat for my brain to register the pain, two more heartbeats to accept it. When it pulsed for a fourth time, I blew out a long sigh as my mind floated into bliss.

Master escalated, and each stinging blow drove me higher as I happily embraced the pain and the endorphin rush that came along with it.

I was so far gone by the time the blows stopped, I barely registered it. Master was suddenly at my back, the heat of him mingling with the warm glow emanating from my burning skin. His fingers found the wetness that coated my inner thighs, and my head dropped back against his shoulder at the sound of his darkly pleased chuckle.

"It seems my little sub does like pain. I wonder how much she can take."

He traced a circle around my pulsing clit. Unable to form words, I mewled and pressed back against him, grinding my ass against the hard evidence of his arousal.

Laughing, he pulled away from me, and I whined at the loss. "I'm not done with you yet, sweetheart."

The next hit came hard and fast, and I let out a surprised shriek. Master had switched to a different flogger, and it *hurt*. The falls were thinner and crafted of smooth leather rather than suede. While the earlier hits had been hot, the burn that accompanied the louder *snap* was fire. I gritted my teeth as the new, more intense pain cleared some of the warm fog that blanketed me.

Breathe.

The breath was my final gasp before the fog condensed to heavy waters that sucked me under. I became weightless in the dark depths, the sound of my sharp cries hardly penetrating the warm sea. I had no worries, no thoughts, no control. Master kept me in this blissful state because that was his will.

The touch of his fingers returned to me, trailing down my belly to tease my pussy. Animalistic sounds of need and pleasure issued from my throat. I was in a base, primal place. Or was it a higher plane of existence? My mind was too far gone to puzzle it out.

"I'm going to hurt you now, girl," Master informed me. "I want you to focus on me and know that I won't harm you. Trust me."

I rubbed up against him in response, physically demonstrating my devotion. Of course I trusted him. I had put myself completely at his mercy, had given him everything.

The fear that exploded in my brain at the sharp crack of the bullwhip shocked me to my core. It didn't touch my flesh, but my terrified scream echoed through the dungeon. Unconsciously, I found the ability to form words again.

"No! Please, no. Please please please please..."

They want to break me. They're going to break me. They're going to slice my skin, make me bleed.

Strong fingers closed around my jaw, and I struggled to twist away, jerking fruitlessly against the chains that held me suspended, vulnerable, helpless.

"Open your eyes, girl. Look at me." The calm command tugged at something deep within me, eliciting my obedience without a thought. His silver eyes filled my vision. "Who am I?"

The molten silver pooled into my being, sending liquid warmth pulsing through my veins.

"Master," I whispered.

"That's right. Stay with me." His breath tickled across my lips as he pressed his forehead to mine, anchoring me to him. "One, sweetheart. I just want you to take one. Can you give that to me?"

I would give him anything; I had already given him everything.

"Yes, Master."

He stayed with me for a minute, running his hands over my body, through my hair, stroking me, calming me. He didn't leave me again until my trembling had stopped.

The whip snapped behind me again, and I couldn't help stiffening.

"I'm here, sweetheart. You're safe. Remember that."

I had barely finished nodding when the ominous whisper of the tail cutting through the air registered. I heard the *crack* of the tip breaking the sound barrier just before the pain hit. The line of fire seared into my flesh with branding heat, and my wail of pain and despair resounded in my ears.

Master was before me instantly, his arms enfolding me as he pressed soft kisses against my wet cheeks.

"Shhh, sweetheart. You're okay. You're safe."

I pressed my face into the crook of his neck, breathing him in desperately. As his rich scent enfolded me, my fear evaporated. Not just my fear of his whip, but all of the terror that had assailed me on the day when that Bastard had thought he had broken me. I had dealt with the memory, had numbed its power over me. But that fear had lingered where it had taken root deep in the most primal corners of my mind. With one harsh lash, Master had ripped it out of me. That unique form of pain was no longer wielded by that Bastard. Master had taken possession of it. And Master would never use it to harm me.

My fresh tears were borne of gratitude, of soul-deep relief.

"Thank you, Master."

He gently gripped my chin, drawing my face to his so he could kiss me sweetly. The demanding, possessive strokes of his tongue reassured me of his love and devotion.

"That whip will never touch your skin again, Lydia," he promised me when he finally released my lips. "I don't want to hurt you."

The strained lines around his eyes told me how difficult it had been for him to inflict that pain on me.

"I needed it," I assured him quietly. "Thank you, Smith."

He kissed me again, long and slow and deep. When I had relaxed into him completely, he began the process of freeing me from my bonds, gingerly rubbing the red marks on my wrists where I had rested my weight on my restraints. He helped me back into my dress, smirking as he tucked my underwear into his pocket. I shivered as lust began to stir to life within me once again. The hungry light in his eyes told me I would receive a very nice reward when we got home.

Once I was covered, he slung his gear bag over his shoulder and scooped me up into his arms. I was grateful he was carrying me out to the car; I wasn't at all sure I would have been capable of walking in a straight line. I was still drunk on endorphins, and my reawakened lust only further weakened my knees.

Decadence's exit let out into an alley to provide an extra layer of secrecy for patrons, and I was glad of the shelter from the chill wind. Master kissed the top of my head as I snuggled into him. The night air was turning cooler with the changing seasons, but his warmth cocooned me.

Master grunted and his body jerked. It took my fuzzy brain a few seconds to register alarm, but panic hit me hard at the sensation of falling. Master had dropped to his knees, but his arms tightened around me, holding me close. I blinked up at him stupidly, confusion and shock coating my brain like molasses.

The fear I saw reflected in his eyes made my heart stop. Master wasn't afraid of anything.

He shoved me away from him, and I dropped to the pavement.

"Run."

The command was garbled, and it didn't hold the usual ring of authority. He blinked rapidly and his muscles tensed once more. Then his eyes closed, and he collapsed beside me.

Panic flooded my system, and I gripped his shoulders, shaking him hard. Something small and silver protruded from his neck. I plucked it out, and a droplet of blood oozed to the surface of his skin where the dart had pierced him.

"Master!" I shook him again.

He had ordered me to run, but I couldn't leave him.

Something sharp jammed into my neck. The large hand that closed over my mouth muffled my scream.

Just like the first time.

"That's right, whore. Master is here."

Insidious warmth oozed into my veins, and my fingers loosened where they were fisted in Smith's shirt.

No!

I couldn't let him go. I couldn't. I couldn't...

Chapter 28

I recognized the smell first: earthy damp, stale sweat, and the metallic tang of fear. Or maybe the fear was a taste on my tongue. The burn of bile in the back of my throat flooded both sensory areas, so I couldn't be sure.

My mind was stumbling, stalling, engaging in internal babbling to avoid the terrible truth.

I squeezed my eyes shut tighter, willing myself to go back to sleep so I could wake up in Master's bed.

Chains clanked above me as my body shifted. Maybe I was still in Decadence. Yes, that was it. I had drifted off into subspace. My body was still stretched taut where Master had positioned me so he could flog me. The crack of the bullwhip had hurtled my mind back to this place, back to my prison. It was just a visceral response to the scene Master had re-created for me. Any second now, he would embrace me, would reassure me that everything was alright. That I was safe.

It's not real. It's not real. It's not real.

Pain exploded across my cheek.

"I know you're awake, slave."

My eyes snapped open at the sound of that chilling, cruelly pleased voice, and my entire world crumbled to dust.

His muddy green eyes gleamed with the sick light that always made my stomach turn. His lips curved in delight, and the back of his hand cracked across my face again.

Everything slammed back into place with the burst of pain. This *was* real. I was in my prison. I had never left.

God, the heroin was crueler than I had ever realized. In the grip of its sweet bliss, I had spun a rich fantasy for myself, a lucid dream in which I had escaped this place.

An inhuman, despairing wail clawed its way out of my soul, ripping up my throat. It went on and on, drowning out the sound of his insanely jubilant laugh.

"Lydia! LYDIA!"

Smith's booming voice slashed through my terror, gripping my faltering sanity and keeping me from going completely over the edge.

I choked on a relieved sob.

I hadn't dreamt him up. Smith was real. *Lydia* was real.

The Bastard's face filled my vision, but I could hear Smith. His string of harsh expletives clashed with the jangling of chains.

Dread suffused me. If Smith was here, the Bastard should be dead by now. The fear that coiled in my belly this time wasn't for myself.

Before my brain could process anything more, the Bastard's fingers gripped my jaw. Steel flashed before my eyes, and I went utterly still as the flat of the knife pressed against my lips. He shifted so that he was standing beside me, and my field of vision was clear for the first time. My cry of alarm at what I saw was stifled behind my closed lips.

The sight of Smith in chains was so disgustingly wrong that I wanted to vomit. Like me, he was suspended by his wrists, but while my restraints were soft leather, iron cuffs had already cut crimson lines into his skin. His hands were fisted around the chain above him, and he jerked at it ruthlessly, fruitlessly, as he struggled to free himself. His face was a mask of savage fury.

"Quiet," the Bastard ordered loudly. "Or I'll cut out her tongue."

Smith's eyes focused on the blade at my lips, and his teeth snapped shut, silent but bared in a rictus snarl.

The Bastard grinned. I recognized the sick, feverish light in his eyes all too well. When he wasn't hurting me, his features shifted in a conventional fashion but his eyes were blank, expressionless. It was only when inflicting pain and misery that they betrayed any reaction at all; a twisted parody of human emotion.

"Good." His soft voice dripped with perverse pleasure. "It would have been a shame to take her tongue. I like how it feels on my cock."

Smith twisted the chain around his hands and dropped all of his weight onto it, yanking at it.

"You motherfucker! Don't touch -"

He stopped speaking abruptly when the Bastard applied pressure to either side of my jaw, forcing my mouth open. The cool blade touched my tongue, threatening but not cutting. Every muscle in my body went rigid as I froze. The Bastard's attention turned back to me, his eyes following the trail of my tear as it slipped from the corner of my eye and fell down my cheek.

Smith said nothing, but he was far from silent. The metallic clanging as he wrestled against his bonds filled the room in a jarring cacophony. His wrists were already torn and bloody. He was going to hurt himself if he kept struggling so violently. I couldn't let the Bastard hurt him.

The blade lifted from my tongue, but rather than retreating, the Bastard eased it further into my mouth. I stopped breathing.

"Isn't that pretty?" He asked softly, watching in rapt fascination as he slowly, incrementally, moved it back and forth in a horrific imitation of penetration. It never touched my skin, but if I moved in the slightest, the knife would slice me open. My lungs began to burn from lack of oxygen, but I didn't dare draw in air.

Black spots were dancing across my vision by the time he released me. As soon as the knife left my mouth, I sucked in a breath, and all of my weight fell on my wrists as my muscles turned to jelly. I blinked hard to clear my vision. Gathering my courage, I looked up at the Bastard.

"Please," I rasped. "Let him go. I'll stay here. I'll be good. Just please, let him go."

Smith snarled his objection, but I resolutely kept my focus on the Bastard. Now that he had me back in my prison, he would never give me the chance to escape again. My life was over. Everything in me screamed at me to fight, to defy him. But I would do anything to get him to release Smith.

I realized with hollow clarity that I had always been meant to waste away and die in this place; the Bastard would never have allowed me to walk free forever. In my brief period of freedom, Smith had shown me greater joy than I had ever known. I could live on that for the rest of my life. However long that might be. Even if pain pushed me to that empty, shattered state once again, I would bury the memory of him deep inside me, providing my soul with sustenance. The Bastard could never take him from me that way.

But he could take him from me if he killed him. He had killed Tucker for being with me. Why else would Smith be here if the Bastard didn't intend to make him suffer?

He studied my determined expression and shook his head ruefully. "All of my hard work undone. I'll have to break you in all over again." His smile was hard-edged. "You'll be punished for trying to run from me, fucktoy. And Agent James has to be punished for taking you from me. His death won't be as easy as your husband's."

The chain that held me jerked as I lunged for him, my body instinctively seeking to hurt him, to mangle him. My pain and fury and desperation left me in a crazed shriek.

He stepped back and watched me with amusement as I writhed and screamed. He had killed Tucker. And now he was going to kill Smith. I couldn't let that happen.

Mastering my instincts, I stopped fighting.

"I'll do anything," I forced out. "Anything you want. I'll be your whore. I'll be your slave. Just don't hurt him. Please."

"Don't you fucking dare, Lydia!" Master snapped as he pulled against his chains with renewed ferocity. "You're mine, goddamn it!"

The knife was back at my lips.

"Shhh," the Bastard practically cooed. His eyes gleamed as he looked from Master back to me. "You think *he's* your Master now, don't you, whore?" The knife lowered, and his fingers touched the tourmaline pendant at my throat. I couldn't help snarling at him as I jerked away.

He scowled. "That's what I thought."

The necklace's delicate silver chain cut into my skin as he yanked down on it. The sound of it snapping was drowned out by my scream of pained protest. He flung it across the room, where it disappeared into the shadows. Although I was still wearing my dress, I suddenly felt as though he had stripped me naked. I was exposed, more vulnerable than I had been since Master had first taken me into his home.

"While your offer is interesting," The Bastard said calmly. "I don't need you to be a willing slave. But we might have fun seeing how far you will go to keep me from hurting him."

Master's inarticulate roar elicited a pleased grin. "He doesn't like that at all, does he? You see, his punishment is to watch me break you. However long it takes is how long he will live. As soon as you call me 'Master,' he dies."

"I will never call you that," I hissed.

His sly smile was his only response. He reached over to the bondage table beside him and picked up an object I didn't recognize. It was about the length of my forearm. The lower half seemed to be some sort of wooden handle, with a metal bar protruding from it. There was a thick, rectangular block of coppery metal at the end, and a long cord ran from the butt of the handle to an electrical socket in the corner.

Fear spiked in my gut as he lifted it to my face. I flinched, anticipating that he would strike me with it. But instead he held it steadily in front of my eyes so I could study it more closely. Artfully styled letters were embossed on the metal block in high relief, protruding from the surface by about half an inch: CM.

"It's an electric branding iron." The Bastard answered my unspoken question. For a moment, the horrific implication of the words didn't quite penetrate my brain. "I'm going to mark you until you accept that I own you. Once you beg me as your Master to stop, you'll get your reward."

He flicked a switch on the base of the handle, and soft heat almost instantly began to pulse from the metal. The sounds of Master's furious shouts and the rattling of his chains faded into the background as all of my focus honed on the terrifying device that was hovering only inches from my eyes, growing hotter by the second.

"I wonder how many you'll take? I'd hate to mark up too much of your pretty skin." The Bastard's gaze roved over me, assessing.

A strangled cry shoved its way past the fear that crushed my windpipe as he reached up my dress and roughly grabbed my naked sex, pressing his thumb into the flesh above my womb.

"We'll start here, whore. You'll never again forget that your cunt belongs to me."

My raw scream of terror clashed with a deafening crash. The Bastard's eyes barely had time to widen in surprise when he was jerked back from me. A heavy chain was wrapped his throat, and Master's hands gripped it tighter. The iron cuffs still encircled Master's wrists, but the ringbolt that had held the chain to the ceiling was no longer embedded in the wooden beam. The Bastard's restraints had never been tested on someone with Master's strength.

The Bastard's hands scrabbled at the chain, clawing at his own neck in a wild attempt to free himself. His face began to darken, rapidly turning from red to purple. When his body sagged, Master released him. He hit the floor with a gasp, but Master was on him before he could finish drawing his first breath. With a feral snarl, Master drove his fists into the Bastard's face over and over again, every hit punctuated by a sickening crunch.

The Bastard's body twitched, and blood gurgled in his windpipe with each desperate breath. When Master pushed off of him, his face was a gory, unrecognizable mess. Master pulled back only long enough to grab the branding iron where it had fallen at my feet. With a vicious, vindictive snarl, he pressed the metal into my tormentor's throat. The Bastard's agonized scream quickly died as Master applied pressure. The brand burned through his flesh, the metal disappearing as it carved a gaping hole in his neck.

Everything went silent and still save for Master's ragged breaths as his chest rapidly rose and fell. The scent of charred meat permeated the room.

Acute fear and shock at the sudden, gruesome turn of events had immobilized my brain. My senses had absorbed everything that happened in sharp detail, but I had yet to process any of it. Now my mind moved sluggishly as my ability for coherent thought slowly coalesced. Disgust, relief, and vindictive pleasure all rose up within me at once, overflowing from my system in a harsh sob.

Master jerked at the sound, but he didn't look at me. Instead, he fished a key out of the Bastard's pocket and unlocked the cuffs around his wrists. As soon as they clattered to the concrete, he stood and strode purposefully away from me.

"Master?" I rasped his name questioningly as alarm tainted my relief.

He said nothing. Bending, he retrieved something from the shadows. When he turned to me, his eyes were wild with possessive fury. Any sane person would have shrunk away from that look, but it made my heart swell.

"It's okay," I said softly as he approached me, trying to soothe him. "I'm okay."

He stopped before me, a muscle ticking in his jaw as he ground his teeth together. He lifted his blood-soaked hands to my throat. Silver and green flashed in the dim lighting. Master stared at the necklace intently as he knotted the broken chain together at the nape of my neck. Tracing his fingers along the line of it, he drew in a shaky breath.

When his eyes met mine, much of the wildness had faded. A sense of completeness, of safety, settled over me as well. The Bastard was dead. He could never hurt me again. Master had protected me, just as he always would.

"Thank you," I whispered.

He pressed his lips to mine briefly, and then he blinked hard, clearing away the last of his consuming anger.

"Let's get you down, sweetheart."

He reached up and unbuckled the cuffs around my wrists. As soon as I was free, I sagged against him, my shaking legs refusing to support me. He caught me up in his arms and eased me down with him as he sank to his knees. Keeping a supporting arm around my back, he reached back into the Bastard's pocket and found a cell phone.

My gaze was drawn to the body. It occurred to me that the gory sight should probably make me want to throw up, but all I felt was a sense of peace. His mucky eyes were still open in his destroyed face, the sick light in them extinguished forever.

"Clayton," Master said into the phone, his voice calm and steady. "Can you trace this call? I need you to pick us up. And bring a body bag."

Chapter 29

"We've finished searching the house and have run his details through the system." There were dark circles under Clayton's bloodshot eyes, but his voice was clear and steady. He had stayed up through the night casing the place where Smith and I had been taken. My prison had been in a basement under a house in a modest, quiet Yonkers suburb. It was hard to believe I had been so close to humanity and yet so far removed for so long.

It was six in the morning, and Smith and I had just been cleared from the hospital. I had some bruising on my cheek where the Bastard had struck me, but other than that I was physically unharmed. Smith's wrists and palms were raw from where he had ripped at his chains, but it had been a fairly simply process to disinfect and bandage the areas where the skin had torn. Even though we were both exhausted, Smith had insisted that we get our debriefing over with as soon as possible.

Now he sat beside me on the couch in Clayton's office, holding me close as we waited for him to tell us what information the FBI had gathered on the Bastard.

"His name was Carl Martel."

Carl Martel.

It was jarring to put a name to the face that had haunted my nightmares. For so long, he had been almost an abstract concept, a remote, powerful being that held my life and my sanity in his hands.

I felt a surge of satisfaction as I pictured his ruined face and blank, unseeing eyes. Carl Martel was just a man, a mortal. And he was dead.

"He spent six months at Lyndon Field Psychiatric Hospital at the age of sixteen for arson," Clayton continued. "After that, he barely exists on the public record. We're checking his financials, but we haven't found anything unusual. He seems to have inherited enough money to live off of when his parents died when he was eighteen. He never went to college, never held a job, and he bought his house in cash. His only other asset is a white GMC van, and forensics are checking that over now to see what more we can find. We suspect that's how he transported you from Chicago to New York, Lydia, and we might recover more physical evidence on the other women's cases from trace evidence in the vehicle."

"Other women?" Smith asked.

Clayton's lips twisted in disgust. "We found video footage and locks of hair in Martel's house. Eight women. We're trying to identify them now to notify their families. Hopefully their cases will help us get new leads on Martel's Mentor. We've come up with nothing so far, but with Martel's limited resources and lack of education, it's seeming more and more likely that his accomplice was heavily involved in facilitating Martel's crimes. He probably helped manipulate the tech to abet in Tucker's murder."

My heart sank. "So you don't have anything on the Mentor?"

The man who had tortured and imprisoned me might be dead, but the man who had taught him how to do it was still out there. He might still be hurting other women. And he was going unpunished for his part in Tucker's murder.

"No, we don't," a voice answered from the open doorway.

An unfamiliar man strode into the room. He was tall and heavily muscled like Smith, and he had the same confident, powerful bearing. His salt and pepper hair suggested that he was a few years older, but his green eyes were keen and youthful. I suspected who he was before he even introduced himself.

"Mrs. Chase." He extended his hand for me to shake. "I'm Kennedy Carver, section chief of the New York office. I just wanted to say that I'm very sorry for what you've been through, and I assure you that the FBI is doing everything in its power to find Martel's accomplice. That being said," he turned his attention to Smith, "our investigation has been considerably hampered by Martel's death. His very violent, very *thorough* death."

Kennedy extended his hand to Smith. "I saw the crime scene photos. Off the record: Good work, Smith."

Smith shook his hand, but he watched his boss gravely. "And on the record?" He asked pointedly.

"You're suspended for a month. With pay. And you're going through a psych eval before you come back."

Smith scowled and opened his mouth to argue, but Kennedy cut him off with a level look. "You can't strangle a man with a chain, beat him within an inch of his life, and then burn a hole through his neck and call it self-defense. You're lucky I'm not doing more than suspending you. Clayton will keep heading up the investigation in New York, and I'm sending Miller to work with Agent Byrd in Chicago. You're going to have to sit this one out, James."

That suited me just fine. If the Mentor had been involved in killing Tucker, then he might still come after Smith. I leaned into Smith and squeezed his hand, calling his attention to me. As soon as he looked down into my silently pleading eyes, his furious expression melted.

"Goddamn it," he muttered, knowing he had lost. He wouldn't leave me to go out in the field if doing so was going to cause me distress. He turned his attention back to Kennedy and Clayton. "I'm taking Lydia home now. You'll keep me in the loop."

"Of course," Clayton answered, even though Smith hadn't phrased it as a question.

Kennedy jerked his chin at me, but he kept his eyes on Smith. "Take the time to look after your sub, James. We'll contact you when we find something new in the case."

I blinked at him, my mouth falling open slightly. Had he really just casually referred to me as Smith's submissive? Smith had told me his boss was in the lifestyle, but for him to tell Smith to take care of me as though I was incapable of taking care of myself was galling. And right in front of me, no less.

Smith laughed at my shell-shocked expression. "Come on, sweetheart, let's get you to bed. I'm sure when you're well-rested you can come up with plenty of cutting remarks to put Ken in his place."

I sighed, inwardly admitting to myself that I *was* far too exhausted to formulate a snappy retort. "Don't think I won't," I said with a pointed look at Kennedy. His answering grin held a taunting edge, daring me to try it.

I rolled my eyes. *Doms.*

Smith chuckled and kissed the top of my head. "That's my girl."
....
Late that afternoon, I awoke to a soft tapping sound. Choosing to ignore it, I kept my eyes closed for a few minutes and savored the feel of Smith's hard body. My arm was draped across his ripped abs, my head resting on his defined chest. The steady beat of his heart below my cheek was one of the most beautiful sounds in the world. He was safe. That Bastard – no, Martel – was dead, and he could never hurt either of us ever again.

Needing to look into his eyes, I opened my own. I immediately understood what the tapping sound was. He held me against him with one arm, but his other hand held his phone. A thin layer of bandages was still wrapped around his palm, but it didn't seem to be hampering his dexterity. Intent on whatever he was doing, he didn't notice me staring at him.

"What are you doing?" I asked curiously.

"Booking a flight," he replied casually.

"What?" My heart stuttered. He was leaving me? "Where are you going?"

"*We're* going to Paris. Tomorrow afternoon. Until they catch the Mentor, I'll feel safer with you on another continent."

My mouth opened and closed a few times as my mind processed that information. He was booking a flight for me? To Paris?

"You can't do that!" I finally managed.

He looked at me levelly and turned the phone so I could see the screen. His thumb hit the "Purchase" button definitively.

"I just did," he informed me.

"I can't go to Paris! What about my school applications? What about my parents? What about therapy?"

He seemed completely unfazed by my concerns. "The colleges will still be here when we get back. You can work on your applications while we're abroad. All of the artistic culture you soak up in Paris will give you more of an edge. And things have smoothed over with your parents, so I see no reason why they should factor into this."

Well, that was true. My parents had called me and made it clear that they didn't blame me for Tucker's death. They wanted me to come home to Chicago, but they had reluctantly accepted my decision to move to New York. But there was a difference between moving to New York and gallivanting off to Europe at a moment's notice. My parents wouldn't think it a responsible decision.

"It will be just as easy to Skype with Dr. Stanger in France as it is in New York," he continued. "Of course you'll continue with your therapy sessions."

But there was another – much more significant – problem with this plan.

"Smith," his name was a firm protest. "You can't spend that kind of money on me. It's too much."

His brows rose. "It's done now. Airlines don't give refunds. Besides, what's mine is yours."

"It doesn't work that way, Smith. I'm your submissive, not your wife."

He shrugged. "You will be."

I gaped at him. "Is that..." I heaved in several gulps of air, torn between annoyance and sheer joy. "Is that a proposal?"

"No. It's a fact. I can promise you the proposal will be much more romantic." He grinned in the wake of my stunned silence. "Do you have any idea how tempting your lips are when they're parted like that?"

Without waiting for me to answer, he took advantage of my open mouth, pressing his lips to mine. He took my surprised gasp as an invitation to explore further, and his tongue stroked in to tame mine. By the time he relented, my head was spinning and my clit was throbbing.

I opened my eyes to find him smiling at me gently.

"I have something for you. And before you protest: it's something else that I can't return, so you'll have to accept it." He kissed me swiftly. "Wait here."

I wanted to question him, but I recognized my Master speaking to me. I decided to wait and see if it was worth arguing over whatever he had gotten me.

He left the bedroom, and I heard the sound of a box being opened in the kitchen. A package had been waiting for us when we arrived at the apartment, but I had been too exhausted to care about what it contained. Now my curiosity burned hotter with every second that I waited for him to return.

When he appeared in the doorway, I couldn't help sucking in an awestruck breath. Every inch of his sculpted naked body was perfect, but it was his eyes that entranced me most. They glowed with an intense, fervent light. My soul instantly responded, opening to him, ceding my body and mind.

He held me in his gaze for a long minute, pulling me further under his power. Then he pointed to the floor in front of him.

I was kneeling at his feet before I could even think about moving. He reached out and cupped my cheek tenderly, and I leaned into him.

A metallic flash caught my eye. In his other hand, he held a solid silver ring. It was about an inch thick, and wide enough in diameter to fit around my neck. A collar.

"Lift your hair for me, sweetheart." His voice was gentle, but roughened by emotion.

Tears made my vision hazy as I obeyed, and I blinked rapidly to clear it. I wanted to fully memorize every facet of Master's glowing eyes in that moment.

The pliant metal parted enough to ease around my neck. I shivered as the cool silver pressed against my skin. Master slipped the staple through the hasp at the back, securing it in an unbroken circle.

"This collar is my promise to care for you, to protect you, and to love you." He hooked a small, silver padlock through the staple. The click of the lock was a soft, loving sound of finality. "I love you, sub."

"I love you, Master," I breathed. "Thank you."

Grasping my shoulders, he guided me to my feet so he could claim my mouth. His hand splayed across my lower back, pressing my belly against his erection. His other hand reached for my sex, dipping his fingers into my soaked pussy. He chuckled in dark pleasure as he pumped them slowly in and out, coating them in the slick evidence of my arousal.

"I can see my sub likes her collar," he murmured against my lips. I moaned as he spread his fingers inside me, stretching me for him.

His touch left me abruptly, and he gave my shoulders a hard shove. My shocked cry at the sensation of falling ended on a huff when my back hit the soft mattress. Master didn't give me a moment to get my bearings. He gripped my ankles, adjusting my body so that my calves rested against his shoulders. As he settled himself over me, his weight pressed my legs towards me, opening my pussy up for his use. His hands ensnared my wrists, pinning them on either side of my head. He bound my body with his, needing nothing more than his own strength to ensure my compliance.

But he had more than my compliance; he had my submission.

He tenderly kissed the collar at my throat when he drove into me in one thrust. His movements were harsh, each possessive stroke holding an edge of pain that only made the pleasure all the sweeter. He caught my nipple in his teeth, and the sudden extra dose of pleasure/pain sent me hurtling over the edge.

"Master!" I screamed out his name as I came, my core gripping him as pleasure wracked my body. He hardened further in response, and his heat lashed into me as he achieved his own release with a rough shout.

He held me close while our breathing returned to a normal rhythm, his fingers idly tracing the line of collar around my neck, as though he was as entranced by the sight of it as I was by the sight of him. His eyes darkened with stormy lust, and his hand trailed down between my breasts and over my abdomen, stopping to tease the flesh around my clit. I gasped and instinctively rocked my hips up into him.

His satisfied grin was wide and almost lazy as he firmly pressed me back down into the mattress.

"Greedy little sub," he chastised. "I'm not done playing." His cock pulsed against my hip as his arousal stirred once again.

I gaped at him. This had to be a new record. "Already?"

"We have," he glanced at the clock on the bedside table, "a little over twenty-two hours before we have to be at JFK. It's an eight hour flight to Paris, and that's a long time for me to have to keep my hands off you. So I'm going to make the most of these next twenty-two hours."

"Who's the greedy one now?" I asked contrarily.

His rich laugh warmed me to my core. "It seems a lesson about flippancy is in order. Again. Do you think we can make it stick this time?"

I grinned. "Probably not, Master."

"Good." His flashing eyes were both pleased and predatory. "I wouldn't have it any other way."

Epilogue

Smith

"Where are we going? The *Mona Lisa* is in the Denon Wing." Lydia's blue-green eyes were alight with curiosity, her cheeks flushed from excitement. God, she was so fucking beautiful.

Seeing the vibrant, strong woman she was now, I felt a flood of immense pleasure and satisfaction. When I had first found her on that terrible night at Decadence, she barely resembled her true self. She had been sick and skittish and chronically deferential. But her trust in me had allowed her to slowly find herself again. After everything she had suffered, she had managed to heal. She had told me she couldn't have done it without me, and that was undeniably gratifying. But it was her own strength that continued to amaze me. The fact that this incredibly strong-willed woman had chosen to give herself to me was both heady and humbling.

And I'd be damned if I let her get away. She already wore my collar, but I wanted another kind of bond with her. I had lost my family through the stupid, selfish choices I had made twelve years ago. With Lydia, I could have a family again.

My own wide smile matched hers as I tugged her along. "We'll visit the *Mona Lisa* later," I told her firmly. "I have a surprise for you."

I lead her through the tightly-clustered crowds of tourists that milled about the atrium of the Louvre, following the map in my head that I had memorized. I hoped to hell I got it right, because I didn't want to fuck up any part of this. It had taken me two weeks of covert research and planning to prepare this for her.

Thankfully, I managed to successfully navigate us to the more secluded Print and Drawing Study Room. A curator greeted us, and I confirmed that I was the one who had made the viewing appointment. Because the particular drawing I was interested in was so delicate, I had to contact the museum and request that it be brought out to view.

Lydia's puzzlement over the arrangement warred with awe as her eyes roved over the room. The white walls were sculpted in relief to form intricate scrollwork and depict mythological scenes, and the vaulted ceiling featured a richly colored fresco framed by gilded molding. The room itself was a work of art.

I touched my hand to Lydia's elbow, calling her attention away from the fresco above us and towards what I had brought her to see. Laid out on a table and protected behind glass was an aged drawing in red chalk depicting a nude woman holding forth an apple. Lydia's expression was enraptured as she stared down at it, her eyes wide and her full lips parted in that way I found so damn sexy.

"It's Correggio's sketch of Eve offering the apple from the Tree of Knowledge," I told her quietly, almost unwilling to break her blissful study.

Her attention turned to me, and the wonder shining in her eyes made my heart skip a beat. I forced my scattered thoughts to gather back together, and I took her hands in mine.

"You told me that my decision to keep you might not have been the right choice, but it was a good one. Now, I'm choosing to believe you. Because I'm not letting you go."

I reached in my pocket and pulled out the small red box. I couldn't hold back my grin when Lydia's jaw dropped as I went down on one knee.

"Marry me, Lydia."

Her gaze jerked up from the sparking princess cut diamond, her eyes narrowing as they found mine. "Is that a question or an order?"

"Does it matter?"

I watched with amusement as she wrestled to maintain her righteous annoyance. After a few seconds, her smile broke free. "No. It doesn't matter. Yes, I will marry you, Smith." She suddenly bounced on the balls of her feet in giddy excitement, all traces of irritation vanishing as her decision sunk in. "Yes!"

I slipped the ring onto her delicate finger, holding it there as I stood. With my other hand, I touched the tourmaline pendant that rested at the hollow of her throat, silently communicating that she was irrevocably bound to me now in every way possible. She touched her hand to mine, curling my fingers around the necklace, silently demanding that I bind her.

"I love you, Smith," she declared fervently.

"I love you too, sweetheart."

At my words, her face lit up with unadulterated joy. This was how she was meant to be. This was *who* she was meant to be: my blissfully happy submissive, my beautiful wife. The love of my life.

Fuck, she was perfect. And she was mine.

The End

How was Martel always one step ahead of the FBI? Who is the Mentor? Reed Miller and Katherine Byrd will be hunting him down in the near future!

Want to know why the FBI was busting Decadence at the beginning of *Knight?* Find out in the next *Impossible* novel, *Rogue*.

I've never been a failure. I don't allow myself to make mistakes. I've lived my life to painstaking perfection.

Until now.

I can't seem to get anything right. And when you work for the FBI, mistakes can cost lives.
Busting BDSM club Decadence for drug trafficking is my chance to prove myself. And no asshole Dominant is going to throw me off my game. Not even sinfully sexy club owner Derek Carter. I have to keep him close in order to uncover his secrets, but keeping him close to my body while guarding my heart is proving more difficult than I ever imagined.

He might just be my biggest mistake yet.

Rogue will be available soon!

Also by Julia Sykes

The Original *Impossible* Trilogy
Monster
Traitor
Avenger
Impossible: The Original Trilogy
Angel (A Companion Book to *Monster)*

The *Impossible* Novels
Savior (An *Impossible* Novel)
Knight (An *Impossible* Novel)
Rogue (An *Impossible* Novel) (Coming Soon!)

Dark Grove Plantation (The Complete Collection)

CPSIA information can be obtained at www.ICGtesting.com
Printed in the USA
LVOW01s1907300714

396753LV00023B/1604/P

9 781494 306670